The Passion of Reverend Nash

The
Passion
of
Reverend
Nash

Rachel Basch

W. W. Norton & Company, Inc

New York   London

For information about permission to reproduce selections from this book,
write to Permissions, W. W. Norton & Company, Inc., 500 Fifth Avenue, New
York, NY 10110

Manufacturing by Quebecor World, Fairfield
Book design by Lovedog Studio
Production manager: Amanda Morrison

LIBRARY OF CONGRESS CATALOGING-IN-PUBLICATION DATA

Basch, Rachel.
The passion of Reverend Nash / Rachel Basch.— 1st ed.
p. cm.
ISBN 0-393-05768-2
1. Congregational churches—Fiction. 2. Belief and doubt—Fiction.
3. Women clergy—Fiction. 4. Connecticut—Fiction. I. Title.
PS3552.A784P37 2003
813'.54—dc21

2003001045

W. W. Norton & Company, Inc.
500 Fifth Avenue, New York, N.Y. 10110
www.wwnorton.com

W. W. Norton & Company Ltd.
Castle House, 75/76 Wells Street, London W1T 3QT

1 2 3 4 5 6 7 8 9 0

For Nathaniel and Hannah

✄ Acknowledgments

My deepest gratitude to Sally Lane Gould for opening the door to faith and to the Reverend Steve Gordon for taking me by the hand and leading me inside.

I am indebted to the members of the Wednesday morning Meditation and Bible Study at Newton Congregational Church for widening their sacred circle to include me. My thanks to Professor Fay T. Greenwald for her insightful reading of any early draft of this work. And my unending appreciation for my first reader and ultimate editor, my husband, David L. Gould.

"My lyre is turned to mourning, and my
pipe to the voice of those who weep."

Job 30:31

The Passion of Reverend Nash

❧ Chapter 1

REVEREND Jordanna Nash lay on the footbridge behind the Hutchinson Congregational Church and listened. But there was no sound. Not from Bethel Falls, which usually rushed under the little span, not from the Potatuck, which had, only last month, surged through the backyards on West Street, not from Osborne Brook or Tibbetts River or any other of the twenty or thirty moving bodies of water known for babbling, even roaring, through the town. There were parts of Hutchinson in which the sound of pulsing water was typically so loud people had to shout to be heard out-of-doors. And Jordanna found that they only bothered when the communication was essential. There was a lot of waving and smiling from cars, hands cupped to ears, the shrugging of shoulders from porches and side lots. Jordanna loved this about Hutchinson, that human chatter could be drowned out almost entirely by the Divine natural monologue. And when she woke in the middle of the night, alone in the parsonage, there had been, until this week, the constant sound of water purposefully headed from one place to the next, the great circulatory system of the town coursing and pumping, testifying that something somewhere was still alive. But it had been a hot dry summer, and now at the end of August, with so many people gone and so much moving water turned to mud, it was as if Hutchinson had lost its voice.

DRAPED like this across the bridge, Jordanna spanned the width of the brook. She was that tall. Dangerously tall, Gael, the church secretary, had told her more than once when Jordanna winced as she got up from a chair or grunted when she reached across her desk for the phone. It was over a year ago that Gael, having broken her oath of hostility toward the new minister, had neatly printed the name of a chiropractor on a large Post-it note and placed it on the back of Jordanna's desk chair—uncannily, Jordanna thought, to correspond with the exact site of the pain. The chiropractor's name was followed by an ever-elongating list of medical and holistic practitioners, one for every disgruntled vertebrae in her too-tall back.

Jordanna never consulted any of the doctors so lovingly catalogued. She tried not to go to doctors anymore; in fact, hadn't been to one in three years, not since she'd turned forty. Gael said she understood the faith thing, and Jordanna just let it go, again and again, at that. But the truth was that she, too, like Gael, had made a kind of pledge based on nothing more holy than ire. Gael had sworn to herself that she would do nothing to cozy up to the new woman minister brought in to replace the defrocked Reverend Hanley, and she had maintained what she considered an aggressive iciness from her first meeting with Jordanna shortly after Easter until the first week after Pentecost. Gael still wrote to Reverend Hanley, now technically *Mr.* Hanley. He'd moved to the Southwest after the disclosure of his affair with a church member who'd come to him for counseling. Gael wrote to him, inquiring about his new life, as well as to Mrs. Hanley and the children in their new home in Massachusetts. It was the only way, she said, as she broke down early last summer and apologized to Jordanna for having been such a bitch for the past few months. Jordanna had nodded and smiled. Then, taking Gael's tiny tanned hands in both of her too-large pale ones, Jordanna said, "And when you're ready, maybe you'll come back to church." At that, Gael cried a little and turned very red, the flush running all the way out to the tips of her freckled ears. The thing was, she said, she had started going to another church, up in Deerfield. Jordanna had smiled more deeply and, still gripping Gael's hands, vigorously shook them up and down in congratulations, as if they were pulling on the great greasy rope that rang the bell in the bell tower. "That's wonderful," she had said.

JORDANNA liked to think of the bridge as her own hot little rack. When the sun heated the uneven pine, lying here for even fifteen minutes usually brought relief. She reached over for her last sip of coffee, then dropped the mug into the leather mailbag she'd hung from the handrail. She pulled up her knees one by one, hugged her bare legs tight to her chest. Nothing. Without the water, gallons and gallons of cold water rushing wildly just inches beneath her clenched spine, lying on the bridge was pointless. It was the river that had been the balm all these months. It was the water's proximity, its continual shout, its thick scent of moss and leaves that worked on her great knot of pain.

Sometimes, very early in the morning or at dusk, she'd come back here to meditate. It had always been difficult for her to be still, and in the past few years it had become nearly impossible. It was as if she'd begun to equate moving with breathing, certain that if she stopped, she would die. When she was alone now, she needed to stretch and shift, rock and tap, insisting herself into life. Even in her sleep she was in motion. At least once a week she awoke to the sound of an intruder, only to realize that it was her own large leg that had slammed into the wall by her bed. But here on this bridge, with the force of moving water below, her body and mind had been tricked into thinking that she was moving, too.

This morning's sermon was *Endings and Beginnings*. Each week she had to give Gael the title by Thursday afternoon so it could be printed in the bulletin for Sunday's service. Occasionally she would announce at the start of the homily that she'd changed her mind, that the sermon advertised in the program was, in fact, not what she would be talking about. Things happened in the course of three or four days. Things happened in the world and in their church community. Sometimes you woke up on a Sunday morning and everything was different from the way it had been when you went to bed. Sometimes Jordanna hoped for that, sometimes she even prayed for it.

Nothing had happened in the past three days to preempt *Endings and Beginnings*. She had the scripture passage and she had the conclusion, the place she wanted the sermon to lead. But not the middle. The bridge between the scripture and the conclusion was where the work lay. She had e-mailed her husband, Daniel, earlier in the week asking, as she often did, for input. And, ever the Jew, he had written back that endings as beginnings were, he was quite sure, the cornerstone of her whole outfit. That was Daniel. When he could go no deeper he made a joke. But the thing she wanted to get at was the notion of transition. The anxiety that was almost always attendant with change. The end of summer and the beginning of fall, the end of vacation and the return to work and school. Ends and *then* beginnings, she wrote back to Daniel, not ends *as* beginnings. There was a difference.

"Trees don't get anxious when their leaves begin to turn," she scrawled, the yellow pad pressed against the dusty floor of the bridge. "Animals don't resist their thickening coats. They know, in that way beyond knowing, that their existence is cyclical, with finishes and starts, ends and beginnings." A poem or anecdote would be good here. Wordsworth, Whitman, Dickinson, the copies of those books in her study were all marked up, their edges paper-clipped. Anecdotes were more difficult to come by, but usually more effective. She often used her nephews, her sister's four boys, when she needed a funny human illustration. She had renamed each of the boys for the purpose of her sermons, and had, in fact, turned the two older ones into characters who appeared and reappeared a couple of Sundays a month, as if in some kind of weekly Christian sitcom. All her congregants knew that she had a sister and brother-in-law and nephews in Hutchinson. Yet the children she conjured in her sermons had, in the imaginations of some, overtaken the flesh-and-blood Healey boys who attended Our Lady of Fatima down the street with their Catholic father. She was frequently asked if she was planning to visit Matthew, Mark, Luke and John in that far-flung place where they lived. Where was that again? What had she sent them for Christmas? Might they come east during summer vacation? Would their parents let them travel alone? And did Matthew, Mark, Luke and John get along with the Hutchinson cousins, Brendan, Christopher, Michael and Gabe? During the prayers of concern one week, a congregant had offered up a prayer of healing for Mark, having remembered that he had suffered a run-in with a goalpost in a sermon two Sundays prior. She had, since then, been conscious of letting the fictional nephews sit out more than a few Sundays on the anecdotal bench.

"See?" Jordanna's sister, Abby, had said, pouring Jordanna another glass of wine one Sunday at dinner. "This is why I pray solo. The preacher is invariably a bullshitter and the churchgoers all idiots."

"But I'm a good bullshitter, the best." She and Abby were alone at the table, and Jordanna reached over with outstretched fork and speared an unfinished brownie from Gabe's plate. She didn't tell her sister that sometimes her preaching involved feelings so real, so pointed that she had to drape them on the fabricated nephews. Abby didn't "do" church. Every once in a while she would turn up in one of the pews, Christmas Eve, Easter Sunday, sometimes when their parents were visiting. Lately, Jordanna had been noticing Brendan, though, tucked away in the back on the occasional Sunday. Both Jordanna and Abby were suspicious of Jordanna's need for Abby to be among the flock, and Abby's need to keep her distance. Abby tried to explain that your sister could not possibly be your spiritual leader, most especially your older sister. She had come to the first few sermons, because Jordanna had begged, had said she needed a focal point, one person amid that sea of polished wood and still-damp hair, gold lockets and rep ties.

In one of those first sermons, Jordanna had said that she thought the *Call* for her to serve in Hutchinson had come from the "river of God," from the river of God right here in Hutchinson. Hutchinson Lake, Black Pond, Valentine Pond, Bethel Falls, Tanner's Kettle and the Potatuck River—how very blessed they all were to live in a place where there was so much water, where brooks and streams, creeks, sluices, rivulets and tributaries ran between backyards, across pastureland, behind schools and minimalls and even over the grounds of some select churches. There had been an audible shifting in the pews at this joke. The search committee had been visibly pained during the interview process. It seemed that they desired little more of Jordanna than to bear witness to their collective shame. Reverend Hanley's sin had been well tended in their garden. How very fortunate, she continued, to live in a place where every day, without much effort, you could hear the sound of the living God rushing and gurgling, calling out to you by name. "Life," she said, "calling to life."

Abby had met up with her later, by the Bess Eaton near the highway. "*I* called you here," Abby said, unrolling the inner spiral of her cinnamon bun. "*I* got on the telephone and called and told you there was a job here, not God." Abby worked as a guidance counselor at the high school. She'd known about the philandering minister before almost anyone else, because the other woman's daughter had broken down in her office after failing a Spanish test.

Of course, Abby was right. Abby had called her here. Abby had called and called, nearly every day, during those wretched years while she was having healthy baby after healthy baby and Jordanna and Daniel were wishing and burying and grieving theirs. Abby had called her back to life in a way that no scripture or prayer or other being, human or Divine, had even attempted. Abby called week after week and repeated the same thing until Jordanna heard it. We need you here. Four is more than any woman's fair share. Consider them yours, too, they can be your children, too, but only if you're here. We all need you to be here. And by the time the offer came, she and Daniel had already begun to confuse their grief about the babies with disappointment in each other. She was no longer even sure she wanted to ask Daniel to leave his job at the University of Maine to move with her to Connecticut. Abby's husband, Jim, had written her a note then, reminding her that she was to go where the need was greatest. Jordanna had cried, then laughed at that. They all knew she was the one with the need, she and Daniel. And they couldn't any longer, for the life of them, be located. So her sister had called, and she had come to Hutchinson to solder herself onto their happiness, wondering briefly if her sister's invitation was bred of guilt or unfathomable generosity. She had come because she couldn't bear her and Daniel's own miserable fortune together any longer. She had come because she couldn't stand to be alone anymore. More than anything, she needed to be touched and hugged and grabbed, kissed and spit up on, licked and loved. And this was the only way. She had reached over that day at Bess Eaton and picked at the icing on her sister's roll. "But you *are* my river of God—you and the kids and Jim."

SHE closed the door to her office and cranked open the two small casement windows. Her office was on the shady side of the church house. In winter she brought in a space heater. In the summer months the slate floor, with its very slight patina of moisture, made the whole room feel like a cave. She turned on her computer and stood in front of the mirror on the closet door. A little boy at Bible camp this summer had referred to her multicolored braid as a snake. She quickly brushed her hair back off her forehead, then worked her sturdy fingers in and out of the brown and red and gray strands. She coiled the long thick braid, then began the slow process of pinning it up. She felt the barrettes and clips with her hands, patted the whole invisible creation behind her and decided it was good enough.

"You'll scare the hell out of them like that," her Divinity School advisor had said before she went out on her first round of interviews for assistant pastor positions. "Too much hair, too much clothing, all those jangling bracelets and those earrings, big enough to receive satellite signals." She was twenty-seven and she thought she looked great, professional but approachable, interesting but not weird. "This is not a star turn, my dear. Who do you think these folks want to hire? Somebody who looks just about like them, but is younger, has far more energy and is willing to work like a dog for peanuts."

There was no point in explaining to him that even without a stitch of clothing or a single accessory, she was excessive. She was big, tall and thick, not fleshy, but solid, everywhere. Even her face was big. Her blue eyes bulged just slightly, and her nose was long and flared a bit at the ends. Her brow was prominent, and her lips were large and naturally red as if she were always sucking on cherry candy. When she spoke, her teeth showed themselves to be as big and tall, as striking, as the rest of her. And if she smiled fully, the potent asymmetry of her looks was readily apparent. She had a dimple in her left cheek deep enough to hold a nut. There was no being demure, she told Reverend Solloway.

"This is not a commentary on your personality, Jordanna. I wouldn't dare alter what God has so artfully arranged. I am merely talking about your getup."

She kicked off her sneakers and zipped the black nylon clerical robe over her T-shirt and shorts. The church was not air-conditioned. She refused to wear a dress and hose at the end of August. She leaned over the laptop and checked her e-mail. There was one from Daniel. She sat down at the desk and pulled herself close to the screen. He had been on a dig outside of Auckland since his semester ended in May. Now that the university had agreed to free him up to stay on through the academic year, they both felt they should meet for a week in October in Melbourne. Without articulating it, their decisions were those of individuals who were "staying together" for the sake of the marriage, much the same way people did for their children.

Separated by three states or three continents, their relationship had a similar ebb and flow. Intent could be expressed in letters or e-mails, articles, books and gifts sent between the two, but, no less pointedly, through silence. Both of them were capable of long silences in their correspondence. The phone call from Auckland was weekly but sometimes the connection was poor, or there was that infuriating delay, so difficult for Jordanna to dismiss as a mere technical problem. There were weeks when she wondered why be disappointed or angry with someone so far away. Why be anything *to* him if you weren't *with* him. There were no passing looks, household duties neglected or completed, no physical quirks or scheduling conflicts or compromises as a means of communicating all the millions of messages spouses usually send. Mostly, there was the written word with its enormous capacity for posturing. There were set pieces they sent to each other one after the other. Emotional or nonemotional stills. Frame after frame of separate lives.

She could hear the organist rehearsing. She had intended to type up her sermon notes. The letter she had sent Daniel last week had been selfish, more purgative than communicative. "There is nothing for it," she had written. "That is the worst realization. No blessing in disguise, no sheep in wolf's clothing, no silver lining, no yin to this hellish yang. There is no metamorphosis for all that we have lost. It is only what it is. And when I wake up too early, before I've established my defenses, the rationalizations, the tools of my trade, for a split second I know it for what it really, really is—eternal pain." She had mailed the letter without introduction or preparation. The context was old. Unbelievably, though, the sorrow revisited itself always as something new. She fingered the frame of the computer screen now. She didn't expect anything from him, but that had no bearing on desire, or worse, hope. She closed the e-mail without reading it, saving it for when she had more time and less need.

❧ Chapter 2

"'THE heavens declare the glory of God, / And the firmament proclaims God's handiwork. . . .'" Jordanna raised the wide sleeves of her black robe out toward the windows on either side of the church. "What a glorious day," she said, striding partway down the aisle, then turning. "What a glorious day to be here together to worship God. Let us all take a minute. How difficult it is to leave behind the self that set the alarm clock and made the coffee and found the clean clothes and got here on time. Well, almost on time." She smiled as a young couple dropped their diaper bag and slid into a back pew with their baby. People chuckled and turned. "But really, isn't it our hearts and souls that require transport to this place this morning? Let us all take a moment to bring our selves, our true selves, into this sacred space. I promise, if you lay down your workaday self, right there next to you on the pew, it won't go anywhere. It will be waiting for you at the end of worship this morning." Jordanna walked farther down the center aisle and slid into the second pew.

She ignored the tap on her shoulder as she carefully lowered her back into the pew. Someone was either saying "Reverend Nash, Reverend Nash" or "Shhh, shhh." She blocked it out. She was unprepared, and she used this period of silence to ask God to, at the least, help her integrate her fragmented self. The tapping continued. It was Carol Chandler with some burning message. The organist had already begun the opening chords for "Praise to the Lord! Ye Heavens Adore Him." Jordanna smiled at Carol, squeezed her hand and strode up to the armchair on the side of the pulpit. The hymn ended and Jordanna waited for the hundred-odd little thuds of the hymnals being returned to their slots in the back of the pews. She waited a moment for the talking, the crying, the errant shout. Fred Rinehardt, the lay minister, was on vacation. Ninety percent of today's service would be hers.

"We come seeking the holy love of God . . ." She began the responsorial reading and noticed a small envelope with her name written on the outside, sticking into the fold of the opened Bible on the lectern. "Let us share a life of holiness, justice and love . . ." She slipped the bulging envelope onto the shelf below, where she kept her glass of water and her cup of coffee. There was a slight rustle of bulletins and then, as always in this precious church, a clear and distinct response from the pews. "Let us worship God." She smiled and nodded and stepped out from behind the pulpit.

"Indeed, let us worship God." The wind had picked up outside and the loping maple branches with their late summer leaves waved back and forth, casting shadows across the pews and back into the narthex. She stepped down the three shallow steps of the altar and looked out at the congregation for the unison prayer of invocation. "Gentle God," she began, "help us to learn more about Your great love for us. We have come here to give You praise and thanksgiving . . ." She closed her eyes, let her own voice trail off and listened to them. This was an indulgence, a reaping of energy, to which she felt unentitled, but to which she was helplessly drawn. ". . . for all the wonderful gifts of creation, and for Your holy spirit living within our hearts." The Sunday worship service was a kind of fulcrum, she on one side, the congregation on the other. How to give to each one of them, how, possibly, would she ever balance out her own needs with theirs, her penchant for procuring from them as well as for them? "Let this spirit gather us in . . ." the congregation continued reading, "and form us into an even stronger community of people who reflect the face of Christ to a world in need."

They were down at least a hundred this morning. The last Sunday before Labor Day was one of the least-attended services of the year. At the UCC national conference in Orlando last winter, a minister from southern California had led a session called "Shaking the Hour." Today was her chance. He had advocated the rearranging of the distance between congregants, the sacred spaces in the sanctuary and the minister. She'd been intrigued by his notion of elevating the sacred quality of the pews and deemphasizing the altar. It was from him that she had adopted the habit of sliding into a pew at random during the prayer parts of the service. He'd also led an exercise in which they each removed one shoe and passed it to the person on the left. She'd forgotten the point and couldn't imagine anything less appealing on an August morning.

"What would you say if we all moved in closer together this morning?" She raised her arms high enough for the sleeves on her robe to slide nearly to her armpits. As she slowly lowered her hands, the large watch face on the inside of her wrist caught the sun, sending a glinting light out across the pews. "Our ranks are considerably thinned here, and from where I stand you all look less like a congregation than a constellation . . . Hutchinson Minor." Jordanna walked back toward the altar, sat down at the top of the three steps and slowly stretched out her legs, relieving most of the twist in her lower back. "Those of you who don't mind sitting on the floor, why don't you come up now and do that. Just find a place . . . anywhere." She readjusted the wireless microphone clipped to the underside of her stole and accidentally hit it with the silver spoon ring on her index finger. A thwack of sound shot through the speakers. "Bring your hymnals . . . and your earplugs."

She waited while people looked nervously at their spouses, friends and neighbors. "And I bet everyone else, well, I bet you could all fit into the first five pews on either side of the aisle. Those of you back and side dwellers, come forward today and cast your countenance into that sometime sun."

This was a risk. You could exhort the group to break convention, but there were always those who insisted on acting on their own authority, whatever the request. Surprisingly, it was the elderly parishioners who were the most obedient. They began to move, so did the teenagers. The kids clambered quickly out of every pew, eager for a spot on the sea of burgundy carpeting. Some lay down, a few leaned against the piano. It was the men in their forties and fifties who most disliked her innovation. She waited. People looked at their watches. There was the coffee hour afterward. There was a schedule. The choir director hadn't been informed. How was it, she wondered, that when everyone was doing the same damn thing, something new and different, possibly something they didn't really want to do, a few middle-aged men insisted on being at once self-conscious and dismissive? You could just see it on their faces.

"Magnificent," she proclaimed, as they all rose, some from the floor, some from their pews in front and a few scattered out in the back. The organ started up and they sang the "Gloria Patri."

"Prayers of concern, prayers of celebration . . ." Jordanna said, slipping the list of ill parishioners from underneath her watch strap. Once last summer she had made the mistake of putting the list in her shorts pocket and had been forced to partially unzip her robe to retrieve it. She had refused to be embarrassed, not an emotion she experienced much, if ever, anymore, and instead she had stood squarely in front of the congregation and kept on talking, willing them to look up beyond the red and orange stole she'd purchased years ago in Turkey, past the weighty turquoise earrings suspended from her earlobes, straight into her dark blue eyes with their seductive mixture of compassion and doubt.

Jordanna read through the names on her list, saying each one carefully and loudly, as if properly calling them out here in this space could cure them. When she spoke the names, she envisioned each person, seeing them as whole and happy and healthy, standing on their own two legs here in church singing loudly. When she visited people in the hospital, she tried not to fix her eyes on the metal bed or the oxygen, the urine bag or the IV. In prayer she needed to eliminate those images of disease. Instead she focused only on hands and faces. And breath. No matter how stale or sour. What was being inhaled and exhaled, she told them, told herself, was the breath of God.

"Prayers of thanksgiving? Prayers for recovery?" Jordanna looked around the circle on the floor and at the pews, craned her neck behind her to the organist and the choir. There never was a Sunday when no hands went up. Someone, somewhere was always sick, or worse. She acknowledged each congregant with a nod. The older women often asked for prayers for more than one person, sometimes named three or four, and Jordanna had learned to hold her eyes on these women until she was sure they had finished speaking.

"A prayer of thanksgiving for my new granddaughter Kimberly Bonner Henderson." Laura Bonner looked around at the group, accepting congratulations.

"How many does that make now?" someone called out.

Jordanna steeled herself. It would be a huge number, she knew. Somewhere in the double digits. She had, in the past fifteen months, baptized at least four Bonner grandchildren, and those were only the ones who lived in town. She closed her eyes, folded up her desire as small as it would go, until it hardly showed, until, even to herself, it was barely recognizable as envy, and asked God to forgive her. No sooner would the word *baby* pass from someone's lips, accepted whole and heavy on her own tongue, than she would petition for forgiveness.

"Thirteen," Laura said.

There was nothing for it. "Blessings to you all," Jordanna said by way of congratulations.

She listened as names of the sick were added to the list she had already read. She kept a pen up on the pulpit for updating her own list of people in need of pastoral visits. Today she would just try to memorize the additional names. The trick was to remember the number of new names. If she could recall the number of additional names, she would eventually remember the names themselves. The wind was loud, unusually loud for a sunny summer morning. The clapboards creaked a bit, and now that the choir was silent, it was possible to hear a kind of groaning up through the bell tower.

"A special prayer for June Nearing and for her family," Carol Chandler said, looking straight at Jordanna. Jordanna had been counseling June since just prior to Easter. June had been despondent since the death of her sister the year before. That's what she told Jordanna. That was why she came. But then it seemed that everything in June's life was not right, her marriage, her relationship with her mother, her life at home all day with three young children. And God. Where exactly was this God of hers? Lately, she had begun complaining about aches and pains, shooting pains in her legs. June's sister had died of breast cancer that had spread to the bone. She had described in detail to Jordanna the pain of cancer in the bones. While it seemed likely to Jordanna that the painful symptoms June was experiencing were psychological, she had encouraged June to go for a physical. Oh, Lord, maybe they had found something. When people came forward in church and asked the congregation to pray for someone and to think of their families, it was never because they'd contracted the flu or were recovering from elective surgery. Something far more grave was needed to prompt that kind of public declaration of suffering.

" '. . . One day speaks to another, / night with night shares its knowledge, / and this without speech or language or sound of any voice. / Their music goes out through all the earth, / their words reach to the end of the world.' "

Tom Stanton, the lay reader for the morning, had walked up to the pulpit and begun the Psalter reading. Jordanna turned awkwardly from where she sat on the steps. The offering and the presentation of the gifts had been difficult, given that the entire floor space in front of the altar was covered with children. Kids had run back to their parents for money. There had been some tripping, even some spilling of change. She was sure she would hear about this unorthodox seating arrangement from more than a few people.

When the reader was finished, Jordanna walked up to the pulpit and gathered her sermon notes. She pulled one of the armchairs from beside the pulpit and dragged it to the middle of the altar.

"Can everyone see me from here?" She sat down in the chair and looked out at everyone. She folded the sermon notes in half and laid them on the floor beside her. "Today's scripture lesson is Philippians, Chapter four, verses four through eight:

" 'I will say it again . . .' " She looked around at the circle before her, looked into as many pairs of eyes as she might. " '. . . all joy be yours. Let your magnanimity be manifest to all.

" 'The Lord is near; have no anxiety, but in everything make your requests known to God in prayer and petition with thanksgiving. Then the peace of God, which is beyond our utmost understanding, will keep guard over your hearts and your thoughts, in Christ Jesus.' "

She always memorized the reading. Earlier in her career, she had been troubled by her attachment to such a cosmetic talent. But her own sincerity was no longer an issue for her. In fact, her lack of concern about performance versus essence had become her greatest strength as a minister.

"What a powerful message from the imprisoned Paul. In *everything* make your requests known to God, then the peace of God will guard your hearts and minds. 'The Lord is near.' Look outside. As the psalmist tells us, 'God's handiwork is everywhere.' Look beside you, look around this very room. Is God not so near? Breathe in, breathe out. Look at yourself; is God not, indeed, so very, very close?

"Funny time of year." A little boy over to the side laughed. "For most of us, the hallmark of autumn is change. For some of us that means the less dramatic change of the lightweight wardrobe for the heavier, the shortening days, the cool nights, the end of the blossoms in the garden. For many it means a new school year, new teachers, new classmates, a whole world of new subjects, a host of new opportunities. How many of us greet change, even the hint of change, with a great deal of wariness, even fear? How many of us met this little change-up this morning, this rearranging of the furniture, with trepidation? Seems to be the human condition."

She had written none of this. It was just coming on her, thought after thought. She reminded herself not to pause midsentence, not to hesitate until one thought was complete, not to fragment. It was thrilling for her when this happened. Not as rewarding as when she'd honed a written sermon, worked long and passionately on transferring the message behind the word to the congregation before her. This was another kind of high. It was like being on a swing. She wasn't pumping, but still she was flying higher and higher, so somebody, somewhere must have been pushing. She was sitting in an armchair talking to a relatively small crowd, but her pulse was beating as rapidly as when she rode her bike up Castle Hill. She could feel that her face was hot, and sweat was beginning to trickle between her breasts under her bra and T-shirt and clerical robe. It was that great trick again. She was sitting still in one spot, but part of her was racing and speeding, flying, soaring.

"How many of us separate ourselves from God by our anxiety? How many of us base our decisions upon our fears rather than upon our faith? How different our lives and the world might be if we were to embrace change. If only we truly operated in this world of ours as if God did keep guard over our hearts and thoughts.

"In what is the last week of summer for most of us, why don't we ask ourselves to accept Paul's message in its fullest sense. 'Then the peace of God, which is beyond our utmost understanding, will keep guard over our hearts and our thoughts, in Christ Jesus.'

"Dear God, may the words of my mouth and the meditations of each heart here be acceptable to You, for You are our rock and our redeemer. Amen."

.   .   .

CORINNE Jenkins handed her some wet paper towels as she walked into the narthex.

"How thoughtful," Jordanna said.

Corinne held her hand open to receive the used towels when Jordanna finished wiping her face and the back of her neck.

"Above and beyond, and muchly appreciated." Jordanna pecked her on the cheek, then took her spot out front on the church steps. In between shaking hands, she looked out past the parking lot to the west. The clouds were skimming past, layers and layers of gray, some black. There was thunder in the distance.

"Is June Nearing okay?" Leslie Ray was holding her little boy on her hip. Jordanna cradled the child's face in her hands, and he grabbed on to one of her rings. She slipped it off her finger and onto one of his. He laughed.

"She couldn't take much more, you know," Leslie said.

Jordanna wondered if Leslie knew she'd been counseling June. She gave Leslie's shoulder an extra squeeze, scooped up her ring and fixed her eyes on the next congregant in line. On packed Sundays, the receiving line sometimes reminded Jordanna of a lifeline in a riptide. Hand over hand, she'd been taught for surf rescue. Only here it was hands crossed under eyes, hands, eyes, hands, eyes, as fast as you could go and still maintain some intimacy. Sometimes it seemed that she was passing them down the receiving line, and sometimes it struck her that it was the congregation that was handing her along from member to member.

"We'll see you downstairs." Jordanna smiled at an elderly couple and patted their shoulders. She glanced at her watch. Abby's eldest, Brendan, was in a soccer tournament at one P.M. Damn coffee hour. She wanted to go back to her office and read Daniel's e-mail. She looked up at the sky, and longingly at the cars pulling out of the lot. She would have loved to get in her car and smoke a cigarette while en route to Bess Eaton and a chocolate donut.

When the last congregant had filed through and she could hear the clinking of cups down in the undercroft, Jordanna closed the church's double doors and flicked off the lights in the narthex. She turned to pick up a dropped bulletin, and saw Carol Chandler. She was holding a little envelope. It was the envelope that had been up on the pulpit, stuffed into the Bible.

"Didn't you hear me trying to get your attention?" Carol said, with a mixture of anger and embarrassment.

"I'm sorry," Jordanna said. "You know how I am. I get swept up in the moment, and I don't always pick up on—"

"June Nearing's been missing since seven o'clock last night. She went up to the IGA after supper to get some ice pops for the kids, and she hasn't come back. Drew was up all night. He called the police, and of course Frank Leahy called me this morning before church."

Jordanna sat down on the long bench under the window that looked into the sanctuary. The glass was streaked with saliva and fingerprints. The crying room, they called it down at Our Lady of Fatima. Every house of worship—every house—should have a crying room, she thought.

June had done this before, twice in the past several months. Jordanna wasn't sure how many people knew that. Carol's connection to June was hardly proprietary. She'd gone to high school with June's mother-in-law, and she owned a police scanner. The first time June had just up and left without a word to her husband or mother, she'd ended up in Point Judith at a friend's. The second time she'd called Jordanna from a Comfort Inn near the Canadian border. It was the driving that helped her, she'd said. She listened to tapes as she drove. She took them out from the library, poets reading their own poetry. She needed a lot of time in the car by herself, she'd said.

Jordanna looked up at Carol standing there expectantly. "I'll run up to the house after the coffee hour. I'm sure Drew could use some support."

Carol put her hand on the large pull to the door going downstairs.

"I have a . . . *sense* that June is all right," Jordanna said, placing her hand over Carol's on the door handle. "I think she's okay."

Carol handed Jordanna the envelope without looking at her. When the door had closed behind Carol, Jordanna carefully unsealed the envelope. The paper was thick, the kind children use for art projects. It had been folded numerous times to fit inside the small envelope. The deeply creased single page was filled with writing, a small hard script in two different-colored inks. At the very top in tiny letters it said "To: Jordanna, From: June."

Jordanna opened the doors to the sanctuary. Her back was killing her again. She stretched out in one of the pews.

The letter was a poem, by Elizabeth Bishop: "The art of losing isn't hard to master; / so many things seem filled with the intent / to be lost that their loss is no disaster." Jordanna stopped, folded the paper on her chest and reached behind her to undo the clips in her hair. She piled the barrettes and the bobby pins on top of a hymnal and pulled her fingers through her braid. She knew the poem, but she picked up the paper and made herself read the words in June's crabbed hand, made herself hear them in June's low voice, a voice that was sometimes so aggressively soft that it ate up parts of words even as it spoke them.

. . . Then practice losing farther, losing faster:
places, and names, and where it was you meant
to travel. None of these will bring disaster.

. . . —Even losing you (the joking voice, a gesture
I love) I shan't have lied. It's evident
the art of losing's not too hard to master
though it may look like (*Write* it!) like disaster.

Jordanna turned her cheek on the cushion of the pew and looked down at her hair, skimming the floor. She pulled up her knees and called out to God in that burgundy seat cushion. After so much Divinity School training and over fourteen years in the pulpit, she could still pray like a five-year old. "Oh, God," she whispered into the nylon and wool, "fix it, fix everything." She looked up, at a water stain on the acoustic tile in the ceiling, at the darkened choir loft, at the brass chandeliers all curve and shine, suspended like crowns in this empty room, and she prayed like the minister she tried to be. "Show me how to help her. Give me the strength to lead her to some kind of hope." Then she pressed her ear hard to the cushion and listened.

❧ Chapter 3

D REW Nearing was making grilled cheese when Jordanna walked into the kitchen through the slider in the back. The two girls were at the table and the baby was in the high chair. Only the baby, Ian, was making noise, shaking his bottle upside down, pressing the nipple against the plastic tray. Carly, the three-year-old, was lying with her face on the table, and the oldest child, Lee, the five-year-old, shut her eyes tightly when the woman who slid open the screen turned out not to be her mother.

"Hey, guys," Jordanna said, sitting down at the table next to Lee. "Can you guys see my bike from here?"

Carly hopped up and ran to the slider. "Yeah."

Jordanna saw that she was still wearing her pajama bottoms, even though it was after one. All three of the children looked damp and mismatched. The girls resembled June, small and fair. The older of the two looked as breakable as her mother. "And do you see anything in the basket of my bike?"

Lee stood up and walked slowly to where her little sister was standing. "There's a white bag," she said, without turning to look at Jordanna.

"Did you bring us a present?" Carly walked over to her and took her hand.

"A little treat, for after lunch, if your dad says it's okay." Jordanna looked over at Drew. Unlike the children, he was dressed up, in deeply creased khakis and a dark green polo shirt, as if he were going somewhere. He hadn't said anything to Jordanna since she'd come in. They'd been through this little dance before. The two other times June had "vanished," she'd called Jordanna and told her where she was before calling her husband. The last time, in July, Drew had told Jordanna that he was getting tired of being at the tail end of June's life.

"Reverend Nash, would you like a grilled cheese sandwich?" Drew added more butter to the sizzling pan.

"Is this one of your dad's specialties?" she asked Lee, who was staring at her.

Lee shrugged.

"Actually, Drew, I'm starving. Yes, thank you." She had stayed for a long time at the coffee hour after worship. She had eyed the donut holes and the pineapple coffee cake. She'd caught a whiff of Terri Martin's banana bread. Someone had fetched her a cup of coffee and brought it to her where she stood, glued, trapped, by a faction of congregants who had resurrected, yet again, this rumor of the church selling the property it owned on the other side of town to a developer. Usually Jordanna did her level best to heighten these concerns by saying that the property would be perfect for a couple of housing lots for Domus with Dignity, and wouldn't that be a wonderful legacy for their church community. But this morning, distracted by June's taunting note to her, she had tried to pass off the question to a Prudential Board member. She looked around the room for one of the trustees, and in the end she had been stuck, her sandals on one rose-colored square of linoleum, her large left hand planted against the painted cinderblock of the undercroft, one cup of coffee and no cake for over an hour. The business of this parcel of land never failed to incite argument. For the fifteen months she'd been in Hutchinson she'd been trying to figure out what that land represented to the church, what selling it would signify. Sometimes entering a church community was like being asked to join in a family game. The family was not hers and although the many siblings fought, and seemed to have invited her in order to serve as both arbiter and entertainer, their loyalty, ultimately, belonged to one another and to the conservation of the game. She'd served in congregational life long enough to know that being a pastor meant being, to some degree, marginal.

"What would you guys like to drink?" she asked as she began opening cupboards looking for glasses.

Carly yelled out, "Soda," as Drew reached into the refrigerator and pulled out a gallon of milk.

"There's paper cups over by the water," he said.

"Well, this is neat." Jordanna pulled a stack of cups from a dispenser attached to an office-size water cooler at one end of the unfinished kitchen. The Nearings were remodeling. Drew and June's brother had spent much of last summer adding on to the kitchen. According to June, the construction had been completed by Thanksgiving, but nine months later, the floor was still not in, the Sheetrock was unpainted, the new windows hadn't even been primed. Tall white cabinets lined one wall like a life-size Advent calendar. The counters were covered with a mix of the things of daily life, bread and tape, markers and bananas, as well as nails, shims and unopened cans of paint. They had lost all forward-moving energy.

"Our grandma's taking us swimming this afternoon," Carly said.

"If it doesn't rain," Lee added.

Jordanna placed two cups of milk on the table.

"We had pancakes this morning," Lee said, by way of explaining the tackiness of the walnut table. Jordanna nodded. "Well, your milk won't spill if it's stuck to the table."

Lee shrugged.

"We can too still go if it rained," Carly said.

"They close the pool if there's thunder or lightning," Drew said, looking over at the table for the first time.

"I'm not scared of that," Carly said.

"You should be," Lee said.

Carly slid off her chair and walked over to her brother and began to yank his toes.

Jordanna walked up behind her. "Let's see if we can make him laugh without even touching him." Her oldest nephew, Brendan, had adored this as a baby. Without touching him, she'd sing or dance or blow on his wispy hair and his body, his whole being, would correspond to her voice or gesture as if they were one, as if he understood how thoroughly he was loved.

"It'll be a contest," she said to Carly and Lee. "Okay. Ready?" Jordanna squared off her shoulders and circled her wrists around, vamping the breaststroke. She pinched her nose and shimmied her way into a crouch. "The Swim," she said, raising her eyebrows high above her prominent brow and flaring her nostrils.

Carly screamed. Lee shrugged, and the baby hesitated a minute before his face crumpled and he started to whimper.

"You want to pick him up," Drew said. "He already ate. We're just keeping him in there so we don't have to chase him."

"Dad." Lee stared at the grilled cheese Drew had placed on the table in front of her. "He's supposed to have a nap after his lunch."

The baby was crying full-tilt now.

"He doesn't seem to want me to get near him," Jordanna said. In church, at baptisms, when the babies cried it always struck her as somehow part and parcel of the scene. She had a hundred ways of either getting them to stop or at least playing on it. She would hold the older, larger babies up under their bellies and arms and fly them over the first few people in each pew, drooling cherubs who swooped and sailed. Sometimes they'd laugh; if not, she'd make sure to hold their mouths away from the mike, and she'd just do a running commentary over the crying, which was never loud enough to fill the inside of the sanctuary. But in this kitchen, today, the crying was as overpowering as an organ. Jordanna felt herself getting tense. "Maybe he's still hungry," she said.

"He misses Mommy," Lee said.

Jordanna nodded. For months she had listened to June tell her story, and she had pictured faces and rooms the way you do when you listen to the radio. She had reweighted almost every one of June's statements, adjusted for jaundice, supplied the unvoiced side of the story. But being in this kitchen with June's children and husband, Jordanna caught a solid whiff of June's desperation. This physical immersion in June's life made her realize how little real empathy she'd had for June these past months. *Compassion,* she had reminded herself more than once while June complained about her three healthy children and her loving husband, *to suffer together with* this woman. The smell of burning butter, the crying baby, the crumbs on the subfloor, the unpainted walls—she needed to commit all this to sensory memory if she was to be with June in *her* passion.

"I COULDN'T wait." Jordanna ran her thumbs around the top of her now-empty lunch plate as Drew came down the hall after putting the baby in the crib. "It just smelled so good." The girls had finished eating and were playing out in the yard.

Drew got a pitcher of iced tea from the refrigerator and placed it on the table. "June does this thing where she brews it out in the sun. It's good."

Jordanna pushed her chair from the table and attempted to stretch her spine. "Did anything happen yesterday? Did she say anything before she went to the store last night?"

Drew got up again and got a pile of napkins from the pantry and placed them down on the table after checking for a clean spot. "Did she say anything to you? You just saw her Thursday."

"She said she hadn't been feeling well, physically. I suggested she go to the doctor." Jordanna circled her stiff neck. She looked down under the table at a hair elastic, some Cheerios, Drew's polished loafers. On Thursday, when Jordanna had met with June, she had asked June if she'd called the therapist Jordanna had recommended nearly four weeks before. June had taken the inital referral as a rejection, and they had spent some of every meeting since discussing it. "And, of course, we talked about her making an appointment with Scott Davis, again."

"Who's Scott Davis?" Drew reached for a napkin and gently wiped his red mustache. The rest of his face was smooth and hairless, half man, half baby. His features were fine, as precise as his movements and thoughts. He was like June, in a lot of ways, Jordanna thought. They were small, gentle people who moved almost silently and slowly, as if never wanting to disturb anything or anyone around them.

"Scott Davis is the psychiatrist I recommended."

"Just this week?"

"No." Jordanna inched to the edge of the small kitchen chair and arched her back. "It was over a month ago."

Drew put down his still nearly whole sandwich. She would have guessed him for a slow eater, too.

"She didn't discuss it with you?"

He shook his head. "If you were worried about her enough that you recommended a psychiatrist, don't you think you should have told me or Bev?"

Bev was June's mother. She still lived in the farmhouse where she had been raised and then remained to raise her own four children. The farmland had been sold off, and now the ludicrous houses of Camelot and Stoneleigh Chase encircled the two-hundred-year-old house. When June's brothers finished helping Drew with the kitchen, they were going to jack up the old farmhouse and attempt to repair the foundation. Jordanna admired Bev. She still kept two cows, some sheep and chickens, all in full view of her neighbors' large decks and elaborate swingsets. She worked part-time in the Hutchinson Library, and after her daughter, Eve, died, she began working in the church's Outreach Program. Three out of four Sunday mornings each month she visited homebound congregants. After Easter, she had come to Jordanna's study. Jordanna had been prepared for her to talk about her concern for June or perhaps her grief over losing Eve. What would it take, Bev asked, to become a lay chaplain? She thought it would be really something if she could give Communion when she visited the shut-in congregants. Some of the older ladies had been asking.

"She's good with sick people," June had said softly one day, as if her mother were on the other side of Jordanna's office door. "She was good with my sister when she was sick and dying. She's organized, and she always has a plan. Maybe it comes from growing up on a farm. I mean, really, when she was a kid it was a big farm. She knows how to do that kind of work. The physical aspects of dying are . . . familiar to her. She knows what to do when people are physically sick." June had mumbled the end of her sentence down into the collar of her shirt.

"My discussions with June are privileged," Jordanna said, looking over at Drew. Other people's marriages never failed to shock her. She had not counted on June telling her minister things she had not confided to her own husband.

Drew chewed slowly. There was still a lot of lunch left to eat. She wondered what it was he attempted to rend from that sandwich. "I'm at the tail end of her life," he said, his voice rising up at the end. Jordanna wondered whether he was asking her or telling her.

"You understand that she is depressed. I don't mean sad or even very sad. She needs to see a psychiatrist. This needs to be attended to." Jordanna reached for the pitcher and poured herself another full glass of iced tea.

Drew put down the rest of his sandwich and wiped his hands methodically, pulling at the grease on each finger as if he were tending to one of his children. He sighed deeply and turned toward Jordanna. His milky complexion had gone blotchy, his eyes pink like a guinea pig, as if he were allergic to what else might be revealed. She wondered what she didn't know. People only told you so much, even when they came to you for help, even when they told you more than they told their spouses. Supposedly at the ends of their respective ropes, their hearts and minds gushing all kinds of apparently uninhibited thoughts and feelings, people still only told you what they wanted you to know. They couldn't help it. Depending on how deep you wanted to go, there was always more. She looked at Drew now and got a sharp pain in her nose, as if she were breathing in ammonia. "There's something you'd like to tell me," she said. She heard the baby roll up against the slats of the crib and listened to the girls outside, the plastic wheels of a riding toy grinding over the gravel in the driveway.

"The awful thing is," he said after a while, his mouth pointed down toward the dark, sticky table, "I'm worried about her. I want to know she's okay. But . . . there has been . . . a peace in this house with her gone. . . ." He sighed deeply and when he exhaled a choked sob bolted out from his chest. "I'm sorry," he said, "I . . ."

Jordanna reached over and placed both of her hands on top of one of his on the table. "There are whole systems of belief in which it is assumed that one's emotions run out beyond the boundaries of the flesh, where one's spiritual life is an essence with dimension, texture and a name by which it can be called forth." She stopped and looked up at him and began again. "Trust me, in a family, a depression can be licked up off the floor."

"I haven't even let Bev take the address book . . . worry everybody all . . . We just went through this . . . what, less than six weeks ago. I called the police around midnight last night because . . ." He stopped and abruptly grabbed the dirty dishes on the table. "This time was different. It was night, and the kids were expecting a treat. They were just sitting out on the steps waiting for her. I don't know. It didn't seem like her to tell the children she was going to do something and then . . . disappoint them."

"Well, then you did the right thing," Jordanna said. "If you were concerned for her safety, you did the right thing."

"They don't consider it official until it's been twenty-four hours.

They take the information, but they don't do anything with it. Things always have to get worse and worse before anyone ever does anything. Have you noticed that?" He was using a brush to scrub the cheese from the plates. He let the water run steadily from the faucet and stared at it.

Jordanna picked up the kids' cups and napkins and threw them in the outdoor-size trash barrel in the corner of the unfinished part of the kitchen. "Would you like some help with the laundry, the house, the kids? You know, the Caring Committee would be glad to line up some people from church."

"It's harder for June when everyone knows she's flaking off, as she calls it."

After one of her trips north, June had told Jordanna that when she returned to church she felt like everyone was staring at her, like her depression emitted an odor that trailed her down the aisle. "It's like I'm wearing shit-covered shoes into the sanctuary," she had said.

"Where do you think she is, Jordanna?" Drew turned from the sink with the water still running.

His invocation of her name caused her to remember the pain in the sway of her back. At least a few times a day people asked her to tell them the truth, as if all that were stopping her was a kind of greed, as if she were a spiritual hoarder amid a town of starving souls.

Drew let the water roll off his hands and drip from the ends of his fingertips onto his spotless shoes. "Do you think she would do something to herself? Is she that depressed? Are we—"

"No," Jordanna said. "I think she's in agony. I think there are days when she cannot grieve her sister and bathe her children. I think she has days when she is so sad, she just can't make it down the driveway. That happens, Drew. That happens to people."

"It's been over a year."

"Well, the grief has brought on a depression. I'm not a therapist, Drew. I've spent these past months talking to her about her grief. I understand about mourning. I see now she's gone beyond my professional reach, and I told her as much. She needs a doctor as well as a spiritual counselor."

What June had said to Jordanna on Thursday was, "So, you think I need drugs?" It had been an oppressively hot day, even in the slate cavern of Jordanna's office. She'd positioned two standing fans on opposite ends of the room, and then she'd had to reposition books and mugs to hold down all the papers on her desk. June was so small and thin, so pale and weak, that she had looked like she might be blown against the casement windows if she hadn't been gripping the armrest of her chair. She'd had to tuck her long blond hair into the top of her shirt to keep it from flying around her face. Eventually, Jordanna had switched the fans to low. They were too loud. How many times could someone be asked to repeat a thought or feeling that had been nearly impossible to speak on the first go-around? And when the fans had slowed, it was as if all the emotion in the room that had been furiously whipping around slid to the floor with a thud. That's when June said, "Even Jesus can't help me now."

"Why would you say that?" Jordanna was sitting opposite June in one of the three duct-taped leather armchairs in the room.

"Well, my coming here . . . my hope was that I would learn a new way of looking at all this, a way that might make it bearable." She fingered the small gold locket that dangled from her neck.

Jordanna nodded. She thought of something a congregant in AA had once told her: *Religion is for people who are scared of going to hell, and spirituality is for those who've already been there.* "You know, the axiom about grief—I'm sure I've mentioned it before. 'There's no way through it, but through it.'"

June was wearing white canvas shorts, so small and so in need of washing Jordanna thought they could have belonged to one of her kids. June's appearance had declined in the past few weeks, and Jordanna was unsure of how to address it, other than to continue referring her for professional help.

"I'm too troubled for spiritual guidance. It's like God's giving up on me."

"No one is giving up on you, June, please believe that. I would hope that you would still come to talk with me, even while seeing Dr. Davis. Please understand I am not closing this door."

She shrugged and some of her hair slid out from her pink-striped top. "I mean, I had already felt like God skipped me by. You pray and pray and pray for someone so young as Eve to get better. You do everything, and no one, no one listens. God ignored me then and he's ignoring me now."

Jordanna reached across the space between them and laid her knobby hands over June's. She could feel all the chewed-up parts of June's fingers as she let the full weight of her hands descend onto June's. "People ignore, June. That's a human response to suffering, not a Divine one. God has not abandoned you, just because you cannot hear his voice right now."

"The thing is"—June slipped her hands out from under Jordanna's and smoothed down her shorts and slid her chair back slightly on the floor—"I don't really care anymore."

Jordanna wondered if she meant this or if it was merely one more kind of goading. June had become increasingly provocative over the months. These sessions seemed less palliative than combative, June often trying to lure Jordanna into a debate.

"How's the sleeping? Are you able to sleep?"

June shrugged. "I only enjoy sleep if I dream about Eve. And God doesn't even give me dreams about Eve. You know all these people in these books you've suggested I read. They all have these great experiences, where the person who has died comes back to them, sometimes in a dream, sometimes when they are awake. And it's all so comforting and wonderful. All that reassurance. I suppose I don't deserve that, either. None of that. I've had none of those . . ." She stopped and exhaled.

Jordanna had led June through a number of guided meditations over the past months, meditations that were meant to help her commune with Eve in some way that might prove spiritually, emotionally beneficial, to stay connected to her. All those attempts at reassurance had failed. "Nothing" is what June would announce as she opened her eyes week after week. "Not a thing." God had left her comfortless.

"What makes you think you are undeserving?" Jordanna continued.

"Experience."

"Do you see that as a choice?" Jordanna was losing patience. "Are you aware that you are choosing to view life as a report card? Bad things happen to people who deserve bad things to happen to them. Where would you get an idea like that?"

"Everywhere." She rubbed her thumb over the filigree on the face of her locket.

"Why would you choose to internalize it? Why not choose a God who is all-loving and accepting? Why not view the joy in your life as of equal importance and value to the pain?"

"I don't think you understand what I've been through," June said firmly but quietly. "How can an all-loving God torture a twenty-eight-year-old-woman with radiation and chemicals for fifteen months, force her mother to watch and then have her die?" Her voice was low and flat. "Where's all the love and acceptance in that kind of a deal?"

"God did not take away Eve's life—cancer did. God is here to help all those left behind. Jesus is a healer—if you allow yourself to be healed."

LIGHTNING flashed in the Nearings' yard for a full five minutes before there was any thunder. Jordanna leaned out the sliding door and called the girls in.

"Now we can't go swimming," Lee said, as if she had predicted this all along.

"We need the rain. The flowers and the plants and the trees are thirsty," Jordanna said as they came inside. "Maybe it will rain really hard for a few minutes and the sun will come out and then you can still go swimming."

"But the ground where we put our towels will be all soaked."

"What about our treat you brought us?" Carly said as the first clap of thunder ripped through the sky.

"Oh, my gosh." Jordanna opened the sliding door and a cool gust of dark air swept into the kitchen. She ran across the deck and into the driveway. She walked back with her bicycle.

"How will you get home?" Lee asked.

"Here's my hat, what's my hurry?" Jordanna teased.

"What?" Lee asked, with the same deadpan expression Jordanna had seen on June's face more than once.

"Is it okay if I wait out the storm? We'll have some . . . of what's in this bag while Dad's doing the laundry." The thunder and lightning continued and the wind caused the swings to twist around wildly, but still it wasn't raining.

"Is our mommy dead?" Carly asked as Jordanna put a large black and white cookie in front of her on a piece of paper towel.

Jordanna's mouth was full of the thick dry cookie. "Oh, no, Carly, no." The words came out with crumbs. "Have you been thinking that?" Jordanna came up behind her and squeezed her shoulders.

Carly shrugged and reached for her cookie.

"We had an aunt who died and she was even younger than our mother," Lee said.

"I know that. Your mom has told me a lot about Aunt Eve."

"We just called her Eve," Lee said.

"Well, if she's not died, then where is she?" Carly said. She continued to eat her cookie, but Lee stopped and looked up at Jordanna.

"You know, when I'm sort of worried about things, or feeling sad, I tell God all about what I'm thinking. We could do that right now, the three of us. Talk to God about your mommy."

"You mean, like, pray?" Lee was studying Jordanna so carefully now that Jordanna reached up to her nose with a napkin to make sure it wasn't running.

"If you would like to do that."

"We need to hold hands all together," Lee said, eyeing the cookie in her little sister's hand. She took the cookie out of Carly's grip and grabbed her hand, then took Jordanna's. Jordanna reached across the width of the kitchen table for Carly's other hand.

"God, tell Mommy that we miss her," Lee began with unusual energy. She had her eyes closed and she was squeezing two of Jordanna's fingers in her whole little-girl hand. "We will be very good if she comes home, because we love her. And baby Ian really needs her, too. Everybody here is sad. And maybe if you tell her to come home this time she won't be sad so much." Lee paused and looked up at Jordanna. "Oh, and amen."

❧ Chapter 4

JORDANNA stopped at the pay phone at the Amoco before heading over Bennett's Bridge to Brendan's soccer game. She'd probably missed the first half by now, even with the delay for the thunder and lightning. A front had moved through, bringing cooler air and strong winds, but no rain. The sky still looked steely, filled with electricity. Jordanna reached into the pocket of her shorts and pulled out a pile of inadequate change. She laid down her bike by the auto vacuum and slowly walked around the empty gas pumps, eyes on the oily pavement, searching for a quarter. She stopped suddenly, bracing her foot against a trash barrel and registering the sharp little sensation in her septum. She needed to call the answering machine in her office. Three or four times a week this happened. She would find herself in the presence of something stronger than an inkling, but weaker than an outright premonition. It was no more, really, than an unconscious redirection of attention, like catching something out of the corner of your eye, something you just can't ignore. A person would pop into her head and she would sense that she needed to place a call, write a note, drop by for a visit. As a kid she just figured she was distractable. Her thoughts would wander and she'd try to rein them in. For much of her life she had treated these urges like cravings for a certain food, or a book, or a piece of music. It had all seemed to be a kind of lust, the product of an undisciplined mind, self-created and therefore completely dismissable. But something had happened after James was stillborn and then Alice. It was like what she'd heard about blind people having a stronger sense of hearing than sighted people. Losing those babies had been like losing vital organs, and now her empty body echoed its perceptions loud and clear. In the past few years these thoughts were almost always accompanied by a strong but odorless scent, as if just for a moment pure oxygen, cold and clean, were being blown into her nose, as if the Holy Spirit were performing CPR.

"Hey, Reverend Jordanna, you know, you really should wear a helmet." Derek Taylor came out of the gas station unwrapping an ice-cream sandwich.

Derek was in Senior Pilgrim Fellowship, the youth group she ran for high school students in her church. "Well, that looks mighty good. You don't happen to have a quarter on you, by any chance, do you? Of course, I'm good for it."

Derek laughed. He stuck the half-unwrapped ice cream between his teeth and reached with both hands below his knees into the pockets of his long shorts.

"Isn't that a nuisance? Your pants always falling off like that?"

"Breeze," he said, pulling the waistband of his shorts away from his nonexistent stomach and handing her a quarter.

"That's true. Remind me about this quarter, okay? I mean it."

He laughed again. "You really should wear a helmet, you know."

"It's not a motorcycle, just a bike."

"Kids look up to you. Think about head trauma."

"Everybody looks up to me, Derek. I'm the tallest pastor east of the Mississippi." She began walking toward the pay phone, then turned around. "The first Thursday night after Labor Day, okay? I'll e-mail everybody. That's going to be our first meeting."

"You know about Tara Sears?" He threw the shredded wrapper

into the blue barrel by the door of the minimart and walked back to where he'd been standing by the motor oil display.

Jordanna turned from the phone and started back in his direction.

He looked around. They were the only two in the whole gas station. He waited until she was close, then took a step forward. "She's pregnant, and her parents are making her have the baby."

Jordanna ran her forefinger around her dry lips. "Are you friendly with her, Derek?"

He shrugged and Jordanna stared at him. Tara had stopped coming to Senior Fellowship sometime during the winter. Jordanna had called once, and then left her alone. "Would you do me a favor? Suggest that she call me. She might need someone to talk to."

"Her parents are, like, sending her away somewhere or something."

Jordanna wondered about the accuracy of this information. "What grade is she in now?"

"She's going to be a junior."

Jordanna nodded. "Would you do me that favor? Tell her she can come by and see me anytime. She can come over to the house, if that's better for her, okay?" Jordanna touched him on his bony damp shoulder and strode off to the phone.

She had four messages. The first was from Abby, reminding her to pick up an ice-cream cake on her way over for dinner. It was Gabe's half birthday. The second was from Daniel, who never called on Sundays. She remembered the unread e-mail, wishing she'd taken the time to print it out. The third was a hang-up and the fourth was from the hospice nurse taking care of Mary Jane Krull. Mary Jane was dying. Today. It was only a matter of hours now.

Jordanna picked her bike up from the ground and headed back up West Street and then onto Conover. She reached down for her bottle of water and slid it out of its holder. "Don't ever get old," Mary Jane had said vaguely on Wednesday, her head barely denting the pile of thin pillows beneath her. It was the first time since her diagnosis that Jordanna had seen her in bed. Only the week before, Mary Jane had brought Jordanna out to her barn and taken her on a tour of forty years of sporting equipment: skis with bear-trap bindings, skinny bamboo poles, golf clubs in tartan plaid pull carts, warped wooden tennis rackets, mouse-eaten life preservers, which Mary Jane referred to as "Mae Wests," figure skates and hockey skates, a croquet set with the totem-pole paint on the poison stick barely visible, battered shuttlecocks, bald tennis balls and, way in the back, hanging on the far wall of the barn, a black tandem bicycle.

"I want you to take the bicycle." Mary Jane had pronounced the word so that it sounded like *life cycle*, and Jordanna had been confused for a moment.

"Well, if you can't take it today," Mary Jane said, nodding beyond the open barn doors into the sunlight and Jordanna's English three-speed bike, "then you'll come back for it."

"A bicycle built for two," Jordanna said.

"Well, somebody built it, but mostly it was bought for two. A bicycle bought for two. Mr. Krull bought that for our fifteenth anniversary."

"You're sure your niece and her children won't want it?"

"I want you to take it, because I know you'll ride it. When your husband comes back, the two of you can ride it all around Hutchinson. Now, won't that be a sight." Mary Jane sat down on what looked like the cabinet of an old television set.

Jordanna laughed. The minister's husband was sight enough standing on two legs. The congregation didn't know what to do with him when he did visit. The idea of him seemed to suit everyone so much better than the reality.

"What was your favorite sport, Mary Jane?" Jordanna said, looking around at all the long-unused equipment.

"Swimming. Was and is." Mary Jane picked up a spider by one leg and dropped him to the dirt floor. "That's what I think about when I'm lying down. There's so much resting and so little sleeping when you're going. No one tells you that, but it's true. What do you need to rest for, I don't know. But when I'm lying down, I close my eyes and I swim all the rivers and ponds and oceans and pools I've ever been

in. I'm working my way though them all. I started with the bodies of
water furthest away. The Pacific Ocean. Mr. Krull and I went to California in 1973, and I swam in the Pacific. Then I just go like that,
working my way east to Hutchinson, and all the swimming holes I
was in as a girl, the swimming pools and the little streams and brooks
we used to picnic by. I'm trying hard to remember them all. There
are ponds that have come to me for the first time in fifty years. It's an
amazing thing."

"Have you always been able to do that?" Jordanna walked over to
an old archery target, with ancient hay poking through its canvas
cover. "Is it just something that's come to you now, that kind of clar-
ity about the past?"

"Now that I'm going, you mean?" She pressed the heel of her
hand into her hip. "Bow and arrows around here somewhere. Mr.
Krull and I used to set that up in the field behind the house after supper and we'd bet each other. Not money, but chores, things like that.
I was an excellent shot. Almost always beat him." Mary Jane moved
slowly toward an old tabletop pinball machine. She pulled back
weakly on the ball release. "I called Herb Kennedy up at the funeral
home and told him I want to be put in my swimsuit and bathing cap.
No shoes, and no polish on the toes. They do that, you know. Ghastly
business. He thought I was joking. But I'm not going to let some no-
mind come in here and pick out a dress I probably bought to wear to
somebody else's funeral, and dress me up in it. When we go up to the
house, I'll show you right where I keep this swimming suit."

They walked out of the barn and Mary Jane tried to stretch to
secure the doors with a sliding bolt, but her body was too hunched
for that. Jordanna offered to help, but Mary Jane waved her away.
"No point, really, in locking it, anyway." She led the way toward the
small white Cape through a gauntlet of hostas. "Now, I know I can
count on you to see that my will is done, because I see that you are a
lot like me."

"I am flattered by the comparison, Mary Jane."

Mary Jane made a face. "Don't be insincere. It doesn't become you." Mary Jane pulled open the heavy screen door with the curly metal K stretching across it. "I can see we've walked the same road."

The house was dark and still. Jordanna went over to a new fan on the coffee table and put it on high. The price tag swung wildly as the fan began to oscillate.

Mary Jane sank into the couch, which was covered with a mended pink bedsheet. There were half-filled mugs and Dixie cups on every surface.

"God hasn't blessed you with children, either. I can see it on your face all the way up when you're in the pulpit." Mary Jane looked straight at Jordanna and motioned for her to sit beside her on the sofa.

"Mr. Krull came home with that two-seated bicycle to distract me, I think. Fifteen years married, fifteen years no children. I was at the end of my rope with want. It was worse in those days. Women around here didn't go to office jobs. Women were wives and mothers. The two went together, wife and mother. People thought nothing of having families of seven and ten children. And here we were out here day after day, night after night, with only husband and wife. Barrenness was considered a kind of punishment. I bet you don't know that."

"I don't think things have changed very much, in that respect," Jordanna said. She eased herself down on the couch, so as not to jostle Mary Jane. She didn't talk about her "losses" to many people in Hutchinson. It was not part of her identity at the church. In some ways that was why she'd come. Nobody here had seen her body rise and fall twice with a growing baby. No one here knew about the two funerals, the two caskets, the two headstones. Her inability to sustain life was not her most notable attribute, as it had been in Maine. Here, the whispers were only about her height, her unorthodox marriage, her unusual fashion sense, her bike, her hair. Here, the whispers were about things that mattered little to her.

"Do you think about that still? Do you still think about not having had any children?" She looked over at Mary Jane. Her head was tilted against the back of the couch and her eyes were closed.

"When it stopped being a physical possibility, I mean, at all, you know, after the change, well, the desire just finds its place. But you don't get old without thinking about children taking care of you. Cripes, that used to be the reason people had so many. At least one was bound to care for you in your old age. Now I think about everything. But of course, that's just as it should be."

JORDANNA rode up the long gravel drive that led to the Krulls'. A new house was under construction down by the main road, but up in the back the property surrounding the little Cape and barn probably looked pretty much as it had for at least a hundred years. There was only one car parked in the turnaround by the old pump, and Jordanna figured that she was in time. She propped her bike against the barn and plucked some daisies from the side yard before going into the house.

The music was on loud, a show tune. Ethel Merman was singing, "No, you cain't get a man with a gun." The nurse walked down the hall when Jordanna entered.

"How's she doing?"

"I would say an hour or two at the most, maybe not that."

"Have you called her niece?"

"Can't get ahold of her. I've left a few messages. August is a terrible time to die."

"Is there ever a good time?"

The nurse smiled. "She liked Ethel Merman, she told me that last week. Loved Broadway musicals. So I thought . . . We've played almost all the show tune albums over the past ten days. She might still be hearing something."

Jordanna walked down the hall to the back bedroom. Mary Jane had not wanted to die in the double bed she had shared with her husband, in the room where she had spent fifty-four years of marriage and six of widowhood. Instead, she had laid down for the last time in what she called the guest room, what Jordanna imagined had once

been considered the nursery. Jordanna pulled a ladder-back chair up
to the twin bed. Before she sat down she leaned over Mary Jane and
placed both her hands on the old woman's nearly visible skull.
Silently, she prayed for the transition from here to there to be easy,
even joyous.

The nurse poked her head in and said she was going to get some
iced tea. "Would you like some, Pastor?"

"I'm sorry, I've forgotten . . ."

"Lois."

"Please, call me Jordanna. Yes, a cold drink would be wonderful."

"Mary Jane," Jordanna said, smoothing the yellow chenille bedspread over Mary Jane's small body. "It's Jordanna, Reverend Nash.
I've just come to sit with you for a while. If you are uncomfortable,
you must let us know. Squeeze my hand or blink."

There was no response at all. Ethel Merman was still quite audible
from the record player in the living room, shrieking that she wanted
"an old-fashioned wedding with champagne and caviar." Jordanna
got up and pushed back the yellow curtains from the two windows in
the room. There was a breeze outside, but none in this boxlike room,
with its low ceilings and its crowd of maple furniture. She picked up
a little porcelain bell from a doily on the dresser. The ball inside
clinked dully against the china. There was a small oil painting of a
boy fishing by the banks of a river. Jordanna ran her finger over the
boy's blond hair, the unbaited hook at the end of his rod. This was
what was sad. Everything in this room, these things, all these things
were sad, but not Mary Jane. Jordanna stood at the end of the bed
and leaned over the footboard, one post draped with rubber bands,
and rubbed Mary Jane's feet under the spread. "It will be wonderful
there, you know, Mary Jane. Maybe all the resting has been to ready
yourself for this passage, this trip."

The nurse walked into the room with the daisies Jordanna had
ripped from the yard. She placed the small vase on the dresser and
handed Jordanna her iced tea.

"I'm going to give a quick listen. There was quite a bit of fluid, even last night. That's what happens. The morphine gets in the way with . . ." She stopped talking as she slid her stethoscope under the top of Mary Jane's nightgown. "It's very labored. Do you think she'd want her niece here now?"

Jordanna took a long drink of her tea. It was unsweetened and she made a face as she swallowed. "I think Julia would want to be here. Whether that is what Mary Jane wants . . . You've left messages. Why don't we just see what happens." Jordanna picked up her sweating glass from the dresser and rubbed at the little puddle that had formed on the dark wood. "Was there any other kind of music Mary Jane said she liked?"

Lois laughed. "There's lots of records in the other room."

"It is Mary Jane's day, but Ethel Merman just doesn't seem conducive to . . ."

"She made sure I would remind you about the bathing suit, too." Lois lifted her glass from the airless windowsill.

"Do you live in Hutchinson?"

Lois shook her head. "Deerfield."

"Have you had many dealings with the Kennedy Funeral Home?"

"Enough. He's usually very . . . prompt . . . about picking up. I had one case a few months ago where they were waiting for one son to get home, to say his goodbyes. Well, you don't keep the embalmer waiting, I guess."

"How do you think he'll respond to Mary Jane's burial outfit?"

"She's a character."

Jordanna reached over the end of the bed and massaged Mary Jane's feet again. "I've only known her for a little over a year. She's been sick probably that whole time. I've had the strangest thoughts, though, of wishing I'd been a contemporary of hers. You know how when you were a kid and you'd read a history book or a biography and you'd try to will yourself back in time. Mary Jane has a way of describing the past, her past . . . It's like I can smell it."

"I think at the end of people's lives the past gets . . . done up a little . . . romanticized."

Jordanna looked a Lois, conscious of not being dismissive. Clearly the woman did not understand what she had meant. Here she'd had the privilege of witnessing a vibrant, effusive woman's last days, and all she'd gleaned from that was a platitude.

"I have enjoyed our talks," Lois continued. "She's a gracious woman. Even in pain, she maintained a kind of calm. She was probably the person least afraid of discomfort, even of death, who I've worked with. I was called in here late, maybe that's why. She'd made her peace with things by the time I got here."

The record had ended and Jordanna listened to the needle running around and around the center of the album.

"I'll see what else is in there. If you want, you can take that washcloth and dip it in that bowl of water and just pat some on her lips."

Jordanna twisted up an old white cloth and dipped it in the saucer of water. She gently touched the wet cloth to Mary Jane's mouth. Her lips looked painfully dry, with thin little cracks running beyond the boundary of color and onto her dusty white skin. "Would you like me to read to you, Mary Jane?" Jordanna said now with her back to the bed. She opened the nightstand drawer, where she knew there would be a Bible. This was the room that husband or wife moved to when they couldn't sleep. This was the room with the Bible. The Bible opened to Psalms, where a business card had been used as a bookmark. It was an ancient-looking doctor's card, with an address in New York City and a phone number whose prefix was written out in letters, MH 3-3232. There were four psalms on the two pages where the card had been. Jordanna read the 100th, the 111th and the 112th all out loud. She walked over for the last of her iced tea and began in on the 113th Psalm. "O praise the Lord. . . . High is the Lord above all nations, his glory above the heavens. / There is none like the Lord our God in heaven or on earth, / who sets his throne so high but deigns to look down so low; / who lifts the weak out of the dust and raises the poor from the dunghill, / giving them a place among princes, among the princes of his people; / who makes the woman in a childless house a happy mother of children." In the small white space before the beginning of the next psalm, written in a tiny cursive hand, were the words "Are not I, your husband, worth more to you than ten sons?" Jordanna pulled her chair closer to Mary Jane's bed and flipped the Bible back to First Samuel, to the beginning, to the story of Hannah. She looked down quickly, then closed the Bible with her thumb in the spine and said to Mary Jane softly, "Elkanah had two wives, Hannah and Penninah. Peninnah had children, but Hannah was childless. This man used to go each year to worship and to offer sacrifice to the Lord at Shiloh. When Elkanah sacrificed, he gave several shares of meat to his wife Penninah with all her sons and daughters; but to Hannah, although he loved her, he gave only one share, because the Lord had not granted her children."

Mary Jane's mouth twitched slightly and Jordanna picked up the damp cloth and pressed it to her lips again. She had lost her place in the story, her recall was thrown, and she picked up the Bible and read from it. "Hannah's rival used to torment her because she had no children, torment and humiliate her. This happened year after year. Once when she was in tears and would not eat, her husband Elkanah said to her, 'Hannah, why are you crying and eating nothing? Why are you so miserable? Am I not more to you than ten sons?'" Jordanna exhaled slowly, deeply, and closed the Bible, her thumb holding the place. First Samuel had deeply troubled her for some time. When infertile couples came to her for counseling she no longer referred to it. They knew all about bargaining with God already. Desperate transaction was at the heart of the quest for fertility, both modern and ancient. She and Daniel had argued about this passage once. Daniel had told her that it was read in the synagogue during the High Holy Days along with the story from Genesis about the binding of Isaac, and that the two stories had always horrified him. She remembered defending his own text to him, trying to explain about the covenant, about total faith and trust in God. "Primitive stories from a primitive culture about human sacrifice," he'd said. "Child sacrifice," she'd heard him mutter to Chip not long after they'd buried James, his academic grip on the phrase slipping and giving way to something on the verge of rage. She and Daniel hadn't yet worked their way to the 113th Psalm. When it seemed right, she did guide couples to it as a means of showing them that there could be many ways to fill a house with children. She guessed it was Mary Jane's husband who had cross-referenced those passages, and she tried to imagine what it might be like to be married to someone who spoke to you in the margins of the Holy Bible.

"After they had finished eating and drinking, Hannah rose in deep distress, and stood before the Lord and prayed to him, weeping bitterly. Eli saw the priest was sitting on his seat beside the door of the temple of the Lord. Hannah made a vow. 'O Lord of Hosts if thou wilt deign to take notice of my trouble and remember me, if thou wilt not forget me but grant me offspring, then I will give the child to the Lord for his whole life, and no razor shall ever touch his head.'"

Jordanna closed the Bible and began to open the drawer of the nightstand from where she'd taken it. She wondered who would come to own this Bible, if anyone would ever again read that handwritten plea at the end of the 113th Psalm. Perhaps it didn't matter. Maybe all that God had intended had, in fact, just transpired. She walked back over to the dresser and tipped her glass up to her mouth, forgetting that it was empty. As she put it down, she saw something different on Mary Jane's face. She was crying. Not with sound or shaking. But tears were coming, one fully formed, then another out of the corner of her right eye. Jordanna walked over to her and bent down and kissed her lips.

❧ Chapter 5

ABBY looked out her bedroom window at the smoke billowing from the barbecue. The fire was hot, and her sister was late. She'd have a good reason. Jordanna always did. Someone was sick or dying, or lonely or crazy. Someone, somewhere, needed her, and dinner was, well, just food. Each time, Jordanna had encouraged them to go on ahead without her, to the table, the game, the movie, the concert; Abby had cautioned that she'd be a hell of a lot happier if she could set some limits. Carve out some sacrosanct time from this omnivorous job. The argument would then unfold with Jordanna saying that it wasn't a job, it was a role—like mother or father. Or aunt, Abby would say. No, not like aunt, Jordanna would tell her. Aunts were ancillary, nice to have, a plus, a bonus, but not crucial or central. Mothers, fathers and ministers were central.

Abby lifted out a pair of boy's underwear from the laundry basket, folded it neatly in thirds and told herself to check her anger at her sister. It's all she's got and she needs to make it all-important. She wondered if she'd bring the ice-cream cake. Jordanna was selfish that way. The details of life were somehow always absorbed by those around her. Maybe that's what came from people deferring to you, entrusting you with their souls: You started thinking yourself above certain things, like remembering dessert.

Abby walked into Brendan and Christopher's room, a stack of briefs and seven pairs of rolled-up socks smashed to her chest. It had shocked her to see her sister's life up close. There was so little that was familiar about it. Shortly after Jordanna had moved into the parsonage, Abby had spent an afternoon there waiting for a fax line to be installed. She'd expectantly placed her key in the lock of the house, looking forward to suspending the chaos of her own life, immersing herself in the mystery of her sister's existence, or at least her stuff. She'd been in the house before, but always with Jordanna there. Why hadn't she noticed how bare it was? Without Jordanna's massive shining presence, the house was frighteningly empty. There were no fingerpaintings or sprouting seeds in Dixie cups, no crude ceramic figurines or listing piles of catalogues, none of the junk of Abby's own house that trailed behind it the material glory of life with kids. There were the few noteworthy pieces Jordanna and Daniel had collected in their travels. A large brass bell they'd brought back from Turkey dangled above the pine plank table in the dining room. Two Moroccan masks interrupted the clean sweep of white wall opposite the navy sofa in the living room. There was one low bookshelf downstairs and a whole roomful of black and olive books upstairs in a spare bedroom that had been turned into an office. Either Jordanna or Daniel, or both, in some misguided conjugal contract, had stripped every single hardbound book of its dust jacket, giving the shelves an institutional feel, about as comforting, Abby thought, as the ancient stacks of a university library. Before Jordanna had moved to Hutchinson, Abby had fantasized that the parsonage might serve as a kind of pied-à-terre within her own town, an oasis, a retreat for the lay mother of four. But the spare house with its functional, dispassionate decor seemed more lamasery than day spa. The place seemed so inadequate to the true needs of flesh-and-blood people. She had tried to explain to her husband that it was more than an ascetic aesthetic. It was as if their lives were being lived out somewhere else entirely.

Jim had laughed and said, "Of course, those two live the life of the mind or the spirit or whatever. Life *is* being lived somewhere other than in the material of that place." Abby had shaken her head. "But where does she rest? Where does her body rest?"

Abby shut Christopher's dresser drawer and looked out the window at the front of the house. Jordanna was coasting down the steep gravel driveway, her torso stunningly erect, her large and glorious head unprotected from the dangers of the road. Why, Abby wondered, had she been chosen to suffer the aching desire to nurture this older sister, and the equally maternal, no less fierce, inclination to reconfigure her? When she had encouraged Jordanna to move here, she had thought she might locate herself at a few key junctures in her sister's life so as to discreetly redirect its flow. But Jordanna had, of course, arrived and made her own life, most of which had little to do with Abby and the kids. Abby had watched her sister roll along, and she'd found herself unable to effect any real change, certainly not the sea change she had wished for.

Abby continued folding clothes and listened to the voices of her sons and husband and sister, first out in the yard, then in the kitchen. There was always a kind of excitement when her sister was in the house. Even in the worst of her grief, she came bearing energy. Her voice was deep, slightly raspy, as if she were about to tell you a dirty joke or order a martini at noon. There was something ever so slightly illicit about Jordanna—both illicit and swollen with a purpose of the deepest kind. In high school Abby knew that both boys and girls had mistaken Jordanna's nearly continual physical movement for sexual energy. They'd been too inexperienced then to know that the attraction wasn't about sex but power. Jordanna could make things happen—in a couple or a family, a congregation or a community.

Abby tucked the empty laundry basket under one arm and picked up the book on the floor next to Brendan's bed. She heard her name invoked a few times, and listened as they talked downstairs about the forgotten dessert. Jim said he'd run out and get something. She placed the book on the nightstand. C. S. Lewis, *Letters to Malcolm: Chiefly on Prayer*. Last summer it had been the Dalai Lama. From below she heard a dining room chair scrape the floor. She pictured her sister, one foot in the middle of the rush seat, retying her sneaker. A ball bounced unevenly. There was a scurry of feet to the living room, to the stereo, and then the distinct sound of speakers being moved. Of course, you had to have music to play football.

Abby washed her face and reapplied her makeup. She was the pretty one, Jim always reminded her. She was tall, but not as unusually tall as Jordanna. She was trim and fair, with no one feature that caused you to say, "Too bad," or stare for just a second too long. She had the kind of face people enjoyed looking at. Her looks were calming and safe, somehow familiar and reassuring. By the time Abby got downstairs, she could hear crying even above the sound of Cheryl Crow belting it out in the living room. Jordanna was sitting at the kitchen table with Gabe in her lap, a dish towel filled with ice held up to his eye.

"Tell your mom how you took one for the club," Jordanna prompted as Abby came in the room. Jordanna squished up her face and shook her head far above Gabe's view. *He's fine,* she mouthed to Abby.

"JoJo's going to teach me the flea flicker," Gabe said in a break from his sobbing.

Abby squatted in front of him and pulled the washcloth from his eye. The orbit was beginning to turn a bit purple. She replaced the ice against the bone and kissed her sister on her cheek.

"Mary Jane Krull passed."

"Oh, I'm sorry," Abby said.

"It's too cold, Mom. Can I go watch TV?"

Abby pressed slightly on the bone under Gabe's eye, then she kissed him and picked him off her sister's lap. "Don't you want to go back outside with the boys?"

He shook his head.

"Okay. Just for a while."

When he was out of the room, she said, "Was it awful?"

"Not at all." Jordanna walked over to the refrigerator and pulled out a bottle of white wine. She held it up to Abby for approval.

"Sure." Abby dumped the dish towel filled with ice into the sink. "Well, it was fine for you, you weren't the one dying."

"Actually, it was quite a powerful experience." She opened the silverware drawer and pulled out the corkscrew.

"I would think so, for Mary Jane."

"Well, I'm not going to share this with you if you're not into it, Abby. It's really an honor to be with someone at the most important moment of their life—I'm not going to betray that significance, Mary Jane's integrity, so you can get off a few good lines."

"Can we just not talk about death today? I feel like talking about mesquite versus hickory and . . . Brendan won his soccer game."

"I'm really sorry about that. The hospice nurse called me around one. She really only had her niece, who wasn't even around today. I couldn't let her die alone."

"It wasn't a criticism. I was really just telling you about the game. Brendan had two assists. They won two to one. It was close, really close."

"June's gone off again. Not a word, not to anyone."

"Nearing?"

Jordanna swept two wine glasses from the top shelf of the cupboard. "Went to get ice cream on Saturday evening."

"It's only Sunday."

"That's what I said to her husband. I was over there after church. I don't know. I've been counseling her—"

"Forever."

"Abby, I've tried and tried to get her into treatment with someone. You know that. I've asked you for a million names. I've made calls for her. The whole nine yards. She's taken the medical referral as a rejection."

"Wouldn't you?"

"She's taken it as a rejection by God, I think."

"That's precisely what depression is." Abby slid a fat clove of garlic into the garlic press and squeezed the pulp over the marinating steak.

"Separating yourself from God is what depression is. She thinks *God* has done the rejecting here."

"Well, you can understand that, can't you?"

"She's not allowing herself to be comforted. That's what God is there for, and she's raising up these obstacles to her belief." Jordanna tugged on the front of her shirt where it stretched too tightly across her breasts. "She's getting in the way of the healing."

"You're mad at her. That must make her feel real good."

Jordanna handed Abby a glass of wine and walked to the other end of the kitchen and examined the bananas hanging in the mesh basket.

"I'm frustrated. She thinks God has taken her sister from her, that God's abandoned her. She's so belligerent in her depression."

"And if she were open to listening to you, then she wouldn't be depressed." Abby reached into the refrigerator and pulled out a fat shiny eggplant. She ran it under the faucet. "She needs drugs."

"And counseling. Drugs don't give you hope."

Abby tucked the eggplant under one arm and ripped a piece of paper towel from the roll. "The good ones do."

"What do you want me to do? I'm just standing here. Give me a job."

"Set the table," Abby said.

"In here or outside?"

"In the dining room." Abby cocked her head in the direction of the next room. She began slicing the eggplant into rounds, listening to her sister opening and closing more drawers than were necessary. She heard the slap of place mats on the table, then the clattering of silverware.

"You want to teach Sunday school this year?" Jordanna called to her while Sheryl Crow continued to sing that car wash song. "We need somebody in third and fifth."

"And exactly what knowledge would I be passing along? My own pet theories on transactional analysis and adolescents, or my advanced cat's cradle skills? Jesus, Jordanna."

"You're good with kids and there's a curriculum. You just follow the curriculum."

"You've gone too long without sex, now. You've completely lost your mind." As soon as Abby said this she knew it had been the wrong thing to say. She filled a large pot with water for the corn, covered it and stuck her head around into the dining room. "It's what the smoking's all about," she said by way of apology.

"What," Jordanna said, the *t* splitting between her lips, "are you so"—she paused in the place where most people would have cursed—"mad about tonight?"

"What?" Abby said self-consciously. She pulled open the pine armoire and took out some cloth napkins.

"You've been pissed ever since you came down the stairs."

"I'm in a bad mood." Abby kept her face lowered, moving around the table with the napkins in the opposite direction from Jordanna. She stopped just before she crossed Jordanna's path. Her sister, she knew, did not believe in moods.

"No," Jordanna said, motioning with a clutch of spoons. "It's something else."

"You've got to learn to give people a little more room, Jordanna. Not everyone operates as cleanly and efficiently as you do."

"Well, what does that mean?" Jordanna pulled out a chair from its neat fit under the table and sat down.

Abby couldn't remember her ever finishing a single domestic task in her house. "You've got the whole deal figured out, and you're impatient with those of us who are lagging behind."

"That couldn't be further from the truth, and you know it."

"You have a way of making other people feel like emotional . . . freshmen."

"Where is all this coming from, Abigail? What's going on? I walk in this house and it's like a firing squad."

Abby stopped when she heard Jim walk into the house. He yelled to them from the kitchen. "Ice-cream cake in the freezer?"

Neither Abby nor Jordanna said anything. Abby wished Jordanna would leave, wished it would sometimes occur to her to just get up and go, but that never happened. It seemed her own boys were more likely to storm out, feel unwelcome in their own house, than Jordanna. Wherever she was, was where she was supposed to be, or some hogwash. All you had to do was look at her to know that she believed she belonged, everywhere. She was at home in every room of the cosmos.

Jim walked into the dining room. And Abby turned to look out the window. Jordanna was sitting with her chin in her hands at the half-set table. "Right as you walk into the IGA, there's this notice about a missing woman."

"Really," Jordanna said. "Already?"

"You know about this?" He looked around the room quickly, then out the window as if his wife really were staring at something significant. "You two were in the middle of a good one, weren't you? I'm gonna go check on the fire."

"It's June Nearing," Jordanna said before he left the room. "A woman from my church."

"Nearing. Don't know them." Jim slid a spoon from the silvery pile on the table and placed it beside a knife.

"Eve Congdon's sister."

"Oh," Jim said.

"Oh, what?" Jordanna said.

Jim shrugged.

"She's not even been gone twenty-four hours," Abby said.

"Honey, if you were ever missing, I promise I'd wait at least forty-eight."

Abby shot him a glance. "The steak is on the counter. There's eggplant and zucchini, too.

"Can we turn off this music?" he said, walking over to the stereo. "Who had the bass like that? You can hear it all the way up the driveway. Thump de dump, dump dump. It's why you two are arguing. It's the music that's driven you to it. If it makes kids violent, just think of what it can do to grown women."

"I think I better go home," Jordanna said, a little too loudly. She grabbed her black leather mailbag from the corner of the dining room and waved to Abby.

"I have to be allowed to have a point of view sometime," Abby said. "We have a ton of food. Come on, JoJo, stay."

"No. I'm expecting a call. Daniel should be calling."

Abby shrugged. She watched her husband put his arm around her sister and walk her into the kitchen and out through the mudroom. There was a big clap of thunder and then some lightning. Through the open windows she could hear her sister's bicycle tires grind over the loose gravel. It probably wouldn't rain before she made it home, and even if it did, Jordanna wouldn't mind getting wet. She knew that about her sister.

ಲೆ Chapter 6

T HE Prices' front door was open. Jordanna stopped in the entry, remembering to remove the rubber bands that had kept her pants legs from getting caught in her bicycle chain on her way over. At least twenty people were in the family room when she entered. The argument about the color of the posters ceased while everyone greeted her. Grant Price stood up and offered her his chair, as did a few of the women. She motioned for them to continue and walked behind one of the large checked sofas to a spot on the carpet just slightly beyond the circle that had convened around the coffee table. Looking around the room, Jordanna recognized most of the Caring Committee as well as two of June's first cousins and some of her friends. Neither Drew nor Bev was there.

"Well, I just think we should ask Drew about the color," Marge Price said.

"Does he really need to be bothered with a detail like that right now?" A woman with graying short hair lay down her knitting on her lap. Jordanna didn't recognize her from church.

There was a chocolate Bundt cake on the coffee table that no one had yet cut into. Jordanna was starving. There had never been time to eat today, to sit down and eat something filling and satisfying, something resembling the appropriate food at the appropriate hour. She'd slept fitfully the night before and had made up for it with an almost comatose sleep early in the morning. It was her day off, she had told herself at five when she felt herself finally losing consciousness. "It's my day off," she had said out loud when the phone rang at 10:40. It was Roy Fenton asking if she might come with him to visit his sister in the nursing home in Deerfield. He didn't like to go alone. The other lady in his sister's room always started undressing when he came to visit. While Roy talked, Jordanna pulled herself up on her elbows in bed. Her back was always better after sleep, when nothing had been asked of it. She looked around her bedroom and said a silent prayer of thanksgiving for the cessation of pain but also for the great vacuum of thought she'd woken to. For a few brief moments while Roy talked of "odors," and "drooling" and "gutturallike noises," she was unaware of any of the specifics of her particular life. It was more than waking up blurry and unfocused, it was as if in sleep she had traded in the literal for the abstract, the terrestrial for the celestial. The body fell away, but better yet, the mind. "We can go to lunch when we're done. There's a very decent kind of a coffee shop just before you get back on the highway." Roy was still talking. She never liked to say it was her day off. Other ministers, she knew, referred to their Mondays as family time. "Well, Roy, do you think later in the week would be all right? I have some . . . personal business to attend to today." She knew him well enough to know that "personal business" would conjure up some horrid mélange of "female troubles." He was off the phone in a flash. In the shower she remembered the fight she'd had with Abby the night before, and of course the e-mail from Daniel. Then all the hard noisy pieces of her life snapped into place, like in that game she and Abby had as kids, Hens and Chickens?

.   .   .

"I T 's cheaper to go with the white paper." Phil Pangrossi was fiddling with an unlit cigarette. "Not to sound crass, but we're talking about quantity here. At least two, three hundred flyers. It'll make a difference."

Ben Hall, Drew's uncle, looked at his watch. "If we could stay on task here, get the damn thing worded, I could be at that Kinko's up near the mall by nine, nine-thirty, and we could be good to go with these tomorrow morning." He stopped and rubbed his large earlobe. "Time is of the essence here. I'm sure we all agree on that."

Nobody said anything. Jordanna put down her slice of cake. She had told herself she wasn't going to speak, that she had just come as a show of support. After all, it was her day off. "Well, you know, Ben"—she couldn't help herself—"now that you mention it, it hasn't been all that long." She folded her hands together and looked around the room. "I think we do have a bit of time."

"Not if she's been abducted." Claire Hancock pulled a blue tissue from the cuff of her blouse and dabbed at her mouth.

Jordanna waited for people to fill in their worst fears, for all the rumors that had burgeoned and ripened over the past forty-eight hours to be admitted, out loud, now in the Prices' clubby family room.

"She was in the car and they haven't found the car yet, either," Marge said.

"We all get a little complacent around here. Just because it's not Deerfield, we think we're safe." Phil Pangrossi tucked his unlit cigarette behind his ear.

"The police *are* investigating this," Ben said, staring at Jordanna. Drew's uncle was a Prudential Board member in the church, and he was one of the few people who openly took a dislike to Jordanna. "Too relaxed in both style and substance," was the way in which he'd phrased it in a memo he'd written to the Pulpit Committee, a memo they had then shared with her.

"Yes," Jordanna said evenly. "Yes, I know, they are treating it as a missing persons case."

There was silence again, and Marge took the opportunity to remind everyone that the coffee was decaf and they should just help themselves.

"I'm sure," Jordanna began, "each of us is asking what we can do to best help the Nearings right now, all of them."

"Caring has already got the phone chain going. We're organizing meals for Drew and the children," Marge said.

Jordanna nodded.

"We've got a heck of a bigger problem than bringing over a bunch of casseroles." Ben stood up and shoved his hands in his pockets and walked out of the family room and into the kitchen. They all listened as his shoes clicked on the tile floor. Some of the women on the Caring Committee shifted in their seats and leaned over to one another and began whispering.

"Let's just decide on the wording of the poster." Ben stood in the doorway of the family room, his barrel chest blocking almost all the light behind him in the kitchen. "I told you I'd pay for them, and I will. But I want to get them done tonight, and we'll need about three times as many people as are in this room right now to go putting them up tomorrow."

"You know, just listening to Jordanna just now, well, I get a sense she has some objections. . . ." The woman with the knitting, whom Jordanna couldn't quite place, talked down toward her lap, her eyes not straying from her work.

"I'm sorry," Jordanna said, lowering her head, attempting to catch the woman's eye, "I'm afraid I don't know your name."

"Debra, Debra Rispoli. I'm . . . I don't go to your church. I'm one of June's neighbors. Sometimes I watch the kids. You know, in a pinch."

Jordanna smiled at the woman. June had talked about a neighbor who occasionally babysat, an older woman with two grown children in a cult. Jordanna studied the woman for a moment, wondering if she knew the history of June's disappearances.

"With all respect to Reverend Nash," Ben began, without an ounce of anything Jordanna remotely recognized as respect, "I'm tired of talking and of listening." He did not like her encouraging congregants, especially children, to call her by her first name. This he had told her, not in a memo, but time and again, to her face. To which she always replied, "I guess we just have a difference of opinion on honorifics, Mr. Hall."

"I think if Jordanna has some real concern about these posters we should hear it," Grant Price said. He picked up someone else's half-filled coffee cup and slid a paper napkin under it.

Jordanna tucked her long legs underneath her and straightened her back as best she could. "I know some posters have already gone up."

"Drew did those," Marge offered.

Jordanna nodded. "I just think we need to realize that by papering the town with hundreds of pictures of June, we are making this family's difficulty very public. I am not, let's be clear about this, saying the action shouldn't be taken." She sighed deeply. "I am simply asking each of you to understand the significance of the step, that's all."

Ben looked around the room with a bully's need for agreement that she was half off her nut. Jordanna thought he would just as soon spit as anything else. "Point taken," he said sarcastically.

"Well, I think Jordanna does bring up something we really need to think about," Debra said, unraveling part of a row.

"You sound like you don't think this is a crime," Marge said. She was sitting at the edge of her own couch as if she were a guest in the room. "I mean, well, now, what do I mean. . . . I guess your tone suggests something else—"

"Criminy," Ben said. "Let's just agree to disagree. Okay? I really don't want to have to go home and call my nephew and tell him we talked all night and didn't do a damn thing. If you people can't get together on this thing, I'm just going to do it myself." He stood up from his armchair, knocking down a little pillow with a needlepoint Scottie on it. He made no move to pick it up and began jingling the keys in his pocket instead.

Jordanna looked around the room. No one here was a match for Ben. He was having a field day with the meek and the mild on the Caring Committee. She bit the inside of her cheek. She thought of June and reminded herself how inappropriate it would be to get in a fight with Ben Hall here tonight over this issue. Betraying June in an argument now could, she thought, hurt the Nearings a lot more than papering the town with posters advertising the most intimate truth of June's life—that she was a wife and a mother and an escape artist.

Alison Congdon, one of June's cousins, raised her hand from her seat on a blanket chest by the TV. Jordanna smiled at her and Ben acknowledged her. "Well, I have two things to say. One is some posters have already gone up about June. The ones at the IGA. So really, that step's been taken. And the other, I just think, you know, this is a tragedy, and people need to talk about it, Ben. Everybody has their own way. You're making it like talking is a crime. If we're talking, then it's probably because we need to, because we're all upset." She punctuated the end of her speech by flipping her wispy blond hair behind her ears, a gesture June always managed to imbue with an aura of defeat, and which this younger, brighter version used to garner the sensual attention of the entire room.

Ben shook his head. Jordanna asked the Prices if they had a computer. She suggested that they all take a refreshment break, and maybe Ben would like to mock up a poster in the other room, and then when everyone was done with their cake and coffee they could look it over.

At ten-thirty, a heated debate broke out about whether to include a photo or a sketch of June on the poster. Jordanna excused herself. Marge walked her to the door.

"The Caring Committee's been doing a wonderful job in general, and especially over the last couple days with the Nearings. I'm sure they greatly appreciate it."

Marge nodded.

Jordanna slung her mailbag across her back.

"You're not on your bike, are you?" Marge said, concerned.

"It's the best time of year for riding."

"Let me drive you home. We'll pop the bike in the back of the Jeep. It won't take but a minute."

"You just want to escape," Jordanna said, tipping her head in the direction of the family room.

Marge let out an unladylike sigh, something much deeper and darker than Jordanna thought her capable of. "You know, of all the things you think you might be asked to do in your life, this . . . well, this certainly . . ."

Jordanna laid a hand on Marge's shoulder. "Maybe, before everyone goes home, you could take a moment and pray for June." Jordanna knew that she should have done at least that while she was here tonight. Unable to reveal to them all that she knew, she might have given them what they desired. A moment of prayer would have defined the efforts of the evening. She let her mailbag fall to the marble floor, and she took both of Marge's hands. "You and me, right now," she said abruptly. "Oh, God, we ask You to watch over our friend and neighbor, June Nearing. May she be safe in the confines of Your love. May You give us the wisdom to help her, to find her, to love her. Even if she is lost to us, we trust that she is present to You. Amen."

It was a cloudy night, no moon or stars to give off light. Jordanna clicked on the little headlamp she'd attached to her bike and swung her mailbag across her back. It was no more than four miles from the Prices' to her house. Mostly flat, with one uphill section and a longer downhill one. On a moonless night, Hutchinson was darker than anyplace she'd ever lived. She'd lived in more remote places. She and Abby had been raised on Cape Cod in a town so underpopulated in the winter months that you could jog naked (which she had done once during an Easter vacation) for a good five or six miles with nothing but gulls and bobwhites, rabbits and chipmunks taking notice. In Beecham, where she and Daniel had last lived in Maine, and in Whiting's Point on Cape Cod, the ocean was all around, reflecting any and all random light, retracting the darkness. It had seemed to her as a child that a little flame burned always just out of view, a night-light low and constant in some unseen corner, illuminating the dark.

As she rode along the winding streets of Hutchinson, branches heavy with chestnuts, leaves big enough to conceal body parts reached out into the road, dangling, rustling, lapping at her. Unless she was passing a farm or a new housing development, the sky was obscured. A canopy of green hung above and around her. Daniel had said that Hutchinson at the end of summer was as dense as a jungle. It made him claustrophobic, he'd told her last year.

She stood on the pedals to go up Castle Hill. The bike was only a three-speed, but it was the bike she'd had as a girl and she was attached to it. She couldn't bear to think about what her back would feel like all hunched over on one of those racing bikes, her breasts scraping the crossbar. On her old Raleigh the handlebars were up high. When they'd first met, Daniel had told her she looked like a character actress in an episode of *Masterpiece Theater,* Mr. Chips in the making, riding around the Divinity School, a wicker basket strung onto the front and everything. "I'm going to take that as a compliment," she'd said. She recognized him from Cross-Cultural Theories of Mortality. On the few occasions when he'd spoken in class, he'd struck her as too cerebral to be a Div School student. "I wouldn't be surprised if you made a left on Elm and found yourself on the banks of the Wye."

They were in front of Battell Chapel. She was late for a prayer service. Her bike lock was in her hand, but she remained seated, her legs in a wide straddle. "Does this particular fantasy end there, or are you just getting started?" She swung one leg over the seat, slid her bike into the bike rack and began threading the lock. She'd been waiting for him to retort, but when she looked up he was halfway down the sidewalk.

Jordanna rested for a moment at the top of Castle Hill and threw the mailbag into the basket in front. A breeze blew up behind her and she lifted her braid from her damp back. He'd always been difficult, always. That first time they had spoken, she'd thought she'd offended him. She'd spent the entire prayer service wondering how to apologize. Part of her motivation for becoming a minister had been her deepening acknowledgment that she needed to be more attentive. Quick to think, quick to act, quick to emote. "Unconcerned with consequences," her father had railed at her during high school. "So hungry, so goddamn hungry," he had yelled. "Absolutely unaware that you need to make room for anybody else. You need to stop storming through life, arms akimbo." She had entered Divinity School as a means of redemption. She had cruised through her teens and early twenties unintentionally hurting people whom she was sure she loved. "It's just that . . . it's like a child who doesn't understand how strong he's become," her mother had said. "You're unaware of your own power." For a long time, Jordanna heard only the thinly veiled pride in this admonition. She was exceptional, and her mother's forgiveness a given.

It had shocked her then, when in the spring of her senior year of college her mother had let the phone line go cold, ending the conversation with, "You're too old now to plead ignorance." Again it involved a boy, a man, this time. Brian Seitz, a Vista volunteer she'd met in a bar in Allston one night at the start of the summer after her junior year. By the end of July he was spending every weekend at Whiting's Point, helping her run the shuttle launch, checking on moorings, towing inexperienced tourists back to the pier. He was from Louisiana and every funny word he spoke came out of his mouth warm, nearly melted, even when he sang above the roar of the outboard or called to her dog down the beach. In the fall she took the train to Boston to visit him. He played the violin for her, classical and Cajun, and he sketched her, dressed and nude. But when he began asking to come down to see her at school, she said no. Having him on campus, she thought, would be like pouring boiling water at an imaginary tea party. By the spring he began accusing her of compartmentalizing, of keeping him at arm's length. She couldn't possibly feel about him the way he did about her. When she said matter-of-

factly that people's feelings, one for the other, were always incongru-
ous, he told her she was very young. He upbraided her for proclaim-
ing emotions she didn't really have, for exaggerating her feelings for
him. It wasn't the first time someone had challenged her capacity for
love, and she couldn't think of a worse insult. Defending her
integrity from a pay phone in the basement of the library late one
night during spring semester, she told him that he was wrong, dead
wrong. She loved him, more than she'd ever loved anyone. The next
day when she left for her nine o'clock class, he was outside her dorm,
sitting cross-legged on a bench, smoking a cigarette and holding a
paper bag. "Reach inside," he drawled. There was a frost on the
grass, and mist rose up all around them in the quad. Her fingertips
grazed what felt like velvet, a velvet box. She didn't know stones, but
this one was purple and the band was silver. It looked like an
antique, valuable for what it had outlasted. As she slid the ring on
her finger and swept her hand away from her body, she registered
its heft. She was slow to shift her gaze from her hand to his eyes,
too slow.

"I'm going to take that particular look for a yes," he said, standing
to kiss her.

"Obtuse," was one of the words he used later.

After driving back to Boston in a white-hot fury, Brian had called
her parents, who'd watched this romance develop, called for valida-
tion that they'd seen what he'd seen, intuited what he'd intuited.
"Moral responsibility!" Her father's disappointment was palpable
over the phone. She had a moral responsibility for other people,
toward their feelings, feelings that she had fueled and flamed,
encouraged and nurtured. When she hung up with her parents that
afternoon, she left her room and moved through the campus nearly
numb from the sting of their disapproval. It was the middle of April,
and the sash windows in the dorms were all wedged open. The peck
and ring of the occasional typewriter served as a reminder of the
studying she wasn't doing while she walked and walked, working
her highly illuminated faults into a cause for justifiable self-pity.

The madgrigal group was rehearsing in the college's chapel, and for the second time in four years she entered the great wooden ark of the Methodist structure and slid into the last pew. She punched her knuckles under the Bible rack and pushed up a copy of the Holy Scriptures. What if her parents were wrong, and it wasn't just that she was callow? What if she were flawed, indelibly flawed? What if she could never make other people feel loved? What if it were like a kind of handicap she'd been born with, a missing piece or a faulty enzyme that couldn't convert what she knew she felt into an effective gift? What if something were horribly wrong in the great equation, and she could only receive, but never give? What would be the point of her life, then? People killed themselves for reasons half as good.

She lay down on the dark wooden pew, covered her face with the open Bible, as if shielding herself from the sun, and listened to the singing. The choral group sang without accompaniment in a language she couldn't identify, the bell curve of their voices glancing off one another, merging, melding, becoming distinct once again. The Bible smelled moldy and she pulled it away from her nose and began to flip through Matthew. Jesus was charging His disciples. She didn't follow it all—Be-elzebul and sparrows sold for a penny and people rising up against one another. Nobody wanted to go through life bringing other people pain. That wasn't how she wanted to be recognized. She was so much more than that. Nothing she did would ever matter, though, if she were remembered for how she'd careered across other people's lives, wounding them. She would have to change. She would pray, right now, beg God to change her, alter her. She sat up. Confirmed, committed. She moved to close the Bible, and her eye caught the last line at the end of the left-hand column: ". . . and he who loses his life for my sake will find it." A sharp pain shot through her nose, and while she knew that the singing still filled the church, a furious silence buzzed in her ears, her brain. God was answering, offering her a proposition. The ministry. As Reverend Nash she would be forced, hourly, to get a grip on herself. There was more than a touch of martyrdom in the decision. It was a form of punishment for an ego that had grown untamed. She would learn to contain herself, to do for others in service to God.

AND it had worked, in a way. She was much better, much improved. Her family had told her so. Daniel was proof. He was the first man to fall in love with her whom she hadn't devastated. Abby had said it wasn't for lack of trying, it was just that he was impervious, but Jordanna knew she'd changed. She'd memorized Philippians 2:3–5: "There must be no room for rivalry and personal vanity among you, but you must humbly reckon others better than yourselves. Look to each other's interest and not merely to your own." The trail of men and women she'd somehow misled, who felt she had welched on promises of intimacy or favor, even grace, had dwindled considerably. By the time she and Daniel were engaged, there was only the occasional two A.M. phone call to the house and the last of the desperate letters. She had, she felt, learned to harness her spirit to magnify the spirit of others. That was a huge step in a person's life. And until she lost James, then Alice, she had construed it as the defining change in her life, the means by which she described herself.

"YOUR life will, of necessity, have to be about something else," Daniel had written her yesterday. She readjusted herself on the seat as she began to coast down the back side of Castle Hill. "Your whole life can't be about this—about this absence. It won't work for you, it certainly won't work for us." She had gotten to that part of the e-mail, the part where he used the word *us,* and she had warmed. "Can you look into the future and identify a point in time when you will look at me and not think of loss? I don't think so."

Each time they made love during the few months that it took them to conceive Alice after they had lost James, Jordanna imagined that she and Daniel were on the beach in the Cook Islands. They'd traveled there together one summer while Daniel was pursuing a

postgraduate research fellowship. The sea was like a gigantic wading
pool. She remembered walking straight out from the beach for half a
mile and the water never covering her shins. Each time they set
about to "try again," Jordanna would ritualistically uncover the
unblemished memory of sex in that warm salty water until the sheets
on their landlocked bed liquefied and lapped the length of their
uncertain bodies. And when Daniel would reach orgasm, she'd picture the tidal pull of her own muscular release drawing the life of the
sea up into her, the monumental leap of faith present at the start of
the cosmos being reenacted within her.

"We loved each other before the babies," Daniel had written in his
e-mail. "Why can't we go back to that? Why not just go back to
where we were before? It seems to me to be the only alternative.
There was an identity we had before we ever began planning a family. There was a love affair and a life together and there was work
that we had. I write all these things knowing they are rhetorical,
knowing that you are incapable of what I ask."

"How dare you, how dare you," she yelled out now as she rolled
down the hill on her bike in the pitch-black. Last night she had sat in
front of the screen for a long time after reading the e-mail, maybe
half an hour. It was nothing new, what he had said. What was different was the tone. There was this awful inevitability behind every
word. He wrote as if she were frozen in place and time, and he was
the only one of the two living in the three-dimensional world with its
abundant potential for mutability. He'd written her off as some
arrested case of grief, a perpetual mourner, like the old Italian ladies
in his neighborhood whom he'd watched as a kid. Every day for a
year, in every kind of weather, they had walked the two miles to the
cemetery dressed head to toe in black. "You're not going to be like
that, are you?" he'd said after the third time she'd driven from Maine
to the cemetery in Whiting's Point during those first months after
they had buried James. She had barely heard him. Nothing was real
about that autumn. She had taken off only one week, and had shown
up again in her office in the church house still in maternity clothes,

breasts leaking, no baby. It helped to be the minister, most everybody knew what had happened, and it was only once or twice a day, when a bank teller or someone from the Faith Food Pantry or the prison up in Leroy called, that she had to say that, yes, yes, she had had the baby, a boy. And then quickly, before anyone began offering congratulations, she had to get in a surgical strike—"but we lost him." Sometimes that's what she said, as if they had simply misplaced the bassinet or the baby had given her the slip in utero. If she said he died, then people wanted to know when and how and why. Stillborn worked best, with its intrinsic irony, its nineteenth century connotations. It stopped people like a brick wall.

I T wasn't a culvert, really, just a place where the newly paved part of Castle Hill was incomplete, as if someone had taken a bite out of the asphalt. The road was broken off on the right side. The bicycle's headlamp only shone six or seven feet ahead, and by the time she saw the gully she was in it, and the bike was skidding and twisting, bucking like a horse as it rode over sizable chunks of broken asphalt, pieces of roadway that hadn't managed to conform to the whole. She pulled up on the handlebars as if she could rein in the bike, regain control over metal and rubber. She swung the handlebars toward the left, trying to jump the bike the way she'd seen her nephews do, the way she must have done herself long ago, attempting a wheelie, turning the bike into a unicycle. Before she could land the front wheel onto the paved part of the road, the back wheel slid out from under her. She landed on her side, just on the cusp of the asphalt. Her left hip and elbow and ear bore the rest of her weight like a faulty tripod. It was her ear that hurt the most, and before she even got up out of the road she felt the blood running down the side of her cheek. One-half of a copper sunburst lay jagged on the pavement by her knee, the rest dangled limply, only partially attached to her ear. She looked around for the bike. It had beaten her down the hill by a few body lengths, the shattered headlamp pointing skyward.

She got up slowly and gently brushed the little bits of gravel from the ripped skin around her elbow. Her hip was bruised, she imagined. Her pants were ripped above her left knee. She waited to register the pain in her back, but it wasn't significantly worse than it had been all week. The rear fender on her bike was smashed in toward the tire. Jordanna pulled on it slightly, and the entire frame seemed to scream at the pressure. She walked past the bike and picked up her leather bag. Keys and Kleenex, pens and paper clips fanned out from where the mailbag had landed. She turned the busted, but still working, headlamp to shine on the stream of stuff, reached down for a tissue and wiped her bloody cheek.

When she got to the bottom of the hill, she looked back once. She'd left the bike propped up against the base of a maple tree, on top of a pile of deer droppings. She'd thought about hiding the bike, worried it might fall prey to some thirteen-year-old. But she knew better. Even though she treasured that bike, no child in Hutchinson ever would have given it a second covetous look.

Without the bike she was free to get to her house on Hull Hill by walking across the playground behind Castle Elementary. "Goddamn you, Daniel," she said out loud as she passed the curving yellow slide. "Goddamn you to hell," she said a little louder, as she pushed through the hemlocks that separated the soccer field from somebody's unmowed backyard. "Fuck you," she said as she slid her key, teeth up, into the back door of the parsonage.

ॐ Chapter 7

ABBY went ahead and ordered Gabe his pancakes. She let him
rip open two of the little creamers in the basket on the table and
watched as he poured them into her second cup of coffee. Jordanna
had called, waking them all up this morning, begging Abby to meet
her at the Hutchinson Diner. Now, of course, Jordanna was late.
Abby pressed down on the spine of Gabe's coloring book and pulled
some crayons from her purse. She knew Jordanna wanted them to
"set aside" their anger. She would show up, her teeth glistening with
goodwill, and say something like, "My love for you is all that's real."
When she was younger, Abby had made the mistake of pointing out
to Jordanna how manipulative that kind of statement was. Jordanna
had stared at her blankly. "No, no, no," she had said. "It's what I feel,
and it's pure. It's true." "For you, Jordanna," Abby had said. "It's true
for you, but what about everyone else?"

The pancakes arrived, and Abby slid the coloring book to the side
and began cutting through the steaming stack.

"JoJo, your tooth broke off," Gabe yelled as his aunt pulled out a
chair across the table and dropped her heavy leather bag. Abby
looked up at her sister. One of her top front teeth looked as if she'd

bitten it off herself. There was a purplish bruise under her left eye, and her left ear looked as if it were being held together by white electrical tape. "What happened?"

"I fell off my bike last night," Jordanna said, sitting down.

"Why didn't you call me?"

"I did, I called you this morning." Jordanna looked around for a waitress. "I need one of those." She nodded toward Abby's coffee.

Abby passed the cup to her.

"Mama, it needs more syrup," Gabe said, looking down at his plate.

"How about a kiss?" Jordanna pushed the little diner chair back away from the table and spread open her arms.

Abby helped Gabe get out of his booster seat. "What's that?" Gabe slowly moved toward Jordanna and pointed up to the side of her face with his fork still in his hand.

Abby hadn't seen the jagged cut running down from Jordanna's ear, just along the jawline.

"Does it hurt?"

"I'm tough."

He quickly hugged her around one arm and ran back to his seat.

"You sure you're okay?" Abby asked. "This is why you have to wear a helmet."

Jordanna nodded.

Abby stared at her sister's ear. "Do you think you need stitches?"

"What I need is coffee." Jordanna stood up and Abby noticed that immediately the atmosphere in the diner changed. The room became smaller. There was a pause in conversation, in the scrape of cutlery on china, even in breathing. And then they were done staring, and there seemed a compensatory acceleration in the breathing and eating and talking. Jordanna's presence, at least when she stood, could reorder time and space and energy. It was like a localized physical law. The waitress hurried over and Jordanna put her hand on the woman's bare forearm, as if the request for coffee were a deeply personal plea.

"That white tape makes you look like you've been to the vet, like you've just had your ears pinned back. Did you even consider going to the emergency room? You have a black eye."

"Not really."

"Really." Abby reached into her purse and pulled out a small compact with a mirror.

Jordanna moved the little mirror around as if she were merely playing with the light coming in from the windows.

"Can I try that, too?" Gabe said, standing up from his booster on the little ledge of the chair.

Jordanna handed him the compact and Abby frowned.

"Did you call the dentist?" Abby watched Gabe press the foam makeup pad to his syrupy lips. She rooted around in her bag for a replacement toy. "Oh, look, a little . . . tool." She pulled a tire pressure gauge from the side pocket of her purse and held it out to Gabe. "You *do* have a dentist, right?" Abby palmed the compact and slid it off the red-and-white-checked oilcloth covering the table. Abby didn't think that her sister had been to a doctor since she'd delivered Alice. It would be three years this October since Jordanna's uterus had ruptured and Alice had been stillborn. Last year, when Jordanna had gotten what she guessed was strep throat, she'd gone through Abby's medicine cabinet thankful to have found remnants from an old penicillin prescription.

"Does it look that bad?"

"Oh, yeah, it's bad," Gabe said, staring again at his aunt's tooth.

Jordanna laughed.

"You didn't injure it at the root, did you?" Abby winced.

Jordanna shrugged. "I don't think so. I think I'd feel it. The ear . . . it's just an awkward place, hard to get a Band-Aid to stay on there. The earring . . ." She made a ripping sound. "It'll heal. I've got Mary Jane Krull's funeral tomorrow. I doubt I can get into the dentist before that."

Death, again. Abby looked at her watch. "I have a staff meeting at eleven at school. Tomorrow's opening day."

"Right, right."

"I'm going to Miss Diane's tomorrow, right, Mama?"

Abby nodded without looking at Gabe.

"I've been thinking about Sunday," Jordanna began. She took the coffee from the waitress and pushed Abby's mostly empty cup back across the table. She opened three little creams, then looked up. "I've gone over it again and again. I was up most of Sunday night."

Abby nodded. The waitress was standing beside them ready to take their order, but Jordanna was unaware of her. She was leaning against the wall, her good ear in her palm, studying the sunflower in the vase on the table. "I come to you, into your house with my whole—"

"Jordanna," Abby said loudly.

"Oh, oh. Food, right. That's what we're all about this morning. Food." She laughed.

After the waitress had finished taking their order, Abby said, "I know what you're going to tell me. You've said it before, that you enter our house in gratitude and with nothing but love and—"

"And always a wonderful sense of expectation. It's one of the few times I'm able to experience that feeling. It's one of the few times . . . I'm rarely thrilled. But riding down your driveway, knowing all those warm bodies, arms and legs and belly laughs are waiting . . . I'm excited. And it's like you want to squelch that, just squeeze the life out of it."

Gabe stopped drawing, and Abby watched him stare at his aunt as if she had just said something he understood and concurred with. This was the whole problem. Now she couldn't say anything. Jordanna's motivations were without blemish or flaw. Love and loss were behind her every thought and deed. There was no way to counter or contradict that. Abby simply nodded.

"I know why I fell off the bike."

"Because I was mean to you, right?" This was one of Jordanna's pet theories. She believed in the psycho/spiritual basis for "accidents," some accidents. Certain mistakes, injuries, slips could trace their genesis to one's emotions, or at least one's energy field. "Or maybe because you're riding all around creation on a thirty-year-old bike."

"Daniel had written me a kind of, well, an inevitable letter, I guess. I was thinking about the letter. Actually, I was hearing his voice, hearing him read aloud the e-mail, and the next thing I know, I'm yanking part of my earring out of my cheek. It was a good accident, really. I needed this accident." Jordanna stuck her finger in the amber ashtray in the spot where a cigarette might have rested.

Abby repositioned Gabe in his booster seat and bit the inside of her cheek. Her sister had been headed in this direction before she lost the babies, but after Alice, this predisposition for tidily packaging everything that happened as possessing meaning had turned into a conviction. "Are you baiting me now, Jordanna, or are you being honest?"

"You mean, am I kidding myself? No clue. And I hate that."

"What did he say? When are you supposed to be going over there?"

"October. He said . . ." Jordanna spun the ashtray around a few times. "He said, basically, get over it. We had a life . . ." She stopped and looked over at Gabe. "You know, before. And we need to just get back there. If we can get back there, together, we can move on."

"Moving on is big with him."

"With everyone."

Abby nodded. "Did you write back?"

Jordanna shook her head. "Nothing for it," she said. "Nothing for it."

Abby told herself to stop staring at her sister. It wasn't the cuts on her face from falling off the bike that held her gaze. It was what always happened when she was with Jordanna. She'd forget to breathe and look around. She'd forget what she was thinking and feeling. Sometimes it seemed she'd forget her own name. She looked over at Gabe and inhaled the creamy wax of his crayons. She looked down at her watch.

"Do you miss him?" she said after a long while.

"You mean, do I miss sex?"

Abby glanced at Gabe, who was engrossed with the pressure

gauge, then up at her sister. She remembered her jibe of the other day. "That wasn't what I meant. I know it came out—"

Jordanna waved her hand. "It's what you meant. But, you know, Ab, we . . . sex is . . . it's like going to a funeral for us. It's not a release or a relief."

When the waitress arrived with the food, Abby watched Jordanna for a signal. Usually she flopped her hands into an attitude of prayer, no matter where they were, and began saying grace. But today her sister just reached across the table for the jelly and started in on eating.

"You don't have enough fun. Amend that, you don't have any fun."

"Mary Jane Krull left me a tandem bike. We should ride together. It'd be a hoot."

Abby stared at her. "We'd probably murder each other."

"She's got a canoe over there, too, archery, everything. It's like Camp Katahdin in her—"

Abby watched as Jordanna dropped her knife loudly on her plate and shoved back from the table. In four long strides she was out the door.

"What's JoJo doing?" Gabe leaned way over to one side to try to see his aunt through the front window of the diner.

"I don't know. Maybe she saw someone she needed to talk to." Abby looked over at Jordanna's Mexican omelet and sunk her fork into one corner. Abby and Jim had lived in town for fourteen years, and no matter where they went with Jordanna, she had to jump up and talk to somebody. Occupational hazard, Jim called it. But it had always been like that, even before she became a minister. Once, on their way to a wedding in Omaha, they'd stopped overnight in Ohio and a girl from Abby's high school class had swum across the motel pool, ecstatic to be reunited with Jordanna, who, of course, only pretended to remember her.

"Have you seen any of these yet?" Jordanna asked, coming back to the table.

Abby took the sheet of bright blue paper and studied the poorly duplicated photo of June. The first posters, the ones Jim had told her about that had gone up almost immediately in the center of town, had been black and white and included only June's name, her date of birth and the color and make of her car. But this poster was more like a résumé than a missing person's identity sheet. It listed her vital statistics, height, weight, age, hair color, as well as the facts of her life—that she was somebody's wife and the mother of three. The poster struck Abby as a reminder aimed at June herself, a crib sheet about who she was and where it was she was meant to be, a signpost leading her back to her proper place. "I'd shoot myself if someone put up three thousand flyers with a photo of me on Christmas morning looking that bad."

"They're everywhere. She's going to be mortified."

Abby shrugged. "It's the front page of the Deerfield paper this morning."

"Shoot." Jordanna put down her fork and choked her coffee mug with both hands.

"That's not entirely a bad thing," Abby said. "She needs help. This way she'll get it."

"Some detective's coming up to the office this afternoon to ask me some questions, anything that might help locate her."

"Are you worried?" Abby asked.

Jordanna laughed. "In Beecham, we had a guy who stole a car and he pulls into the parking lot of the church one night and bangs on the door to be let in. We happened to be downstairs having a meeting. So I ran up to see who it was, and the guy just blurts out the whole thing as we're standing there on the steps. He thinks that the church can offer him some kind of absolution or immunity, like we're the American Embassy and he's in a foreign country. I was probably involved with the police twice, three times a month in that church. Then there were the men I worked with in the prison." She stroked the sunflower in the center of the table. "This is different."

"All those months of her coming in and talking to you"—Abby

pushed her empty plate toward the center of the table—"did you ever talk about yourself, about your losses?"

"I couldn't." Jordanna began lining up sugar packets inside the fortress of jellies that Gabe had erected.

"Why not?"

"The gracious reason?" Jordanna ran her tongue over the broken part of her tooth. "She was already burdened. You don't tell a sad story to someone who's morose. And selfishly and not the least bit having to do with any kind of grace, I don't choose to talk about the babies to anyone who can't hear it, can't feel it. Depressed people . . . Besides"—Jordanna nodded toward Abby—"it's therapeutically totally un-PC, right?"

"Well, that's the advantage you have in pastoral counseling. . . ."

"To tell my own sob story?"

"Hardly, Jordanna," Abby said gently, rearranged by the sudden urge to touch her sister, even kiss her. At some point in their cycle of talking and arguing, of grating and grinding on one another, this moment always arrived—when Abby would crack open for Jordanna, straight down the middle and to the core. "June Nearing thinks she's the last sad woman on the face of the planet. It might have been a point of entry, a way in, maybe, for her not to feel so all alone."

Jordanna shook her head. "*You* can tell about the babies, Ab. You can use that story in counseling, because it's a story. But I'm not there, not yet. It's not a story for me. It's skin and blood and bones and milk." She stopped and touched her taped ear. "It will only be mine to tell when I expect nothing in return, when I need no response. I'm only a couple of steps ahead of June. I don't think her knowing that would have helped anyone." Jordanna picked up the check from the table. "What's Gabe going to do while you're at your meeting?"

"Brendan's going to watch him at home." Abby looked down at her watch.

"Would he like to come over to the church house with me, and you can swing by and get him when you're done?"

Abby looked over at Gabe, who had balanced the tire gauge across two towers of jelly packets, high above a river of Sweet'n Lows. "You want to go to JoJo's office for a while, or do you want to go home with Brendan and the kids?"

"Can we go on the playground?" he asked, looking up at Jordanna.

"The playground isn't open until the nursery school opens next week," Abby said.

"No, Mom, 'cause Gael always can open the gate and we can just go in. Right, JoJo?"

"There's a lot of stapling to be done today. . . ."

Gabe jumped up and down and grabbed onto Jordanna's hands.

"Taping. JoJo means taping." Abby widened her eyes at her sister and mouthed, *No staples.*

"I also have a calculator you'll need to fix. You'll have to take it apart, though."

Jordanna and Gabe started out of the diner, and Abby collected Gabe's crayons and restacked the little jellies into their holder. She turned back to the table as she neared the door and pulled out three singles from her wallet. Jordanna had forgotten the tip.

Abby pulled Gabe's car seat from the backseat of her car and walked with it over to where Jordanna had parked.

"You know, maybe every Sunday is too much."

"What do you mean?" Abby opened the passenger door and pushed the bucket seat forward.

"Your family needs its own Sunday dinners, too. I mean, I'm . . . I'm still sorting out what happened the other day."

Abby slid a copy of the *Christian Century* to the far side of the backseat and reached around for the seat belt. "The kids count on your coming," she said with her head buried inside Jordanna's car. She backed up out of the ancient Volvo and looked at her sister.

"Maybe you should just invite me when you want me, and it shouldn't be a standing deal, you know? Then, when you're not in the mood . . ."

Abby looked down at the gravel parking lot. Gabe had already climbed into the driver's seat and was trying to turn on the radio. She looked at her watch. There wasn't time now. "Do you really want to talk about this, Jordanna?"

"It's why I woke you up this morning."

Abby had had fantasies about telling her sister everything. She imagined it would be like the final moments of a computer game that Christopher and Michael played, in which the loser got buried by an unending truckload of animated grammar school jibes. "I didn't feel like hearing about somebody dying, not that day."

"But it wasn't about death. That was the point of my telling you about Mary Jane—"

"It doesn't matter what it was really about. I asked you in a number of different ways if we could please not talk about death. But you don't listen, not to me, Jordanna." Abby waited until she had taken a few deep breaths before looking up at her sister.

Jordanna was holding her own hands, gripping them together, her silver rings clicking against one another. "I have that problem, I know, Abby. I can get carried away, I lose . . . I'm sorry."

Gabe leaned on the horn, and when both Abby and Jordanna jumped, he laughed and did it again.

"Gabriel," Jordanna said in an uncharacteristically stern voice.

He turned to his aunt and his eyes filled up.

"Pop in the back, now, honey," Abby said.

Jordanna leaned in and buckled Gabe and whispered something that Abby couldn't hear. The boy laughed and he waved to Abby. "See you later, Mom, when you swing by to get me." He laughed again.

Abby put her hand on Jordanna's shoulder, and Jordanna pecked her on the cheek.

◎ Chapter 8

JORDANNA'S bike was still being fixed, and so she walked—
through backyards, side lots, playing fields and the occasional
patch of woods, challenging herself to see how far she could get without hitting pavement. By the time she had reached Hart Hill, she
could hear the bands warming up for the Labor Day parade. The
Hutchinson Labor Day parade was the biggest one in the state, big
enough to draw the governor and at least one U.S. senator each year.
Some of the churches had floats, and the ones with schools always
had great phalanxes of children marching in freshly minted T-shirts.
It tended to be a last-minute scramble to see who was around from
the Congregational Church. She'd marched last year with a few of
the preschoolers and a couple of dogs, and the following week a Prudential Board member had delicately pointed out that the only other
clergy who'd actually marched were the assistant pastor from Our
Lady of Fatima and the spiritual leader of Heavenly Chalice Evan-
gelical Ministries. So this year Jordanna had decided to watch the
parade from the sidelines with Abby and Jim and the kids. She was
taking her time meeting up with them in front of Hutchinson Sav-

ings. Neither her body nor her mind could tolerate two and half hours in a lawn chair.

It had been a wretched week. The choir director had given her notice. A licensing group from the state had cited the preschool for unsafe wiring and the continued drought had begun to have an impact on the well, which supplied the water for the school, the church and the church house. There were pressure problems, Gael said. And every day, people were calling about June. Would she like to become part of the prayer chain that had formed for June, or perhaps take part in one of the teams being organized to comb the woods up by Palestine Road or down along Hanover? More than a few congregants had called asking Jordanna to urge the Congdon and Nearing families to post a reward. And then there were the police, not just the Hutchinson police and the state police—now the FBI was involved. There was the whole matter of her privileged communication with June, what to tell and what to conceal. Though it seemed to Jordanna that anything that might help locate her was already public knowledge. The police were seriously beginning to consider foul play. And that suspicion had come over the town like a rising nausea. Everyone was looking for June's car. The story led the local TV news each night, and every morning June's picture could be found above the fold on the front page of the Deerfield paper. At yesterday's worship service, Jordanna had offered up an extensive prayer for all the Nearings, but she had not addressed June's disappearance directly. The coffee hour had been hell. She was amazed at what people were willing to say to her. She was backing away from the coffee urn when Dee Cimino and Sally List asked her if she might encourage the police to contact a psychic. She'd laughed, and when they didn't join her, her face lost its usual joyous visage, a pose her mentor Reverend Solloway had referred to as her cup-runneth-over demeanor. She told them that spirituality and spiritualism were two entirely different notions, and that while she believed humans capable of incredible connection to one another, she certainly could not be manipulated into condoning a practice that ran counter to the notion of faith in God, one that also might inspire a kind of communal hysteria. There was a long silence, after which Dee said she was sorry, she had thought that Jordanna was more open-minded, that she supposed she was mistaken about, well, about what she seemed to represent. By the time they were done, at least seven to ten people were pressed up close behind Dee and Sally, in a kind of second circle of coffee hour hell.

At the top of Hart Hill she turned onto Lower Meadow and then cut across the Hutchinson Golf Club. Carts motored across the expanse of browning lawn. The water hazard at the edge of Upper Meadow Road appeared to be nothing more than a slight puddle. The town was parched. Lawns looked bleached. The day was no different from the past six, overcast with a chance of rain that never materialized. Hutchinson's drinking water came from two aquifers that crisscrossed the town. Gael had told her that Hutchinson Lake and Black Pond were down a couple of feet, boats were actually running aground. Gael's boyfriend had a Boston Whaler and Gael told Jordanna that they'd gone out at sunset on Thursday evening, and she'd spotted a group of congregants, Drew Nearing among them, on the little unnamed island on the north part of Hutchinson Lake. "It was so sad, like they're looking for a needle in a haystack," she told Jordanna as she handed her the day's mail. "She always looked so, I don't know . . . you know when she'd come in to see you . . . didn't she always look so . . . little? I'd think, how can someone that little be a mother? You know?"

Jordanna rolled up the mail inside a catalogue for Sunday school texts and tucked it under her arm. "She's no smaller than you. I think what you picked up on is the way she seemed to have pulled back from the edges of the world. It was all too big, too loose on her, like she was lost in it."

"Do you think she's dead?" Gael said, turning away from Jordanna to fiddle with the lid on a half-eaten box of donut holes.

"Do you?" Jordanna sat down in the folding chair by the side of Gael's big metal desk.

Gael turned, looked out into the hallway, then at Jordanna, and nodded.

"Why? Why do you think that?"

Gael shrugged. "I dreamt it."

"You had a dream that June Nearing died?" Jordanna heard her own voice come out more harshly than she would have liked.

"Not exactly," June whispered, glancing out into the hall again. "I dreamt that a dove picked her up in its mouth and flew away with her."

"Wow," Jordanna said.

Gael nodded.

"Doves are very symbolic."

"June was all limp in the dove's mouth and the dove flew straight up, like a plane when it takes off, but it just kept climbing, you know, I mean up and out, out of this world."

Jordanna placed the roll of mail on the floor and looked at Gael. "Was it a sad dream, a happy dream, were you—"

"It scared the shit out of me. Sorry."

"Afterwards, or while you were having it?"

"Both."

"Why?"

Gael shook her head. "I don't know. It was eerie. Nothing felt right. Nothing that happened seemed to be what was supposed to happen." She ran her slender fingers over the bones in her clavicle. "I don't know how else to explain it."

Jordanna nodded slowly. "When did you have this dream?"

"Weeks ago. Way before June disappeared." Gael sank down into her desk chair. "I've been feeling bad that I didn't tell you about it, before. I mean, I know that's kind of crazy. What was I supposed to do, 'Hey, Jordanna I had this, like, weirdo dreammmm, so don't, like, let June, you know, leave here today'? But, still. You know, we think we'd like to have knowledge or preknowledge, but really, we're all scared to death of it."

"Dreams are tricky animals, Gael. The world is filled with signs and symbols. Divining what they mean is a whole other business. I'm not sure it's ours to do. I mean, doves—what do they mean to you? First off, what do you think of?"

"Peace."

"Or—" Jordanna motioned as if they were playing charades and she was entreating Gael to move in a certain direction. "Noah . . . the first time a dove is mentioned . . ."

"Peace," she said flatly again. "Oh, oh, the flood, after the flood, right?"

"And what has everyone around here been obsessed with, before they became obsessed with June's disappearance?"

"The drought, I guess."

"And when did the drought begin, officially?"

"The beginning of summer."

"In the month of . . . ?" Jordanna wheedled.

"June," Gael said, halfheartedly. "Oh, oh, June. Do you really think—"

"It all depends on the interpretation."

EVE'S grave was on a slope under a cypress tree. Someone must have been coming up to water every day, because the stone was sur-rounded with burgeoning yellow wax begonias. Jordanna had found the grave fairly easily. She'd buried enough people in the year since she'd come to Hutchinson to have a general sense of where certain families had laid claim. Jordanna spread her legs and slowly folded her body at the waist. Her oversize head and long thick hair acted like a counterweight on the tangle in her spine. She hung like that, stretching, her sneakers growing damp from the dew on the grass.

"So," she said softly, "where is she, Eve? Almost ten days, now. I'm not a worrier, but now I'm worrying." She listened to her own breathing, to the geese overhead. She swung her body just slightly so that her hair brushed Eve's stone and even the tips of the flowers. She could hear the drums from one of the bands, maybe a fife and drum corps, marching in the parade along Main Street. It was a still day. The little flags, now faded since Memorial Day, were not flapping against the graves. The pinwheels some people staked beside head-stones were not spinning. The plastic flowers, the cards, letters, can-dles, charms, the inscrutable totems of animated grief that adorned the graves of the most visibly mourned, were motionless, quiet, per-fectly still. She slowly raised her head and sat down on the grass in front of Eve's grave. "Eve Crane Congdon / Born March 1, 1963 / Brilliant Spirit / Died March 28, 1999 / Diminished World." June's recitation of the inscription in her hesitant and angry little voice bore no relation to the experience of seeing these words cut into the sur-face of a granite slab. Like most epitaphs, Jordanna thought, this one read like a message in a bottle wildly cast back into the offending waters by a desperate survivor, rather than the attempted distillation of a life lived. Jordanna traced her index finger along the carved let-ters and numbers and reflexively thought what she always thought at James and Alice's graves. What if this were like touching? What if this stone had nerve endings connected to yours, what if it could transmit even the slightest bit of feeling to the flesh-and-blood you? The stone was warm from the slant of the sun and she placed the back of her other hand on her own forehead to check if it was body temperature.

James and Alice were buried in a cemetery near her parents' home on Cape Cod. In the months following James's stillbirth, Jordanna would drive the five hours from Maine at least once a week so that she could have her postpartum body near James's dead one. Some-times she would stay with her parents, sometimes she would get in her car and drive back to Maine, and sometimes she would rent a motel room. Her parents never said anything about the frequency of her trips, neither did the senior pastor at the church she was serving, but after a few months, Daniel became impatient. She tried to tell him that this was exactly how she felt. She'd be home in the early morning and she just knew that she'd jump out of her skin if she couldn't touch that stone right then, and with little explanation she'd hop in her car. Every trip she'd play the same tape, Polish Christmas carols sung by an all-boys choir. Driving home was different. Driving home she could listen to the radio, music or talk shows, but not news. The news was still too painful. It was a year before she could read a newspaper or listen to news on the radio or television. She had tried to explain that to Daniel, tried to tell him not to point out things in the paper to her. She knew now that he had probably interpreted her news whiteout as an unwillingness to move beyond herself, but really it was just the opposite. She was everywhere. Her nerve endings had been stretched to Bosnia and Rwanda, Oklahoma City and Jerusalem. Her loss, still so palpable, so physical, became a link, as strong as genealogy, as unavoidable as heredity, to the men and women, even animals, and of course children, in these stricken places. Grief, pain, misery, torture, trauma, anybody's became as real for her as her own. Her suffering was boundless and so was everyone else's, and it merged and melded like a torrent without clear origin but with immeasurable power. To hear about suffering no longer meant merely bearing witness to it, but literally bearing it, and she found herself physically incapable of bearing too much of it on any one day. Reverend Kirk, whom she was working under, relieved her of all counseling and life cycle events. He found previously ignored administrative duties for her, as well as work with the choir, the thrift shop, the interfaith council, and, after a while, back again with the youth group.

There were babies everywhere in Hutchinson Cemetery. The cemetery dated back to the founding of the town. The old and the new stones were intermingled, and more than half of the old graves were for children and babies. There were whole families of children all dead by the age of twelve, their names and dates carved in descending order into limestone obelisks, like some kind of deathly yardstick. Sometimes Jordanna accompanied congregants as they picked out a plot. And when they were busy conferring with the sexton, she'd wander, comparing herself to mothers in the last century, who in the course of a couple of seasons climbed this hill again and again, each time to add one more child's name to the family stone. In the last century women did what she had done all the time.

She prayed now; she prayed to James and Alice to help her. "Strength," she said out loud. "All I ever ask for is strength." She walked around to the blank side of the stone and sat down with her back against it. She closed her eyes and slowed her breathing. She placed her hands across her heart and felt her own life for a while. She pictured Jesus coming over the crest of the cemetery, walking toward her. He was not the translucently pale, painfully thin Jesus of sanctimonious paintings, but a robust Jesus, confident, hearty. He moved toward her in strong sturdy strides, and she could feel warmth, almost a hot light as he approached. He sat down without being asked. Confident, she thought, again, the very thing she was accused of, as if it were a sin.

She breathed deeply and tried to get herself back to the meditation to ask Jesus to help her find June. In the ten days since June had disappeared, she hadn't meditated, hadn't even prayed about June as passionately as she might have. Until this morning, Jordanna had considered June's disappearance primarily June's domain. Jordanna had assumed that June was concealing herself and when she wanted to be found she would be. It was a matter of will and desire. Jordanna tried to recapture her meditation, to block out the distant trombones and devote her heart and mind to the problem of June. She thought about what Abby had told her not that long ago, that she didn't like June, that she was turned off by her. What Jordanna disliked was that expression, "turned off." It had only one connotation for her, sex. She had contrived to bring this two-dimensional Jesus to within touching distance, and now she was wasting his time, or at the very least keeping him in a metaphysical bullpen, while her mind wandered to sex and her sister.

"Finite," she said out loud. It doesn't matter what I think, she pleaded to the robed figure just behind her clenched eyelids. What I think is irrelevant. What I feel only needs to be perfected, trained and retrained toward love. Just a clue or hint. What haven't I considered about where she is? What have I missed? Just a nod in a certain direction. Jordanna's grandmother, her mother's mother, used to play Hot and Cold with Abby and Jordanna. She lived in an old Tudor-style house in Bronxville, and when she had tea in the afternoon in the room she called the library, she'd hide a chocolate bar for them to find. The room contained a leather hassock that opened up to store sewing, or a book or even a lap blanket. She'd only hidden the chocolate in that hassock one time. It was no good after that as a hiding place. But when Jordanna remembered the game, when she thought about her grandmother, it was always that one instance she pictured. After twenty or thirty minutes of searching, Abby had given up and cried, while Jordanna had only become more animated. She dug all around her grandmother's birdlike body, thrusting her hands down between the cushions of the armchair, turning over the end table, removing its lone mahogany drawer, spilling the Pan Am playing cards and the leather coasters. She lifted the chintz skirt that flared from the bottom of the armchair. It ripped, and later, after her grandmother had finally revealed the chocolate and they'd eaten it, and Abby had stopped crying and Jordanna had calmed down, her grandmother made her stitch the little skirt back on, using infinitesimal back stitches that she had taught her on a sampler.

It was just like that with God, she remembered thinking later that night upstairs in one of the underheated rooms in that house. Abby was mad. She said the game was unfair, because Gran never told them that the footrest opened up. Lying under the pink sateen duvet, ancient feathers slipping through its seams every time she moved, Jordanna realized God was always somewhere you hadn't really examined before, inside something you didn't even know had an inside.

Jordanna had played Hot and Cold a few times with Abby's boys. It had been her idea for them not to know what it was they were looking for, an added degree of difficulty and mystery. Abby had walked in once and watched for a while and told Jordanna she thought it was too hard. How could you search and not know what you were looking for? Later on, after the saltshaker had been found at the base of the potted palm and she and Jordanna were alone, Abby told her she thought it a cruel game.

"REPELLENT, maybe," she said now, to her Jesus. She repelled me a bit, and maybe I, her. So now what do I do? Did I fuck up? Jordanna leaned her head back against the rough top of the gravestone. And whether it was that motion, or her own doubt and anxiety, or a clear Divine verdict on her behavior that caused the spasm, she didn't know. For all the pain she'd experienced in her back, she had never had this happen before. It was as if her whole spine seized up into a writhing, ramping mass of nerves. She yelled out, a gasp, really, and grabbed on to the flowers on either side of her, clutching as if for a hand. Breathe, breathe, she commanded herself. Breathe deeply. Maybe if she lay flat on the ground, if she pivoted around . . . But the slightest movement of her head caused her back to torque even more tightly. Jesus, I can't go to the hospital, she thought. I won't. I won't do it. She'd rather stay like this all day, all night, which was a real possibility. The wrought-iron gates at the entrance to the cemetery's driveway had been locked, and she'd come through the little swinging gate by the side. Nobody else would walk up here today. Maybe tomorrow a worker might come to mow. Worse things have happened, she told herself, way worse. There is no fear left. She breathed as deeply as she could without hurting herself, without causing her lungs to inflate so much that they disrupted the arrangement of her vertebrae. It's only physical pain, nothing compared to the other, she told herself.

She closed her eyes and willed that sandal-wearing, toga-clad Jesus to come back for just a moment. She would envision heat, a giant heating pad pressed to her neck and her lower back reaching past her buttocks down to her calves. Her mind could trump whatever the hell this was, this physical aberration. The pain came in waves. Only as it was waning could she register its severity. With the diminution of each wave she told herself not to anticipate its return, not to tense up. It's only pain. She tried to picture Jesus laying his hands on her back, his touch permeating her T-shirt and shorts, the layers of skin, the muscles and nerves. In the distance she heard a jingling, like change in a pocket or an AWOL triangle player from one of the marching bands. It grew a little louder and she thought of the great black gate at the entrance, the antithesis of the Pearly Gates, being unlocked with an impressive set of keys.

The noise turned out to be none of these, but rather a dog, his collar heavy with metal tags. He was trotting quickly, almost as if he were being chased, but still with the integrity to stop and urinate on as many gravestones as possible. If she weren't sure that it would cause extreme pain to yell, she would have. What she really wanted was to throw something. Why did people think of cemeteries as public parks? At the cemetery where James and Alice were buried, she'd seen two young men playing Frisbee, barefoot, each with a beer. She had watched them for a while, given them the chance to infer from her glaring that it was inappropriate, and when she had finally been forced to confront them, they had looked confused, as if burial grounds, even death itself, were foreign concepts. It's an awesome open space, they'd told her in defense. What about the beach? she'd said, gesturing toward the bay, which could be seen from one end of the cemetery. It's windy down there, they complained. Well, it's holy in here, she'd said, walking away.

Now she watched the spaniel run up to where the newest graves were. Out of the corner of her eye she spotted the owner, throwing the end of his cigarette on the gravel drive. Maybe she should try acupuncture or deep-tissue massage or one of the millions of remedies Gael was always suggesting. What if this happened in the middle of a worship service or in Australia or on the plane to Australia? The owner of the dog lit another cigarette and looked in Jordanna's direction. She didn't know if she was visible in among the stones, but even sitting down, she assumed she stood out. He started walking toward her, turned and whistled for his dog. He stopped for a moment as if he were searching for something, then began picking his way through the nonlinear rows of graves along the hill.

"Do you need some help?" he said. He was staring at her from a respectful distance, his cigarette cupped in his palm.

She didn't know what to say. She watched him touch his own cheek in response to the healing scar on her face.

"UPS," he said after a while.

"Hmm?"

"You're trying to figure out where you know me from, right?"

She hadn't been, really. She didn't think she'd ever seen him before. His legs bowed out slightly, as if he made his deliveries by horseback all day. She lifted her eyes to his narrow waist, accentuated by his snug dark blue jeans and large belt buckle with some kind of brown stone set into its center.

"You're the reverend up at the church on Bethel Road, right? I'm probably in your office every other day."

She smiled. Nodding would have hurt.

"Sorry to intrude," he said.

She breathed in deeply. "Do you always walk your dog in here?"

"I live right over there." He motioned to one of the small ranches that lined the western edge of the cemetery. "He gets out, and when he does, he always comes over here."

"People visiting graves might find it disrespectful," she said, unable to muster much righteousness in her tone, given her pain and her dawning realization that she was using a gravestone as a backrest.

"My mother's right over there." He pointed a few stones away.

Jordanna couldn't read that far, couldn't tell if the loss was recent. "I'm sorry."

"Thank you," he said. "Did you know Eve?" He nodded at Jordanna's stone backrest.

"No, unfortunately."

"We were in high school together. She was wild. Not so much as she got older. She was up in Storrs getting a special degree, English, writing or something, when she took sick. The Hutchinson paper did a whole thing on her poetry, published a whole page of it when she died." He stopped and shook his head. "Her mother's up here all the time. I can see about as far as this from my deck. It's like every time I look up in the early evening, she's over here."

"Really?"

"It must help. It does for some people. Usually in those first months after the funeral, you'll see the same people week after week, like an appointment, and then after a certain amount of time it's just holidays, anniversaries. Are you sure you're okay?"

"Do you know Eve's sister?" Jordanna asked, avoiding his question.

"God, that's a shame. I feel awful for old Mrs. Congdon." He raised his eyebrows and shrugged. "I just hope they find the body, you know. It's awful for a family, I'd guess, without a body." He motioned down behind Jordanna at the grave she was leaning against.

Jordanna winced at the start of another spasm. Now she knew she was tensing her back.

"Well, I'll let you get back to your—"

"No, it's fine. I was really just resting."

"At first I thought maybe I was interrupting a séance or something." He laughed. "Kind of strange on a nice bright day like this."

"Actually, I was meditating."

He nodded at her.

"I'm Jordanna," she said, just before he was about to turn to leave.

"Russ," he said, extending his arm.

She looked up at his outstretched arm. "Got a little bit of a back thing going on, so I think I won't shake right now, if that's okay. But before you go, I really did want to ask you something. Is it always Mrs. Congdon you see tending the flowers and visiting the grave?

Do you ever see June? I don't know if you'd know her by sight. But actually, it occurred to me that maybe if I came up here, I might get a sense, a hint about where she is now. She was, I think, very close to her sister."

Russ looked in the direction of his house, as if judging the distance. Jordanna doubted he could individuate somebody from that far away. What he saw on a regular basis was somebody stopping or crouching around this spot. And he figured it was the mother.

"It's not like I stand out there and spy over here all the time. I mean, I know at first it might have sounded like that, what I said about the mother."

Jordanna nodded very slightly. Everyone exaggerated, embellished the truth. Everyone.

"You sure you don't need a hand? I mean, how are you going to get up? Your car down by the gate? You going to be able to drive home?

Jordanna noticed for the first time that his left arm was far darker than his right: driver's tan. His hands seemed large for someone of such a slight build. She thought for a moment what it might be like to grip his hand. "No, thank you. I'll be fine. I think it's just like a little . . . attack. A little back attack. I should be fine in a few minutes."

" 'Cause you're welcome to come in, use my phone. Call your husband or something."

"Thank you," Jordanna said. "I'm used to this. It'll pass in a bit, and I'll be fine. It's an opportunity to look around, listen to the band music . . . at a distance . . . not such a bad thing, really."

He laughed. "Suit yourself. If you yelled really loud, I just might hear you over by my yard."

"Nice meeting you," she said.

He nodded and turned and whistled halfheartedly for his dog. She watched as he walked away, her eyes on his back end watching it go up and down as he picked his way through the gravestones. It reminded her of watching someone recede from view on a busy city street after you'd said your goodbyes when the light changed for him but not for you. She didn't think she could have let the UPS man help her up. She probably would have toppled him, and besides, she didn't really need assistance.

It was almost noon before she'd made her way to a pay phone. The parade was long over, Main Street was littered with campaign flyers and candy wrappers, coffee cups and a few broken flags. She'd sat against Eve's grave for a good hour after the UPS man had left. She'd tried to meditate, but she couldn't. She'd tried hard to bring June to her, to somehow summon her, to uncover whatever knowledge she already possessed but had not yet tapped. She loved to tell congregants faced with difficult decisions that the answers were there. The truth, the right path, the gut instinct was there, it just needed to be uncovered. How far one would have to dig depended on how deeply buried the truth was. But once unearthed, the treasure trove was never empty, there was always the gift of an answer. Well, she would have to go down quite a bit further than she seemed capable of today, Jordanna thought as she slowly walked the half mile from the cemetery up to the pay phone behind the news store on Church Hill Road.

Halfway through the cemetery she had come upon the least painful means of propelling herself. If she leaned on the ball of her left foot, as if she had a splinter in her heel, and dragged the right just a bit, it seemed to trick her body into thinking that she wasn't really bearing all her considerable weight. She wondered only briefly if she was doing permanent damage to her back.

She left a message on Abby's machine and hung up the phone. She looked at the series of hills running down toward her house and it made her tired and sad. There were no cab companies in Hutchinson. If you needed a cab, you had to call to Deerfield. She wasn't about to do that. The church house was a lot closer than home. She could go in there and lie on the floor and read or work. There was mail to be answered. Labor Day was another one of those days when the absence of a family hung around her like a cumbersome dog tag.

Labor Day was the kind of day to play badminton or croquet in your yard and trip on the wickets as you ran through the dark with a flaming marshmallow. It was a day to be at a picnic or at the beach or in bed with a lover with the air-conditioning blasting. It wasn't really the kind of day to be a minister in excruciating pain in the middle of a parched town.

ॐ Chapter 9

T HE first thing Jordanna noticed as she entered the waiting area
was a little shrine with burning incense, a wooden bowl filled
with what looked like milk and a delicately trickling fountain
plugged into the wall. The smell was vaguely familiar—sandalwood
or patchouli, something that brought her straight back to 1973. Gael
had made the appointment, even offered to drive her the fifty minutes it took to reach this "practitioner's" office. Jordanna looked
around the little room for a license or diploma. Her back was getting
better each day. She'd only had to stop once on her way up here.
She'd pulled to the side of Route 7 and had stretched across the hood
of the hot car for a few minutes.

Suki Rahmlow was a deep-tissue masseuse as well as a . . . ? Jordanna could no longer remember. Gael had said that Suki was a
deeply spiritual person, and she was sure that Jordanna would like
her. "It's okay," Jordanna had assured her on her way out of her
office. "Whatever it is, it'll be fine."

"Well," Gael had said, "It's not exactly cheap, and it's far. I mean,
it is a commitment, and she does a few things . . . you know, you have
to kind of go with it, you know what I mean?"

Jordanna had laughed.

"Well, call me as soon as you're done, okay?"

Jordanna thought this was more like a blind date than a quasi-medical appointment. She had agreed, finally, to come, because she didn't have a strong sense that she shouldn't, which was what she always experienced as soon as anyone mentioned a visit to the doctor. Last week, in what Abby referred to as a major inroad, Jordanna had allowed Abby's dentist to cap her tooth. Jordanna knew she needed to do it. Sunday after Sunday standing in the pulpit with a broken tooth would prove an insurmountable distraction for many in the pews. Why doesn't she have it fixed? Is it the money? Doesn't the congregation provide her dental insurance? And she doesn't use it, flagrantly disregards it? It's a shameful waste. Worse, it's an insult. Could she be afraid? Reverend Nash scared? Vulnerable? Does she think a broken tooth is God's will, and she should just live with it, suck it up, accept it as a "gift"? She knew that an entire theology could be spawned from her not fixing that damn tooth. So she'd gone to the dentist.

She'd tried to explain to Abby that she just didn't like people handling her anymore. Haircuts were kept to a minimum, the optometrist was avoided, as were shoe salesmen, even yoga instructors—anything where she might be messed with in some way. She couldn't abide it. Abby said no one liked to go to the dentist. She didn't understand that Jordanna was no longer comfortable as the *object* of whatever little activity was being engaged in. When she was in Dr. Freedman's office with the giant metallic tooth dangling from the ceiling only inches above where she lay prostrate under the interrogation-strength lamp, her neck draped with a light blue bib, her feet dangling off the end of the chair, it was impossible not to feel like something was about to be perpetrated upon her, and in the case of things medical, that something was tragedy. Abby thought that maybe the trigger was sensory. The smell of a certain antiseptic or the dental chair perhaps reminded her of the exam chairs that turned into tables, so popular with ob/gyns. Maybe the little bib was too like the paper smock. If she could identify the one causative agent, then perhaps she could eliminate it or acclimate to it. But Jordanna knew there was no controlling the lessons your body had incorporated from experience. She had managed Dr. Freedman by borrowing Brendan's CD Walkman. It actually had been his idea. She popped in the Brahms Requiem before she got out of her car. Once seated in the chair, she informed the dentist not to ask her anything. She told him she had a pretty high tolerance for pain, but Novocain was fine with her, if he thought she should have it. Then she cranked up the music until the volume itself bordered between obliterating and painful, and she meditated her way far beyond the realm of the blue plastic chair.

"Reverend Nash? I'm Suki." A small dark woman with long black curly hair thrust out her hand. She was wearing a flowing print skirt and a tank top. Jordanna stared first at her voluminous hair and then at her arms. Her shoulders rose up above the straps of her shirt into white boulders that only barely tapered down toward square hands.

"Did you find your way okay?"

"Please, *Jordanna.*" She followed the woman into her office, which was in the back of the house overlooking a pond and a gazebo. In the center of the pond was a little spring or fountain, fully operational even in this drought. The water must have been delivered, and the fountain wired somehow.

"What I like to do, to begin with, is take a medical history. And the medical history I do will be quite different from the traditional kind. Some of the questions might seem strange, beyond the purview of—"

Jordanna exhaled loudly and stepped in quite close to Suki. "It's magnificent here. Really peaceful. The little spring is just, just right." She placed her right hand with its sizable silver ring on Suki's well-developed forearm. "I much prefer the present. I'll give you my medical present." Jordanna laughed, alone. "My presenting injury, as doctors like to call it."

Suki sat down in a saucer-shaped leather chair, watching carefully as Jordanna lowered her body into a similar chair beside her. Suki nodded and continued to stare.

Jordanna stared back, attempting to mimic the same beneficent gaze. After a long silence, Jordanna smiled and finally said, "Will that be all right with you?"

Suki nodded very slightly. "For today, yes. For today."

Jordanna focused on the fountain while Suki asked her things like whether she preferred salty or sweet foods, whether she needed an alarm clock to wake up. Did she sleep throughout the night? Did she sweat at rest? Did she sleep on her left or right side, back or stomach? She wrote down the answers to these questions in a large leather-bound notebook. She asked Jordanna to hold out both hands, and she carefully examined the short square nails, then her tongue. She told Jordanna to "hop up" on the examining table, then apologized and asked if she thought she could comfortably make it up there.

"It's getting out of this chair that's the problem." Jordanna braced her right arm behind her and pushed off against the back of the chair, slowly, until she felt she could stand. She walked across the room to the black leather examining table, which looked more like Danish furniture than medical apparatus. The top was covered not with paper, but with a tan linen cloth, like something the Episcopalians would use on the altar during one of their services. Rather than attempt to seat herself on the table, she merely leaned against it. Suki placed her child-size fingers first on the inside of Jordanna's wrist, then stretched to place them under her jaw. Without warning, she dropped to the floor and pressed her second and third fingers on the inside of Jordanna's bare right ankle. Jordanna laughed, and Suki just sat on the backs of her heels, eyes closed, counting. She rose slowly, and unhooked a stethoscope from behind the door and without intrusion placed it perfectly on Jordanna's heart. They stood there like that for a while, as if it were completely natural for two people to be connected ear to heart, each gathering and sending some kind of information. When she had replaced the stethoscope on its hook, she wheeled out a blood pressure gauge from under the table, cradled Jordanna's left elbow in her hands and folded the black nylon cuff around her arm, as if it were a special seal.

"You're extremely gentle," Jordanna said after the cuff had been removed and the little machine wheeled back out of sight.

Suki smiled and nodded.

"So?" Jordanna crossed her arms over her chest.

"Is that comfortable for you, standing like that?"

"It's all relative," Jordanna said.

"Well, when you are home alone—"

"I lie flat on the floor, with my legs up on a chair."

Suki nodded and then opened the door to the waiting room and returned a few moments later with a small wooden chair painted sky blue. "Please," she said, motioning for Jordanna to lay down. Jordanna eyed the spot on the wood floor where she eventually pictured herself, and slowly began the incremental movements needed to get there. Suki positioned the chair for her and Jordanna carefully raised her legs, her flax-colored pants sliding down to her knees as she did.

"What do you think is wrong?" Suki pulled her legs into the large white leather chair and balanced her notebook on her knees.

"My back's flipping out." From where Jordanna lay on the floor, Suki looked like a fairy-tale character cupped inside a cabbage leaf.

"And these . . . lacerations?" Suki gestured toward Jordanna's cheek.

"Oh, that's nothing. Just a little bike accident. Nothing to do with my back."

Suki nodded slightly. "How long have you been in pain?"

Suki was writing down much more than Jordanna was offering. "For about three years—not this badly, of course, the entire time. Labor Day. This happened on Labor Day."

"And three years ago . . . your back began hurting after an illness, an accident?"

"Do you meditate out by that fountain?" Jordanna said.

Suki nodded and said nothing for a long while. "What healing modality do you think would be best now, for your back?"

Jordanna smiled. Even the way this woman pronounced the word *healing* had a palliative effect, as if menthol, eucalyptus, frankincense and myrrh had just wafted through the room. "Any kind of healing would be welcomed," Jordanna said.

"Would you like to lie down on the table, then?" Suki said as she began moving around the room, closing the wooden blinds that covered the sliding doors to the outside and striking a match to light a candle. "I work with a variety of practices. And perhaps today it would be best for us to begin with a certain kind of acupressure called Jin Shin Do."

Jordanna rolled slowly from her back to her left side and began the long process that was standing up. She watched Suki glide through the scented space of the room.

"It is only my thumbs," Suki said, as if she had been asked. "I press on various acupuncture points for a few minutes, at most. The result is the release of both physical and mental tension. The ultimate goal is the unblocking of your *qi,* your vital energy."

In order to lie down on the leather table, Jordanna first needed to get into a kneeling position, then slowly lower her chest and then one leg at a time down flat. When her cheek finally rested against the soft cloth covering the table, she breathed in the distinct smell of oranges and lemons. It reminded her of a cake that someone in her last congregation used to send over to grieving families. Jordanna must have been offered a slice of that cake forty or fifty times in the four years she was in Beecham.

"Forgive me, Jordanna." Suki appeared at the side of the table. "The accupoints I will be working on today are all on the front of your body. I'm happy to help you to turn, though I sense you are more comfortable doing things yourself."

Jordanna let out a few low grunts as she turned her too-large body onto its back. The room, which had been perfectly cool when she first entered, had grown warm. She had expected to be asked to disrobe. And even as a film of sweat broke out across her forehead, she was grateful to have been allowed to keep on her clothes, just the thinnest layer of the nonobjectified self.

"As I press each spot for about three minutes, I would like you to begin to release the source of your pain. Your back is the expression of an emotional . . . of a loss . . . I think. All that . . . sadness is locked into the back. But the poor back, no, the back is not the origin, only the manifestation. My words are making you very tense, I can feel that. Okay. No talking. Okay, Jordanna, what I'm about to do will seem very odd."

Jordanna's eyes were closed and she was trying to breathe deeply and thinking how lovely it was that someone had anthropomorphized her back like that, so sweet. No one in her life spoke to her that way, not anymore. In the first few months of knowing Daniel, when she found herself in his bed more often than her own, he used to call to her body parts in all the Austronesian languages he'd studied. If she accused him of making up the word for pubic hair in Maori or nipple in Malay, he would get out of bed and walk slowly across the cold floor to the shelf where he kept no less than twenty foreign dictionaries, as unselfconscious about his naked body as she was with her desire for it. No matter how many times she challenged him, the words were always real.

How could you not love a man who knew so many words for clitoris? she told him one night. It was Reading Period, and they had no business lying intertwined on Daniel's platform bed on the Sunday before exams began. "That's not why you're attracted to me," Daniel said, propping himself up on one elbow.

"It's not?" She dragged her many-ringed fingers across his dark chest hair.

"You don't know, do you? Incredible. Don't you have to be introspective to be a woman of the cloth?"

She sighed. This had happened before, with other men, men whom she liked a lot, a few whom she even thought she loved. At some point, and for some reason that at twenty-seven she hadn't fully figured out, they all felt the need to try to pound her down a bit, whittle off a few of her seventy-five inches. Because she didn't distrust her own powerful instincts, didn't inspect herself hourly for rust and rot the way most women did, she'd unnerved every man she'd become involved with.

"You love me because we're alike," he said, clasping her hand.

She laughed. They couldn't have been more different. He was small-boned and lean, shorter than she was. He was studious, circumspect, maddeningly patient and socially aloof. And Daniel Greene was Jewish, Hebrew, dark-skinned, hirsute, intense, foreign.

"You're a much better student than I am," she said, not sure she wanted this conversation to get too deep.

"That's because I'm smarter."

She laughed again.

He adjusted the pillow so that he was sitting upright now. "I am. And the cool thing is that you know it, and it doesn't bother you one bit. Not today, not ever."

"How can you be so sure?" she said.

"I knew it the minute I saw you pull out a notebook from your book bag. And when I watched you ride that ludicrous bike around campus my intial findings were corroborated—"

"And now that you know me . . . carnally?" she asked.

"You don't start every day with some deep deficit. You're not going around trying to prove anything—"

"But—"

"Wait," he said. "Except for one thing. You want to be good, whatever that means. Or, you want other people to think you're good. I'm not sure yet. That little martyr chant you mumble about personal vanity and looking to other people's interests—"

"It's from Philippians."

He shrugged.

"It's not really about being good." Is that what it looked like to him? "It's more about . . . loving . . . having your love accepted."

"See, you can say something as . . . bald as that, unconcerned that you'll be teased for it."

"And that makes us alike?"

He had begun braiding the loose strands of her hair that had fallen across his arm. "In a way. You have a kind of . . . certitude that I recognize. I don't want to say presumption, because that sounds so . . ."

"Egotistical?"

"There's a word for what I mean used by this tribe I'm studying, where the language hasn't been all fucked up by Freud. They have this word that means both well water and self-possession. This confidence is not an attribute you acquire genetically or environmentally. You can't learn it or lose it. They believe it's part of your soul."

SUKI had moved. Jordanna felt it, insistent and slow through her clothes, a finger being pushed down in her groin, about two inches below her navel.

"You must tell me if I hurt you."

"Very little hurts me," Jordanna said, as the woman began pressing down on what used to be her uterus.

"Shhh," Suki said, and the sound came out as an intimacy more than an admonition.

The little woman was strong, and determined, apparently, to put her firm finger straight through Jordanna's—

"Conception vessel," Suki said.

Jordanna stared up at her and Suki nodded. "It's all right. Yes, I know."

When June returned, Jordanna would send her to Suki. The calm was remarkable, the reassurance.

"You must help here, too, Jordanna. Your mind right now is everywhere, I can feel that. What I need to feel is your pulse here. Try to focus, as people do in meditation."

"I do meditate."

Suki nodded. "I could tell from your pulse rate, before. And you run?"

"Bike, I bike. Well, I did. I took a bad fall about ten days ago, and then my back . . . I haven't been able to ride in a while. I miss it."

Suki nodded again, as if she were hearing everything Jordanna said for the second time. She very gradually released the pressure on her groin and moved one finger's width up and slowly began depressing again.

"Inhale, now, slowly and deeply," Suki said, her tongue wet on the *l*'s.

Jordanna had always begun her guided meditations for her congregants with a chant of, "Breathe in the breath of God," and she intoned it now silently to herself. If Suki came to her office in the church house and Jordanna led her through a meditation, who would the little woman envision? What form would God take in her mind? That was a kind of sight she wished she could have, to be able to see what others saw when they envisioned God. Was it an endless variation on a familiar theme, or did the ultimate truth give onto a bigger and bigger room with each person's view?

"You need to try to . . . open." Suki herself was sweating now.

"What makes you think I'm not open?"

"The capacity is without limit." Suki gently began decreasing the pressure. She measured a thumb's width above Jordanna's navel, closed her eyes and began once again to exert pressure.

"Most people think I'm *too* open."

"Breathe," Suki whispered.

Jordanna wondered if she could ever get Daniel to come here. Could this kind of healing work on couples, could it work on men? Daniel would say that he believed in the mind-body connection, but that's as far as he'd commit. He said he believed in God, too, but whenever she pressed him to translate for God, he would shrug or smile, sometimes saying the ways of God are beyond all understanding. He accused her, before the babies, of always trying to humanize God, describing the Divine in terms of the mortal, making God relational. Big mistake, he told her. After James died he refused any invitation into such a discussion. It hadn't stopped her, of course. To not talk about God in their house, to not give the Divine a thorough going-over, an airing, would be like not talking about James, or Alice, or her purloined uterus and ruptured future.

When she was pregnant with Alice and every day was both miracle and trial, she'd asked Daniel if he found Henri Nouwen's notion of the Eternal Now comforting—that we come from God and we return to God, dwelling in that matrix for ninety-nine percent of our existence and spending only one infinitesimal fraction here on earth in this thing we call life. It was late spring and he was making carrot soup. The blender was going, with the steaming carrots whirling orange inside. Jordanna sat at the kitchen table, her feet stretched out on the chair in front of her, picking the croutons out of the salad with her fingers. He didn't answer at first and she rubbed her bare toes on the floor, rubbed her hands together and moved to the counter so he could see her. She asked again, where in the time line he thought our existence here on earth fit in. Maybe this was the unimportant part. He pressed the puree button and pulsed it, on, off, on, off. In the silence she could hear the echo of the grinding motor.

"Not interested in God, Jordanna."

"Really?" she said, sticking her finger into the steaming carrot puree when he lifted the lid on the blender.

"Really," he said, spooning the thick stuff into the soup pot on the stove.

"Well, I have to talk about God, it's what I do. I mean, what if I were a stockbroker and you said you never wanted to talk about money again—"

"I didn't say *never*. Don't be dramatic. Just, now."

"Can other people talk to you about God, or is it just me?" She looked over at him, at the stove: His lips were pressed together and he was humming softly.

"Daniel, we've lost a lot already, tons. I mean, you can't boot God out of here, too."

The humming got a little louder. It was something cheesy and familiar, something people played at catered affairs—the "Mexican Hat Dance," something like that.

Had she been able to feel anything then, really feel, she would have been mad, mad enough to hit him, maybe, but instead she began singing in her loud, theatrical voice, "Ave Maria." And it was only when she got to *benedicta tu in mulieribus,* and breathed, that she realized he wasn't humming the "Mexican Hat Dance," but "Hava Negilah."

"BREATHE," Suki whispered. "This is the last pressure point I will do today." She leaned in on both thumbs, as if she might balance all of her muscular self right there on those little pads, and pressed just below Jordanna's throat, midway between her collarbones. "Lightly," she said. "Lightly."

When she finally pulled away from the last pressure point, Suki walked to an armoire in the corner and pulled out a large muslin sheet, like a shroud. She draped it over Jordanna, first tucking it in under her feet and then moving carefully, almost ceremoniously around the black table and sliding the cloth just under Jordanna's body. Jordanna braced herself for pain as her back was moved, but it was gone. The cloth smelled of lilacs or violets, floral and springlike. When Jordanna was all wrapped up, her arms tucked to her sides, swaddled like a newborn, Suki dropped a dot of oil on the crown of her head and then on her forehead. The oil, too, was perfumed— rosemary, perhaps, an herb you might cook with. Suki rubbed gently, one thumb at the top of Jordanna's head, one on her forehead. Jordanna closed her eyes and imagined herself being laid backward, like a baby, anointed in baptism, cosseted, secured, treasured.

ᔓᕽ Chapter 10

ABBY wondered whether she should answer the phone. She had let herself into Jordanna's house because it was Friday afternoon and she doubted Jordanna would be home and she needed a waystation while she made the switch from concerned guidance counselor to loving mother. Gabe was at Miss Diane's waiting to be picked up and the other three would be in the house now by themselves, boxes of cookies, bags of chips, Gatorade, the screen door wide open. She didn't care.

It was cool and quiet in Jordanna's house. The shades she had sewn for her sister when she first moved in were pulled down and the house felt womblike. The wood floor was cool on her bare feet and nothing interfered with the smell of the verbena soap drifting out of the little downstairs bathroom. Right when she'd come in, she'd slipped *Blue* from its cardboard sleeve and popped it onto Jordanna's old record player, expertly lowering the needle to the start of "A Case of You."

The phone rang while she was peering into Jordanna's refrigerator. There was an avocado, which everyone knew should be out on the counter, two Yoo-Hoos, some eggs, the end of a loaf of french bread, garlic, wilted scallions with the rubber band still around them and an entire shelf of little yogurts, the kind she would never buy her kids because they had marshmallow cereal mixed into them. "God, how does she live?" Abby said out loud, and the phone rang again. She pulled a pack of Marlboro Lights out of the butter compartment and counted the cigarettes left. She waited for the machine to pick up and put the cigarettes back in the refrigerator. After four more rings, she walked into the hall, angry at being interrupted in the middle of her date with the desultory.

It was Daniel. "You'll probably want to hang up. This is Abby. Jordanna's not here and I know this is an expensive call." Abby pushed her index finger up through the black vinyl coil of the phone cord.

"How are you?" Daniel asked.

"How are *you*?" she said.

"Tired."

"How's the . . . digging going down there?"

"Good, interesting. Some good stuff."

"So . . . is it Saturday there already?"

"Yeah. How are the kids? Jim?"

"Good, everybody's good."

"Jordanna?"

"Well, I just let myself in. I'm not sure where she is. I don't know if she told you . . . her back's been pretty bad. I've been trying to get her to go see a doctor."

"Yeah," he said, as if she had just asked him a question or he was speaking to someone on his end of the line.

"You know she had kind of a bad bike accident last week or the week before."

"Really?"

"Cut up her face, chipped a tooth. She was a mess."

"She didn't tell me."

"Oh."

"I probably should go, and try her again later tonight or tomorrow."

"Yeah," Abby said. She pulled on a rubber band that was wound around the basement doorknob. "Jesus," she said, hanging up the phone. "How *does* she live?" She walked over to the sofa and put her legs up on the coffee table, something Daniel had brought back from somewhere. In its original incarnation it had been some semiprimitive culture's communal milling table or something. Her parents hadn't really warmed to him at first, and she had been his defender. Her mother thought he was too serious, that he didn't laugh enough. "You know," she had said to Abby one night when Daniel and Jordanna were visiting, "the conventional wisdom about laughter?" They were walking the dog out on Perry's Way. There was no moon, but lots of stars. It was colder than it should have been, and they were wearing parkas. Abby was home from college and Jordanna from Divinity School.

"No, Mom, I don't know the conventional wisdom about laughter."

Her mother pulled on the leash a little and looked across the road in the direction of the marsh and the cattails. "Laughter and sex, you know, there's a direct correlation."

Abby laughed.

"People who are willing to laugh are willing to—be pleased. He doesn't seem to be easily pleased."

Abby's father objected to Daniel's lack of interest in things mechanical. He was urban and pale and bearded and intellectual, not to mention a good inch shorter than Jordanna, and none of those things sat well with Abby's parents. Jordanna accused them of anti-Semitism, and, deeply wounded, they responded by saying no one could be more politically liberal than they. Abby defended their parents to Jordanna by saying they really were liberal, they just weren't used to men marrying their daughters.

Now it was all complicated. Abby's father thought it was ludicrous that Daniel should leave his childless wife and move to east Oshkosh, as he referred to it, for a year. And Abby's mother had told Abby that she prayed for Jordanna to find love, something to supplement God's love. She hoped Jordanna would find real physical love again. Abby and Jim had benefited from all the tension between Jordanna and Daniel and their parents. They had met and married and started having children all fairly quickly, and as far as Abby knew there had barely been any concerns. Jim was Catholic, but he didn't seem very Catholic, Abby's mother had told her when they were planning the wedding. It's because he's a Christian, Jordanna had said. It's comfortable for them. The truth was, Jim seemed at times as if he might have been raised down the street from them, if not in the same home. He was familiar, and he rarely pushed them into places they were unwilling to venture. That, and the fact that he owned a set of ramps for changing his own oil, was handy with a shovel, a paintbrush and a circular saw, endeared him to her parents. Abby knew that what comforted her parents about Jim was that in their presence he successfully veiled his sexuality with his functional masculinity. Daniel's sexuality, on the other hand (in direct opposition to what Abby's mother had feared), was far less coy or apologetic. Abby remembered spending an entire Christmas morning watching Daniel read. As she moved around the dining room, collecting wrapping paper, vacuuming tinsel, setting the table, she watched him in the family room where he was reading, continually running his thumb and forefinger around his mustache and then slowly down the sides of his beard before bringing them together at his chin. If he could caress his own hairy face like that, again and again, in that ongoing circular, meditative, rhythmic motion, she could only imagine what he might do to her luxuriant older sister in bed.

She and Jordanna used to talk about sex all the time. It was actually one of the topics they didn't argue about, that didn't split them. Sex was what had brought them together as teenagers. Jordanna had pulled off this incredible feat of having a lot of sex in high school and feeling neither terribly guilty nor proud of it. She made it clear to Abby that it was their birthright. "Orgasms are there waiting to be had—all the time," she'd told her. In the last few years, when Abby had attempted to bring up the nature of intimacy in marriage, her own or Jordanna's, Jordanna had stopped her. What had she said the other day? Sex with Daniel was all about loss now, something like that.

SHE took one of the cigarettes from the refrigerator but didn't light it, and went up into Jordanna's room to get back the sun hat she'd lent her. Jim had suggested they come over here when Jordanna was in Australia, which was coming up, she thought. "Your sister always has candles. We'll bring some wine, some CDs." He asked Abby if she thought Jordanna or Daniel still had any dope anywhere. Abby thought it was possible. She surveyed the bedroom now, the platform bed, the prayer wheel, the singing bowl, the mandalas and kabbalas and whatever else it was she was looking at. The dorm room look and feel of the space never failed to make her nostalgic for marijuana. In one corner of the room, Jordanna had a little prayer space with a rag rug and three white candles in various states of melt. There were prayer stones and a Bible. She looked over at the nightstand. She didn't want to open any drawers, but she did need to look in the closet for the hat. In high school and college, Jordanna used to keep her pot in a little crewelwork pouch. They each had received one, a gift from their mother when they'd begun to menstruate. It was intended for sanitary napkins, and Jordanna had kept everything she knew her mother didn't really want to see in that little pouch with its scene of the shepherdess and her flock under a blossoming tree.

Abby looked on top of what she guessed was supposed to be Daniel's side of the low sleek dresser and then shifted her eyes left, to Jordanna's side, with its earring tree and raku pinch pot filled with foreign coins. There was a cassette entitled *Sunday Sermon, Nov. 7, 1999 Do You Know the Ways of Dorothy Day,* a small cruet of yellow oil and a beige linen pocket square. And then, of course, her niece and nephew, James and Alice, each in a silver frame.

Abby remembered the first time Jordanna had showed her that

photo of James. She had ritually unfolded the rectangle of blue-black velvet in which the picture was wrapped and pressed the framed photo into Abby's hands, as if she still possessed something that might yet be lost. Jordanna had told her that the pictures had been taken a few hours after the delivery, and all Abby could think of were those death portraits the Victorians were so fond of. She would, she knew, say that the baby was beautiful, or at the very least precious, or something, but she was scared that the photo would be a better representation of death than of a baby. She herself had brought home three babies by then, and it had shocked her to see stillborn James dressed as her sons had been, in a little hat with the name of the hospital on the turned-up part. Jordanna had told her that since he had died in utero maybe three or four days before the delivery, the bones in his skull plate had begun to override, and they'd slipped the hat on him as soon as he'd emerged, the way they did with the other babies to keep them warm. They'd wrapped him in a towel, Jordanna said, and then in a blue and white hospital blanket. His face reminded Abby of dead faces, the way they filled and bloated. His eyes were closed, his skin a bit gray and his lips a frighteningly deep red. "Perfect," Abby had said. "He's perfect."

She looked at the photos now, side by side. They looked like siblings. It was more than that they shared not being alive. They had Daniel's little nose and Jordanna's bowed lips. Abby remembered seeing her grandmother's open coffin when she died. Abby was thirteen, and their mother had brought them into a special viewing room before the funeral and the funeral director had lifted that little Dutch door that coffins have, and there she'd been, with a corsage on her bosom, as if it were Mother's Day. Jordanna had leaned over their dead grandmother, her long loose hair sweeping across the old woman's waxy face. And Abby thought she had kissed her, though Jordanna never did tell her whether she had really pressed her lips to the dead woman's. Abby had reached out and gently touched the chiffon sleeve of her grandmother's dress. And then she watched the corsage, waiting for that small bony bosom to move and heave, for the flowers to rise, even the smallest bit. She looked at the babies in the pictures on the dresser now, at the blanket swaddling Alice, which she had made, and wondered what might happen if she stared long enough.

"Abby?" Jordanna called to her from the front door.

"Hey. I'm just up here looking for my hat." Abby repositioned the frames the way she thought they'd been and walked toward the top of the stairs.

"The police think they've found June's car." Jordanna dropped her mailbag and her keys onto the telephone table, then draped her jacket over the banister. "I've just been at the Nearings'. It seems the car was by Snow's Lake, but they hadn't seen it before because it was a ways in. In the woods, I guess. There's an old fire road in there."

"I'm sorry," Abby said, meeting Jordanna at the bottom of the stairs. "Do they—"

Jordanna walked into the kitchen and reached into the refrigerator for her cigarettes. "Sorry, but I have to."

Abby shrugged.

"I'm not sure yet what else they've found. They'll be getting back to Drew."

"How was he?" Abby followed Jordanna out the kitchen door onto the small back porch with its two rusting green metal chairs separated by an old milk can painted black, which served as a table for Jordanna's ashtray.

"He's scared. We're all scared of hearing something we don't want to hear, something violent. He thinks she's dead. I think he's jumped to that. So has Beverly."

Abby remembered the cigarette she'd left on the dresser upstairs. "Jumped?"

Jordanna looked down at her hands.

"It's been a while—what, two weeks? What do you think happened to her?"

"That's a really complicated question." Jordanna tugged hard on her cigarette. "Is the stereo on?"

Abby nodded.

"Was it on when I walked in?"

"Yeah."

"I didn't even notice it."

"Daniel called."

Jordanna took another tantalizingly long drag of her cigarette and tipped her head back before exhaling upward. "Did you talk to him?"

"For a minute. He said he'll try you tomorrow."

"My ticket's for the beginning of October. I guess I have to go. We've got this Divinity School intern. The hat's in the downstairs closet. You and Jim should use the house while I'm away." Jordanna looked at Abby.

"You don't want to go?" Abby said.

Jordanna stubbed out the cigarette and sighed. "I can't not go. I mean, if I don't make this visit . . . It'll mean too much if we decide we can go for nine months without seeing each other. It's just easier to go."

Abby looked out at the tire swing hanging from a limb of a chestnut tree. It had been Daniel's idea, for the boys. He'd bought everything, then called Jim to come and help him. "We're going out for pizza tonight, you want to come?" The phone rang, and Abby reflexively stood up to answer it.

"Let it ring, Ab."

Abby was already in the kitchen. "It might be the kids," she yelled back. She ran into the hall and picked up the phone. She said hello nicely twice, then a little more harshly and then she hung up.

"I'm not here," Jordanna yelled over the music and through the screen door.

"Don't you have anything to drink here? Beer?"

"Irish Mist," Jordanna yelled. "Who was it?"

"Hang-up."

"You should have called me in." Abby heard the loose-hinged metal chair clang and creak and within a second Jordanna was crowding the little doorway. "Did you hear anything?"

"I think it was probably a wrong number," Abby said measuredly. She pulled a kitchen chair over to the counter and reached up above the refrigerator for the Irish Mist.

"Shit," Jordanna said, slamming her fist on the counter.

"What's the matter?"

"Well, it could have been June." She grabbed a hank of her hair from behind her and twisted it rapidly as if she were wringing it. Abby took a step back as Jordanna flung the hair angrily across her back. She turned toward the freezer for some ice and listened as Jordanna pounded across the hardwood floor of the living room and pulled the record off the stereo.

When she reentered the kitchen, Abby handed her a short glass of whiskey. It was so rare to see Jordanna angry that Abby found herself watching her sister with an unusual degree of remove. "I'm going to go in a minute," Abby said, taking a sip of her drink and staring at Jordanna. "Let's go outside. So few days left like this, you know?" She reached for her sister's hand the way she would have with Gabe and pulled her gently toward the porch. "What's the worst—"

Jordanna cut her off; she held up that massive stop sign of a hand and placed it too close to Abby's face and then she opened her eyes and said, "Pray with me, just pray with me right now."

Jordanna closed her eyes again and Abby watched her clutch her drink with one hand and reach up and out with the fingertips of her other. "Oh, heavenly God," she began firmly and with conviction. "Oh, heavenly God . . . Oh, heavenly God . . ." she repeated, and then she began to cry, her face not hidden, but tilted upward. Abby watched as tears came from the corners of her sister's eyes, her nose, her mouth, as water just flowed and flowed off her face, as if from abundant reserve. The tears ran down that large upturned face and only after a great while did they begin to sail over her chin and in fat consistent drops onto her blouse and skirt, her hands, her drink.

Abby thought about continuing the prayer for her sister, but she didn't know what to fill in, in that large blank. *Oh, heavenly God, make June not dead, make Daniel a loving husband, make Jordanna a mother to live children*. She searched, trawling her memory for some bit of remembered scripture, something general but uplifting, something she did not have to create, something Jordanna might relate to. Their grandmother had taught them that there was only one legitimate prayer when you were praying for yourself. "You may," she would say precisely, "for yourselves ask God for only one thing . . . strength. Pray for strength." Abby had been in junior high school before she realized that her grandmother had not been referring to the power to leap tall buildings and bench-press cars. The adrenaline they were to pray for was that other kind of inspiration. Abby put her glass down next to the ashtray and grabbed on to Jordanna's free hand with her ice-cold hand and said in an amateurish, self-conscious voice, "Oh, God," which sounded less like an invocation than a complaint. "Oh, God, we ask you for strength. Make us strong."

Abby watched her sister, the tears continuing to spring, and then she felt that proprietary squeeze of the hand, that patronizing, loving, infuriating, comforting and powerful claim. "Amen," Jordanna said loudly. She stood up and embraced Abby, pressing the glass of whiskey into the small of her back. Abby allowed herself to be hugged. It was diagnosable, really, if you stepped away and looked at it objectively. General Jordanna. She thought about the boys, about Jim, about anything that made her less like an adjutant in Jordanna's life and more like the subject of her own.

"I should go," Abby said, her face still pressed to the front of Jordanna's wet blouse. "The boys are home alone." She didn't repeat the invitation to join them for pizza; once was enough.

"Your drink," Jordanna said, pointing at Abby's glass with her own.

"I don't think I can really drink this stuff."

Jordanna had still made no move to wipe her face. She didn't even dab at her eyes, the left one brimming, the tears just barely contained by her lower lid. She couldn't possibly be able to see out that eye. Abby picked up the drink from the top of the milk can and started for the kitchen. "We're going to the House of Pizza around seven."

She opened the screen door, poured the whiskey down the drain and put the glass in the dishwasher, which was sadly empty with only one of everything. She walked back to the screen door and looked out at her sister, who was holding her own glass against her forehead. "You know, you're under a lot of pressure. This is a lot to deal with, even for you." She walked farther into the house, ran up the steps for that lone cigarette she had put down next to the pictures of the babies. Just as she was trying to remember where Jordanna said that straw hat was, she heard the doorbell ring. She didn't know if Jordanna could hear it out back. She ran down the stairs to the front hall and opened the door. There was a young girl standing there, someone Abby vaguely recognized as a student from Hutchinson High.

"Oh, sorry, I thought Reverend Nash lived here. I just wanted to—"

"Tara," Jordanna called out from behind Abby on her way into the front hall. "Tara, this is my sister, Abby."

"Mrs. Healey?" Tara said, somewhat alarmed.

"You know her?"

"From school," Abby said to Jordanna.

"Oh, of course. Right. We've really missed you in Senior P.F."

Tara attempted to look past the two women into the darkened house. "Are you having a party or something? I can come back another day."

"Of course not. It's wonderful you've come."

"I was leaving anyway." Abby turned toward Jordanna and touched her on the arm. "Maybe we'll see you later, then."

"Okay, then," Jordanna said, not focusing on either Tara or Abby. Abby walked down the brick steps bisecting the sloping front lawn, to the street where her car was parked. As she got in and turned on the ignition and the air-conditioning, she looked back up the hill toward the open front door, to her sister folding the girl up under one arm, ushering her deeper into the house.

℘ Chapter 11

A PHOTOGRAPH of June's white Chevy station wagon was on the front page of the Deerfield paper on Saturday morning. Jordanna had tucked the folded newspaper into the basket of her bike, and as she rode up to the church house she read the caption and the beginning of the corresponding article. Waiting for the traffic at the corner of West Street, she opened the paper, spreading it across the new leather grips of her handlebars. She had just picked up the bike on Wednesday, and it looked as it must have the morning she turned twelve and woke to find it by her bed—the indigo paint unblemished, the fresh rubber scent of tires with discernible tread, a small chrome bell bolted on the right handlebar. She realized she'd felt somehow diminished those weeks while the bike was in the shop and she'd been forced to travel through Hutchinson at a remove, separated by metal and glass.

She ignored the green light and continued to read the story that ran alongside the color picture of June's car, neatly parked between two pine trees. A Detective Wilroy from the Hutchinson Police Department was quoted as saying that the car had not been vandalized and did not appear to have been stolen. Drew was "unavailable for comment," but his mother had said that "the family remained hopeful and continued to pray for June's return." Jordanna thought June's mother-in-law made it sound as if they had a lost a family heirloom, or perhaps a pet, its value highly subjective, proportional only to its owner's sense of loss. Because of the continuing drought, there had been a number of brush fires in the woods around Snow's Lake the past few weeks, and the police thought it best to remove June's car as quickly as possible. When asked if the lake would be dragged for the "body," as the reporter called it, the detective said he was not sure yet what the next step in the search would be.

Jordanna leaned her bike against the church house building and reached into her bag for the keys. She moved along the main corridor flicking on the lights and walked into her office and turned on the computer before heading into Gael's office to start a pot of coffee. She had a counseling session at ten with a couple new to the church. If she didn't check her e-mail she might actually have time to look over the sermon notes she'd written. Romans 8:24—". . . hope that is seen is not hope. . . ." To avoid addressing the community's concern around June's disappearance would be callous. People came to church on Sunday wanting the minister to voice the burden they could not name. A preacher was simply a canary in a coal mine, the Lenny Bruce of the soul. The problem was to speak about faith and not seem as if you were instructing adults to behave like children, to blindly place their trust in something larger than themselves. The essence of faith was not about God's dominion over us. She hated that word *dominion*. No, no, the essence of faith was inner strength, not abdication, which is how it was so often taught in Sunday school. Faith as surrender, mindless surrender. She would have to propose an active, life-affirming faith, faith as movement and power, faith as one's fully realized partnership with the Divine.

"Reverend Nash?"

Jordanna jumped. She'd been standing in the hall, staring at the painted cinderblock, tracking her own inner monologue, possibly

aloud, she wasn't sure. Jordanna hadn't heard Tara come in or pad
down the hall in her sneakers.

"Are you okay?" Jordanna said. The girl looked sick. She remembered that feeling in the mornings, light-headed, easily pushed over
the edge by the hint of diesel exhaust or the idea of a cup of coffee.
When she was pregnant with Alice was when she had discovered
Yoo-Hoo.

"Come, sit in my office. Is the smell of that brewing coffee bother-
ing you? I'll shut the door."

Jordanna snuck a look at her watch as she went to close her office
door. The computer was humming, the icons glowing behind her as
she sat down on the desk.

"I think I might need you to talk to my parents for me."

Jordanna stared at her. Tara Sears seemed to have gone out of her
way to make herself appear menacing. Her hennaed hair looked as if
she had trimmed it with a steak knife. She was wearing what looked
like black eyeliner on her lips, and she had punctuated each side of
her mouth with a silver stud, giving the effect of a nihilistic smile.
For the portion of last year that Tara had attended Senior Pilgrim
Fellowship, Jordanna had found her difficult to penetrate. Some
inscrutable joke or restricted cultural reference was central to everything Tara said and did. When she'd appeared on her doorstep yesterday, Jordanna had been shocked. She'd called Tara's house once,
about a week before, and she'd left it at that. She doubted that Tara
would do anything as prosaic as come to her minister asking if it
were really wrong for her to go and get an abortion and keep the
whole thing from her parents. She was about seven weeks along, and
contrary to what Derek had told Jordanna two weeks before in the
gas station, not only weren't her parents making her have the baby,
stowing her away on some mythical baby farm, they seemed to be the
only people in Hutchinson who didn't yet know that their middle
daughter was pregnant.

"Did you do what I suggested, last night?" Jordanna had play-acted with Tara yesterday afternoon in her living room. She had encouraged her to approach her parents much the same way she had approached Jordanna. She had counseled Tara that in the act of telling the news and of asking for help, something positive might transpire. She had tried to get her to see that the pregnancy was, in fact, an opportunity to bring the family closer together. Parents want to be needed, she'd said. They want to be allowed in. What will hurt them, ultimately, is that you have gone through this alone.

"Why do you think you're having such a difficult time telling them?" Jordanna switched off the computer monitor behind her. "You were so candid with me."

Tara shrugged, and pressed her arms down through the space between her skinny legs. "It's your job to be . . . understanding. I knew you wouldn't get mad at me."

Jordanna laughed. "And your parents' job is something other than to be compassionate?"

"You know my dad."

Jordanna vaguely remembered the man. He didn't come to church much. He had found her first "children's message" far too unorthodox, and he had written her a note on the Monday morning after that worship service to tell her so. He didn't think the sanctuary was the appropriate place for props. Did the gospel really need a yo-yo to help put across its message?

"What's your biggest fear, Tara? What's the worst thing that can happen?"

"He'll kill me."

Jordanna stared at her until the girl shifted and shrugged and said, "Already, he's not my biggest fan, you know. I mean, he'll hate me even more than he does. He's, like, so suspicious anyway. He'll probably get one of those collars for me, like they put on dogs when they put in an electric fence. I'll be like getting these little electric shocks every time I try to step off the curb for the next twenty years."

"What's the best-case scenario?"

"That this will just go away. That I never have to tell them. That this . . . this just dissolves." She slammed her lower abdomen with her clenched fist.

Jordanna hopped up to the door. "Excuse me for a moment," she mumbled as she moved out into the hall. She pressed the heel of her hand to her heart to stop the pounding. She stood in the hall, confused for a moment about which way to walk for her mug, her coffee. All yesterday afternoon, she hadn't been thinking about babies. Tara needed an abortion, June was missing. Tara was scared of her parents. June's car yielded nothing. She was there to help Tara wend her way through this difficult time. She was there to help the congregation with June's disappearance. But sometimes the babies, her babies, jumped out, their souls pressed through hers, and there was blood, and steel on steel, buckets and beeping and the white sheets smooth as skin, sheets that had covered thousands of sad, sick bodies, the dying and the dead. The baby wrapped in the towel. The feel of terry cloth on the fingers, not of skin, the skin too dead to stay on the body of the baby.

She poured the coffee and carried it back into her office.

"I'm sorry," Tara said.

"For what?"

Jordanna pulled her chair around from behind the desk and placed it so that her knees and Tara's knees were nearly touching. She lowered the hot mug to the stone floor and took hold of the girl's hands with their peeling silver nail polish. A smudged phone number written in purple ink was still barely visible on the inside of one index finger. "We'll work this out."

Tara began crying and Jordanna got up and, acknowledging her back, knelt in front of her, pulling the girl toward her.

"Can't you tell them for me? Please, Reverend Nash, please help me do this."

"Remember we talked about your writing a letter, Tara. Have you tried that? If you like, you can sit here and do it now. I'm meeting with a couple in a few minutes. I can bring them into the library, and you can sit in here and work on my computer. Sometimes it's much easier to communicate something difficult in a letter. That way you have time to say it just as you want, without the fear of being interrupted. It also gives your parents the chance to compose their response."

"I'm too scared, I'm too scared." She pushed at her eyes with her awful nails. "What if they come here to talk to you? What if I bring them here? Then it won't be like what you said, your interfering. If they come here . . . I might be able to tell them, if you were sitting here with me."

"Don't you think, Tara, love, that they will feel ganged up on?"

"Why do you care about them more than me?"

She slowly bent down for her coffee, her back tightening noticeably now. June had said something like that to her during counseling, and it had irritated Jordanna, the neediness of the statement, the lack of integrity. But coming from this girl who was young enough to be her daughter, it made her smile. "I hope you don't see this as my sacrificing your feelings for theirs, that's not my intent at all. But sometimes, if you look at a situation from the point of view of the others involved, you'll be better prepared for how they might react. More importantly, you'll be attempting to move towards a solution with love, through love. Does that make any sense?"

Tara pulled on the beads that were wrapped around her wrist and let them spring back a number of times. "I told them you wanted to talk to them." She aimed at the vein inside her left arm again with the stack of colored beads. "They think it's about Senior P.F. or something."

Jordanna stood up and turned from Tara. She placed her coffee cup on the desk and walked around a little. She looked out the window. There was a dad and two little boys on the jungle gym outside the nursery school. "Now that you're in here, in this room with me"—Jordanna turned to face her—"how do you feel about having done that?"

Tara shrugged.

Jordanna walked up and stood right in front of her, blocking the girl's view to anything other than her massive presence.

"I'm a fuckup anyway, what does it matter?"

Jordanna nodded, inclining her chest down into the girl's face. "You're nothing close to a fuckup, Tara. On the contrary, you're a highly skilled manipulator. I hear that corporations pay big money for people who can do what you've done so effectively here. We can all be arch, you know."

"What does that mean?"

"Too cool for school."

Tara half laughed, her black-lined lips slightly curled.

"Look it, my job is to help people. What's yours?" Jordanna stepped back from the girl a bit.

She shrugged.

"Come on, what's your job?"

"Like, what do you mean?" she said, her eyes at half mast.

"Your purpose on this planet."

"God, how should I know?"

"You do know."

"I mean, what do you want me to say? Being good? Taking home wounded animals . . . ?"

Jordanna just stared at her. She knew the girl was smart enough to get this. She was also tough enough to foil Jordanna's need for resolution. She was not interested in pleasing anyone, including herself. "It's not random, hon, your being here. It's part of the design, and you have a role, now you just have to figure out what it is. We all have something to give and something still to learn. The sooner you pick up on what that is, the easier your life will be. And I suspect that your telling your parents this hard thing, by yourself, without me, is part of your job. It's part of the plan." She stopped for a while, looked out the window, finished her coffee.

"What if they don't let me get an abortion? What if they make me have it?" She spit out this last word. "I mean, then will you at least help me? Will you make them understand that my whole life will be wrecked?"

They had talked about this yesterday in Jordanna's living room.

Tara had pulled out a pack of cigarettes as she sat on Jordanna's couch, and then, while she was sliding her little painted fingers between the cellophane and the pack, feeling for the matches, Jordanna had said, "There's no smoking here." The girl had then made a big huffy display of putting the cigarettes back into her jeans pocket, where there didn't look to be room for lint, let alone a dozen cigarettes. She had thought for a moment about them both lighting up. She was careful not to smoke anywhere anyone in the congregation might see her. Mostly, if she smoked she did it out-of-doors, and ever only in front of her sister. Daniel hated cigarette smoke. While she thought about cigarettes, she told Tara that life was sacred, everyone's life. And while she personally believed in a woman's right to choose, Tara was a member of a family, a family with feelings, opinions and rights as well. "You are a minor and there are laws about consent. Whatever your decision, I'll be there . . . be with you."

"What's the point of believing in abortion if you don't stick to your guns?" Tara said now.

Jordanna looked at her watch openly. "I have a scheduled counseling session in about two minutes, Tara. So we'll have to continue this. But let's get something clear, okay? No one, no one, *believes* in abortion. Do you understand? There's nothing to believe in there. When I say that I believe in a woman's right to make that choice, what I'm saying is that you are as precious to God as the baby you're carrying. That's what that means, okay?"

She watched Tara cry for a moment before comforting her. It was, she thought, perhaps the first time either of them had used the word *baby,* instead of saying, "the pregnancy," or "it," or "the situation" or "the eventuality." *Baby,* a word that unfolded into a hundred joys and a hundred heartaches.

Jordanna heard the sound of high heels on the linoleum outside the office door. She stood up and walked to Tara, who was cradling her wet face in her dirty hands. "Will you let me pray over you?"

Tara shrugged. Jordanna knew that Tara was familiar with what was entailed. She had on occasion prayed over the kids in Senior Pilgrim Fellowship and had encouraged them to pray over one another. She had ended the meetings with them pairing off and taking turns praying over one another. "Let me just tell these folks outside that I will be another minute, okay?"

Jordanna opened the door only slightly and walked into the hall. Mr. and Mrs. Sears, not her ten o'clock counseling couple, were standing in the darkened hallway, holding hands. She had underestimated the girl's brazenness.

"Good morning." Mr. Sears thrust out his hand for Jordanna to shake.

Jordanna took their hands in hers and squeezed them. "Tara suggested you come by this morning," Jordanna said, the intonation somewhere between a statement and a question.

"We're early," the mother said, echoing Jordanna's uncertain tone.

"Not at all," Jordanna said. "But I do have something of an emergency, so if it's all right . . . Here, come, Tara's in my office. Come on in for a minute and we'll work up a plan." It occurred to Jordanna as she opened the door into her office that Tara might not still be there, that, like June, she might just have vanished. But she was just as Jordanna had left her, bent over a bit, holding her head in her hands.

"Your parents have arrived," Jordanna said with a ridiculous note of gaiety, a small but pointed punishment for the teenager. "I explained to them about the small emergency I have with another family. What I'd like us to do is this. Why don't the three of you go on into the library and begin talking." Jordanna stopped and looked at the Searses. "I believe Tara has some issues to discuss. And when I am done in here I'll join you. There's coffee down in Gael's office, help yourself. Sometimes she even keeps a box of cookies in there, okay?" Jordanna leaned over Tara in her chair and kneaded her shoulders a bit, and as soon as she touched the girl she knew she wasn't going to move. She heard more people in the hall now. They were walking slowly, asking each other if they were, in fact, in the right place.

"Better idea," Jordanna said, placing her large palm on Tara's head as if offering a benediction, "you three stay here. And when I'm done I'll come back in. Please, please, pull up some more chairs." Jordanna walked quickly to the door, before Tara could bolt. She closed the door loudly behind her and looked up to find a startled young couple slowly making their way down the dimly lit corridor.

Their name was Nyquist, and they were, they said, really sorry to have to trouble her with something that was, well, they were sorry that this was her introduction to them. The wife did the talking. Peggy was a cherubic-looking woman in her early thirties, and something about the way she was dressed, all primary colors, and the high polish of her cheeks, let Jordanna know that the this story would not be terrible, and she felt at once immensely relieved and slightly let down. She knew they would tell her that they had been transferred from the Midwest and then they would add something about the church they had belonged to out there, and how it wasn't exactly Congregational, but . . .

"Back in Indiana . . ." the woman began. And there ensued the story of the man's father who had recently remarried, to a woman really no younger than himself, and was lavishing her and her grown children from another marriage with all kinds of gifts and interest-free loans. He never called his son and daughter-in-law in Connecticut and showed no interest in their children, his grandchildren. He seemed to travel all over the country with this woman, but he never visited his son, or his daughter, who lived not far away at all in Indiana. At a family wedding two weeks before, he told his daughter-in-law—this apple-cheeked farmer's daughter—"not to count on anything, you know, when I go. . . ."

Jordanna watched the man, the son, the injured party in the story, look around the cluttered library as his wife spoke. It wasn't a space that inspired confidence, she supposed. The room seemed to be part library, part walk-in storage closet, the rear of the room piled to the ceiling with boxes and cast-off furniture being collected for a Kossovar family that had been resettled in the area. Whenever the wife paused while recounting the story, Jordanna tried to listen, for sounds of crying or shouting, or anything at all from across the way in her office. Nothing.

"This all must be very painful for you," Jordanna said after a while, directing her comment to the husband, Clark. He nodded. He was wearing a tweed jacket, and Jordanna suspected that he was roasting. They had gotten dressed up to come speak with the minister who was wearing what looked like Chinese silk pajamas.

"We have two little boys," Clark said. "Before he married Libby, he always remembered their birthdays. He'd call, he'd send cards. I mean, well, the thing is, I called him this week on the anniversary of my mom's death, and he told me he couldn't talk."

Jordanna nodded.

"Clark's mother died when he was only fourteen."

"I'm sorry," Jordanna said.

"It's just like he's totally forgotten my mother, and my sister and I are just part of that whole package. I mean, I'm sure this sounds ridiculous to you. It's not like I'm fourteen now or anything. I mean, we probably shouldn't even care."

"Of course, of course you care," Jordanna said. They were sitting in a strange configuration. Husband and wife on an old blue sofa, and Jordanna pulled up close to them in a bright orange butterfly chair.

"We were hoping you could show us the 'Christian' way to deal with this situation. I mean, we certainly don't want the children growing up thinking bad things about their grandfather or hearing us—"

"It's not the money—" Clark said.

"Though it was your mother's inheritance and—"

"I could care less about the money," Clark repeated.

Jordanna nodded. "Money's rarely money, anyway, is it? It's never simple. When someone tells you not to expect anything in the future, in a will, they're really telling you something far more complicated."

The man nodded and readjusted his tie way up at the Adam's apple.

"What should you say when someone says something like that to you? I mean, how do you handle that sort of a thing?" Peggy said. The pink in her cheeks was spreading to her forehead now.

"The fact that you're here is really moving. Think of all the vengeful ways you might have of responding to a situation like this. The fact that you're seeking a peace-filled resolution tells me so much. I'm going to ask you a question, and I'd like you to think a bit before you answer—even if it comes to you right away, sit with it for a minute, meditate on it. What's your goal in all of this? When the film finishes rolling, what do you hope the outcome will be? Let's write the ending you would like and then try to work backwards to make that happen." The chair was terrible for her back. She excused herself and rooted around by the back wall before coming up with a nice old-fashioned student desk chair. She dragged it over to where the Nyquists were seated.

"Go ahead," the wife said to her husband, managing to sound both selfless and controlling all at once.

"I want him to love us and show it, and I want to be able to love him in return, without any . . . bad feelings." Clark pulled on his tie again and closed his eyes.

Jordanna shifted her gaze to Peggy.

"Well, mostly I want not to be angry. I hate to be angry. It's not me. I mean, that would be my immediate goal. Beyond that, well, if I had to be honest, and this sounds ugly, I know—well, I'd like him to divorce that woman. I guess I just wish she wasn't making him choose between us and her. That's my goal, that he not be forced to choose." Peggy jiggled her wrist, resettling the small braided gold bracelet on her arm.

"In a church where I served as associate minister years ago, there was a woman who came to me with a similar problem. Her mother had died, her father had remarried, and basically cast her aside. This young woman had some other troubles in her life at the time, but it was this disconnection from her dad that was seemingly insurmountable, and really unbearably painful for her. And I remember she said to me, 'How can you make someone love you they way they're supposed to—'" Jordanna stopped for a moment and looked at the couple. "There is so much wrong with that sentence, isn't there? For starters, I mean, I sometimes find it helpful to think about God's love for us—completely unfathomable, right? Not at all partial to being fit into any understandable, recognizable kind of human model. Divine love is beyond our comprehension. Well, perhaps human love is sometimes, too. No 'supposed to's,' is what I'm getting at. We know love should never look like abuse—but beyond that who are we to say that I love you thus and so, therefore you must love me thus? Is love quantifiable?

"The second thing troubling about that sentence of that former congregant was that as soon as you say you want someone to love you like they're supposed to, you immediately feel frustrated and powerless. It's just not in our power to make other people feel things. That's not the way it works. So what are our options? Hmm? All we can really ever do is affect our own behavior. What do you truly possess? Only that which is yours to give freely, only that which truly belongs to you—only love. All you can do is show your constant, steadfast and unswerving love for your dad. That's what's real. That's what you have to give. The truth is, no matter what his behavior, he's your father and you'll continue to love him."

"And we're supposed to just ignore his . . . rudeness?" Peggy said, and Clark placed his hand on his wife's leg, as if to suppress her outburst.

"Not at all. You're free to respond in whatever way, as long as you're clear that you're speaking because it's helpful to you and not because you're going to change him. We're going to mix a little Buddhist philosophy in with our Christian love here. Detach from the results. Love him because that's pure. Love him without expectation, and if you feel the need to tell him that his behavior is hurtful, well, do that purely, too, without expectation."

"Don't expect anything and you won't be disappointed kind of a thing," Clark said, seeming to warm to the idea.

"I don't know." Peggy moved away from him on the couch and

shook her head. "It just doesn't seem fair, you know. I mean, there are consequences for treating people certain ways, right?"

They all stopped for a moment as a door slammed across the hall twice. Clark looked up at Jordanna. "We've probably taken up too much of your time already."

"No, though I should probably just go check on that. But please, I would like to continue with the two of you, and we haven't even gotten to talking about how you came to move out here. And I did want to tell you one or two things about the church." She stopped again now, as they listened to Tara yell "fuck" three times in a row, as if she were casting a spell or perhaps cheering for her team.

"Really, I'm so sorry. You know, maybe we'd better reschedule. At least now I know why you're coming to talk with me, and I'll be prepared—"

"Well, actually there were a couple of other things . . ." Peggy said.

Of course, there always were. Jordanna squeezed the woman's hand tightly and tried to read her face. She glanced quickly down at her round body and had a few ideas about what those problems might be. "Come now into the secretary's office. She keeps the calendar. Have you met Gael yet?" Jordanna kept up a constant babble as she led them down the hall, trying to drown out the yelling that was increasing from behind the door to her office. Next week looked completely booked. They had hired a sitter to come here today. Okay, Jordanna said, what if she came to them some night? It might be on the late side. She had meetings most nights. Would nine-thirty on Tuesday night be okay? She walked them out the front door and embraced them.

Chapter 12

THE rain started in the middle of the opening hymn at Sunday's worship service. It didn't begin as most rainfalls do, with a sprinkle that steadily increases, but instead seemed to land all at once on the roof of the church, accompanied by thunder and a crack of lightning so violent the earth rumbled. The lights flickered a few times, then went out. That ambient noise that man-made electricity generates, the white noise of the church, went dead. The four large fans stopped, the blades making the last revolutions on their own stolen momentum. The mikes cut out. The organ sounded different against this backdrop of ancient silence. The choir kept on, though the congregation's singing seemed to peter out, as if their power source had also been cut. There were a few gasps and much whispering, some people clapped and a few cheered. Two of the deacons ran to shut the windows as the rain began to splash in through the screens of the bright white double-hung windows. The choir continued with "Gather Us In" as Z's of lightning appeared in the field on the west side of the church. The few children who were in the sanctuary, too young for Sunday school over at the church house, cried out. And when the choir finally straggled in with the last few notes of the hymn, no one sat down. Jordanna walked from the altar into the center aisle and said loudly in her unamplified voice, "Let us offer thanks for this rain."

She could tell that people were expecting her to lead them in a specific prayer, one that surged and swelled with gratitude and crested in sparkling metaphor, but instead she hung her head, her chin resting on her vestments, and she was still. She listened and she hoped that they would listen, too. No one in Hutchinson had heard rain since July 10, two months. She stood there with her eyes clenched tight and imaged all those dry riverbeds and pond bottoms, all the little bridges in town, their backs bent over hollows of dirt, and she pictured them all filling, filling up with this water. She listened to the rain running now too fast for the gutters along the east side of the church. You could hear water being poured down upon the building and it was not rhythmic at all, it was wild and loud and alarming, and she stood there on that sea of dark red carpet in the center aisle of the Hutchinson Congregational Church and she could almost feel the water rise up from those fibers, tinged with that red, rise up through the soles of her shoes. This was not a cleansing rain. This was the stuff of floods, a busting loose of everything that had been held back in that polluted sky. This, she would remember, was the weather the morning she received the word about June.

She had stood there in silence for too long now. There was stirring, some coughing and shifting. People were fanning themselves with their bulletins. She slowly opened her eyes and saw through her tears that people were staring at her. She stared back, smiled and walked briskly in large determined steps back up to the altar. "Let us join in the call to worship." The lay reader for the morning, Ron Ciccilone, came up to the altar, and Jordanna sank down into the armchair by the pulpit.

The police had found the note in the car. A detective had called last night and asked if he could come by this morning, before she left for church. He hadn't said what it was about, and she had assumed there were more questions. When she answered the door in her bathrobe, her wet hair towering above her in a twisted towel, she saw two policemen, and she knew they hadn't come to ask her questions. She could tell by the way they stood on the steps, their eyes never coming to rest on her face or her robe or even that ridiculous old pink towel on top of her head. They came in and sat down in the living room, and she sat, too, as if it weren't her house, or a house at all, but rather some dislodged antechamber, a nonlocalized waiting room specifically designated for the receipt of only the worst kind of news. She moved her body around a bit in an attempt to regain a foothold on her own life. She was readjusting her shoulders, stretching out her arms, when the older of the two men stood up and took something from his breast pocket. She stood, too, and so did the other officer. "We found this on the front seat," he said, handing Jordanna a two-inch-square envelope, the kind that comes when you buy a little gift card. She saw her name written on the front in pen. She noticed that the seal on the back was opened.

"We had to read it," the officer apologized.

She nodded, then sat back down and looked at the front of the envelope, then up at them.

"It's a suicide note," the younger officer said. "There was one for her husband, her mother and her children."

Jordanna realized she'd been holding her breath, and she exhaled and inhaled a few times.

"We, uh, came this morning, figuring that, well, there's a chance that the recovery of these notes may be reported in the paper tomorrow."

"You've spoken with the Nearings?" Jordanna said. "June's mother?"

"Yesterday," the older officer said.

Jordanna looked at her watch. It was eight. She couldn't make any kind of announcement at church without talking to Bev and Drew first. She was surprised they hadn't called yesterday.

"You have to understand, Pastor," said the older officer—Detective Wilroy, she saw on his nameplate. "We read these notes not to invade anyone's privacy, but this is an investigation, and we are still looking for Mrs. Nearing's body."

Jordanna ran her thumbs around the perimeter of the tidy little envelope. "Nothing about that in here?"

"Later on today or tomorrow, you might be getting a call to speak with somebody else. Now that we're certain it was a suicide, there's a limit to the manpower, the . . . we'll spend on searching for the body. That will somewhat be up to the family, costs incurred, et cetera."

Jordanna nodded. She looked down again at the envelope and was dismayed at her total reluctance to read what was inside. She wondered if the officers would simply sit here until she did. She looked at her watch again, and then stood up. "Thank you," she said, "for taking the time to come over this morning."

"THE Sacrament of Baptism this morning is for William Hallstead, the son of Maryanne Peters Hallstead and Richard Hallstead. . . ." Jordanna walked down from the altar to the front row on the left side of the church, where the parents and godparents and infant boy were seated. She motioned for the group to stand and reached in toward the mother to take the baby. He was sleeping and she snaked her robed arms under his blanketed body and cradled him. The power was still out and she didn't want her voice to wake him. So she walked with the baby up the center aisle of the church, dipping him in the direction of one side, then the other. People slid in their seats to have a look, as if he weren't just any baby, as if they truly appreciated the miracle. He was warm in her arms, and Jordanna rocked him a little. The weight of him was as reassuring as the line in June's note, "God does not leave us comfortless." It was from a poem June had written out in a flowing script by a poet Jordanna had never heard of before, Jane Kenyon.

Let the light of late afternoon
shine through chinks in the barn, moving
up the bales as the sun moves down.

Let the cricket take up chafing
as a woman takes up her needles
and her yarn. Let evening come.

Let dew collect on the hoe abandoned
in long grass. Let the stars appear
and the moon disclose her silver horn.

Let the fox go back to its sandy den.
Let the wind die down. Let the shed
go black inside. Let evening come.

To the bottle in the ditch, to the scoop
in the oats, to air in the lung
let evening come.

Let it come, as it will, and don't
be afraid. God does not leave us
comfortless, so let evening come.

Jordanna swung the baby in her arms and turned to face the congregation. "I know all of you will join me in the lighting of the Christ
candle. I know that you will stand with me now, a symbol of support
to this child as he makes his way, that you will, each one, be there to
aid him in his attempt to live a Christian life." It seemed to Jordanna
that people were slow to stand. She began to walk with the baby up
toward the altar and the candle. Frank Leahy motioned to her from
the first pew. He was the deacon sponsoring this morning's baptism.
Fred Rinehardt touched Jordanna on the arm as she held the baby

and began to light the candle. He leaned in to her and whispered, "You forgot to baptize him?"

Jordanna finished lighting the candle and nodded slowly. She waited a moment before she turned around, the baby still asleep in her arms. She looked out at the congregation, listened to the rain continuing to pound down on the roof and the wooden sills. You could almost hear the brown grass suck and slurp. "It seems I've become unplugged as well, this morning. By what name will you call this child?" she said, moving now down to the parents and godparents. She tipped the baby backward. "William Peters Hallstead, we baptize you in the name of the father"—she moistened his forehead—"and the son"—again with her thumb—"and the holy spirit"—one last time. "Amen and so be it." She leaned down and kissed the baby's forehead. She whispered to the parents, "Now you'll have a story to tell him about his baptismal day." She squeezed the mother's hand.

Jordanna sat with her eyes closed while the choir sang the morning's anthem, "Come Let Us Join with Faithful Souls." She really hadn't allowed herself to consider the possibility that June was dead, though everyone had been encouraging her in that direction, June most of all, it seemed. Drew had begun to suspect that June was gone for good as much as a week ago, so had Bev. But Jordanna had spoken intimately with June for months, wouldn't she have seen it coming? June was angry, bitter, even. She was depressed, so listless that Jordanna couldn't picture her having the energy to plan this out—to copy these poems, write these notes. Orchestrating one's escape took vision. For weeks, Jordanna had been trying to instill in June some kind of desire or wish, a scheme for how life might be. But June's spirit had been this nonarable little acre where no positive thought or forward-moving action seemed capable of taking root. She remembered Drew's guilt at saying the house was lighter without June's presence. She thought of her own relief at not having to deal with June's determined darkness these past two weeks. Now she would have to consider June for the rest of her life. This would be another wholly uncategorizable event. June's suicide would run over into everything. Into every glimmer of change, or joy, there she'd be, as needy and demanding in death as in life, a reminder of every one of Jordanna's weaknesses.

Jordanna watched the collection plates being passed. She ran her eyes through the pews, picking out people she knew who had lost jobs and spouses, people whose children had died in car accidents, who had lost limbs, who had lost their minds. Not one of these people had demanded of her the way June had. Not one of these people had killed himself. There were people in this congregation who had been convicted of crimes, who had been arrested for solicitation, who struggled daily with alcohol or drugs. People who'd been beaten and raped as children, and they were still here this morning. They had each of them put one foot in front of the other and kept on going, through pain and fear and devastation. You could cry out, "My God, my God, why hast thou forsaken me," but you kept on going. You breathed in, you breathed out.

The ushers carrying up the offering waited on the second step for Jordanna to come over and take the bowl. She led the congregation in the doxology, her thoughts running down and out like the overwhelming runoff of rainwater. She looked at the clock above the choir loft. There was still nearly half an hour left in the service. There were the scripture readings, there was the sermon . . . and then there was everything that would come after she walked out of this church this afternoon. A funeral without a body.

"Oh Lord, thou has searched me and known me!
Thou knowest when I sit down and when I rise up;
    thou discernest my thoughts from afar.
Thou searchest out my path and my lying down, and art
    aquainted with all my ways.
Even before a word is on my tongue,
    lo, O Lord thou knowest it altogether.
Whither shall I go from thy Spirit?

Or whither shall I flee from thy presence?
... For thou didst form my inward parts,
   thou didst knit me together in my mother's womb.'"

This was not the psalter reading listed in the bulletin, but Jordanna stood at the pulpit and recited it, loudly and from memory. When she got to the end, she instructed everyone to turn in their Bibles to Psalm 139 and she read it through one more time.

"... The Spirit helps us in our weakness; for we do not know how to pray as we ought, but the Spirit himself intercedes for us with sighs too deep for words. And he who searches the hearts of men knows what is the mind of the Spirit, because the Spirit intercedes for the saints according to the will of God.... Who shall separate us from the love of Christ? Shall tribulation, or distress, or persecution, or famine, or nakedness, or peril, or sword? ... No, in all these things we are more than conquerors through him who loved us. For I am sure that neither death, nor life, nor angels, nor principalities, nor things present, nor things to come, nor powers, nor height, nor depth, nor anything else in all creation, will be able to separate us from the love of God in Christ Jesus our Lord.

"When I was a child I had a terrible habit, a habit I was sure would keep me from progressing in life, a habit that nearly kept me from progressing from one grade to the next."

She had written the sermon two days before, *Seeing Faith*. It was not really specific to the Nearings. She would never mention them by name, but rather would allude to those things that happen for which there seem to be no answers, no conclusions. Just keep standing and reading, she told herself.

"I daydreamed. Harmless enough, right? That's what childhood is for. Why else would they put windows and posters in schoolrooms? But my daydreaming was much like my build, even back then—big, free-ranging, not easily contained. My daydreams threatened to outpace everything else. And the very worst part of it was how these reveries always ended, with my coming to in the middle of a lesson."

She breathed in deeply. There was no microphone to help her to get the message across, just her breath, her larynx, her insistence.

"Often what brought me out was the sound of my name being repeated, as if it were a curse, by my teacher. We all know that feeling, I'm sure. You look up and so much is happening all at once. You are trying to think while the sound of your own pulse thrums loudly against your temples. Your eyes are everywhere at once, trying to do the quick study, figure out where on the page you're supposed to be, or in my case, even what subject was being discussed. I did terribly in school because of this. I got bits and pieces of information and always I was struggling to put together a sensible equation with these scraps of knowledge."

She was needing to take deeper and deeper breaths. The sanctuary had become almost unbearably humid. The windows steamed with moisture from the inside. She could see the sweat, an almost solid substance, lining brows and lips. Outside the rain continued, not a cleansing rain bringing relief to a parched town, but a rain so late in coming that it no longer qualified as an answer to a prayer.

"The test would begin and I would not have heard the instructions. It would suddenly be my turn to read and I wouldn't even have my book out, let alone be able to find the page. I was always looking all around me for cues and clues, as if knowledge were a five-hundred-piece puzzle and all I had were a few pieces of the sky. The picture would never be whole for me.

"Well, I suspect it's something like that for most of us and the stories of our lives, the story of the world we live in. We are on the receiving end of crucial bits of information, but we're on a cheap car phone and we're only really sure that we're hearing every tenth word. We think we're looking at the whole picture, but in fact the picture is still in process. It's a Brueghel, or a Hieronymus Bosch, one of those Flemish painters whose canvases are filled with literally hundreds of people in a village. It's incredibly intricate, and it's not even one-one-millionth finished, but we're trying to come up with the whole definitive story by looking at it from inside our infinitesimal corner of the canvas. Not only is our perspective of looking at it from within, one that is bound to fail us, but the work is not nearly finished, the tale not completed. How could we possibly make a judgment about the theme, then?"

She kept on with the sermon. Emphatic, assured. It's what they all responded to, the declarative nature of her speech. She was never tentative, not in anything. People swarmed to certainty. She wasn't being insincere. It wasn't that simple. Truth, falsehood. Honesty, dissembling. Faith and doubt did not fit into that paradigm.

"But we do it. We all do it. It's human nature, is it not? We are always summing up and concluding, supposing and denoting, inferring and determining, gathering, deducing, ascertaining. But our disadvantage is considerable, though we never, ever recognize it. Our perception is compromised. There is a bell tower from where the view is total, but we do not have access to even the first step on that tower staircase."

For the first several minutes of the sermon as she lifted her arms, palms raised in an attitude to give and receive, she told herself that the trouble with her breathing was climatic. The sanctuary had begun to resemble a terrarium. But now she listened. She listened to what she was saying, exhorting the congregation to believe in something beyond their capacity to conceive, and she felt a kind of dread.

"Well, you know, God calls our names, too, always when we are daydreaming. And we wake to our lives, which may seem incomprehensible. Tragedy, tragedy always is incomprehensible. We go after it with reason and knowledge and logic. We try to dismantle the thing, attempt to get it to give itself up to us, give up its internal organization. Bad things happen to us, really bad things happen to people we love, things for which we cry out to God. Outcomes we think we cannot bear. And we come to the conclusion, based on these tragedies, that we are unworthy. We might, on occasion, feel singled out, as I did as a child. We look around at the other kids in the room, at the rows of desks, and no one else seems to be struggling the way we are, and we arrive at the conclusion that God has found us unworthy of God's love, that, in fact, God has done this to us, taken our parent, sickened our child, removed love and health from our life. We have all had times when we've reckoned our sense of God, and God's love, by looking at the facts of our life. But we are doing the subtraction without knowing all the factors. We are concocting an entire story about our relationship with God based on forty threads in a tapestry that's composed of a hundred thousand strands of silk."

She sounded so full of conviction. Somebody, somewhere truly believed exactly what she was saying. Like clothing, theses ideas fit someone perfectly, but with her fingers pressed now on her rising collarbones, she realized that person wasn't her.

"We are slow, each one of us. We are disadvantaged when it comes to Divine knowledge, and we need to forgive ourselves for it. We need to forgive ourselves and not be too quick to judge God for what we see as the story God's written for us. We are in the terrible habit of assuming that God is about like us, only kinder and everywhere at once. That God's love is just a bigger version of human love. How dare we try to fashion God in our own limited likeness.

"In one of the last chapters in the Book of Job, God responds to his plaintive, if faithful, servant, upon whom unthinkable tragedies have befallen, with much this same explanation:

"Where were you when I laid the
    foundation of the earth?
Tell me, if you have understanding.
Who determined its measurements—
    surely you know!
    Or who stretched the line upon it?
On what were its bases sunk,
    or who laid its cornerstone,
when the morning stars sang together,
    and all the sons of God shouted for joy?

Or who shut in the seas with doors,
    when it burst forth from the womb;
when I made clouds its garment,
    ˙ and thick darkness its swaddling band,
and prescribed bounds for it,
    and set bars and doors,
and said, 'Thus far shall you come,
    and no farther,
    and here shall your proud waves be stayed'?

"Bad things happen, and more bad things will happen, and we will struggle to make sense of them. We look for blame. We're big on that, we humans. It's one of the surest ways to closure—another big idea of ours. There is no closure in God's Kingdom. It is forever. There is nothing apart from it. 'I am the Alpha and the Omega, the beginning and the end.' We attempt to comfort ourselves by understanding what has happened to us. But remember that of all the gifts God has bestowed upon us, perfect sight is not one of them."

These words, trusting that the story was being written all the time, that you were inside the miracle as it was happening, that it was all an unfolding and not a straight line, that somehow pain and loss, suffering and grief were part of some ultimately beneficent story— she couldn't swallow that, not this morning. Belief was a kind of trick. As if, by looking at death in a different light, it might not seem like some cheap fabric God was trying to pawn off on you, but might, in that light of Christ, look like the very richest stuff on earth. It was a trick that might last a minute or two, an hour or a week, but then there would be June's children, especially that oldest girl. Jordanna would be forced to look into that motherless girl's face and think, Well, now I've fucked up her life, too. There would be the physical separation of mother and child, husband and wife, child and mother. One could not wait hopefully for the resurrection in the throes of that kind of physical pain. June was really dead, and Jordanna was standing up here in front of June's community telling them all that what might look like dark clouds now was really . . . what?

"As you come to when God calls your name, your pulse should not beat wildly against your temples, but rather steadily and with the knowledge that what is perfect in your life is that you are perfectly held in God's love."

And then, like that, she was out in the narthex shaking hands. There was a bunch of bodies up by the open double doors. The threshold looked like something from a movie set, with a wall of water falling straight down just beyond the end of the church's red carpeting. There had been a closing hymn. There must have been a final benediction in which she had probably said, "Let us keep God within us on this day and every day, and let us share that God within with each and every person we encounter, Amen." But she didn't remember saying it.

"Wonderful sermon." A woman she recognized, but couldn't place immediately, took Jordanna's hand. "I'm a neighbor of the Congdons."

Jordanna smiled and nodded.

"I will keep it with me all week," she said, moving on out into the rain. Jordanna turned to the next person and smiled and shook hands, and then Fred Rinehardt, one of the lay ministers, came up from behind and asked her if she felt all right. The question had been prescient, she was sure, because at that moment a young woman with a small spiral steno book approached her from within the line and asked if she might ask her a few questions for an article for the Hartford paper.

Fred now leaned over Jordanna again and said, "Please, this can wait."

"Well, what I wanted to know—"

Jordanna stopped the young woman from speaking by gripping her hands. "We are so glad to have you in church today, and as soon as I'm done saying goodbye to everyone here, I would be happy to speak with you."

"It's about June Nearing."

The notebook had caused some attention, but now the narthex grew quieter. Through the noise of the rain, and the clicking of teeth and tongues as people talked about everything that had happened since they'd seen one another last Sunday, the mention of June's name sounded like a bell.

"Please," Jordanna said, not with her signature command, but plaintively. "Please, wait." Her uncharacteristic desperation seemed to draw as much attention as the reporter's invocation of June's name.

She smiled and shook the reporter's hand perfunctorily, working her way to the end of the line, telling every third person, "See you in a minute," or "See you for coffee downstairs."

Jordanna walked back into the sanctuary and down the center aisle to the first row, where Fred was standing, wiping the fog from his glasses and keeping guard over this reporter.

Fred placed his hands lightly on the reporter's shoulders and introduced her to Jordanna as Karen Tiernan from the *Hartford Times*. He then motioned with his hand for the reporter to sit in the first pew. He sank in next to her and Jordanna stood in front of them both, still in her clerical robes.

"You look as if you need to sit, too," Fred said, holding out a hand for Jordanna. She took it in both of hers and shook her head.

"Reverend Nash," the woman began. "I'm sorry if this is how you are first learning of June Nearing's death. Mr. Rinehardt here, well, he didn't know, so I—"

Jordanna turned her back for a moment on the woman and looked to the altar. It was about eight feet between the first pew and the steps up to the altar, but she knew if she didn't sit now, she would find herself on the ground in a pile. She sat on the top step and planted her feet in their black pumps on the first step. "Excuse me," she said, without any tone of apology. "I want to be able to face you and sit at the same time." The distance between them was awkward. They would now have to talk quite loudly to be heard over the still-rattling rain.

"Karen, why don't we see if we can bridge some distance here, fig-uratively speaking. You've come to my church this morning to do your job, which is to ask me about the death of one of my congre-gants. Writing about the circumstances of her death is your job. Car-ing for the feelings of the people in this church community is my job. As far as I know, not a one of them was aware this morning that June Nearing had committed suicide, not for certain. I only learned just before arriving at church for worship service. For a moment there, it seemed as if your job and my job might have conflicted. Let's begin again, all right, and see if we can work together. I see no reason for the successful completion of your job to be mutually exclusive from the goals of mine."

The reporter allowed about a two-second pause, then said, "Is it true that you were counseling Mrs. Nearing prior to her suicide?"

"Why is your newspaper even covering this story? This is a tragedy that's happened to our community. I can't imagine that peo-ple fifty miles away would be interested."

"We've been following Mrs. Nearing's disappearance for the past week. We've had a picture of her in the paper. Yesterday we ran the picture of her car abandoned in the woods."

"Do you know why you're writing this story?" Jordanna asked.

"Because my editor assigned me to it, Reverend Nash." The woman looked up and stared at Jordanna straight in the eyes.

"What do you want people to come away with when they read this piece?"

"The facts."

"The facts will never satisfy here. We are talking about a suicide which is, by its nature, provocative and elliptical. It's slightly lurid—that's always our attraction to it, isn't it? Because unthinkable pain precedes every suicide, unimaginable human failure and weakness. That's really what we always want to get at in this kind of a story—right? That's the story—not the death, but what prompted it."

The reporter sighed loudly, rudely. Jordanna stopped and looked at her shiny black pants and tight pale blue blouse. There was a seventy percent chance that these were the very clothes this young woman was wearing last night until quite late. "Would you like some coffee?"

Fred stood up.

"Thank you," Jordanna said to him.

The reporter waited until he'd left the room and then closed her notebook. She looked up at Jordanna on the steps. "Are you concerned that the family might bring a lawsuit against you?"

"Every day, people rap politely on my door, with concerns they could never have imagined would be theirs the day before. It would not help anyone for me to worry about what I cannot control."

"How old was June?"

"Have you interviewed her family?"

"One brother." The young woman flicked something from the corner of her eye.

"I'm sure he can give you all that sort of detail."

"Did you take part in the search efforts?"

"I prayed for June. I continue to pray for June and for all those people who love her and whose lives will never be the same without her. But, no. I did not look for her in the way that you mean."

"Do you have an attorney?"

Jordanna removed one of the clips from her hair. She'd thought about this once or twice in the past few weeks, just in passing, much in the same way you think about jumping when you are somewhere very high. "Not on retainer," she said finally.

"Is there some church spokesperson I should contact? The head of the—whatever the equivalent of the diocese is?"

"You could call the Central Conference up in Hartford."

"Do you do a lot of counseling?"

Jordanna stood up when Fred came through the little door that led from the back stairs onto the altar. She took the two coffee cups and saucers from him and handed one to the reporter.

"No, thank you."

Jordanna looked at Fred and he shrugged and accepted the cup.

"I was asking about counseling?"

"I think most ministers would tell you that more and more of our time is spent in pastoral counseling."

"And you are a licensed therapist?"

"I took a number of counseling courses in Divinity School."

"And do you think that qualifies you to—"

"Excuse me," Fred said. He had this courtly manner that always reminded Jordanna of a rounded, midwestern version of Ray Milland. "There are quite a few people waiting to speak with Reverend Nash downstairs."

Jordanna was still standing over the reporter, saucer in one hand, nearly empty cup in the other. She turned her wrist to look at her watch. She placed the cup in the saucer and extended her hand. "Thank you so much for visiting our church today." Then she walked up onto the altar and out through the door that led down to the undercroft. Jordanna stood in the narrow hall at the top of the stairs and listened in two directions. From the undercroft came the sounds of clinking cups and laughter. A few voices were distinct, Shirley Reese and Ambi Fowler. Somebody was coughing. The tap in the kitchen was running. She tried to listen for the reporter and Fred. She knew he was escorting her out of the building. There were no windows in this narrow space. The stairwell was dark; the only light was what crept beneath the door from the sanctuary. It would have been a great place for hide and seek. The rain drummed against the outside wall of the church, every once in a while it sounded as if the water were lashing the clapboards. The wind had picked up. She wondered if this was what it was like inside a coffin.

≋ Chapter 13

"CAN you be me this morning?" she'd said to Fred, explaining that she couldn't go downstairs for the coffee hour. In the dank stairwell above the undercroft, Fred pretended to primp his nonexistent hair. "No," she said, "better than me." She slipped her hand up the wide sleeve of her clerical robe and stroked her own bare arm. "I need to be with the Nearings."

But she hadn't gone to the Nearings' house; instead she had unlocked the church office and, dripping wet, had sat down in Gael's chair and played back the phone messages. There was only one, and it was from Buck Sears, Tara's father. He needed to speak with her—immediately. The Nearings hadn't called. They hadn't called here. She wondered if they didn't want to see her, if they thought they didn't want to see her right now. Buck's message had been left at ten, at the start of worship. It had occurred to her yesterday that Tara's manipulativeness was a teenage variant of the father's take-charge aggression. Her meeting with the family yesterday had centered on only one topic, keeping an open line of communication between parents and child. Jordanna had said very little. She was the fifth wheel, functionally superfluous, potentially destabilizing. In her presence they were forced to be true to their best instincts, to don itchy woolen motivations they'd strip off as soon as they were back home. Yesterday had been devoted to going back over a year's worth of lying. Yesterday was spent focusing on the family that already existed, not the one now in the offing, and Jordanna imagined that between the time they'd left her office and this phone call, Tara had announced her intention to have an abortion. From Buck's tone, she was sure that Tara had said that Reverend Jordanna agreed with her.

She turned off the lamp on Gael's desk and walked down the hall toward her office. Before she had even opened the door, she heard the splattering of water on flagstone. She moved slowly across the darkened room to the window near her desk. Water was bubbling in along the length of the sill, forming a steady thin waterfall that pooled onto two and half squares of slate flooring. Jordanna thought about Thomas Merton and his malfunctioning fan and decided against flicking on the lights. She locked the door from the inside and rolled her chair back against the far wall, where Buck Sears wouldn't be able to see her even if he cupped his hands to the glass on the office door.

She dialed Auckland and stretched the cord all the way to her perch by the closet. It was nearly four in the morning, tomorrow, there. She let the phone ring twice, then hung up. She needed to center in, to draw God close, to hear what Henri Nouwen called "the inner voice of love." The inner voice of love was not Daniel's voice. She needed to pray, to summon the God from within. "'Be still and know that I am God,'" she said out loud, her voice cracking in the damp room. "I'm not alone," she whispered to herself, above the syncopation of her own doubt. If we were truly capable of believing that we were not alone, why then was touch such desperate proof of our theology? If the massive idea of God's love were really adequate, we wouldn't need sex or babies. Our bodies would be meaningless, the laying on of hands vestigial. But physical life, physical love, was the source of our most profound joy and our most devastating sorrow. It stunned her to think that June had received the courage to die alone, separating herself from the physical, forever. She had relinquished the need for the God of the phallic and fecund, the God of music and movement and color and odor, of heat and pulse and flesh and flesh.

Buck Sears had a slow and heavy stride. It was a long time between footfalls. Jordanna had heard the front door open and clank shut, had heard him clear his throat. The corridor was dark. He stopped more than once. Even Buck Sears could hesitate. She knew he would rap his knuckles against the glass on the door and not the wood. She jumped when his large class ring clipped the glass. "Reverend Nash. Reverend Nash, I . . . Jesus," he mumbled. "I was hoping to catch you."

Jordanna stood up from her chair. His voice was breathy, tentative. "I am . . . I'm really . . ." She heard him crack into a sob. She turned the key on her side of the door and found him, his head pressed up against the cinderblock in the hall.

"It's wet in here," she said, placing her hand on his heaving back. "Why don't we go down into the library." They walked down the hall, her right hand grazing his back, imperceptibly pushing him ahead. When they came to the doorway of the library, she reached across with her left hand and guided him inside. He stopped before sitting on the couch and pulled out a handkerchief. "Please, I am . . . Oh, I'm really . . . I don't ever . . . I'm whoa . . . so sorry." He blew his nose loudly.

She reached for the box of Kleenex on the conference table and blew her nose as well. "Tell me," she said, sitting down beside him on the old sofa.

He was a large man, broad-shouldered and tall. For a while he sat sniffing, his closely cropped head in his hands. "I . . . I've known for a long time that I was failing Tara. I've done it all wrong with her. We've been butting heads. . . ."

Jordanna looked down and realized she was still in her robes. It was close in the library, and she began to sweat, but she didn't want to do anything to dissuade Buck from what sounded like a confession.

"I bet you looked at us, the three of us, yesterday in your office and thought, man, has he screwed up this little girl. I bet you heard her yelling all those obscenities. I mean, all you have to do is look at her, the hair and the holes she's pierced in her skin." He folded his handkerchief and slid it into his pocket. "I know what you're thinking. I come across like such a rigid person, right? And she's what happens when you run your household like the Marines. But you don't have kids, do you?"

Jordanna shook her head.

"You know what I think? I think it's just the sins of the fathers, right? I don't know where that passage comes from, 'the sins of the fathers will be visited on the next generation,' or whatever—something like that, right?"

She didn't identify the quote for him—Exodous by way of Euripides and Shakespeare. Instead, she reached over and spread her hand on top of his. She knew that in a moment everything would be different for Buck. He would say aloud something he never had said before. In the long silence while Buck was summoning his sin to his tongue, Jordanna listened to the rain and the sound of water coursing more certainly onto the floor of her office across the hall.

"My wife . . ." He stopped and took a deep breath. The effort he was expending in trying not to cry was causing his face to redden, as if he were single-handedly holding back an oncoming torrent. "I've been married to Louise for nineteen years. She doesn't know that when I was seventeen, a senior in high school, I got a girl pregnant. This girl . . . she was so goddamn shy . . . she never really . . . Jesus. You know, she told me, and I just acted like it had nothing to do with me. It was like it was a storm or a flood, some act of God. She went to a different school. We'd met through some . . ." He stopped and shook his head, and Jordanna couldn't tell if he was about to laugh or sob. "I mean, get this, we met in a church youth group. I didn't even know her that well. After she told me, I never went anywhere I thought I might run into her. I acted like nothing had happened. I graduated a few weeks later, and I never saw her again. I mean, I don't know if . . ." He stood up now and walked back and forth between the faded floral couch and the bookshelves on the opposite wall. "It's one reason I've been so hard on my girls. You know, because there are guys like me out there. . . ." He slid his oversize fingers into the pockets of his trousers, and Jordanna listened to him toss some coins inside one pocket. Jordanna took the opportunity to unzip her robe and then fan herself with the long opened panels. It was only after the fact that she realized she'd steeled herself to hear Buck confess that he had impregnated Tara. She lowered her shoulders now and unclenched her toes inside her pumps. She leaned back into the couch. This, though, of course, was what she should have expected. How many times had she seen someone respond to a life challenge by splitting open his past, stem to stern, and letting loose the gestating sin, as if adversity were merely God calling your bluff?

She looked up at him, waiting for some signal that he wanted her to respond. Sometimes, when someone confided a secret he'd been hoarding for half a lifetime, the moment would become sanctified, as if a transfusion had taken place, the bleeding out of the guilt in exchange for forgiveness and love. But this afternoon, she felt only that a transaction had occurred. He had offered some old transgression in return for some vague assurance about the present. Jordanna heard the phone ring in Gael's office, and she realized that she hadn't thought about June or the Nearings for at least fifteen minutes.

She looked up once again at Buck. "How do you feel now?" she asked. "You've just done something extraordinarily difficult." She wondered if she'd suffer a wave of dread every time someone mentioned the name of the sixth month of the year. Would *June* take on the power to disintegrate her, the way *baby* and *expecting* already had?

He nodded and paced once more back toward the shelves. "Maybe a little less fake. You probably think I should tell my family, don't you?"

She was listening to the river in her office. Either the leak had progressed or the echo of the empty church house had just become more profound. "What do you think would be best?"

He nodded his head thoughtfully up and down. "Well, what did I just get after Tara about yesterday, the whole time we were in your office? Honesty, that was my big thing with her. Trust, respect, blah, blah, blah."

"What are you afraid of, Buck?"

"I want my family to respect me. I mean, we all have a way we want people to think of us. We want people to see us in a certain light. I've worked my whole adult life for that."

She watched as he paced back and forth again. Every part of his body seemed pumped full of muscle threatening to burst the seams of his clothes. Dressed in dark pants and a starched white shirt, he looked like a missionary on steroids. "John said that the truth will set you free, that everyone who commits sin is a slave. Only you can know if not sharing this part of your past now with your family will set you apart, separate you from them and from God. That's the definition of sin." She leaned forward from her place on the couch as he paced back toward her, and she touched him on the arm, to still him for a moment. "What's happened to Tara, with Tara, with your whole family, is an opportunity. You have been offered this chance, and it's no accident, Buck." She gripped his hand firmly. "Trust me, it's no accident."

He hung his head down in front of her, and then turned away. "I don't believe in a God who's a puppeteer."

Jordanna smiled. "Neither do I. We're all given numerous opportunities, and mostly we don't even recognize them as such—but here, well, you've been fortunate enough to be alerted to this one."

"So you're saying I should tell them?" He sat on the edge of the conference table, his legs sloping toward the couch.

Jordanna slowly shook her head. "It's not my place to tell you anything, only to point you toward the source of the answer. I think you know."

He walked past the bookshelves and the two towers of black file cabinets, toward the door. He blew his noise loudly. Thunder rumbled as if it were coming from the ground and not the sky. "You know, you've got to watch out for something, Reverend Nash," he said, now, spitting the words at her. "You might have all the answers, you know, but the rest of us poor slobs, well, that's why we hire you, to help us. I'm not sure it does much for either one of us for you to make it seem like it's patty-cake, you know. I told you a hard truth—about my life—"

"And I respect that," Jordanna said, somewhat awakened now that she was under attack.

"Well, what I do next, that might seem easy to you, but not to me."

She should have predicted this, too. Now that he had made himself vulnerable to her, he had to regain some ground; what better way than to accuse her of being sanctimonious or uncaring, or whatever it was he was trying to say. "I'm sorry," she said. "If I have hurt you, please, know that it was inadvertent."

"Life is hard," he said quietly. He looked at her on the couch, and she nodded in agreement.

"Tara wants an abortion," he said.

"Would it be helpful for the three of you to come together to discuss this?"

"Do you think it's a sin?" He crossed his arms in front of his chest.

She stood up and walked toward him. "What I think doesn't matter. Tara is your little girl. And she still is, you know. She still is a little girl."

He passed his fingers over his lower lip, as if feeling for something distant.

She needed to leave. She needed to be with the Nearings. Usually, when she wanted to end a counseling session, she would suggest a closing prayer. But she didn't think she could pray just now. She knew she couldn't. There was no way to bridge the gap between her and the Divine, not now. She looked at her watch and told Buck that she was sorry, but there was someplace she was supposed to be. She offered to stop by the house later on. She jotted down her home phone number. She would be home all evening. Why didn't they talk, as a family, about what they wanted to do.

. . .

THERE were a few cars parked in front of the Nearings'. She sat there for a while and looked at the house, a small tan Cape. June had planted marigolds all along the front walk, orange and yellow. Someone must have watered them. After a summer-long drought, there they were, ridiculously hardy, sturdy, stupidly bright, a flower without any subtlety. She should have thought to bring the children something. But what? What really could it have been, something that they would for the rest of their lives associate with the day they found out their mother was dead? Music. She should have brought them a tape. She wondered if June had ever sang to them. All mothers sang, though, didn't they? She tried to remember if she ever saw June sing at church. Jordanna liked to close her eyes during the hymns. She loved to listen to the confluence of all those voices without being distracted by looking at their individual faces. She wondered if June had ever thought to record her voice, singing or reading a story. She hoped there were plenty of pictures of her with the children. After James, Jordanna had planned that when she did become a mother, she would make certain to create a trail of relics leading straight to the heart of who she'd been here on earth. That's what tragedy taught you, to be prepared for instant death, the complete rearrangement of every given in your life. She knew June hadn't thought of this. How could she have? In planning for her absence, she would have been forced to imagine that her children were about to be as wounded as she already thought she was.

Of course Jordanna would go in. It was her job to comfort the bereaved. There was a service to plan. This was what the congregation paid her to do. Abby had told her once, years ago, that she couldn't fathom having a job in which death figured so heavily. It was worse than being a doctor. At any time, any place, someone could die and you'd be brought in to tie it all up, to enter the room most people couldn't wait to flee. Jordanna had tried to explain that it wasn't like that, that it was an honor to be invited into people's lives at their most significant junctures. A kind of irreducible, pure truth suffused thought and action after abject loss. In the past few years she had wondered if the meaning of her having lost the babies was to draw her closer to the grief of others. But now she looked across the soaked sidewalk. The flower beds were floating. She wondered how to will herself from here to there. She felt no call to go into the Nearings' living room. Her need to stay in her car, to drive to her house, to sneak into her bed, seemed the true call. She looked at the dashboard clock and told herself she would only stay for forty-five minutes. She could endure anything for that long. She would just *be* in their presence, that was all. She didn't need to *do* anything.

Lee was in the hallway when Jordanna walked in and shook out her wet hair. Jordanna smiled, and Lee, who was hanging onto the doorknob of the coat closet, just stared back.

"Is your dad home, honey?"

"He's in the kitchen with Grandma . . . and everybody."

Jordanna nodded. "Where are Carly and Ian?"

Lee shrugged.

"How are you?" Jordanna said.

"We're looking at pictures of my mom. Everyone is saying that she died."

Jordanna crouched down on the front hall rug and nodded. "It's very sad."

"Ian is too little to understand. He just keeps calling for Mommy. Carly cries sometimes, but then she forgets and I have to tell her it again."

"That must be hard."

"No."

Jordanna looked down at her feet. The mat was pink and fluffy, as though it had once been used in a bathroom. "Do you think it would be okay if I went into the kitchen and saw your grandma and your dad?"

Lee shrugged and grabbed the doorknob, swinging her feet off the ground.

Jordanna walked to the hall mirror, stooping to get a look at herself. Her hair had mostly abandoned her braid, and the makeup she had applied at eight-thirty had been washed away by rain and later tears. She had attempted to cover the healing scar on her cheek, but now it seemed even ruddier and more visible. She pressed her palms down over her blouse, felt for the choker around her neck and quickly squeezed her own hand for comfort.

Bev saw her first, or, at least, was the first to greet her. She pushed back the clunky walnut chair and embraced Jordanna. Jordanna looked over her shoulder at Drew, at the two men she guessed were June's brothers, and at Sheila Nearing, Drew's mother. There was a bottle of Seagram's Seven in the center of the table and some coffee cups and a tin of butter cookies. Jordanna could hear a TV in the next room. She walked over to where Drew was sitting and reached down to hug him. He didn't move, didn't look up at her. Bev introduced her to her sons, Kent and Miles, and later, when she came in from the living room, to her daughter-in-law, who was very pregnant.

"We're making a list of all the things that need to be done," Sheila said.

Miles brought in a chair from the dining room, and Jordanna sat at the table, next to Bev.

"Are you making some plans?" Jordanna asked Drew. He was looking out the window. The grass in the backyard was tall and a small stream coursed down the children's plastic slide. Jordanna slowly looked around. The seams from the drywall were visible under the primer. She wondered if the box of nails and the hammer on the counter were unmoved since the last time she'd been here. The cupboards were still propped up against the unfinished walls.

"Drew," his mother said loudly, as if he were deaf rather than bereaved, "Reverend Nash wants to know if she can help with the plans. Is there something you would like her to do?"

Drew lifted a plastic glass to his lips, and Jordanna heard the cubes slide together.

"We've decided not to wait," Miles, the older of the brothers, said. "We think it would be best for the kids and all if we had a funeral service. And then when . . . well, we can have a burial or whatever. . . ."

Jordanna looked at Drew, who was now scraping his thumbnail across the poinsettia design on his plastic party cup.

Leaning toward Jordanna, Bev whispered that perhaps she would like to talk with Drew alone.

"We all failed her," Drew said, a bit too loudly. Jordanna scanned the table. Everyone except Sheila and the pregnant woman had one of those Christmas glasses in front of them. She would have to wait a few more sentences to tell if he was drunk.

"Maybe if we'd met like this when she needed us to, when we still could of helped her, we wouldn't be here now."

Nobody spoke. Jordanna listened to a teenage girl in the next room repeat something tenderly to one of the children.

"I try, you know, but . . . I can't picture it. Waking up every day . . . with this. It wasn't my plan, you know."

Anna, the pregnant sister-in-law, got up and pulled an accordion door shut between the kitchen and the room with the TV. Jordanna watched her cradle her stomach in one arm as she walked back to the table.

"Now's the time to focus on the kids. Your kids need a strong father." Sheila sounded practiced in her impatience.

Bev glared at Sheila, but Drew seemed not to have heard his mother.

"What have you told them?" Jordanna asked.

"The pediatrician suggested we not tell them all the same thing." Sheila poked her lipstick-stained coffee mug slightly to her right. "Of course, Ian . . . who knows what they understand at that age?"

"He knows she's gone," Drew said. "He stands at that window and looks for her, calls, 'Mama.'"

"The children's doctor," Sheila began again with authority, "said to tell Lee that Mommy was sick and the sickness affected her brain and it was a very bad sickness and it killed her. And to Carly, he suggested, for now anyways, just saying she died. 'Mother has died.' He says that at Carly's age, she won't get it. She'll keep asking."

"Jordanna," Bev said, "there are other things we should be telling them, don't you think?"

What she thought was that she smelled June. That mix of baking soda and boiled-over coffee that she'd associated with June's body, she now realized came from this house. Something acrid or very nearly burnt underscored that joyless, utilitarian smell of bicarbonate. She closed her eyes and thought that perhaps her smelling June now meant that she was here. Of course she was among them, but how close? Was she hovering in the room or hanging on Jordanna's shoulder, just enough to tug her lower back? Or was she even closer, inside her head, or resting on a valve in her heart? She hadn't realized that she was crying until Sheila coolly pushed a large box of Kleenex in her direction. Bev reached under the table and placed her hand on top of Jordanna's. She wasn't just teary, she was weeping, ostentatiously, the kind of crying that can never be confused with an expression of sympathy. She breathed in deeply and smelled June again in all her desperation, and for the first time in years, Jordanna was afraid, truly afraid.

"How can I tell my kids their mother killed herself? I mean, really."

"Shhh," Sheila said.

Jordanna plucked tissue after tissue from the box, like pulling weeds, and attempted to turn in Drew's direction. She was grateful that he was drunk and ignoring her. "It was wonderful to think to call the pediatrician. Your love for your family is going to guide you to making the right choices, Drew."

"*I* called the doctor," Sheila said.

Jordanna nodded. "The family, all of you, will need the support—"

"Yeah, it takes a village," Drew said snidely.

"We should be talking about a date for the service," Miles said.

"Tenth of never." Drew rolled his now-empty cup on its side.

Bev pushed back her chair and leaned over him. He hung his head down and then stood and followed her through the hall toward the bedrooms.

"He never drinks," Sheila said.

"Well, he's entitled today," Kent said.

"It won't help. And I don't want these kids seeing him like this. It won't help them, either."

"He's going to need all of you," Jordanna said, hoping to stem the rant. "This kind of healing . . ." She pressed a wad of Kleenex into her eyes. "To heal from something like this could take a very long time. The children and Drew will need to see that the world is filled with people who love them, care for them. Their life experience has just taught them otherwise."

"We'll all need to be on the receiving end of that, you know," Kent said. He was standing at the kitchen counter working a hand through a coffee can filled with nails, like a rosary. "This is the second sister to die on me in less than two years. No one better be looking at me to show them how *loving* this fucking world is."

Miles went to his brother's side and clamped a hand behind his neck as if he were bracing him.

"Your losses have been . . . enormous." Jordanna recoiled at the emptiness of the statement. She'd spoken without the proper intonation, hadn't taken the time to connect up sentiment to words. No matter how hard she tried to steer herself toward the needs of this family in this moment, she sensed herself drifting, again and again.

"We've been getting a lot of phone calls, from newspapers and stuff, even Channel Three up in Hartford. . . . We're not ready right now . . ." Miles said

"I told you Jonathan will handle all that." Sheila now turned toward Jordanna. "Jonathan's my daughter's husband. He has his own PR firm in Greenwich."

Jordanna nodded. "Do you think one of the detectives might help . . . run interference? You certainly don't need this right now. I know that when this woman from the Hartford paper showed up at the end of today's worship—"

"To talk to *you*?" Kent said derisively.

"Well, she's been counseling June for half a year—had been, *had been* counseling," Sheila said.

Miles sighed heavily, exhaling whiskey in Jordanna's direction.

"What about?" Kent said. "What were you counseling her about?"

"She can't tell you that, right?" Anna looked at Jordanna.

Jordanna now sighed and closed her eyes and there was June, just a flash of her behind her lids, that damn stringy hair, the yellowing T-shirt. "She was . . . despondent over Eve's death."

Sheila shook her head silently.

"*What?*" Kent accused.

Sheila raised her eyebrows. "Nothing."

"My sisters were tight, very tight." Kent moved from the counter toward Sheila. "June saw everything, man, everything, at the end. She and our mother . . . I mean, they never got in a nurse. You know, that's like being in a war or something. People go to Vietnam and they're allowed to come back fucked up for the rest of their lives. No different watching your sister die a slow, disgustingly painful death right in the house where you grew up. You don't forget that shit, you know."

Jordanna wished someone would pour some rye into one of those Christmas cups for her. June had told her details of Eve's death, and Jordanna had counseled her to let go of those images. She had asked June what was to be gained by holding on to that final tragic reel. June had told her that in the last forty-eight hours when Eve's kidneys had failed and the toxins had backed up into her body and she had become completely deranged, Eve had reached down and smeared her own feces over her face. "And I have to live with that image of her as one of my last. I have to remember her doing that and yelling and cursing awful things at me and my mother, things she never would have said, words I never heard her say in her whole lifetime. Why would God do that to her and us, make it so we had to remember her that way? Bad enough to take her life, but to humiliate us all . . ." And what had Jordanna said to that? She remembered June's demand of her that she answer for the eventualities of this world, that she explain God's plan, that she be accountable to June for the work of the Divine, as if she were his operative here on earth. She only remembered being annoyed and provoked by June's weakness. She didn't remember what she had said.

"Other people bury family members and they're able to move on. Not every soldier comes back from war not right in the head," Sheila said, not making eye contact with anyone.

"I think Kent makes an important point," Jordanna said softly. "Perhaps society is not as compassionate towards mourners as it might be. Maybe there wasn't enough room made for June's grief."

"You include yourself in that, Reverend Nash?" Miles said now.

"Miles." Bev uttered his name from halfway down the hall. No one spoke as she walked slowly back into the kitchen.

"What, I can't question the minister?"

"Blame is very small, and nothing about what has happened to your sister is small." Bev set her lips and began to cry, the tanned flesh of her arms wobbling as she hugged herself.

"Mother," Miles said gently, "we have to be able to express ourselves. When Eve was dying, we challenged the doctors, questioned them, asked them what was going on. This isn't any different."

"What is it you want to know?" Bev said. She sounded as if she had been working long and hard, as if she could barely concentrate on the conversation. Jordanna looked over at her and saw it happen. Like the tenth or twentieth division of cells at conception, Bev had just registered the slimmest bit of the whole enormous encoded truth, that yes, her daughter, her June, was dead. Each time this happened it was news, shocking again and again. And in that moment it was impossible to know anything else but that the universe had just been reorganized.

Nobody said anything. A female voice was singing on the television in the next room. There was an uneven plunking from a downspout outside the kitchen window. And maybe there was the faintest sound of weeping from down the hallway. Jordanna left the kitchen and walked toward the bedrooms. Drew was on the bottom bunk in the room the three children shared. It smelled slightly of soiled diapers and talcum powder. There were toys, doll clothes and pressboard puzzle pieces in piles around the room. A pillar of stuffed animals wound about a pink plastic chain attached to the ceiling. Drew was awake. He looked over at her as she entered and then turned to look up at the slats in the bunk bed above him.

"When I first put this thing together last winter, I lay down here and thought how great it would be to be three again, for this to be my bed, to only have to worry about whatever three-year-olds worry about. But I can't do that now. It'll be worse for them than me, all this. I wouldn't ever want to trade places with any one of them now. I got to live until now, thirty-four, with my mother alive. They'll always be different because of this."

Jordanna sat down on the scatter rug between the bunk beds and the crib. It was a baby-blue rag rug and she thought about June carrying it outside in the back to beat.

"We all fucked up, you know, Jordanna, down to a man." Drew's face was flushed and his eyes were bleary.

"You loved her, Drew. You loved her as best you could. The only thing we have to offer the other is our love—"

"And it wasn't enough. My love for her wasn't enough. It's a terrible thing—to know you gave completely to someone and it wasn't enough."

Jordanna looked over at him. He was running his eyes up and down the rails of the bed. Not such a terrible thing, she thought. In fact, it was a holy thing to give utterly of one's self and to know it, to be sure that you had held nothing back, kept nothing in reserve, secretly, selfishly.

"Go home," Drew said. "I can't plan a damn thing today. I just have to miss her today. That's all. Today, I just have to think about her never coming back."

ᘒᘓ Chapter 14

EARLY Wednesday morning as Abby was getting ready to bring Gabe to day care, he asked her if it was going to rain so much that the people in the graves would start floating around. Abby was walking ahead of him quickly through the garage, wincing at the decided smell of mold that had developed during the ten days it had been raining.

"Hmm?" she said. She had heard him, but she was thinking about whether Christopher and Michael would miss the bus, and if Brendan had remembered his key, and cursing that she had agreed to this early morning PPT.

"Will that happen?" he said impatiently as she buckled him into his car seat in the back of the van.

"No," she said. "They bury people way, way down deep in boxes. No. Dead people will not start floating around." She backed out of the driveway and waited until they were on their way to ask him where he had gotten such an idea.

"Why?"

"Why what?" she said.

"Why won't they?"

"Why won't dead people float around?"

"Yeah."

"I just told you. They're very far under the ground. Are you worried about dead people for some special reason today?" She turned around to look at him, and he shrugged and took a triangle of his cinnamon toast out of the baggie. There had been a significant amount of press about June Nearing's suicide and the continued search for the body. Brendan had been talking about it at dinner last night, before Abby had told him to please wait until later. The guidance department had pulled together a quick staff meeting last week to discuss the possible effects of this very public hometown suicide on the high school population. Certainly, these kids would not identify with some disthymic homemaker. On the other hand, June Nearing had just made suicide a very real possibility for everyone in their small town. It was like hearing that a Hutchinson resident had picked the winning lottery numbers or flown to Paris on the Concorde. If someone from their neck of the woods had actually done it, maybe they could, too. Of all the black scenarios she faced in working with kids in grades nine through twelve, suicide was the one she feared most, even more than school violence. If someone in her school, a kid, committed suicide, she would feel as if she had personally failed. There were days when her job as a school counselor seemed not much different from the one she'd had twenty years before as a lifeguard at Cold Storage Beach. Roam the halls, scan the rolls, use your eyes and ears and nose if you had to, sensing potential trouble. There were always those kids with enough reason to kill themselves, but it was usually the ones you knew little to nothing about who proved the biggest dangers.

The guidance staff had agreed that since it wasn't a peer suicide, there was no imminent copycat danger. And then Leilei Schoen had joked that maybe somebody ought to set up some grief counseling for the young mothers in town. Abby had thought about suggesting to Jordanna that she make Hutchinson Congregational a kind of drop-in center for the week, provide counselors for people to talk with. But she hadn't been able to reach her sister at all last week. Jor-

danna did that sometimes. She would just go underground. She'd
been doing it since high school. Whenever something un-Jordanna-
like transpired in her life, she would hunker down somewhere, waiting until enough time had elapsed so that the event lost its novelty,
put on some of the weight of history. She had tried to do it when
James died, but Abby hadn't let her. Abby had stayed on her, phoning, visiting. Jordanna had called her "the hound of heaven."

"Mama, if you get dead, will JoJo take care of me?"

Abby turned around and stared at him. "I'm not going to die, not
anytime soon."

He shrugged and scraped the little border of toast crust along the
window. "Michael said JoJo would watch us if you and Daddy got
dead."

"He's right," Abby said. "Is there some reason you're worried
about me and Daddy?"

"Old people die."

"We're not old."

"Miss Diane's really not old."

"Has someone been talking to you about parents dying?"

"Ohhhh, no."

"What happened?"

"My toast bird broke into where the window goes."

"Shit." Abby pulled over in front of Gabe's day care and shut off
the engine. "Unbuckle and climb over," she directed. "We need a
mega-hug before we say goodbye today." He climbed over the center
console, and she slid back the seat to accommodate him and the steering wheel. "I'm going to be your mama forever," she whispered into
his dirty little neck.

He nodded and reached for a baseball trading card that Michael
had left on the dashboard. "JoJo says that even when we get dead, we
still work."

There was a small river running the length of Miss Diane's rutted
driveway. "What do you think she means by that?" Abby said after a
while.

"Well, if you do get died, it's okay, 'cause JoJo's very fun for us."

"I'm not dying," Abby said. She ran her thumbs up under his armpits and he squealed.

"I'm bringing this card for show and tell."

AT the beginning of third period, Tara Sears appeared in Abby's office doorway. Tara was a junior, and Abby's advisees were all in the sophomore class.

"Hey, there," Abby said, looking up from her desk at the henna tattoo, very likely a dragon, on Tara's bare midriff.

"Mrs. Thurman's my advisor, but she's got a pole up her butt. I'd rather talk to you."

Abby waved Tara in and got up and closed her office door. "If we're going to talk, we need to be honest. And honestly, I'm not interested in hearing my colleagues referred to with disrespect."

"Sorry," Tara hissed. She slumped into the chair by the side of Abby's desk with her backpack still strapped to one shoulder.

"What's going on?"

"You know."

"Actually, I don't."

"I thought you were Reverend Nash's sister."

Abby nodded.

"So."

"So."

"Well, I'm like two months pregnant or something," she said, as if it were Abby's doing. "And I want an abortion and my mother, of all people, is freaking on me about it."

"Is Reverend Nash your minister?"

"You know she is. You saw—"

"You sound really angry," Abby said, unfolding a paper clip she'd picked up from her desk.

"Are you going to put this in my chart?"

Abby nodded. "Is that a problem?"

"Shit, it's such a fucking small town, anyway." She pulled her backpack around onto her lap and hugged it.

"Do you have people to talk to about this? Have you talked to anyone else?"

"Reverend Nash."

Abby stared at the girl. Sometimes it seemed that this generation had taken a ton of shrapnel as babies, and in adolescence it had floated up and broken through the surface. Her theatrically pale face was riddled with silver studs. What kind of mindfuck was she into here with the minister and the guidance counselor? Very ballsy. Abby wondered how Jordanna had dealt with this kid. Had the pregnancy obscured everything? She'd seen her sister flame from within, redden and very nearly shake when people sprang on her that they were "expecting." Certainly she was better now than earlier on. And Abby knew that Jordanna had very nearly lost her first job for lacing a sermon with pro-choice sentiment. But when faced with a sixteen-year-old asking for a ride, the idea of terminating a pregnancy might have become as tangible and unbearable as a granite marker. She wondered what Jordanna had counseled this girl to do.

"Have you been able to talk to your friends about this?" Abby chucked the now-broken paper clip into the wastebasket.

"You mean, the guy?" Tara said, as if correcting her.

"I mean, any of your friends."

"He's not really my boyfriend. He's a guy friend, that's all. We were just fooling around. My dad keeps asking if he took *advantage* of me—Jesus, like it's tennis or something. I mean, what the hell does that mean, anyway?"

Abby looked up at the clock on her bookshelf. She had a meeting in seven minutes. "It sounds as if your father is concerned."

"No. He just wants to know who to flip out at. I mean, what does he think? Like this guy pulled one over on me or something?"

"Do you think it would be helpful for all of you to get together and talk? There are a number of things we could do. I could set up a meeting with you and your parents, and if you like . . . the father of the baby."

"It's not a baby, yet."

"Or . . ." Abby stuck out her tongue slightly and pulled out a hair, which may or may not have been there. This girl was bugging her. "You and me and your male friend could arrange to talk together. Perhaps we should start there. What do you think?"

For the first time since she'd sat down, Tara looked vulnerable. She stared out the window toward the patio outside the cafeteria. It had finally stopped raining, and kids were sitting at the still-wet picnic tables. She tucked her chin and fixed on her blue toenails. "I don't think it really has anything to do with him, you know."

Abby rolled her chair farther away from her desk and faced the girl. "Most everybody else is walking around here worrying about tests and games and clothes. This is a lot. It's one of the biggest decisions you'll ever have to make. It would be difficult if you were twice as old."

"If I were twice as old, I wouldn't be in this situation." She lowered her chin onto the top of her backpack and for a moment Abby wondered if she was actually going to suck on the large metal zipper pull. "I would just . . . what about that pill, anyway, that pill that just dissolves the whole thing?"

Abby was anxious to pull this girl's file and see what kind of student she was. Why had she come in here? She wasn't even her guidance counselor. She knew enough to know about a drug that wasn't even on the market yet. She seemed bright enough to navigate the logistics, if in fact that's all there was to it. Abby wondered about the parents, if they were together, or what else was going on, that she wanted yet another adult female to weigh in.

"Are those all your kids?" Tara was standing now with her backpack slung over one shoulder, a girl with an old woman's hump.

Abby looked confused for a minute and then she saw that Tara was looking at the pictures on her desk. She nodded.

"How many?"

"Four."

"Jesus, and all boys. Oh, I know him. He goes here. He's a freshman, right?"

"Brendan," Abby said.

"You must be Catholic—that's what my father would say."

Abby smiled.

"I have a class next period. Are you going to tell Reverend Nash that I came and talked to you?"

"Do you want me to?"

Tara moved toward the door, signaling the end of the meeting. Without turning around, she said, "The guy's in her youth group, Senior P.F."

Abby listened to the spat-out sentence as it traveled through the girl's bony chest and then that enormous sack of books. "Have you told her that?"

Tara made a face.

"Perhaps you should," Abby said.

"It's none of her business."

"Would you like me to set up a meeting with you and your friend and/or your parents?"

"I've got to go to my locker before this class." She swung open the door, then closed it loudly behind her.

While she waited for Tara's file to come up on her screen, Abby realized she had asked nothing about how this pregnancy had been confirmed, if she'd been to the doctor, if she was taking care of herself. If she really was as unsure about what to do as it seemed, then she needed to be attending to this pregnancy now. So many clueless parents. She looked at their address. Both parents had a work number listed. There were two other siblings, one was a senior. The father had some military prefix. The girl was in accelerated math. With the exception of freshman-year Latin, she had nothing less than a 3.6 in any course. Not a lot of sickouts. She could go to the file drawers outside of Doreen Thurman's office to look for the teachers' written comments, for anything that wasn't apparent about this kid by looking at her GPA.

JORDANNA was sitting at the center island drinking a martini when Abby came home at four-thirty. Gabe pushed past his mother. "JoJo's here!" He ran to her and raised his arms, waiting to be picked up.

"Hi, sweetheart," Jordanna said vaguely. "Do you mind?" She raised her glass toward her sister.

Abby shook her head.

"JoJo," Gabe commanded, "up."

Jordanna looked out the window over the sink and then at the refrigerator. "Jim had that good stuff in the freezer."

Abby nodded again. "Gabe, will you go see if Brendan's upstairs?"

Gabe started to walk away, looked back at Jordanna, then at his mother. Abby heard him kick off his sneakers as he passed through the dining room, then try to stomp loudly up the stairs in his socks.

Abby put down her briefcase and her keys and tried not to stare at her sister. She couldn't remember the last time she'd seen her hair loose, completely unbridled in any way, maybe the hospital. There was so much of it. That hair, loose like this, was almost scary, like something separate and in addition to Jordanna. Her eyes were red and her lips were fatter than usual. Jordanna did that when she cried, she pressed down hard on her lips, as if stopping the blood flow, and later, when she'd lost the energy to bite down, the lips would fill with all the blood that they'd been denied. "What's going on?" Abby said softly.

"Do you have . . . I need tweezers. I think I have a tick. On my back. You know, I'm not sure . . . there's no way for me to know for sure, you know. I can't see back there." Jordanna reached her right arm across her body and pulled her top up over her head. "It's on the left, my left," she said from inside the sweatshirt.

Abby went to the sink and washed her hands and then walked to where her sister was sitting.

Jordanna attempted to slap her long fingers up toward the spot on her back. "And Brendan said he wanted to borrow . . . I left it in the dining room . . . *The Seven Storey Mountain*."

"Here?" Abby said, touching a spot that looked irritated. She could feel her sister's body nod yes, the long spine curved down more deeply, bowing into the countertop. Jordanna's back was a pink expanse of flesh with hundreds of honey dots, some moles, some age spots. She pulled slightly on the grayish bra strap. "I think it's a mosquito bite, or some kind of bite. I don't see a tick, though." She ran her hand across the well-muscled and abruptly fleshy parts of her sister's wide back. She patted her gently, and then began to pull down her top for her. "You having a bad day?" she said, still standing behind Jordanna.

"A day I could handle. No, sweetheart, I'm having a bad life."

Abby walked around the other side of the island and pulled out a stool. She didn't think her sister had ever called her "sweetheart." It was off. Not fake or phony, just not Jordanna. She stole another look at her sister. She was dressed wrong, as if she'd grabbed at the dark green print skirt and the orange fleece pullover without registering their colors or textures. While her sister never liked to admit it, she paid attention to clothes. She affected a certain style, much as she pretended that it was somehow just an extension of self and not an act of artifice or deliberation.

"I canceled my trip to visit Daniel. I . . . I really can't leave now. Not with everything . . . with June."

"Wow."

"He sounded relieved. Didn't even ask me that many questions about it. He said he was sorry, but he wasn't." She spun a silver bangle around her wrist as if it were her turn now to move her piece around the board. "I think he's involved with someone over there. I can hear it in his voice, this kind of . . . a kind of happiness or something."

Abby had been waiting for this to happen. "I'm sorry."

"Yeah."

"Is that student minister still coming? Maybe you should try to take it easy, even if you do hang around. Really, everyone needs a vacation."

Jordanna sipped her drink. "I'm tired," she said, as if it were a non sequitur.

"How are the Nearings?"

Jordanna shook her head, slid off the chair and pulled open the freezer. "Want one?" she said, holding up the small bottle of vodka.

Abby didn't really. She looked at her watch. She had to drive Michael to soccer practice and make dinner. There was homework help, phone calls to be returned. But it was depressing to see her sister perched high above her all-white kitchen dressed for Mardi Gras, drinking alone.

Jordanna had already taken down another glass. She poured vodka into it and handed it to Abby.

"I have a lemon. I have vermouth, and probably olives," Abby said. She took a jar of peanuts from the pantry.

"Do you ever read the Hartford paper?"

"Why?"

"This reporter came to church a week ago Sunday, then interviewed all the Nearings and some other people and she writes this feature about June in which I'm like . . . Well, let's say that June's seeking counseling from me is what made it a feature. Basically, she implies that I'm responsible for June's death. 'Psychological, if not spiritual malpractice,' that's what she calls it. That's how I started my day. Fred called, Fred Rinehardt, to kind of warn me. Poor guy, he'd been going out and buying the Hartford paper every day this week. He said he knew, he had a sense. So . . . I mean, I can't even think about Daniel. Daniel doesn't even fit into the same frame with all this, you know. And I've lost all ability to be angry. I should be mad. This woman maligns me like that. I mean . . . what do you guess the readership of that newspaper is? And I can't even work up any fury.

Not mad at Daniel. I'm just . . ." She lowered her head to her drink. Abby could hear the determined sipping behind the veil of hair.

"How's June's family doing? Her kids are little, right?"

"They don't know what to do without a body." Jordanna slid her bracelet from her wrist and set the base of her glass inside its circle. "You know about the notes?"

"Just what's been in the Hutchinson paper. I've called you like a hundred—"

"She sent me one, too, a poem. This really . . . But she wrote notes to her mother and to Drew and she sketched a whole scene, a picture for her kids."

"I'm sure they are aching for some kind of closure."

"I hate that word, Abigail."

"See, you still can get mad." Abby pulled on a hank of her sister's hair, which spread from her lowered shoulders like dark mountain ranges across the map of the tile countertop.

"There's no closure when people die. Closure is for the people who *comfort* the bereaved. They want to know when it'll be over, when their job will be done, when it'll be okay not to have to mention the death again. In real life, in the life of the person with the loss—*the loser*—it never happens." She slid the bracelet up the glass, collaring the cocktail, lifting the great V of cold vodka to her lips.

"All I meant was, they probably need some ceremony, something to make them start to feel as if this is real, that their mother, wife, daughter, sister is really dead and gone. They need to begin to bury her, even if they don't have a body. Don't you think?"

"What I think, more and more, every day, is that it's all about the body. The *idea* of June isn't going to do a fucking thing for those kids. They want her hands and arms, and lap and breasts. It's the body. If I had paid more attention to the body and less to the soul . . ." Jordanna removed her hand from the glass and the bracelet clattered against the counter. "One more body, one more dead body that . . . You know, I mean, you can't keep your congregants from getting killed in car accidents or by tumors, but good God, the least you think you might be able to wangle is to keep them from killing themselves, especially when they've fucking come to you for help, you know? I mean, what on God's green goddam earth does it remind you of, Abigail? When, precisely, twice, have I been guilty of this kind of—what? Negligence? Murder? It's just another body that was my responsibility. Stewardship, shepherding, guiding. I'm supposed to be out there saving souls, and I can't even keep the bodies alive, the flesh."

Abby stood up and came around the counter to Jordanna's chair. She pulled her sister's arms off the counter and forced her to fall into her. "It wasn't yours to do, you know? It wasn't yours to fix." Jordanna's chin settled on Abby's collarbone, and she shook and heaved and sobbed. Abby heard Gabe sliding down the stairs on his bottom. Jordanna inhaled as if she were returning to some kind of calm, then a cry cracked from her throat. "Please, God, no," she pleaded into Abby's neck. "I can't. I can't do it."

Gabe came running into the kitchen and tried to squeeze between his mother and his aunt. Abby sneaked an arm down to try to comfort him, and Jordanna stepped back from her sister. She blew her nose into a paper napkin and sank down onto the floor. "It's okay," she said to Gabe. She held open her arms and he climbed into her billowing skirt and laid his face down on her thigh. Jordanna leaned over him and rested her cheek on his back, her head moving with each one of his confused sobs. "My boy," she whispered, "my boy."

"Don't be scared, honey," Abby said. She was torn between comforting her sister and reassuring her son, unsure which to do first, whose feelings took priority in this triage. "JoJo's just sad, lamb."

He twisted his head from under the considerable weight of his aunt's face and hair, butting her slightly on her already swollen lips, until she picked her head up. "She's sad about baby Alice, right?"

Abby nodded toward him. Jordanna would make much of this mention by name of one of the babies. She would, as she had on numerous other occasions, chalk up his consciousness of Alice's loss to their "twinned" gestations. She was convinced of some kind of otherworldly bond, a link, a connection that was evidenced again and again by things that only Gabe said or did. Abby figured Jordanna's pleasure at this would last another year or so, and then Gabe would, like his older brothers, find James and Alice subjects so embarrassing that they had to be relegated to distant memory, suitable only for discussion by adults, who were getting closer and closer to their own deaths.

"Sorry, guys." Jordanna ran her thumbs down the inside corners of her eyes and twisted her hair into a knot behind her head. She reached out her hand for Gabe to help her up.

"You're too big," he said as he pretended to lift her to her feet.

"You need to talk to somebody, Jordanna," Abby said as she picked Gabe up in her arms.

"Hey, that's what you're for, Abs," she said, working hard to sound breezy.

"No, really, I mean it. Even if it's just that guy, that older guy, that professor from Divinity School."

"You mean, even if it's just a minister." She drank the rest of her martini and walked with the glass to the sink. "Start with the minister, anyway, what's the harm, and then, when he proves incapable, go on to the big guns, the real pros, right?"

This sarcasm was as anomalous as her outfit. Jordanna was many things. She was conceited, she was myopic, grandiose, but Abby could not think of a time when she'd bristled with sarcasm like this. Her karma didn't allow for it. She wondered if Jordanna was drunk. "How long have you been here?" she asked, ridiculously late into this conversation.

"Maybe I shouldn't have canceled those plane tickets. Fight for your man and all that, right? Is that what you're thinking? That I'm just giving up too easily on Daniel? The divorced female pastor—I'm telling you, it's so clichéd. I should be able to do better than that, huh?"

"You sound funny," Abby said, walking Gabe to the edge of the kitchen and whispering for him to go outside.

Gabe walked as far as the coat hooks, then hid behind his father's cracked leather bomber jacket. Jordanna stood at the sink letting the water run over her martini glass.

"Did he say anything when you talked to him the other day?" Abby listened to Jordanna's voice cut in and out over the running water. "Even on the phone, there's that sense of . . . expectation in his voice, like something wonderful is on the verge. . . ." She pulled down hard on the faucet, as if she were shutting off the water at its very source. She leaned over the edge of the sink and Abby watched as her hair dangled down into the wet porcelain.

"Maybe you and me should drive up to the Cape this weekend." Abby had the desperate idea that their mother might now somehow help. "I'll leave the kids with Jim. . . ."

Jordanna raised her right hand, as if signaling for air or motioning for a time-out.

Abby stopped talking and they froze like that, Jordanna at the sink with her back to Abby, and Abby not far behind her, as if they were lined up and waiting for something.

Michael skidded into the room, oblivious to everything but his urgent need to fill his water bottle. "JoJo"—he pushed his way to the faucet—"what are you guys doing? Tai chi or something?" He didn't wait for an answer. "Mom, we gotta go, it's already fifteen after."

"I'll take him," Jordanna said, turning suddenly from the sink, drying her face on a dish towel.

"Aren't you hot in that?" Michael said. He pushed down the cap of his water bottle with his two misshapen front teeth.

"I didn't see your car when I drove in," Abby said, wondering again at Jordanna's heavy pullover. "Or your bike."

"I left the car at Caraluzzi's." Jordanna was studying her reflection in the microwave above the stove.

"That's like five miles away." Abby looked down at her sister's feet. She was wearing little brown suede boots with narrow heels. "Is something wrong with the car?"

Jordanna shook her head. "On the bridle path it's only about two, two and half miles. It finally stopped raining. I needed to walk."

After Abby dropped Michael at his soccer practice, she drove Jordanna to her car. Caraluzzi's Bakery was closed, and Jordanna's was the only car in the lot. "You okay to drive?" She shut off the engine.

Jordanna nodded. "I figure I've killed enough people for one week—got my fill."

"Stop it," Abby said.

"Okay."

"What're you going to do when you get home?"

"Call you?"

"You're scaring me," Abby said. She lowered both front windows.

"Why? Because I made a joke, and usually I'm so . . . what? So unfunny, so . . ."

"Do you have food for dinner?"

Jordanna placed her left hand on top of Abby's, which was resting on the steering wheel. "I'm going to go home and go to sleep, okay? I'm going to sleep, and before I do, I'm going to pray to God to . . . I'm going to sleep, okay?" She picked up her bag from the floor of the van and swung her feet out onto the pavement, the only person Abby knew who didn't need to use the running board to disembark. She shut the door and then banged three times on top of Abby's hood, as if it were a signal they'd previously agreed upon.

❧❧ Chapter 15

O N Saturday morning Jordanna met Drew at Snow's Lake. It had been her idea that they come out here, just the two of them. It was an anniversary of sorts, one month since June's car had been glimpsed through the pines on the north side of the lake, as if the fire road she'd traveled for half a mile had suddenly disappointed and she'd blazed a new trail. Jordanna was hoping that this morning in the presence of the water, of what the *Hartford Times* had deemed June's "alleged final resting place," they might bring her close to them. The paper's continued coverage of the "unfolding story" surrounding June's disappearance had included a feature in last Sunday's magazine section, "Heartbreak in Hutchinson: How One Community is Coping with an Uncomfortable Mystery."

The hastily clipped story had been lying on her desk Tuesday morning when she'd come in after her day off. The accompanying full-page photo showed a steely Kent Congdon dwarfed by the deeply shadowed, "picture perfect" Hutchinson Congregational Church. Both of the Prices were quoted, as was Ben Hall, Al Taylor and Fred Rinehardt. Not one of those interviewed had picked up the phone to tell Jordanna, not even Fred Rinehardt. When she asked Gael how she'd heard about the article, she said she hadn't.

Jordanna had found herself incapable of a sequential reading of the story. She picked up the paper, then laid it down, her eyes running to the outside edges of the columns, scouting for names, slowing when she found them, forcing herself to both breathe and comprehend at the same time. Neither Drew nor Bev were directly quoted, and she had no way of knowing if they'd been interviewed. The reporter, Karen Tiernan, had devoted three paragraphs to June's "pastoral counseling at the hands of Rev. Jordanna Nash," without having spoken to Jordanna, apart from that one time after church.

Jordanna had readied herself for a torrent of calls and queries following the publication of the feature, with it's sidebar entitled, "Religion as Therapy, a Dangerous Practice?" But the story had been like the proverbial tree in the uninhabited woods. No one in Hutchinson bothered with that faraway newspaper, and no one who read the big-city paper had, as yet, uncovered a personal stake in the literal details of this case. It was the idea of it, Jordanna told herself, that made it provocative. It was the line drawing of a church pew made over into an analyst's couch that would interest readers, not the now-dead body of the aforementioned young mother or even her still-living, too-tall minister.

"Tell me if this is too difficult," Jordanna said, greeting Drew at the head of the path that led from the parking area to the beach.

He nodded and held up a small wreath made of miniature white roses. "Anna made it, Miles's wife." He slipped the wreath up his forearm as if initiating a magic trick.

"It's beautiful."

"No service," he said, as they began to walk. "It wouldn't be right . . . without everybody else."

Jordanna nodded and watched him look up at the gray sky, then back at the parking lot, everywhere but the water.

"I just thought that we might find some sense of June here, this morning. She's been so lost to us."

Drew turned and looked at her blankly. He was pale, even his red hair had lost its brilliance, like the foliage this season, diminished and foreshortened by so much rain and wind. In the past month Drew's few coarse strands of silver had developed into thick patches of white. She wondered if he was listening to her. She knew there was a distance that needed to be crossed to reach the bereaved. There were wind tunnels, long corridors that sucked up sound and vaporized it. There was the continual loop of film, the before and the after that needed to be replayed. As if one might really achieve editorial control over tragedy. She knew she needed to shout to be heard above the whir of that overworked projector. The din of grief could be deafening. "Thought we might walk for a while." She motioned toward the path.

It had rained for seventeen of the last twenty-eight days, and the water level of the lake was approaching normal after the long drought of the summer. Jordanna wondered at Drew's choice of moccasins in all this wet sand and mud. They walked for a while without talking, Jordanna nearer the water, Drew leaning toward the woods, the parking lot. Occasionally she blew on her hands to keep warm. There had been a frost this morning, and she'd rooted through her closet for the cranberry wool jacket she shared with Daniel in the cold weather months. The jacket was styled like a man's shirt, thickly lined with quilted gray silk, and the heft of it had always been reassuring, as if she were cloaked in an ironclad promise. She'd even swung by the church house on her way here to meet Drew, with the vague but inaccurate sense that she'd brought the jacket there last spring for days when the office never quite warmed. She rubbed the sleeves of her denim baseball jacket and picked up her pace a bit.

"I've been reading up on suicide," Drew said after a while. The sentence struck her as unbearably sad with its implication of preparation, like reading a Baedeker before a planned trip. "You know much about suicide?" he said.

"A bit."

"Teenagers seem to be the most common victims. Most of the stuff you read is about that age, that or the Kevorkian kind of suicides."

Jordanna nodded.

"In one of the books I've been reading, they interviewed this one guy, failed attempt. He said he thought all suicides were a kind of euthanasia. Of all things that I've read or that people have said to me, that's the most helpful. Sometimes I try to force myself to think about the worst pain I can imagine. You know, when you're so sick you feel like dying, you actually wish you would die so it could be over."

Jordanna's face was wet with tears. They just came lately, a kind of emotional incontinence. She pulled a handkerchief from the pocket of her jacket and tucked it up under the sunglasses she shouldn't have been wearing. She wondered if Drew loved June more today than he had a month ago. She wondered if his passion for her, even his remembered passion, informed his compassion. Jordanna had been surprised when, during their first meeting together, June had told her that she was married. It wasn't that she was unattractive, but there was a flatness to her; her body, her face, her spirit were without curve or hollow, interest or embrace. She had tried to imagine this husband June referred to. She wondered now about the intensity of Drew's feelings for his wife. How wholly un-Christian for her to presume that love was different from one person to the next, that her passion for Daniel had been in any way greater than Drew's for June.

"I didn't do it when I should've, though," Drew said.

They stopped as they crossed an egress for one of the fire roads. Drew sat down on the remnants of an old charcoal grill. "When she needed me to walk in her shoes . . . it wasn't that I blew her off, I just . . . nobody likes to set themselves a problem they can't fix, or at least figure out. And the way she would get . . . depression, I guess . . . there was no getting in there and organizing or fixing it. It was like this fog, this thick fog."

Jordanna had to shove her hands into the side pockets of her baseball jacket to keep from touching Drew, from stroking that purity of feeling, the uncompromised truth of him. June would have fared far better had she opened up to her husband rather than her minister.

"The weird thing is, now I know. She was so upset about losing Eve. My dad died when I was eighteen, so it's not like I didn't understand. I don't know, maybe the sting of it, maybe I'd just forgotten. You don't think you ever will. The intensity of that pain. But Jesus, she's made sure we all get it now, huh?"

Jordanna crouched beside Drew and pulled out her handkerchief again, along with a Percocet, which she popped into the back of her throat and swallowed dry.

"You okay?" Drew asked.

"It's for my back."

He nodded. "I've never liked this lake, not since I was fourteen. A kid we all knew dove in from one of the lifeguard chairs one night, broke his neck and drowned. I've never felt easy here. The bottom must be filled with dead bodies. In this book, a psychiatrist says that the way people kill themselves is important. People who drown themselves, he says, are trying to return to the womb."

Jordanna sprang up from her squat and ran into the woods. She didn't pay attention to whether she was on the path or not. She could feel the blood draining from her face as she hopped stumps and piles of fallen leaves mixed with beer cans and condom wrappers. She was either going to faint or throw up. She hung her head down between her knees. She hadn't eaten today, just that Percocet. She wasn't sure about yesterday. She lowered herself onto a pile of soft moss and bent her head down in an attitude of prayer, supplication. She knew Drew wouldn't come after her, and she was grateful. She was not a woman who inspired the nurturing concern of others. When she was ill or injured, people instinctively left her alone. When she was a child, her mother had ministered to her sicknesses at a respectful remove. "Jord's tough," she woke to hear Daniel say after she'd bled out with Alice and nearly died. "She'll come out on top." She wiped the sweat from above her lip and hugged herself to stop the shivering.

She'd been awakened last night at two by the unfamiliar sound of the furnace rumbling on. And when she'd finally fallen back asleep, she'd dreamt that she was in a cemetery, maybe the one in Hutchinson. She'd stood there under an olive tree, watching for something or someone. She waited hopefully, that's what she remembered most about the dream, an almost luxurious quality to the anticipation. The certainty that something wonderful was about to transpire was as startling as the real sense of lust in an erotic dream. A man appeared very slowly from the other side of a hill. First, only his head emerged, then slowly, his face in increments, like a rising sun. But as he continued to reveal himself, head, then neck, then shoulders, she saw that he had no arms. This poor Jesus of the mind and not the body.

The shivering slowed and she pressed her brow down into the moss. The feeling of the ground rising to meet her was the gentlest touch she'd felt in months. If she were describing this moment to a vulnerable congregant, she would have said, "and then when I most needed to feel God reach out to me, God was there, in that soft protrusion of earth, an herbal baptismal blessing." And at some point she might have actually believed that. But in this moment, without pulpit or robe, when it was just the two of them, her and the Divine, and their well-honed skills for disappointing each other, she was just a woman folded into quarters on the dirty floor of the earth, with no instinct, basic or sacred, for how to proceed.

The splash was close enough, but she didn't think loud enough to have been something as heavy as a body. She stood up and jogged back to the rotted grill where she thought she'd last seen Drew. She turned toward the lake, slid her dark glasses on top of her head and looked across. How far could he have gotten in five, ten minutes? Slowly, she began to inch her eyes counterclockwise around the shore of the lake, in the direction they'd been aimlessly walking. Her heart was pounding, beating wildly, even after she glimpsed the brown sleeve of his coat waving, beckoning her to where he stood, on a rock around the next bend. Trees, some still flocked with russet leaves, obstructed her view of the lake as she moved along the path to where she thought Drew was standing. She jogged, picturing the spot where she expected him to be, even when she could no longer see it. As she got closer, it was apparent that he was crouching, squatting the way kids did when they first learned to dive. She pushed past saplings and climbed over fallen limbs, making her way down to the edge of the water.

"I frisbeed it," he said. "Pretty far, really."

She pulled her feet through the mud at the edge of the shore and stepped up onto smooth gray rock. The small ring of white roses and baby's breath floated about twenty feet out in the lake, as if this white laurel wreath were all that remained of the submerged bride or Grecian goddess below.

"Bev thinks we should have a memorial service pretty soon. She thinks it would be better for the girls."

Jordanna nodded. "What do you think?"

Drew was still hunched on the sloping rock, his fingers tensed on the stone to support himself. "I don't think it matters." He stood and twisted his wedding ring. He looked out at the lake, then without speaking headed through the trees back onto the path. Jordanna followed him, breathing in the musky smell of the fallen wet leaves and warming mud, as they continued moving counterclockwise around the lake.

"My mother found a suicide survivors group. She thinks I should join." Drew didn't bother to turn toward Jordanna as he talked. Instead he pushed ahead, stopping only to toe at an outcropping of mushrooms.

"You might need some time before you're ready. Support groups depend on your sharing your story. But you also need to be capable of hearing someone else's. When you're still so roughed up yourself, it can be very difficult to—"

"Are you in AA?" Drew pulled the cap off the biggest mushroom and brought it up to his nose.

"No," she said. "No." She moved closer to him, ready to knock the toadstool from his hand should he bring it any closer to his lips.

He shrugged. "You said support groups."

"I was thinking mostly about bereavement groups—which is what your mother's suggesting. As painful as your experience is, you've spent time now, a month already, beginning to make it real. But other peoples' stories can be shocking, and, well, there is a time when listening to those stories can be traumatic itself, like putting yourself every week or month in the presence of a new train wreck—"

"That's the give and go of the whole thing, right?" He jettisoned the mushroom cap and they both listened to it tick through the leaves.

"Yes, it is." What was she going to tell him, that she'd gone to a support group meeting once for people who'd suffered neonatal losses, and it had been literally unbearable? Abby had gotten all the information, had driven to Beecham on the first Monday of the month just to bring her to that brightly lit room in that community hospital across the border in New Hampshire. And for weeks after, the weeping porcelain dolls and crucified Virgin Marys of her own continuous-play nightmares began to appear clothed in Sallie's bloodied maternity jeans, awash in floods of Darla's thin blue breast milk, rocking in Pamela's child-size rocker, the sole stick of furniture left in the room that Katherine's mother scrubbed and repainted, never comprehending that even the sensory memory of loss, even death, can be precious to a childless mother. Abby had wanted her to go again the next month, and Jordanna told her no. No. Among those grieving mothers, James would grow up to be nothing more than another dead baby, as unexceptional, as predictable as all the live babies crawling the earth. Talking about losing him reduced him to a baleful plea, as if his graying, cherub's body were the source of her pain, the site of an unhealable wound, an unforgivable injury. No. He was none of those things. He was her boy. Even dead, her greatest joy. Abby had insisted that support was crucial. It's important you know you're not alone, Abby had told her. That's never a problem for me, Jordanna reminded her.

Drew slowed his pace a bit and wrapped his arms around himself.

"June's brothers have been talking to a lawyer. They . . . Kent's pretty angry."

"They hold me responsible, don't they?" Jordanna was walking beside Drew now, close enough to occasionally bump shoulders. She pulled the sleeves of her jacket down over her fingers, even as she considered taking his hand. She wondered if she still had the power to redirect feelings and thoughts by impressing herself on another, by pressing her hand to his.

"Not Bev. She doesn't. She has this big picture."

"And you, Drew?"

"We're all guilty. Kent and even Miles are hung up on the fact that you never told me or Bev you'd given her the name of a shrink, that you should of communicated with us better. Kent thinks there was this crisis and you treated it like a cold."

Jordanna nodded. *Lawyer,* the word worked on her like an awl.

"But, Jesus, I was the husband. Bev was the mother—you were only the minister. We're the family, and we dropped the ball. . . ." He pulled a piece of bark from a white birch. "I'm not sure we're within our rights to find fault with you."

"It's not a matter of rights," Jordanna said. "We're talking about how you feel." They were nearing the parking lot. The sounds of car doors and motors were becoming audible. People walked here in the fall when they didn't know what else to do. It was a place to bring dogs and toddlers and old people who needed fresh air. "When I turn up at the house . . . would you rather I stopped coming around and calling?"

He looked down at his pocket as he reached in for his keys. "I know that Bev appreciates your calls."

Jordanna looked back toward the lake. The wreath was too small, and they were too far now to make it out. She wondered if it had sunk. "You were kind to come, then, today."

He shrugged.

Jordanna moved in toward Drew and took the hand without the car keys and held it in both of hers. "I received June in love, in the love of Christ, each and every week she came to talk to me. I just want you to know that. If that love was not enough for her then, I know beyond a shadow of a doubt that it is everything to her now. Everything."

Drew nodded, gently pulled his hand away and turned toward his car. Jordanna stayed where she was at the edge of the lot, willing him to turn around, praying that this would not be the end of the conversation.

"This isn't about religion." He turned just before reaching his car and shouted to her from forty feet away. "You make it sound like she died because she didn't believe in God. Like believing in God is the only thing anyone has to do, and presto, all problems solved. God has nothing to do with this. She was in agony, and you were throwing little God sugar pills at her. You rely on God to fix everything—that was the whole problem, wasn't it? Instead of intervening the way a professional would have—you just trusted in God. 'Let go, let God.' Where was *your* responsibility? Where was your compassion—real compassion, like when one person sees another one who's hurt and risks something, anything, even everything, to save that person? This was all some kind of—"

Jordanna had been moving toward him as he shouted at her. By the time she held up her right hand to halt him, she was close enough to notice a tiny twitch under his mustache. People who'd at first only been stealing glimpses of them now seemed to have ceased slamming trunks and unfolding strollers so they could stare.

"You're very angry," she said without any inflection. Then she turned her back on him and walked to her car.

SHE stopped at a K mart outside Waterbury and bought a toothbrush and some underwear, a soda and a pack of cigarettes. She walked to an outdoor pay phone, lit a cigarette and dialed Gael's home number. Gael's boyfriend answered, and without making conversation, she told him that she had been called out of town suddenly, and that Gael should contact Fred Rinehardt or Seth Hardesty, the Divinity School intern, and let them know that one of them would be leading the service tomorrow. She got back onto the highway heading east, wondering how far she would have to drive before she convinced herself that her life was something other than a continual descent, with the only potential turnout her ministry. She'd been going along through losing her babies, and now watching from a distance as her marriage expired, and she'd thought, Okay, so this is just where God wants me, in church, focused on the congregants, that's what my life is about. But now what was the message God was sending? That she wasn't meant to work with people at all? She was hazardous? A peril to others? "A spiritual Typhoid Mary," she said out loud in the car. She would tell that one to Abby when she saw her. Abby would laugh, because Abby loved her. That was it. Forty-three years and her circle of love wasn't any bigger than it had been at five. Her parents and her sister. By anybody's definition, that was failure.

"*Failure?* As long as you characterize what happened in those terms, you will have difficulty going forward." That's what her mentor, Chip Solloway, had told her three years ago. "It's not and never has been about your personal success," she said now, mimicking his Brahmin vowels. She pushed in the lighter and pulled out another Marlboro from the pack on the passenger seat. "Cancer sticks," June had called them one time during their endless discussions of "why." Jordanna had encouraged her to rephrase the question. "If we can move from 'why me' to 'what does it mean,' then our potential for insight, wisdom, blessing, knows no bounds." June had stared without affect at the floor and said, "But I'm not asking 'why *me*,' I'm asking 'why *her*.' When you're not the one dying, you have the . . . luxury to be all accepting, maybe. But what about the person in all that pain?"

Jordanna slowly tapped her cigarette against the nearly full car ashtray. She couldn't remember what she had said to that. She had spent a lot of time—whole, immobile hours, trying to comprehend what it felt like to James and Alice to die. She'd driven with Daniel through a late spring snowstorm to keep an appointment she'd made with a fetal medicine specialist at Harvard on the outside chance he might have the guts and the imagination to answer that question. Afterward, walking through the slush to the parking garage, she'd said to Daniel, "When ministers fudge like that, people call them facile, dispensers of pap. But when doctors say that same kind of stuff, everyone thinks they're only human, and aren't they admirable, humbled in the face of the unknown."

"What good's science," she said now, shouting at the windshield, "if you can't get the fucking answers to the questions about the body? Simple questions—does it hurt to get strangled by your own umbilical cord? Straightforward." After Alice had died, and she was still in the hospital recovering from having lost her uterus, a resident stopped in one night to dutifully check on her stitches. Her voice still raspy from having been intubated, Jordanna had whispered the question to the young woman. The resident had kept writing in the chart, looking down at the lined paper with the hospital insignia faintly bleeding through. "I'd imagine it's similar to drowning," she'd said.

She stopped at a rest area outside of Worcester and emptied her ashtray and got some coffee. She dialed information for the church house at Concord Congregational Church. It was a little after two, and Reverend Solloway picked up the phone.

"Very good, Jordanna. Very good. I am absolutely never here on a Saturday, but I'm preaching tomorrow and I wanted to tidy up one part of the—"

"I had a feeling I'd catch you there."

"You always do . . . have those feelings."

She sighed. "How far is Grafton from Concord?"

"Is this a quiz?"

She laughed. "No, I'm at a rest stop near Grafton, I think."

There was a long silence. "Of course," she continued, "you probably have a wedding today or something. The only reason I'm not doing one is that someone brought in an ordained uncle to marry a—"

"Shall I come and get you, dear?" he said.

She waited for a wailing child to be carried out of earshot. "No, the car's fine, actually for once in my life—"

"I didn't suspect the car, Jordanna."

"You're good," she said.

"I know you."

"Yeah, but can you stand me?" She laughed, and watched a man dump his car ashtray at the edge of the parking area.

"You're about fifty-five minutes from my house."

"You and Helen probably—"

"Do you have a pen?"

SHE had been to Chip's house in D.C., and the one in Deep River, but since he'd become semiretired and moved back to his old church where his title was minister emeritus, she hadn't visited him. He had come to see her in Maine often. The first time was at the hospital in Portland. She'd been in the maternity ward for forty-eight hours waiting to deliver James, who had died in utero some days before. He had just stopped moving, and she hadn't realized, hadn't been paying attention. It was her last scheduled appointment, and she and the midwife were talking about stuffing pumpkins with rice and nuts and baking them whole. Thanksgiving was a week away. And then she noticed that the midwife stopped talking and looked out the window as she moved the Doppler thick with jelly around the impressive acreage of Jordanna's abdomen, like a toy mouse roaming a make-believe countryside. But there was nothing. No sound. It was as if the great engine inside had cut out. In that moment Jordanna knew something she wasn't even conscious of knowing. She felt the baby slip down—sink, really, like her heart into the birth canal.

The next morning she and Daniel went to Portland Medical Center for her to be induced. It was Daniel who called Chip. It was Daniel who called everyone. But Chip they allowed into the room. He came toward the end of the second day. She watched the Pitocin drip into her arm and waited for the contractions she'd been hearing about for half her life to finally begin. Daniel rolled around on the little stool that was meant for the doctors, just the right height for them to reach in with their hands where they needed to. Chip loomed above them both, pacing the length of the hospital bed until Jordanna told him it was making her sick, all that moving. He talked for a while, repeated something from a eulogy William Sloane Coffin wrote for his own son. Jordanna only half listened. And then he asked Daniel if it would be all right if they prayed together. Chip placed his long cool fingers on Jordanna's rigid abdomen, and before he could say anything he began to cry. Jordanna looked at Daniel first and he nodded to her, as if to say he would handle this. Jordanna had never seen Chip cry, not when he'd done the funeral of a colleague, a Divinity School professor who'd been murdered, not when he talked of his own work in the slums of Paraguay. She registered Chip's loss of control the same way she'd acknowledged the bawling of the newborn baby in the room just beyond her head, followed by the distinct pop of a champagne cork. She was strangely unmoved. It was as if she were in the audience of an archetypal pageant. From her perch in the last crumbling row of the Colosseum, she realized that no act of will or faith on her part, no sentiment or affect, could ever alter the imperative of the grim plot. She was unable to comfort him. He kept his right hand on her stomach while he reached into his camel hair blazer for a handkerchief. He averted his face and blew his nose, and there was a moment when she caught a glimpse of her loss, as if sorrow could, like a specter, appear in human form.

Chip prayed over her uterus, over the baby that they had only just learned was a boy. Then he motioned for Daniel to stretch out his hands from the other side of the bed, and Chip and Daniel locked hands and held them over Jordanna's belly, a canopy. And the prayer had been a reading from Jeremiah and then the Twenty-third Psalm. And then, without segue, he walked to the head of Jordanna's bed and placed his hands on the top of her head as she had seen him do countless times, as if to make a benediction. But instead he leaned down and murmured. She wondered if she was meant to hear what he said, or if this was between him and God, merely by way of her flesh. Then he touched his right thumb to Jordanna's lips and made the sign of the cross on her forehead up at her hairline.

He walked around the bed to where Daniel had rolled in his stool and, without asking permission now, wrapped his steeplelike fingers around Daniel's head and held them there for what seemed to Jordanna a very long time. When he was through, he bowed his head slowly and placed a kiss on Daniel's scalp.

SHE slowed to read the numbers on the townhouse units and thought how Chip had always known to pray over a person's head, as if half the pain or illness and even the dying were happening there, as well as in the heart or lungs or liver. Besides the doctors and nurses, Chip had been the only one to see James. Jordanna had called him in about twenty minutes after she had delivered. She wanted Chip to baptize the baby. "Normally we'd wait a month or three or six to have a baptism," she had told the nurse as if she were still the authority, the teacher. For the two days that Jordanna had been in labor, Daniel had been anxious about what the baby would look like. With each shift change, a new nurse had come in and made it a point to talk about the importance of seeing and touching the baby once he was delivered.

She was told she had done a great job. Three pushes and James had emerged into a room where the light had been dimmed, and where no one was talking. For forty-eight hours she had been listening to the noises in the rooms around her. She knew that the advent of a new baby was met with laughter and screams, not silence. The room was quiet, except for the clink of metal tools, the thwack of bloody pads tossed into a bucket. "Is this what would normally happen? Would you be doing this anyway? In a regular delivery . . ." She needed to know, as she reminded them, "I've never done this before."

They held him up first thing for her, the resident reaching over, too quickly, to close his one open blue eye, as if he were a corpse.

They wrapped him in a baby blanket, and put the blue and white newborn hospital hat on him, just like a regular baby, and then they handed him to her. In the months of nights that followed that one, awake with regret about never having looked into his eyes, she would read, among other things, that the startling red color of his lips, the berry red of those bowed lips, was a hallmark of a dead baby. In the initial moments of their only meeting, she had secretly believed that the intensity of color in his lips was a sign of vibrancy and vitality. "Be careful with him," the nurse had instructed her and Daniel. She laid him down on the bed in front of her, and she and Daniel unswaddled him, needing to look at every little part that they would never see again.

"He's not ours to keep," she said to Daniel, the tears running down her face and dripping onto the baby. Daniel reached with his forefinger to wipe Jordanna's tears from the baby's cheeks and a nurse cautioned them to be careful. "The skin will flake and peel. Limbs might not hang together . . ." she went on, as Jordanna gripped a tiny ankle and raised it to look at the baby's bottom, the way she'd seen her sister do with her nephews countless times on the changing table. Jordanna nodded to the nurse. Bad enough she had borne him dead, now she might rip him. Daniel swaddled him again, like a package, a gift, and she watched as her husband brought the baby to his chest and rolled with him on that little stool. They had picked a name. They'd been ready for the only two possibilities they thought there were—boy or girl—not dead or alive. Daniel had asked her if she wanted to save the name, save it for the next boy, one they could call to from another room. No, of course not, she told him. "It's his name. It's all he has." And so they asked Chip back into the room, and Daniel said, "Fine." She knew that in that moment she could have asked her husband to become a Hare Krishna and he would have said, "Fine."

Chip sat down at the foot of the bed and watched her hold the baby. As he walked to the sink to wash his hands, Daniel said, "Maybe his mother should baptize him." Chip turned off the water.

He nodded. He reached into his pants pocket and pulled out a little vial, the kind used for blood, and he handed it to Jordanna. She lay the baby in her left arm, the way she'd seen other mothers do when they were about to nurse. "By what name do we baptize this baby?" she said, looking at Daniel.

"By the name of James Nash Greene."

"James Nash Greene, I baptize you in the name of the father . . ." She looked up and Chip took her palm as if he were doing a reading and sprinkled some of the holy water in her hand. She dripped the water onto the baby's forehead. "And the son . . ." She spread the water with her thumb horizontally. "And the Holy Spirit." She dragged the drop of holy water downward, completing the sign of the cross. "Amen." She lowered her face to the baby, her hair spilling all around him, and kissed the top of his covered head the way she'd done to the hundreds of babies she'd baptized in a decade of ministering.

THE pale yellow garage was topped with a brass 62. She pulled into the empty driveway and flapped her clothes a little when she got out of the car, trying to disperse the smoke smell. She slowly rolled her shoulders forward, incrementally curling herself to relieve the habitual, though tolerable pain in her lower back. As soon as she slammed the car door, she heard Chip clear his throat. He was somewhere behind the house.

"Around to the left, I'm on the deck."

"Stentorian," Daniel had said about his voice, the first time he'd met him. He taught, among other things "The Principles and Practice of Preaching," and Jordanna remembered her first class with him, where he preached from Jonathan Edwards's *Sinners in the Hands of an Angry God*. "The sound of him reading the class list could make you quake," she remembered a fellow student saying. But it was precisely the thunderous grandeur of his speech that made her seek him out as her advisor.

Jordanna followed the weathered wood walkway around the side of the house. Each of the townhouses was looped with one, as if eventually all the occupants would roll in and out in wheelchairs. Chip was sitting, as always, with his back erect, in a frayed director's chair. As she approached, his long narrow face cracked open and widened in a dozen places. "If it isn't Reverend Nash," he said, not moving to stand, but rather simply reaching up his long thin arms, as she'd seen him do so many times with the offering, willing her to place her face in his hands, a gift given and received all in one gesture.

He kissed her wetly on the forehead. "You're hot," he pronounced, and patted a newer canvasback chair beside him.

"Where's Helen?" she asked.

"She's giving a seminar in town. All-day affair—'Hip, Hip, Hypnosis,' you know."

She laughed.

"You need this." He reached to his right, where there was a little tea trolley with a glass pitcher of ice water and a stack of paper cups. He handed her a Dixie cup filled with water.

"Lovely," Jordanna said, glancing around at the backyard for the first time. The lot was perfectly square and flat. The dark green grass, striped slightly, as if someone had just run a vacuum across, was bordered on all sides by a fence of rigid hemlocks.

"God's waiting room," Chip said, reaching to tug ineffectually at a sagging navy sock.

Jordanna sat down and there was a long silence in which he stared at her unfocused smile, and she tried to think how to begin. She looked down into the now-empty paper cup. "I've come for some career counseling. I'm toying with the idea of leaving. Leaving this call, and doing something . . . something more concrete, less people involvement. Maybe something with Christi Publishing or Broadcasting—something legitimate." This always happened in Chip's presence, she began talking like him, the pause for effect, the precise enunciation, the diction, even. "You know, with spirituality on the rise, the scores of books—"

"Publishing," he said, nodding. "Something literary where your religious training might be put to good use?"

"Exactly," she said, as if they were playing a guessing game.

He set about staring at her again, and this time she stared right back for as long as she could. She nodded now, acknowledging his power. "Okay." She folded the empty cup in half and flattened it. "Have you ever done a memorial service when the body hadn't been . . . recovered?"

He nodded.

Of course, it had been an ignorant question. He'd been a pulpit minister during the middle years of Vietnam. "For a civilian," she added now.

"Yes, once."

She placed the ruined cup on the tea trolley and waited.

"It was quite difficult. The service was for a young man, a boy, really. This was, oh, I'd guess, '69 or '70, and this young man had disappeared while hitchhiking on the New England Thruway. About five years after his disappearance, his parents decided to have a memorial service on his birthday."

She nodded and licked a piece of wax that had adhered to her lip. "My situation . . . this young woman, three small children—under five . . . well, it seems she committed suicide and has somehow made her body disappear. And in the place where she used to be . . . is this enormous, enormous crater of pain and anger."

He reached down for another swipe at his sock. "Was she a friend of yours, Jordanna?"

She let out a low laugh. "She should have been. Had I been doing my job. No, she was a . . . customer. A dissatisfied customer, let's say."

"Ah," he said, loudly enough to startle a squirrel who'd been scaling the ivy along the chimney.

"I'd been counseling her for nearly four months, and then she just . . . apparently, she killed herself."

"I'm sorry," he said.

She nodded and swung her legs under the chair. The pain in her back was needling past tolerable. Angling her body, attempting to brace her back against the laxness of the cloth, caused the chair's little dark wood legs to groan. She tilted her head back and ran her hands across the plaits of her braid, then she snapped up and looked directly at him. "I have been counseling congregants for nearly fourteen years. In the past eight, I'd say, it has been the lion's share of my business, you know. I mean, that's the way the ministry is going. And I'm good at it. I mean, if I weren't good at it, why would the line outside my door be getting longer and longer, right? I think people find me easy to talk to. I'm not judgmental. And unlike lay counselors, I actually give something back. I offer a way for people to proceed with hope and love, and maybe faith."

Chip nodded and folded his tapered fingers in his lap.

"I've had everything walk through my door. Everything. All kinds of abuse, elder abuse, drug abuse, incest. Theft. Every humiliation possible on this planet. And so this woman comes to me, a case of grief. That's what it seems. Her only sister has died of breast cancer. There are other siblings, but this sister is her soulmate, and she's young. They're both young. And she just cannot seem to lick this grief. Hell, this should be my specialty. This is a subject I know. I can talk from ample experience. It won't be like the advice I offer on . . . child-rearing or gambling. Grief is my language. 'My lyre is turned to mourning, and my pipe to the voice of those who weep.'"

She shook her head and looked out on the doormat of a backyard. "I really made a hash of it. And I knew it. That's the thing. From about the third time I met with her, I knew. . . . I began talking to my sister, trying to get some pro psychology advice, beause I sensed that we should have been humming and clicking at a different pace. And way back then, my sister offered that maybe this congregant of mine needed professional help. That it sounded like a clinical depression. That maybe she needed medication. And that maybe spiritual advice, alone, would not be enough. And I balked at that. You know, it was a challenge. My faith has gotten me here—has gotten me through . . . so I know that faith is capable of anything, of everything.

I work from that, Chip. You know that about me. That this is the place where I begin each day. Faith brought me here. Faith delivers us. God saw me through the worst pain. God will see you through—"
She realized that as she'd been talking, she'd been swinging her legs, and she'd accidentally kicked Chip in the shin.

She hopped out of her chair and began rubbing his leg. She slid his khaki trousers up to his knee and examined his papery white skin.

"Jordanna," he admonished, motioning for her to stand.

She walked toward the screen door that led to the kitchen, then turned. "I couldn't move her. Literally, she was unaffected, nearly inanimate. I have had congregants who have lusted after me and those who have loathed me, to the point of threat—but I have never encountered anyone, I don't think, upon whom I had no effect. My words, *the Word*—nothing moved her—not prayer, not meditation, not ritual, not exhortation. And I did, you know, finally I did suggest she consult a psychiatrist. I got a name of someone for her to see. Maybe I waited too long. I don't know. I gave her the name and nothing. She didn't do anything. I asked, week after week. Sometimes we met twice a week. I mean, I did not abandon this woman in her pain. I did not."

Jordanna was pacing the deck, planting her heavy-soled boots with such determination that the small pressure-treated structure shook with each footfall. She was pleading her case in front of the one mortal judge whose opinion truly mattered to her. It would be nothing like this in a real courtroom, if it ever came to that. There, her responses would be cut off at the knees, the discourse scripted to fit the limits of a two-dimensional story. "Now the family says I should have called them in. Well . . ." She swung her right arm into the air. She couldn't bring herself to say the word *lawyer* in the presence of the pastor she so admired. "You know, now we are into all this confidentiality . . . my responsibility . . ." She blew through her mouth as if her lungs were filled to bursting with something that needed to be expelled.

She shook her head and sighed again. "As soon as I mentioned that she might consider going to a psychiatrist, she felt I had rejected her. And so this is what we began to focus on—how I, and of course, here, I was a stand-in for God, the God who let her sister die, the God who had not consoled her, either—how I had let her down. She told me that I was trying to pawn her off." When Jordanna finally looked up, she saw that Chip was steadying the water pitcher with one hand. With each of her heavy steps, the tea table was jumping.

"Poor Jordanna," he said now, "poor Jordanna." He pronounced her name with each syllable distinct from the next, as if he were examining an artifact. She remembered going to his office once to talk with him about a paper. He'd looked down at her name on the top of her essay and had said, "Ahhh, Jordanna. Descending." And she'd thought he was referring to her academic standing in his course until he clarified. "Jordanna . . . Hebrew for 'descending.'"

"When did all this happen?" he asked looking up at her leaning against the side of the house.

"Today," she said, and tried to smile. He was the one who had first introduced her to the concept of the eternal now. "I'd been counseling her since about Easter. She disappeared at the end of August. The suicide notes were found about four weeks ago. I was supposed to go . . . I should be visiting Daniel in Australia right now."

He stared at her and she released as much as she could to him without speaking.

"This is not an easy time of year for you, either," he said softly.

She had written to him last fall that the sound of leaves under her car tires, the great piles of gourds and squashes at the entrance to the market, anything burnt orange or russet-colored pried at the wound. "A few weeks for Alice, a few more after that for James."

"Three years since Alice. James would have gone to kindergarten this year. Thank you, for remembering."

"The weeks before an anniversary can be like running a gauntlet, don't you think?"

She stared at him.

"Just take into account the additional strain of memory right now."

"No additional strain needed for this to be—"

He held up his right hand, the second and third fingers together, like Giotto's Christ riding into Jerusalem on a donkey. "I am not suggesting that the suicide of a congregant isn't the stuff of crisis."

"Is that what I sound like, like I'm having a 'crisis'?"

He smiled and she told herself that she would not accept his patronizing. "Does it have to be a crisis situation for me to come and talk with you, as I pass by?" She had forgotten exactly where she had told him she was going. Maine, she thought she'd said, to Beecham, to her old church.

"It's unlike you to be defensive."

"And unlike you to be judgmental," she shot back.

"Not true," he said. "I'm extremely judgmental. I'm also extremely tactful." He winked, and again she was irked at his attitude, as if he knew something she didn't, had been somewhere she hadn't, as if her life were somehow not as integral as his own.

"If I excuse myself for a moment, you won't leave, will you?"

"Of course not."

He nodded and smiled a genuine smile at her. She watched as he reached around the tea cart and gripped the gray rubber handle of a cane. It was not the kind of elegant walking stick she might have imagined him affecting in his older age. The metal shaft of the cane branched into three rubber feet. She stood and stared, making no move to help him as he began the slow process of lifting himself from the deck chair.

"We haven't spoken in a while," he said, not looking at her, his voice preoccupied with the strain of standing.

"No, we haven't," she said. "What's going on, Chip?"

"Not certain yet," he said, now standing. "I've been having some weakness in my left leg for a while now. Still undergoing tests. Not sure just yet."

"I'm sorry."

He waved away her concern. "Jordanna, do you know how old I am?"

She had always guessed that he was in his mid-fifties when they'd first met seventeen, eighteen years before. "Sixties," she said.

"I'll be seventy-nine in January. I'm entitled to some dry rot."

She moved to slide open the screen door for him, and he said, "I'm fine, just fine, right here. As long as I'm not required to dance . . ."

"You know me, Chip. I stormed in and set to unburdening myself. We don't usually do pleasantries, the two of us—how are you, fine, how are you. I've always felt my time with you is too precious—"

"It's not a concern, my dear," he said.

"I might have noticed the cane, though. I might have . . . This is precisely what my sister finds fault with . . . this . . ."

"You hold that thought," he said, and he moved his eyes quickly, indicating some urgency. "I'll be right . . ." his voice trailed off as he moved through the unlit kitchen and beyond to where she could no longer see him.

She walked the length of the deck, pounding back and forth, her energy causing a domino effect. As she paced, the weathered planks shook the tea cart, which created waves in the blue and green glass water pitcher on top of the cart, a biosphere with its own tidal pull. She peered back through the slider into the kitchen. She knew Chip wouldn't be hurt by her sin of omission, her "myopia," as her sister called it. People like Mary Jane Krull, Bev Congdon, her brother-in-law, even her husband, none of them went through life looking to be wronged. They were strong people who expected nothing, who experienced her for what she had to offer, not what she lacked. But Abby and June, they made themselves so available to hurt. They lay down in the middle of the road, and then accused her of a hit and run, never comprehending that if they'd gotten up, raised themselves up, she would have seen them, and would have stopped and bundled them into her car. No, she knew Chip wouldn't take offense that she hadn't spotted the cane. He would still love her and would know that she loved him. He would know that her concern for his health, her fear of losing him to infirmity or death, was no less real simply because she hadn't made it visible. He would take it on faith that his pain mattered to her. He didn't need continual proof. Her failure had been in misreading June. June had needed proof. Her faith in everything, in anything, had been flimsy, as bent and bowed as she was; what she had sought from Jordanna was proof.

Jordanna heard the rubber bottoms of the cane squeak on the linoleum in the kitchen. She slid open the screen door and stared as he lowered the cane down the one step, poking at the deck as if he were testing the thickness of the ice on a skating pond.

"You know, Chip, I use you all the time. I rip you off—" She released her grip on the screen door just as his left foot, the bad leg, failed to clear the slider's track, and he came lurching forward. She caught him with her arms and her left hip, almost as if they'd planned it.

"Forgive me, forgive me," he muttered, as he tried to right himself. He'd dropped the cane, and he was using Jordanna's arms to fully straighten himself. "Have I hurt you, dear? I'm so sorry. Let's have a look. . . ."

"I'm glad I was here."

"Providential," he said.

She saw the sweat on his scalp bead up beneath the sparse wisps of steel-colored hair. She knelt down for the cane and handed it to him. "You just tripped," she said, her voice rising, a plea for reassurance embedded in the dismissal.

"The leg just buckles without warning. Difficult to plan."

She walked him to the chair. He slipped his hands into his pants pocket, unfolded a white linen handkerchief and wiped his brow.

"I should probably go. You look like you could use a rest."

"That bad, huh?"

"I've interrupted your perfectly peaceful Saturday. It seems I still need mentoring."

"Thank goodness." He patted the chair next to him. "You didn't kill her, you know?"

Jordanna jerked her head toward him.

"Well, let's start there, shall we? Then we can move on to why you want to become the checkout girl at the Stop and Shop, all right? Firstly—and you really should have done this weeks ago—what did I always say . . . if you are confronted with a problem, you research it. You go back and you see what others have done in similar situations, for there have always been other pastors who've faced these problems. Much as we like to believe that we are singular, we are not. In this case, and really, I must say I'm quite disappointed . . . you need to reread *Mourning and Melancholia,* then get yourself Durkheim and Alvarez, for a start. You are so quick to abandon the intellectual for the emotional. It won't do."

"What makes you think I haven't read about suicide?"

"Don't make me answer that, dear. You need to place yourself in this event. You are now a victim of this woman's suicide as certainly as if there had been a murder and you, too, had been wounded. You can help no one else without understanding some of your own psychological responses to this trauma. Secondly, you must think long and hard about the conscious or unconscious associations you are making with this trauma and some of the others in your life." He nodded toward her. "Everything is connected psychologically, as well as spiritually. And this thinking cannot be done in the five minutes between the prenuptial counseling and the meeting with the new Sunday school teachers. I am talking about the kind of rumination, introspection, meditation and prayer that can only happen in complete removal from the rest of life. Preferably in silence. No one would benefit more from silence. You need to separate yourself from the congregation and regroup. You are free to tell yourself that this is as much for them as it is for you—"

"Are you done?" she said, interrupting him. "You talk to me like I'm still twenty-six, like I've learned nothing, as if I haven't evolved spiritually—"

"Not at all. But no one in his right mind is ever tough with you, and passionate rigor is precisely the kind of unyielding stripe to which you respond." He turned his wrist and looked at the time. "I would like you to stay here tonight. You'll find at least two of the three books you need to read inside in the den. I also think that you need to talk to Helen and me about Daniel. Actually, you are free to stay here for the next week. Helen and I are going to California Monday morning. I'm giving a talk at UC Davis, and we're going to visit Robert and his wife. If nothing else, Jordanna, your congregation needs to see you draw into yourself. Take time for intensive prayer and meditation. Model for them the way through this crisis."

"By abandoning them?"

"A few weekdays does not abandonment make. Do you have someone lined up for tomorrow?"

She nodded. "I have a Divinity School student."

"How just," he said.

She didn't smile. She wasn't listening to him anymore. There were birds cawing, and wind chimes somewhere, low Asian-sounding tones, and very faintly an aria from a few units away. She looked down at her boots and across the deck floor at Chip's slipping socks and his undependable legs, and she knew that the instinct that had driven her here, that need for communion, was not enough to connect her in this moment to him or to anyone. God had cut her loose. "I need . . ." She began, and then stopped. She needed everything. She was starving, voraciously hungry and tired and thirsty, paralyzed and frenetic. She was still, as still as her babies, and she was jumping out of her skin. "I need you to pray over me," she said, sliding her palms up and down her arms.

Chip inched forward in his chair, one hand on the wooden armrest, the other on that tea cart, in order to raise himself.

"No, don't get up," she said, moving toward him.

She should have realized he would not pray for her without touching her. He would try to bridge this gap, cross the distance.

"Chip, please—" As she went to grip his hands, insisting that he stay seated, one side of his face went slack, as if the muscles had been cut.

She heard the crash of the glass pitcher as it struck the deck railing. Then the loud splash of water. And then the slip and slide of

Chip's long, uncertain body as it came to rest at her feet. His eyes were open, and he nodded at her.

She knelt and pulled at the cuff of her jacket, pressing it against his bleeding nose and lip. He must have hit the table on the way down. The blood was thin and it quickly soaked her sleeve. She looked in his hair and along his back. She cradled his neck and lifted his head into her lap. She placed her other hand on the top of his forehead. The pitcher had fallen on the far side of the table and the blue and green glass had mostly shattered away from him.

"It's all right," he murmured. She nodded and began reciting from Lamentations 3:22: "The steadfast love of the Lord never ceases, his mercies never come to an end. . . ." She brushed his nearly bare scalp. His eyes had been fixed on her, but now they seemed to be straining for something. She followed his gaze upward, tilting her head back, and when she looked down at him again, his eyes had rolled beyond the sky.

She pinched his cheek and leaned over him, putting her mouth on his, yelling his own name into his mouth, "Chip, Chip," as if calling him from inside. She didn't want to lay his head down. There was so much blood coming from his nose, she was afraid he would choke. She closed her eyes and yelled, first his name and then simply, "Help! Help! Somebody! Oh, God, help me!"

❧ Chapter 16

ABBY was planting bulbs and Jim was raking when the white station wagon bearing the Deerfield Taxi logo turned into their driveway. It was nearly six and still light out, the last weekend of autumn before they'd have to change the clocks and the darkness would set in. Abby had just sent Brendan inside to start making supper for the kids. He'd placed a note on the kitchen table when he woke up stating that he was observing "silent Saturday." He wasn't going to talk, though if you had to, you could talk to him. Writing was preferable. To his father's first query, he'd scribbled on a pad, "I'm trying to separate from the material world today." Abby had rolled her eyes and said he still had to babysit tonight. Did he think he could get Gabe to go to bed without talking to him? She and Jim were supposed to be in Ridgely by seven-thirty for a surprise party for one of the attorneys Jim worked with. When she saw the cab, Abby's first instinct was hopeful, that something, someone had come to deliver her from having to attend what she knew would be a dreadful affair. And even after she realized the mysterious stranger was Daniel, she allowed herself the ten-second fantasy that Daniel was finally here to help.

By the time the boys were done opening the gifts he'd brought, whatever primitive optimism she'd felt was replaced with cultivated dread. He'd been elaborate with the presents. A carving of Tangaroa, a Maori ocean god, for Michael, and a manly-looking coral necklace for Christopher. Gabe got a felt pirate's hat, and Brendan an audiotape. "It's a recording of a karakia," Daniel said to the nodding Brendan. "It's an incantation to the forest god Tane-mahuta, for the felling of a tree to build a canoe. The chant requests Tane-mahuta to give up one of his 'children' to be used by the humans."

Before Daniel told them that he had come back to ask Jordanna for a divorce, that there was indeed someone else, someone he wanted to marry, he talked and talked. About the questionable dating of some Polynesian artifacts they were finding and the implications then for rewriting the history of the arrival of the Maori in New Zealand. As Abby dug at the soil beneath her fingernails and watched the dirt and vermiculite circle around the drain, she half listened to some long, supposedly humorous story about a graduate student, an accident, the trip to Rotorua. . . . As she pulled out the glasses and opened a box of crackers, she heard "Manukau" and "Waikato" and then, "Ellen." She got down the cheese board and planned what she would tell her sister. He looked thin, she would say, but he always looked thin. Grayer, definitely. Taller. She wouldn't say this to Jordanna, though. Without her by his side, he really did look taller. He was louder, somehow, funnier.

"This trip came about suddenly." Daniel leaned back into the sofa and rested the base of his wine glass on the knob of his knee, the bony outline visible under his khakis. "Seems there's a tenure vote that's come up, potentially divisive, some kind of shakedown in the department. I promised I'd fly back. We're going up to Orono tomorrow morning. I thought I'd try to see Jordanna today."

Abby could feel Jim look over at her on the *we,* but she didn't return the glance. She pulled her legs up under her in the overstuffed chair.

"Is she on retreat? I called at around noon from the airport. I had the cab go by her house first. I called over to the church office."

Abby shrugged. She hadn't seen her sister in over a week. "Have you guys talked to each other recently?"

Daniel nodded.

"She's got a lot on her plate right now," Abby said.

"She always does, doesn't she?" Daniel said, with genuine fondness in his voice. "She didn't go up to the Cape, did she?"

"I don't know. I could call my parents," Abby said, reaching for the wine bottle.

"I meant to the cemetery. She's not back to that again, is she, Abby?"

"I wouldn't know. She's been quite busy with a number of people in the church. There've been a lot of funerals lately. . . . She's trying to plan a spring trip with the youth group. They're trying to revive the lay-led Bible study up at the prison—"

"Who's the 'we' who's going with you up to Maine?" Jim cut right through her babbling.

"The young woman I was telling you about before, Ellen McNamara, a graduate student on the dig with me—I think there might be an opening for her for next fall. We . . . actually, we've been talking about her coming back to the States with me in June."

Abby stood up without excusing herself and walked out of the living room into the kitchen. "You fucking asshole, you fucking, fucking shithead." She had waited until she was in the pantry. She pulled the door closed behind her and left the light off. She stepped up onto the footstool and rested her head on the empty lip of the shelf with the flour and the sugar. Her first thought, for which she immediately berated herself as being thoroughly childish, was why did he have to tell her this. It was like watching one scene too many in a movie that was scaring the shit out of you. If only she had shut her eyes, put her fingers in her ears. If only she hadn't been home this afternoon when he'd been so certain they'd be there. Then Jordanna could know first. He'd planned it this way, the prickhead, the manipulative . . . He knew she would do his dirty work for him. He probably thought she was in here right now calling her sister. Their relationship had always been cartoonish to him, some hormone-hyped love-hate thing that he could reduce to a derisive one-liner. What did he know about anything? What did he know about hurting Jordanna, killing her? What did he know about everything that might happen now?

Abby dragged her pinkie through a dusting of flour on the pantry shelf. She had thought that bringing her sister here, keeping her close, would protect her. She had steered her sister toward a good job, one that distracted her from the loss of her maternity and fertility. But this bad shit just kept on happening to Jordanna. Had it always been like that? She tried to think back to a time when her envy of her sister hadn't been mixed up with pity, when Jordanna's pain wasn't as outsize as her frame or her ego.

"You all right?" Jim opened the door to the pantry and reached in for a box of crackers. "He doesn't want us to say anything to the kids or your parents, until Jordanna—"

"Oh, but it was fine for him to come over here and tell me, before he tells his own wife." She stacked a can of artichoke hearts onto a flat tin of smoked oysters, smacking the metal together. "But now it's dawned on him that word might spread in some unseemly fashion. What a first-class prick, really. I mean, he doesn't even seem sad, does he? Or guilty? It's a fait accompli in his mean little mind. I want him gone." From the footstool she was taller than her husband, and the extra height gave her an added power. She spotted the red and green crystals she'd looked for last Christmas when she and the kids were making cookies. "He fucking thinks that I'm going to tell her, doesn't he? What's he going to do, walk in with this little grave digger or whatever the hell they're doing down there and introduce her to Jordanna and say, by the by—"

"Abby." It was Daniel.

Abby looked at her husband, who had been leaning into the little closet, his hand on top of the door. He closed it partway, and she saw by his expression that Daniel was there, just on the other side.

"Abby, I came here because I'm worried about Jordanna. I'm worried about her response. I told you first, hoping you might—"

"Hoping I might, what? Make it easier for you?"

Jim reached in and helped Abby down from the footstool and guided the three of them back to the living room. "I think we need to keep our voices down," Jim said, nodding up toward the staircase.

"Fuck that," Abby said.

"We've been moving toward it being over for a while now. It won't come as a shock—maybe consciously, but not unconsciously. I mean, if she thinks about it, she'll realize that she knew it was coming."

Abby screwed up her face. "What the fuck does that mean?"

Daniel exhaled loudly. "When I got this grant to continue, she never asked me not to, never suggested that she might come along."

"She had just gotten a new job here, a big job."

He nodded. "That was my first indication, when she applied for this job down here—she made it clear. I have tenure in Orono, Abby. She knew what that meant. The two of you cooked up this scheme to bring her down here. You both wrote me out of the picture with that move."

"You're unbelievable, you know that?" Abby stood up and shoved her hands into the pockets of her corduroys. She moved past her show of hospitality arrayed across the coffee table—the wine, the olives, the little votive candles. The room looked foreign, as if the furniture had been rearranged, some trick played on her domestic comfort. She walked to the bay window, then back toward the fireplace. "It's my fault that your marriage is breaking up—is that the deal, here?"

"I'm not saying it was causal—that you were causal. You were prescient. You know how Jordanna thinks she knows things before they happen—that third eye thing, or whatever she claims to have? You suggested she come move here because you *knew*, on some level—"

"You're . . . Why didn't you move with her? That's the sixty-four-million-dollar question. Why didn't you even look into the departments at UConn or Fairfield or Trinity or any of the hundreds of universities down here?"

"You know what, guys, this is not—" Jim began.

"Hey, he's blaming you, too, in case you didn't realize." Abby looked into the unlit fireplace.

Jim shook his head. "You're way off here, Ab, way off."

"Where were you"—Abby pointed at Daniel from across the room—"when I was talking to your wife three, five, seven times a week? Where were you? I talked her back from hell—and what the fuck were you doing?"

"Abby." Jim moved toward her, but didn't touch her.

"Don't turn my support of my sister, my empathy for all that the both of you went through, into a scheme. How dare you. How the fuck do you dare to come into my house and tell me that my, my compassion was what severed your marriage."

"You done?" Daniel was sitting in the middle of the sofa, the good anthropologist, more observer than participant.

The phone was ringing, and she heard one of the boys run and slide along the upstairs hall to answer it.

"I didn't come here to argue with you, Abby. I'm worried about Jordanna—just from our e-mails and the few phone conversations, she seems . . . I don't know, more penetrable than usual. I didn't want to just dump this on her. Really, I wanted your advice."

"Hey, Mom," Christopher yelled from the top of the stairs, "it's JoJo."

The room changed again for Abby. It sharpened, its edges grew more defined, as if a mist had cleared. Jim walked into the kitchen and picked up the phone.

Abby and Daniel stood together in the candlelit living room. Abby went over to the piano and switched on the little music lamp. Daniel pulled out his pipe from his shirt pocket, but he didn't light it. She remembered Jordanna telling her once a long time ago that sometimes when she kissed Daniel, his bottom lip would be hot from the pipe. How could her sister have ended up with so little, so little love?

"Do you think he'll tell her that I'm here?" Daniel said, removing the mouthpiece of the pipe wetly from between his lips.

"Do you want him to?"

"I don't know."

"She's going through a very bad time right now." She hadn't wanted to tell him that—hadn't meant to color her sister as more vulnerable. But now there seemed so little left to lose. "Someone she was counseling—a woman—committed suicide about . . . I don't know, five or six weeks ago. The family is pretty angry. Jordanna had referred the woman to someone else for treatment. Well, anyway, it's something of a mess. The newspapers are covering it. I wouldn't be surprised if it led to some kind of litigation—"

Jim walked back into the room, his face flushed.

"What's the matter?"

"She wants to talk to you," he said, nodding toward Abby. "She's outside of Boston. She's in the lobby of a hospital. Chip Solloway's had a stroke or something. She was visiting him at his house. . . ."

Abby began walking toward the phone, and then came back. "Did you tell her Daniel was here?"

"Christopher did, when he first picked up the phone."

"Did she ask why?"

"I said he came looking for her. . . ."

Abby looked at the phone receiver resting in the drying rack. She picked it up. Through the window above the sink she could just pick out the piles of leaves that they had raked earlier, large mounds scattered across the lawn, like some otherworldly distress signal.

"Abby?" Jordanna's voice sounded heavy on the end of the line.

"Where are you?"

"Chip's in the emergency room. We think he's had a stroke."

"Where? Where are you?" Abby watched the dog run around the leaves with the kids' old Nerf football in his mouth.

"Outside of Boston. Emerson. No, that's the name of the hospital. I don't know, Lexington, Concord, one of those towns."

"I didn't know you were going away for the weekend. Usually you—"

"I needed to drive."

"Is his wife there?" She wanted the dog to come in. It was long past dark. She wondered if they would still have to go to this party.

"She is now. I had to ride with him in the ambulance. I . . ."

"I know," Abby said. In Jordanna's second pregnancy she'd hemorrhaged and had been taken to the hospital by ambulance. The ambulance, the emergency room would reactivate that whole experience. Alice's birth was why Jordanna never went to doctors anymore. "It's normal. You do know that? It's a natural post-traumatic stress response. You're having to relive all that."

"It's plenty bad without having to relive anything. The present—"

"I know," Abby said. God, maybe she wouldn't ask about Daniel. "Do you want me to come get you?" she asked, without thinking. She wondered what she would do if her sister said yes.

"My car's here."

"We can figure that out."

"I think I need to . . . step out."

"Oh. Okay. Get some air. Can I call you back there?"

"No." Jordanna laughed. "No, I mean, I need to get checked in somewhere. Check out of this life for a little while. I had been hoping that Chip would arrange for me to go on retreat. The unstrung ministers—that kind of thing."

"Oh," Abby said blankly. Abby had thought she should take a mental-health sabbatical three years ago, after Alice died. Daniel had thought so. Chip had thought so, too.

"How does he look?" Jordanna asked.

"Daniel?"

"Yeah."

"He's got that Down-Under academic thing going on. Thin, hairy—"

"Tanned?"

"Yeah."

"It's the 'Dear Jordanna' letter in person, isn't it? The sick thing is . . ."

"What?" Abby listened to her sister cry on the other end of the phone.

"They're moving Chip to intensive care. I need to go."

"I'm going to come and get you." She heard her brother-in-law walk into the kitchen. Those damn boots. She didn't turn around, but kept looking out at the dark hillocks on the lawn, a suburban Stonehenge. "It's seven-something now, seven-twenty. I can be there by nine-thirty, ten o'clock. We'll be home around midnight."

"Is the girlfriend there, too?"

"You need to talk to him, Jordanna."

"Can I talk to her?" Daniel said loudly. He ran his hands over the wrinkled surface of one of Gabe's paintings.

"I'm right, aren't I? I'm always right," Jordanna said. "Has he been standing there the whole time?"

"No, he just walked—"

"May I?" Daniel said now to Abby.

"Love you," Abby said into the phone as she moved it from her mouth to his. She grabbed an unopened piece of junk mail and scrawled on the back of the envelope, "You should go and pick her up, you bastard." She crossed out "you bastard" almost entirely before placing the note on the counter where Daniel was perched with the phone.

"THESE kids are starving," Jim said. He had just gotten out of the shower. She sat down on the edge of the bed and watched him dress for the party.

"It's not that late. They'll live."

"It's nuts for you to drive up there and back in one night." Jim rubbed at a spot on his shoe with his dampened thumb. "She'll be fine."

"You don't know that." Abby lay down on the pile of clean, unfolded laundry covering the bed.

"I want you to come to this thing with me. I need you to drive me to . . . what town is it in again?"

"Ridgely."

"Yeah, Ridgely. I need you to be my designated driver."

Abby laughed and turned her face into Christopher's flannel shirt. "I think I'm my sister's designated driver. . . ."

"She's got God. God's her designated driver. Let her put the pinch on God for a change, instead of you."

"You're mad," Abby said, looking up at the ceiling and all the dead bugs in the frosted lens of the overhead light.

"Leave them to work it out, okay?"

"You think I'm interfering?" She was no longer distracted. She propped her head up on one elbow and turned to face her husband.

"Don't take another step closer into that mess they've made between them." He moved toward the closet and his tie rack.

"What does that mean?" She shook her head. "Don't wear a tie. You'll be the only one. You make it sound like it's all their fault. They've had an awful lot of misfortune."

"Yeah, and you can't make it better. You can't save your sister from the bad stuff that's happened to her. You'd like to, but you can't. She needs your love, your—"

"It's that attitude that . . . sucks. What if everyone thought that, and no one ever extended themselves?"

Jim sighed. "I'm tired, Ab. I'm exhausted from all this." He motioned with his head toward downstairs. "I don't understand it. I don't understand anything about how he's dealt with her, and I can't fix it. I love your sister and I—"

Jim stopped when they heard Daniel yell up the stairs to them. Abby smoothed down her hair and opened the bedroom door. Jim came around and put his hands gently on the tops of her shoulders. "Don't blow me off, Ab. I'm not as dramatic as Jordanna—but I'm equally as deserving of your attention, you know?"

She sighed and went downstairs.

❧ Chapter 17

T HE Sunday service at Chip's church had been nearly full, and
now Jordanna stood on the steps outside the church overlooking the green and watched the congregants greet the senior minister.
They stood in groups of twos and threes, murmuring and clucking,
frowning, shaking their heads. Daniel was to meet her here, on the
steps, and then she supposed they would walk or sit somewhere with
coffee. On the phone last night, when she had talked to him from the
hospital and he was still at Abby's, she had said that she would like to
meet his young woman sometime, but not yet. In fact, she asked him
to do her a favor, something she could not remember ever having
done before. Or more precisely, she couldn't remember phrasing a
request that way. She asked him if he would, please, leave the girl
behind somewhere. "Give her the car and have her drop you off a
few blocks away. And tell her to drive, not around town, but out into
the country. And when she picks you up, have it be inside somewhere. Do you understand that, Daniel?" This last line had sounded,
even to her, as if she were dictating the terms of a ransom.

He had offered to come and get her last night, but then there
would be the problem of her car left here. More to the point, she

didn't want to have their last conversation trapped in a rental car, hurtling down the Mass Pike at seventy miles an hour in the middle of the night. She had waited with Chip's wife until the first of his children arrived. Then she'd taken a cab back to the Solloway's house to get her car and checked into the ancient inn across the green from Chip's church in the center of town. She pulled out the Bible from the nightstand drawer and allowed herself Job 30:20–22:

> I cry to thee and thou dost not answer
>   me;
>   I stand and thou dost not heed
>   me.
> Thou has turned cruel to me;
>   with the might of thy hand thou
>   dost persecute me.
> Thou liftest me up on the wind,
>   thou makest me ride on it,
>   and thou tossest me about in the
>   roar of the storm.

She fell asleep reading, and when she woke up with the first church bells at eight, she found herself on top of the opened Bible, Job 29 and 30 irreparably wrinkled. She showered and put on the same clothes she'd worn to go on that painful little hike with Drew the day before. It had only been twenty-four hours, but it seemed like that whole event had occurred on another continent. Oceans, time zones, international date lines must have been traversed between then and now.

SHE watched the church members disperse. The young helped the old down the cascade of shallow steps. Two children with unbrushed hair hid behind a spindly mountain laurel and tried to scare a third. The senior minister, a man about her age, waved to her one last time before going back inside. They had talked by phone last night. Helen had asked Jordanna to inform him of the uncertain extent of the stroke Chip had suffered. And then she had spoken to the minister again this morning, after she'd heard from Helen that Chip was alert but having difficulty speaking.

She sat down now on the cool stone steps and opened her purse. She popped four Advils, and forced herself to swallow them dry. Was there a limit to what you could lose? Did God ever just say, enough and no more? Or could it just keep on going, an endless river of hope flowing into a boundless sea of emptiness, the tide never turning, the movement always in that singular direction? After James and Alice she'd kept her grip fairly loose, her desire at a minimum, so as not to be undone ever again. She and Daniel had been releasing each other for three years, incrementally, as they dangled from an ever-diminishing height. But with Chip, she'd forgotten to transpose for loss. He was a constant, perhaps the only constant. How exactly was she to proceed without this mentor? It wasn't as if she called him all the time. Months and months went by when they didn't communicate. But he was out there, this inexhaustible resource, sustaining and protecting.

June, July, August, September, October—four months since she'd seen Daniel. She tried to guess which direction he would come from. How far off would she be able to spot him? As she slid into the hotel bed last night, it had occurred to her that she might never have sex again. Of course, she couldn't have sex with Daniel now anymore. So, the last time had already happened. It had been the day before he left for New Zealand. Daniel had run up to the attic to get something, and when he came back into the bedroom, Jordanna was in their bed, in the middle of the afternoon, naked. She had accidentally knocked over his half-packed suitcase, and she watched him hesitate when he entered the room, wondering if he would pick up the clothes that had tumbled onto the wood floor, or unzip his pants and climb into bed beside her. They had both cried afterward, and it seemed to her now that their mutual dissembling had been no match for the honesty of the body. Some more essential part of them had known it was the end.

Daniel's hand was on her shoulder before she realized he was there. She had been sitting with her face tilted into the sun, and she hadn't seen him approach. She stood up, and Daniel leaned in to kiss her on the cheek.

"How's Chip?" he asked.

"He's awake, but he's not talking."

Daniel nodded. "Do you want to walk?"

"Coffee would be good, I think."

She watched him look up and down the street, as he had done so many times in airport terminals, in foreign cities, and even at the fork of a hiking trail. "There's a—"

"Not Starbucks," she said.

He shoved his hands in his pockets. He looked leaner than usual, as if he were in training, about to compete and certainly win. His hair was long in back and shorter on the sides. She could tell he'd paid attention to having it cut. Perhaps someone with a keen interest in such things had stood beside him as he sat in the barber's chair or had even cut it herself. The gray streaks were less noticeable for having been exposed to so much sun. His face was honey-colored, tan for autumn in New England, where the pallor of winter had already overtaken most faces.

"I stayed there, last night," she said, nodding in the direction of the inn. "We could probably sit in the lobby." As they walked away from the church, Jordanna thought about what the facilitator in the support group had said the one time she'd attended: "When you marry a guy at twenty-five, you don't think you've just chosen the person who'll help you to pick out a casket or a headstone. You don't realize you might be selecting a grief partner as much as a bedmate."

The hotel lobby, with its fraying velvet settees, was crowded with people waiting to be seated.

"Should we go somewhere else?" Daniel asked.

Jordanna surveyed the room. People were eating waffles and

berries, bacon and eggs and scones. There was a thick smell of coffee and maple syrup, steam heat and newsprint. She wouldn't have minded waiting on this line forever. "I'm in no hurry," she said.

"What happened to your ear and your face?" he reached up and touched her cheek. She felt the scrape of his index finger with its cracking skin.

"You can hardly see it. Little bicycle accident a while ago."

"Still not wearing a helmet?"

"No, I thought I'd just wait around for the halo."

He nodded as if he were listening and she had said something of value. He combed his fingers through his beard. "Abby told me some of what's been going on."

"Wouldn't it be simpler if we just talked . . . about what we really need to?"

"It's just that I want you to understand . . . I had no idea all this was going on . . . My timing is lousy, to say the least. Really, I thought you were thriving in Hutchinson."

She turned abruptly toward him in response, her large bag knocking against a blue and white ginger jar. "Thriving?"

"I mean, aside from us. It just sounded, from your e-mails, that your life in this church had really—"

"I like that word, *thriving*. It's filled with this generative quality." She whirled her thumb around the top of the porcelain jar. "Hutchinson's been the right place for me. And this, these last few weeks . . . Clearly God thinks there's something I'm still not getting, something that burying two babies and one uterus didn't make clear to me." Jordanna looked across the sea of little tables. She knew there would be a long silence on Daniel's part now, that he would look down at his boots and his cheeks would go slack underneath the beard.

"Just two?" A young Irish hostess snaked her way around the couplings of laced-topped tables and cast-off chairs, turning now and then to make sure they were behind her.

"Thank you," Jordanna said, clamping the girl's elbow. "You just helped us to avert what might have been our last argument."

The girl blushed and smiled and handed them their menus.
Daniel shook his head.

"I know. You don't like being exposed. . . ."

He opened his menu and stared into it. "It's just that it's not true."

"What?"

"We weren't about to have an argument. And even if we were, it certainly would not have been our last. I'm not looking to—"

Jordanna coiled her hair and threw it behind her like a lodestone. "You want to get married."

He looked up at her now, his eyes welling.

She lifted one shoulder. "I know. I think I've known all fall."

"I'm not looking to have a life without you in it. You make it sound—"

"Yes, you are, Daniel. That's what getting divorced means. If you weren't looking to have a life without me, you wouldn't have gone to New Zealand for a year."

He capped his hands over his empty, overturned coffee cup. "It was the sadness . . . that's what I went to get away from."

"They don't have grief Down Under?"

He looked up at her, wounded. "Nobody could have been expected to weather that intact. Something was going to give. It had to. Something had to give."

"People get through all kinds of things."

"And still live? Make jokes? Have sex? Move on—together? I don't think so."

"We're always moving on, Daniel. The minute after James died, we started moving on—"

"I'm not talking about after James. After James, you got pregnant again. We were—"

"There's no standing still. Things might not unfold the way we want, but we are always moving—"

"Moving and moving forward. . . ." He shook his head.

"What?"

"I don't know. It's different for you. You have this, this spiritual

prism. You can filter experience so that it refracts . . . all this meaning. Perhaps that's the real difference for us. My moving on has to be
active. It can't be simply . . . meditative. It has to involve physical
change. Locus—"

"Why do you think I went to Hutchinson?" They were saying
nothing new, just stating it more clearly than the last time they'd had
this discussion. With each chronicling of their fate, their roles
became more stylized. It had occurred to her that if their marriage
continued, in a year or two they'd be as dimensionless to one another
as characters in a morality play.

After they ordered, Daniel got up to go to the bathroom and Jordanna was left alone at the table. She moved into his chair and
slipped her arms into his oilcloth coat. She lifted the inside lapel up to
her nose in what she knew to be an atavistic move. She rubbed the
flannel lining on her upper lip and pulled the jacket tight around her.
The waitress came by and poured the coffee. "Drafty in here, isn't
it?"

Jordanna smiled and slid her hands into the pockets of the coat.
She closed her eyes and felt a set of keys, some gritty change, his
pocketknife, the one she'd given him with his initials engraved on
the cover. As she encircled her fingers around the objects in each
pocket, attempting to identify them, testing if they belonged to his
old life or his new, she felt her hand being held. Not her whole hand,
just that same little grip, that Daniel had told her had been a halluci-
nation from the morphine when she'd abrupted with Alice. Always
the last three fingers of her left hand. Heat, real heat. Touch. Almost
flesh to flesh. And when she experienced this little grasp again and
again, weeks, months, years later, he had told her that the mind
could reach back and replay any scene, especially in times of stress.
Her metaphysical experience was nothing more, he said, than a psy-
choneurological event. He was probably right, of course. Humans
were so primordially afraid of isolation, of being alone, that for mil-
lennia they had created spirits and angels, even an ever-present God.

"Cold?" Daniel sat down in the chair across the table.

She nodded. She wanted to tell him about her hand being held, and she wanted him to thrill alongside her. But that could never happen, and maybe that's why this would be their last meal together, their last long look at one another. "What's her name?" Jordanna said, as if she were asking one of the baptismal parents, *By what name do we baptize this child?*

"Ellen."

"Have you told Ellen about our babies?"

He nodded.

"Did she cry?"

"She said she thought it was the saddest thing she ever heard."

"Then she must be very young."

"Ford was president when she was born."

"Have you shown her their pictures?"

He nodded.

"Did she say they were beautiful?"

He bit down on his upper lip, taking his mustache into his mouth. "She asked me why we didn't adopt."

"Did you tell her that we didn't so that you could fall in love with her? Now it makes sense. All that seeming inaction."

They had talked about adoption before Jordanna took the job in Hutchinson. They had taken turns promoting the idea, the one trying it on the other, a homemade bandage over a too-fresh wound. The last time Daniel brought up the idea, Jordanna said she wasn't ready. She was waiting to hear a kind of call, one she felt she had to heed. And when she raised the issue last spring, he said, "I just want James and Alice back, my babies, the ones I was promised." People asked all the time why they didn't just adopt, hoping to catch her and Daniel in some failure of liberal thinking, some small-minded phobia. But the truth was they'd become incapable of forming any joint desire. Their sense of themselves as a couple, potent, fearless, fecund, had been damaged after James's death and incinerated beyond any possible resurrection with Alice's. It took so much less energy and material to refashion the self than it did the couple. Individually, they might be able to transcend their losses, the construct of the future having only to bear the weight of one. But to envision a shared future they would have had to erect a bridge solid enough to support the staggering burden of their combined sorrow.

Daniel was weeping now, openly, and Jordanna reached into his jacket and pulled out a handkerchief. "Do you ever think that we shouldn't have gotten married—all the misery we created . . . literally?"

He reached across and took the handkerchief and blew his nose. "Never," he said.

One afternoon some months after Alice had died, during that winter when it had snowed so much and so often Jordanna thought they might suffocate, she and Daniel had taken a walk through the woods behind Beecham Congregational Church. She'd been told by any number of congregants about the salt lick set way back beyond a grove of birches. They had pushed their way together along no particular path, removing hats and unwrapping scarves, wet with the effort of moving through thigh-high snow. Jordanna remembered thinking that this was what they needed to do, set a goal, make a plan, endure the pain and the labor of seeing it through, even if it was something as inconsequential as finding this salt lick. It was sunny and cold. They hadn't worn sunglasses and as they pressed through the snow, they were forced to squint. Daniel turned to her and said she actually looked like she was smiling. They walked and walked and they could tell from the sun that they weren't walking in circles. They commented on how good this was for them. All the bereavement books stressed the importance of exercise. They walked for over two hours, never mentioning the salt lick, their failure to locate it, the possibility of backtracking. Just when Jordanna thought she heard the not-so-distant sucking of wet tires on a wet road, Daniel pulled off his glove and swiped a sweaty red hand along a snow-lined limb. "Do you ever think what it would have been like if we'd never wanted kids?"

She was sure then that it was the interstate she heard. She

glimpsed a swath of glistening black macadam amid all the mindless white. "Do you think that would have been better?" she asked him.

They kept moving toward the road, and she knew that without talking about it they would not walk back to where they'd begun but instead would stand on the edge of the sanded interstate and hitch a ride home.

"Do you?" he asked. In that moment she had the sense that the gap between her knowledge and his could never be closed up. Was he really asking her if she would trade eighteen months of feeling her children move beneath her own skin, of having them as close as they could ever be—to any mother? He had only known them dead, but she had experienced the whole trajectory, the entire spectrum of their lives. What she had lost would never be the same as what he had lost.

DANIEL pulled his chair in toward the table and cupped her face in both his hands. "We . . ." He stopped for a long while and Jordanna watched him try to get beyond the ache in his throat. "We're joined in a way . . . that will never be undone."

She turned her face in his palms and kissed the inside of his hand.

ELLEN was going to meet him at the Concord Reader at one. Daniel and Jordanna walked slowly across the green. Jordanna had changed her mind. She wanted a look at this girl. She wondered if he was marrying the same physical type, starting over with a younger version of herself, or if he had picked someone as different as New Zealand was far. Her mother, when Jordanna finally got around to telling her, knowing that Abby had already done so, would ask if it wasn't, in essence, just a midlife crisis. And Jordanna would tell her that if she had the chance to marry someone who could give her children, she'd jump at it, too.

But when she saw the girl, she saw that it wasn't that simple. Jordanna watched Daniel wave to a small dark figure seated at a white metal table out on the sidewalk nearly a block away. How could he see that far? As they walked closer, Jordanna could feel a kind of excitement come off him, it was what she had been hearing in his voice over the phone these last few months—a breathlessness, an urgency. She couldn't remember if he'd ever exhibited that with her when they'd first met. She hadn't been thinking about his own expectancy then, she was sure. Daniel was a few steps ahead of her now. He turned and waited for her, as if the excitement were mutual. The girl stood as they approached. She was small, with a delicate face and jet-black hair. Her hair was so short that Jordanna wondered if she had gone through chemo not long ago. Her cheeks pinked up and set off her little pearl earrings as Daniel approached.

"She's beautiful," she said, right before she thought they were in earshot. Later, when she would tell her sister about this moment, she would say that a kind of grace had descended on her as they walked on that sidewalk. Just at the moment when a comparison between this exquisite physical specimen and herself would have proved painful for Jordanna, she'd had this odd rush of pride, as if somehow she had provided this for the two of them, as if she, too, were integral in the orchestration of this love affair and would bask in the reflected glow of that passion.

Abby would tell her that that was one of the most twisted, denial-rich responses to being dumped that she had ever heard. "It's always a choice," Jordanna would tell her. "And since I'm doing the choosing, I'd rather believe that it was a moment of grace and not delusion."

Daniel had said that she was twenty-eight, but she looked younger. Her skin was smooth, and her face reminded Jordanna of the inside of a pink conch shell. It made you want to run your finger over its features, to trace the small nose, the large eyes, then place your ear to the coral lips to find out what you might hear. But Jordanna didn't touch the girl's face, she touched Daniel's. She ran her left hand, still with its wedding band, down through his beard, and said, "Make sure to introduce Ellen to Mark and Janine when you're in Orono."

She turned to Ellen now, and saw her staring at her face. Certainly she must have seen a picture, maybe not. "You'll love Orono."

"I've been there once before, for a conference."

"Actually, we probably met before, but we don't remember," Daniel said.

"Daniel doesn't remember," Ellen said. "But I remember him."

Jordanna would relay this moment, too, to her sister. "I suddenly had this barely repressible urge to rip at those perfect pearl studs in her ears, to somehow disassemble that delicate whole."

"Where's your car?" Daniel asked.

"Behind the church." She pointed across the green.

"Is it running okay?"

"What happens next?" Jordanna asked.

Ellen politely walked back to the table, where she'd left her tea and a book. Jordanna strained to read the title. The desire to hurt the girl had, thankfully, lost its urgency. Ellen slipped her purse from the back of her chair and walked inside the store with her empty mug.

"I'll talk to Lou Pearsall tomorrow," Daniel said.

"And am I supposed to find a lawyer, too?" A lawyer. That awl again. "You'll have to school me on this."

He nodded.

"We should say goodbye while she's inside," she said. "When will we see each other? I don't know what you're—"

"I'll call you. We'll still talk, Jordanna."

She had already stepped backward on the pavement, moving where she could no longer touch him. He was saying something, but she turned toward the church and her car. With her back to him she mumbled to herself, "Nothing left."

෨෦ Chapter 18

O N her way home from Massachusetts, Jordanna left a message
on Abby's answering machine. She told Abby not to worry.
She was going to unplug her phone for a few days, meditate and
sleep, and yes, they would talk soon, just not today or tomorrow.
Then she had stopped off at Villa Bianca's and placed a take-out
order for a large pizza with clams and ricotta and spinach and bacon,
and while she was waiting for it, she sat at the little service bar drinking Chianti and smoking the bartender's cigarettes. There was a TV
suspended from the ceiling, reminding her of a hospital room, and
she and the bartender sat there silently watching something called
Touched by an Angel, which left her even colder than she had been
already.

She unlocked the front door and attempted to examine herself.
She'd been coming home to an empty house on and off for a year and
a half. Was it different now that she knew it was permanent? Supposedly, Daniel's absence had been devoid of meaning before, and
now . . . She turned the oven on to reheat the pizza and while she was
looking around at old newspapers and unopened mail and the darkness extending up to the second floor, her heart did that thing it had

done ten or twenty times a day after she'd lost James. It was that rush of anxiety that was brought on by nothing, by the crushing weight of nothingness. It was a physiological reaction to the truth of her life. Back then, she had learned to hold a lavender sachet up to her nose when she felt that way. She'd been given it by a friend of her mother's who had lost two adult children. Attached to the sachet was a little tag, like a luggage tag, with two interchangeable cards inside. On one was printed "Choose Life," and on the other "One Day at a Time." That sachet and Bach's Double Violin Concerto in D, over and over, had carried her to Alice's conception, and through most of that pregnancy. Then after Alice there had been puzzles, jigsaw puzzles. Abby had sent them in big cartons, always nautical motifs. Then when she was ready for music it was only clarinet music. Eventually she worked her way to books. She reread every Henri Nouwen book she owned, keeping them in a stack by her bed. She wrote in the margins of the books, as if she were writing to him, as if they were engaged in a discourse on pain and loss and the presence of God in that pain. And Nouwen had, really, provided the staircase up and out, or as far up or out as she was going to get.

She smelled the cardboard from the pizza box beginning to singe, and she wondered what would provide comfort now. Jim had always wanted to get her a punching bag. Maybe she could punch her way out of this loss. She sat on the living room floor and placed the hot pizza box on her lap. She flipped open the top, trying to surprise herself. "Say grace," she commanded. "Thank you, God," she began automatically, then there was a long pause during which she felt her mind pull away from the moment. It was only after she realized her pants were damp from the steam that had condensed on the underside of the box that she whispered, "for letting this pizza warm my lap."

She slept in the living room that night. In fact, she didn't make it up to the second floor until late Monday afternoon. She had taken a Percocet and poured herself a scotch, and now she wanted a cigarette. If there were any cigarettes at all in the house, they were ancient, stashed upstairs in the bedroom closet from one of last year's attempts to quit. She couldn't remember how she'd left the bedroom on Saturday morning. She'd visited congregants who maintained rooms for deceased family members, at once preserving the life and the loss, showing it off to guests, museum-quality replicas of unvoiced absence. Daniel and her mother had taken apart the nursery before she returned home after losing James. She had been disappointed, but had never said so. They had emptied the room of the new crib and the secondhand changing table, leaving only the yellow checked curtains and the dark green rug. When Daniel was out of the house, Jordanna sat in the empty room. Her mother had efficiently boxed up the package of newborn-size diapers, the wipes, the ointments and the baby powder. Jordanna had looked throughout that little house one morning, desperate to find the pacifiers and washcloths, the baby thermometer and the undershirts. They were under the bed, hers and Daniel's bed. She slid out the plastic container, too recently stowed there to be dusty, and she ran her hands over the terry cloth bibs, the two plastic bottles, the nipples still hermetically sealed. She pulled out the baby powder and brought it with her into what should have been the baby's room and sprinkled some under each of the four corners of the brand-new green rug.

The cigarettes were up in an old backpack on a shelf in her closet. She crossed the threshold of the bedroom and moved around the bed. She realized she was holding her breath, the way she and Abby used to whenever they drove by a cemetery. What was the origin of that? she wondered now. Inhale as you drive by a graveyard and you'll breathe in death and catch it? She'd buy a new bedspread, and bring this one to the Mustard Seed, the thrift store run by the church. The spread was a deep garnet color. Somebody's kid could use it for a costume if he ever had to be a king in a play, Herod or Louis the XIV. The room would be a problem. Maybe she could seal it off and just live downstairs. She knew that people often moved after divorces. But this was the parsonage. She opened the closet door and reached above the clothes Daniel had left behind, the ones that hadn't made the cut. She pulled down a box filled with beaded clutches that had belonged to her grandmother, a pair of flattened tan sandals and, in the back, a musty orange knapsack she and Daniel used when they hiked. There were three Parliaments in a zip-lock bag, upright and unbroken in a side pocket.

She picked up a pack of matches next to a nub of a candle in an old juice glass. She turned the pictures of James and Alice to the wall, for now, lit the cigarette and sat down on the bed. She wished she'd brought her scotch up with her. She looked down at the jewel-toned spread and thought about burning it. When she'd been a youth pastor in Latham, there'd been a kid in the church who'd been into self-mutilation. She had touched a lit cigarette to each of those unguarded places between her toes. Jordanna had believed what she preached to that girl then, nearly fourteen years ago. She'd said your body's as precious to God as if it were God's own. She lay back on the bed and blew smoke up toward the ceiling. It was far more than a matter of belief. That idea and dozens of others had been like a quickening within her. She was convinced, beyond a shadow of a doubt, that nothing was more important than making the stunning truths of the Gospel real to everyone she met. God had blessed her with this outsize passion so that she could deliver it to others.

"Fuck you," she said now out loud, as she pushed and turned the cap of the Percocet bottle. She didn't yell it, she stated it in a normal conversational tone, as if she might have been saying something else, like "See, see what you made me do," or "Now what." God didn't care about bodies, not James's, or Alice's, or Chip's, or hers. Only people cared about physical pain and physical pleasure and physical love. She walked into the bathroom and angled her head under the faucet. Was there ever a kind of love that wasn't registered physically? Why introduce the physical world if it didn't really count, if it was merely the misleading first chapter of eternal life? Why get us attached to other bodies? For the fun of watching us writhe when it all got ripped apart?

"Your theology is weak," she said, this time more loudly, tapping the hot ash of her cigarette into the folds of her gray sweatshirt. If she were a priest, someone would do her laundry. Hell, if she were male and Catholic, she'd be a bishop by now. Too bad that wasn't an option, really. Celibate, childless, religious, it would have been a perfect fit. One more Divine screwup. She put out the cigarette in the melted candle on the dresser and lay back down on the bed. Even as it was happening she conceded how miraculously easy it was to fall asleep here in the middle of the afternoon.

It was dark out when the voices of her parents woke her. She heard her father's laconic love hiss and spit over the answering machine, "missing . . . wishing . . . thinking . . . " Then her mother chimed in with a joke, the end of it folded into "concerned . . . Daniel . . . Abby." The machine clicked off and the house was silent and unlit by even a single lamp.

JORDANNA arrived at the church house early on Tuesday morning. She had decided to announce the divorce at the staff meeting, and she wanted to wade through some of the correspondence on her desk before the day got derailed. She heard Gael running the tap in the bathroom, filling the coffeepot. There were seventeen new e-mail messages on her computer. She pulled out a bottle of Advil from her desk and took four, as she skimmed over the list of senders, ignoring all those from the UCC central office. Who was Singurl? The subject box was blank. She sat down in her chair and clicked open the e-mail. It was from Tara.

> You weren't in church on Sunday. And you weren't home on Saturday. My parents want me to talk to you again. My father's all obsessed with the guy. Who's the guy, who's the guy? The guy's not the point. Anyway, I'm only writing this because my parents want me to talk to you. It's not like I don't have friends.

She clicked on "Reply."

Tara: I'm sorry I missed you. I was out of town this weekend, but I would
very much like for us to talk again. If you like, you can call Gael to set up
an appointment here, at the office, or call me at home. You have my number, and you can come over one night during the week. In the meantime,
please know that you have been in my thoughts. And trust me when I tell
you that I know, I really do know, how truly difficult this is.
Peace,
Rev. J.

She looked at her watch and scrolled through a few more messages, before stopping at one from Scott Davis.

Just wanted to touch base with you, see how you're faring in the wake of
June Nearing's suicide. I still have the name written down in my planner
from the day you called me about her. I know you have a lot of inner and
institutional resources at your disposal for dealing with this, but I know
from colleagues who've lost patients that this kind of thing can be pretty
tough going. Don't hesitate to give a call. I'm here.

She pulled her swollen Rolodex toward her and dialed Scott's
number. She had met him through Abby before she ever moved to
Hutchinson. Abby had done some postgraduate training at Yale, and
Scott had taught the class. By the end of the semester they had figured out that Abby and Scott's wife had known each other in college.
Abby had pointedly seated Jordanna next to Scott at a dinner party
not long after she'd lost James. They'd spent the evening talking
about Meister Eckhart. He had quoted to her, "The eyes with which
I see God are the eyes with which God sees me." He'd been memo-
rable to her as a therapist who seemed unashamed of his own spirituality. She doubted he'd pick up the phone now, and as she dialed she
wondered why she was calling him. To be polite, she guessed. "Oh, I
was expecting the machine," she said, when he did pick up. "You
must be about to go into a session right now." She looked at her
own watch.

"Nope."

"Well, I really just wanted to acknowledge your e-mail."

"How are you?"

"What's that curse about living in interesting times?" she said, knowing she sounded disingenuous, and not really caring.

"This must be extremely difficult."

"I think the family is struggling. They'd been through a lot prior. Suicide . . ." Jordanna simply stopped talking. She couldn't think of how to finish the sentence, or what sort of a segue or departure she could possibly make. It was almost as if she forgot what she was saying.

"Jordanna?"

"Yeah."

"You okay?"

"Oh, yeah, I . . . someone just walked in here. I should probably let you go—"

"You ever been to The Walrus in Deerfield?"

She didn't answer. Suddenly she wasn't so sure she wanted to talk to him. In fact, she thought it would be a bad idea. Shrinks, after all, were doctors. "You know, I'm going to be working straight through today—"

"How about Friday? You know where it is? A little hole in the wall, right next to the Duck Pin Bowling on Hayestown. One o'clock okay?"

"Sounds good," she said firmly. She would have Gael call him Thursday afternoon and cancel. "See you Friday."

JORDANNA always started the staff meeting with a prayer. Everyone was gathered when she entered the library. She placed her cup of coffee and her notes on the table. "I thought I might read a little scripture today, instead of starting with a blessing." She could read, that she could do, but she certainly couldn't invoke. "This is from Romans 8:22–24. 'We know that the whole creation has been groaning in travail until now; and not only the creation, but we ourselves, who have the first fruits of the Spirit, groan inwardly as we wait for adoption as sons, the redemption of our bodies.'"

She sighed when she was done and then asked Gael to lead off with the continuing discussion of the interim choir director. The principal of the Sunday school asked for more volunteers and for a better mechanism for sharing the burden of volunteering among the congregation. The water pressure at the church house was an ongoing problem. There had been several requests by congregants for a divorced persons support group. The synchronicity of the universe never failed to amaze her. There was a lice outbreak at the nursery school, which really wouldn't have been an agenda item, but, well, given its proximity . . . Everyone went around the table, taking turns, apprising, irritating, challenging. Jordanna looked at her watch, as if it were a holy oracle, again and again. She left the room twice, once for more coffee, once just to walk down the hall and breathe. They were making popcorn upstairs at the nursery school, and for a moment the smell was almost comforting.

"Before we all get back to work, I just want to let everyone know of something that's come up in my personal life that should, for all intents and purposes, have no real effect on the congregation. Really, just a heads-up. Daniel and I will be parting ways, it seems. I will inform the Prudential Board when we meet tomorrow night. I do understand that as a role model . . . well, I do understand how this is less than ideal. But truly, my commitment to my call has, in part, something to do with this divorce. His work has called him elsewhere. My service and his are not really compatible. I don't feel that we are so much tearing something asunder as making an informed decision, and a choice about where our duties really rest."

When she finally stopped talking she looked up at Fred Rinehardt and Tim Boyle, who had their eyes closed, as if they were praying. Gael was crying and Angela Stanton, the Sunday school director, and Seth Hardesty, the Divinity School intern, were simply staring at her. The kids upstairs were playing some kind of elimination game; there was the faint downbeat of a singsong tune, then frantic running and the scraping of chairs.

"Would you like to take some time off?" Tim finally asked.

"How thoughtful," she said. "No, truly, I can't think of anywhere I'd rather be than here, surrounded by all of you. But thank you."

When Jordanna turned down the corridor toward her office, she thought she saw June, for just a moment. She let out a little gasp, she must have, because the woman turned to face her. It was Bev Congdon, June's mother. Their builds were similar, narrow, vulnerable, and they had that same unnerving ability to stand or sit, or simply be, perfectly still. But Bev had a mass of gray curls around her head, nothing like the dirty blond hair that lay flat against June's neck and shoulders. Bev moved her body through space and time with purpose, even zeal, while June had shuffled, pressing up against some unseen resistance, both hesitant and provoked. Bev didn't return Jordanna's smile. Still Jordanna extended both arms toward her and cupped Bev's shoulders beneath her hands. "I'm so glad you're here," Jordanna said, as they went into her office together. Jordanna walked behind her desk and closed the e-mail from Scott Davis, which she'd left open on her computer. She dragged her chair next to the one in front of the desk.

Bev placed her purse on the floor and crossed her legs, her black wool pants bagged around her hips. "Did you keep notes?"

Jordanna readjusted a clip in her hair. "When I talked with June?"

Bev nodded.

"Therapists do that. Pastoral counseling is different. I was guiding her, trying to guide her towards a path. I think the relationship is vastly different than between therapist and patient." She was having trouble pulling up the words. "The distinction . . . it's about walking beside the congregant. Taking notes—"

"How much do you recall of what she told you all those months— almost five months, right?"

"Everything," Jordanna said. "Everything that was important." Jordanna wondered if Kent had persuaded Bev to pursue this legally.

Bev sighed. "I need to know—" She stopped, reached down for her purse, unzipped it and pulled out some Kleenex. "Why didn't she feel loved?"

Jordanna looked out the window. The tops of the trees were bare, like tonsures, and a brilliant, cold light poured through the leaded windows. It seemed a second ago that June had been sitting where Bev was now, fans whipping air about the room. "That is the definition of depression: 'No feeling.'"

Bev shook her head. "She felt things. She must have felt something so deeply. She was in enough pain to kill herself. Even her sister was never in that kind of pain when she was dying." She rose slightly from her seat, as if preparing to stand, then lowered herself again. "No. June was dying, all that time, too."

"What was she like before, before Eve got sick?"

"Pretty. Lovely. She was never very outgoing. That was Eve's job, the little sister. But June was like a kind of . . . gemstone, solid, dependable, silent. In the right light she sparkled, almost. She was always quiet, always on the shy side, but not unnaturally so. Eve was much more adventurous, always putting things in her mouth as a baby, like she wanted to experience the whole world. Not June. June was a homebody. She never talked about living anywhere but Hutchinson, never wanted to go away to school. Even as a little girl, in grade school, she asked me once if you had to sleep away at college. She was someone who needed to stay close, to me, to her dad when he was alive, to her kids. That's still the part . . . Lee was over six months old before she left her with me. She was so tied to place, to the farm, to family. That part doesn't make sense." She slid her watch down toward her wrist. Jordanna recognized it as June's. "I've moved in with Drew. He thinks I'm there to help with the children. But it's selfish. June's still in that house. Of course, I see her in the kids. But in the house I can touch her things, not just her clothes, but her pots and pans, the pattern she'd already cut out for Lee's bumblebee costume, the birthday present she'd bought for Carly, still in the plastic bag in her closet, the paint chips in eight different shades of blue, the coupons for a sale in September, the grapevine stencil for the border in the new kitchen. I listen to her music . . . I picked up the book . . .”

“Was it like that with Eve, too?” Jordanna said, not looking at Bev now, but only at the faded red of the burning bush at the edge of the nursery school playground.

“My own mother died when I was eleven. It was quite sudden. She just collapsed and died in the yard on her way back from collecting eggs. I found her with broken yolk running down the front of her. She’d clutched the eggs to her chest before she fell. The house filled with people, and my grandmother must have set my cousin Jack to the task of keeping watch over me. He was about my age, and he came into my room with a deck of cards. And we played cards, then checkers, and every time I began saying something about the horror of the day, he would pick up the *Guinness Book of World Records* and read aloud. He must have been told to keep my mind off it. And in a way, everyone is like that eleven-year-old cousin. If I mention Eve, people change the subject. Not June. June . . .” She sighed deeply and smoothed the pleats of her slacks. “For the past year or more, for June, there was no other subject. The only person who allowed me to talk about Eve was someone . . . Well, now if I want to talk about my daughters, the way mothers do, I’ll have to be talking about dead people.”

“They’re still your girls, Bev. Mothers need to feel free to talk about their children.”

“You must have things to do.” Bev uncrossed her ankles and leaned forward.

“Nothing as necessary as this.”

Bev picked up her purse, getting ready to leave. “I’ve heard in town, through people . . . that you’re worried we’re going to sue you.”

“I’m sorry that you’ve heard that, but it didn’t originate with me. It’s not something I think about.”

“Kent and Miles have been in touch with a lawyer. That reporter from Hartford calls us just about every day. June's death must be a career opportunity for her. I haven't spoken with her. I wanted you to know that."

Jordanna nodded.

"I need to be able to go to church. I don't know if we can come back to Hutchinson Congregational. Our family has been attending this church since they settled . . . I hate to sever that tie—"

"Then don't," Jordanna said.

"You know, after my mother died, I never could eat an egg again. You understand, it's the association."

"You associate Hutchinson Congregational with June's death?"

Bev looked at Jordanna almost pitifully. She parted her lips slightly, as if she were about to speak. And then she stood up.

"I think we might want to meet again, Bev."

Bev turned from the door and looked around the room, as if she were afraid she might have left something behind. She ran her eyes the length of Jordanna, making sure there was nothing more she wanted there, either. Then she walked out the door into the hallway.

JORDANNA moved through the week guided by a mantra Daniel had created when James died: "Now, you do the next hard thing." Her calendar filled with a string of different groups and committees she needed to inform about her divorce, the inverse of the receiving line. The Prudential Board met on Wednesday night, and that would be the worst. When she was first interviewed for the position, Chip had counseled her to make it clear that she was the one who would be serving the congregation. "Make sure to put across the idea that this is not two for the price of one." Of course, being a female minister, that was a much easier sell. No one expected the minister's husband to host the Lenten luncheon series, or supervise the Greening of the Church during Advent, or organize the mitten drive. But they probably had expected Daniel to sit in one of the first seven pews on Sunday mornings. She had been up front about his being Jewish, and she described their lack of cohabitation as a commuter marriage. It wasn't as if divorce would change the face of their relationship as far as the church community was concerned.

When she arrived at the church house for the Prudential Board meeting at seven-thirty on Wednesday night, Grant Price was on the phone in Gael's office and everyone else was standing out in the hall. It seemed that the bathroom upstairs in the nursery school had sprung a leak, and the library, where they were to meet, was now ankle-deep in water. Jordanna moved past the orderly grouping of Prudential Board members and went to reach for the light in the library. Ben Hall roared at her and snatched her hand away. The ceiling, which had been peeling to begin with, was mapped in brownish red stains. "Grant's on the phone with the plumber right now," Laura Bonner offered. Claire Hancock asked if she should start in on the phone chain for the nursery school. She couldn't imagine how they could hold school tomorrow. It couldn't possibly be safe to be on the second floor, or the first floor, for that matter. It was forty minutes before they decided to move the meeting to the sanctuary, while Grant waited at the church house until the plumber arrived.

In retrospect, it was good of Ben to have held it in as long as he did. They had formed a circle on the altar with chairs they'd pulled from the choir section. Tom Stanton had just turned up the thermostat, against protest, when Ben said, loudly and to no one in particular, that he was sorry to hear about her trouble.

"I'd like to lead us in a centering prayer before we start." She reached her hands to those on either side of her in the circle. Closing her eyes, she began, "Oh, God, giver of wisdom and insight, may we ask that You shower us with the gifts of guidance, leadership and, above all, loving compassion, that we might better serve You and Your people, in Christ. Amen." She remained for a few moments with her eyes closed. "The next hard thing," she said, not wholly sure if she had done so aloud.

"As some of you already know, my husband returned from New

Zealand this week to tell me that he would like to get divorced. I mentioned this at the staff meeting yesterday morning, and I apologize if this information has trickled out in the manner of gossip."

Claire Hancock got up out of her seat, crossed the circle and embraced Jordanna. "I'm so sorry," she said, kissing Jordanna on the cheek.

"Thank you," Jordanna said.

There was a long silence after that. Laura Bonner broke it finally by saying, "Well, you know, I'm not a hugger, but that doesn't mean my heart doesn't go out to you, Jordanna. I know that a divorce can be like a death, in a way. I have read that."

"The last thing the church needs is another scandal." Ben Hall tipped his chair, forcing the two back legs to cut deeply into the red carpet.

"Why, Ben, have you been doing something you ought not have?" Laura teased with a hard edge.

"I'm deadly serious. We're not even two years removed from that other ungodly business with Hanley. Jordanna, I think you owe us some kind of explanation."

Al Taylor, who was sitting next to Ben, turned and made a face at him. "What scandal, what are you talking about?"

"I want to make sure that the church isn't tainted, that there isn't some story behind all this."

Jordanna looked around the circle. Her eyes moved to each one of the Prudential Board members, and she wondered, again, why Jesus had even bothered to invite the Apostles to Gethsemane.

"Taint?" Phil Pangrossi said. "If you're worried about taint, then you should worry about our young people. I'm talking about kids in our Senior Fellowship. I understand one of these kids got pregnant, quite possibly on a church retreat."

"What?" Laura Bonner half shouted, leaning onto her knees so she could get a good look at Phil. "Jordanna, do you know about this?"

"I'm not sure this is something we should be discussing in this group, in this—"

"Well, I very much beg to differ with you, young lady," Ben interrupted her.

"For crying out loud, Ben," Grant Price yelled as he walked down the aisle and up the altar.

Jordanna held up her arms and placed her palms facing out. "Peace," she said softly. "Let me see if I can't clear up a few things for all of you. Then we will make sure that each and every heart here gets to express itself, all right?" She closed her eyes and took a deep breath before beginning. "Yes, a sixteen-year-old girl in the town of Hutchinson happens to be pregnant. And yes, she happens to be a member of this church, and yes, she was a sometimes member of Senior Pilgrim Fellowship last year. Those are facts. As far as I know, nothing else that was mentioned about this deeply upsetting situation is fact. This is a personal situation. It is being handled by the family, who I have counseled, along with the girl. I do not think this is something that the Prudential Board needs to take up. I am, in fact, uncomfortable with any further discussion of this. I do not want to be forced to identify this girl or this family. As for my personal situation, there is nothing about my marriage ending that should . . . bring shame to the church community."

Ben Hall let out an audible sigh, and Jordanna didn't even attempt to ignore it. She got up out of her chair in the circle and walked over to Ben. Looming over him, she began, "Would you like to hear the details, Ben? Perhaps that might put your mind to rest. My husband, Daniel, and I have been through a lot in the past five years. We have had two stillborn babies, and I nearly died during the second of those deliveries. I lost my uterus, nearly bled to death. We failed, as a couple, to overcome that grief. Not very admirable for a minister, I'm sure." As she talked, she stared at a mole just at the edge of his hairline, and she paced first to the left, toward Claire, then to the right, to the chair Grant had just taken. "I'm not in the business of hiding things, Ben," she said, moving outside the circle now, resting her hands on the back of her own empty chair. "There is nothing that I would knowingly keep from all of you, nothing that might hurt this church family. I really feel the need to be clear about that. I promised you that from the beginning. I do understand that you remain burdened by what the church went through two years ago. I wish I weren't getting divorced. I wish you could hold me up as some kind of human ideal, but that you cannot . . . Well, that is precisely where I will be most helpful." The phone rang down in the undercroft twice before Tom stood up and walked through the door behind the pulpit to go answer it.

"Jordanna," Phil Pangrossi said, lifting his chin from his cupped hands. "Do you think there are couples now who, you know, let's say things aren't going so well for them, say . . . do you think they wouldn't feel so comfortable coming to you for marriage counseling?"

Ben Hall began to nod vigorously. "For that matter, what about performing weddings—"

"Honestly—" Laura Bonner began.

"Hey, folks," Grant interrupted. "We've got plumbing to talk about, we've got Gael's contract renewal, the choir director search. We've got a damn full agenda. Are we really going to spend all night . . ."

Jordanna leaned over the back of her chair and closed her eyes. She let them talk at each other, and she thought about the fluorescent-lit rood on the wall behind her. She imagined it giving off another kind of light. She tried to feel the heat of it along the cross of her own aching back. It was late; suddenly it seemed like she was in the sanctuary with some strange sect in the middle of the night. She opened her eyes when she heard someone say, "June Nearing."

"Well, it's something of a PR problem," Phil said. "We've got a national newspaper covering the story. You know we made it onto the AP wire."

Jordanna slid into her chair. It had only been a few days since she'd been sitting with Chip on his deck talking about what she might do with her life if she left parish work, and here it was, the eventuality unfolding already. Maybe it was all meant to be, this massive failure, the unraveling of everything she knew. Maybe that was the plan. Lose the babies, lose the organs, lose the marriage, lose a parishioner, lose your job and by extension your house. She had seen a magazine at the supermarket recently called *Simplicity*. She was in the vanguard. Her life had been stripped down to the bone. They were yelling at one another now, and she let them.

Claire finally clapped her hands together like a Girl Scout leader, and in the split second of silence that followed she shouted, "I'm really uncomfortable with all of this. I'm not sure this is how we should be discussing these things."

"Perhaps this would be better handled in a closed session," Ben blurted.

Jordanna turned her wrist to look at her watch, then stood up.

"That's not what I'm saying—" Claire said.

"No, I think Ben is right. You all seem to have a lot to talk about. And I don't think my presence here tonight is particularly helpful. I would, though, ask for you to appoint one person to communicate with me about whatever you do decide."

"Personally, I don't think we need to decide anything," Laura said.

Ben let out an almost animalistic grunt.

Jordanna walked around the outside of the circle of chairs on the altar, picked up her raincoat from the first pew and started down the aisle. Sometimes this space felt even more sacred on a weekday when it was empty, as if the prayers and the meditations, the pleading and the gratitude hung around, hovering above the pews, after the bodies were long gone. But tonight, walking down the aisle of this church felt about as spiritual as deplaning through the jetway of a fogged-in terminal on an unscheduled stop.

❧ Chapter 19

"No." Abby wrapped the bread in foil and turned the oven to 350.

"Why not?" Brendan looked down into the stock pot on the stove. "You're just being random."

Abby didn't need this now. It was already seven. The All Souls service started at seven-thirty, and she still needed to change. "You were out last night. One school night a week is plenty."

"Mom," he said, packing the word with all the emotional ambivalence it could hold, and then some. "That was Halloween, and now I'm asking if I can go to church. How is that 'going out' on a school night? I'm just not getting that."

Abby didn't think he needed to *get that*. "I want to talk to JoJo after, alone, okay? It's really the only reason I'm going."

"You can bring me home first, or Dad can come and get me."

"And leave Michael, Christopher and Gabe alone?"

"Oh," he said.

"Get out the butter and the salad dressing." Abby poured milk into four plastic cups on the table and turned to look at Brendan, who was leaning against the refrigerator. He twisted the pewter rune dangling from his neck so that the black rawhide appeared to be strangling him. "Stop that."

"It's a memorial service, right?"

She motioned for him to move from his spot in front of the refrigerator, and she reached in for the butter and the salad dressing. "Yes."

"It's mostly silent."

"How do you know?" she said.

"JoJo's told me."

Abby placed a colander in the sink.

"What are you afraid of? That, like, I'll get un-Catholic? Why should you care?"

Abby lifted the pot of boiling linguine from the stove and carried it to the sink. She poured the pasta into the strainer and let the steam climb toward her face. Now that she had a child the age of the children she worked with during the day, she'd begun to wonder if her job was a good fit for her life. Dealing with adolescents could be energizing and amusing, even enlightening, especially when she'd been able to leave them behind at three-thirty and return to the simple world of the latent seven-year-old. Tara Sears had been in her office today, during her gym period. She'd complained that Jordanna was giving her a "raft of pro-life shit," "fucking" with her head, telling her "some couple out there would have their prayers answered" if she carried this baby to term and gave it up for adoption.

"Why are you telling me this?" Abby had said, closing her office door and cracking the window slightly.

Tara had rummaged into her army surplus knapsack, hunting for something intently. "I guess I confused you with someone who actually gives a damn."

"Nice talk. If Reverend Nash is not providing the kind of counseling you're looking for, stop seeking her out."

Tara pulled a pen from her bag, uncapped it with her teeth and started drawing on her exposed knee. "You don't get it. She's, like, hounding me."

"Really?" Abby said, not meaning to sound so invested. She'd been trying to reach Jordanna for a week. She'd left messages at work and home. Last night she'd brought Gabe and Michael over in their costumes, but the lights were out and Jordanna didn't come to the door, not even when Michael tossed a jawbreaker up at her bedroom window.

Abby opened a file drawer and pulled out a sheet with the phone number for Planned Parenthood in Deerfield. "They provide counseling. There's even directions to the office here. You'll need an appointment first."

Tara stared at the sheet but didn't take it.

"What?"

"Why didn't you give me this the first time I came in here, like, almost a month ago?"

Abby shook her head and closed the file drawer with her hip. What brass, Jesus. "I thought perhaps you had some other issues."

"Oh, yeah, right. The guy."

"Have you told Reverend Nash that he's from your youth group?"

"It's not like Senior P.F. is *my* youth group."

"Have you told her?"

"Have you?"

Abby slid the window open farther, sucked in the cool air and reminded herself that Tara was still a child. "You know that I haven't."

"You talked to my parents."

Tara's parents had called Abby three weeks ago to tell her that they were handling things as a family. God, by now, she had to be, like . . . "How far along are you now?"

Tara shrugged.

"Have you been to the doctor?"

"My mother took me—to the guy who delivered me, if you can handle that one. I'm, like, sixteen weeks or something."

Abby looked at the girl's body. Her small breasts looked different, strangely plump on her still-reedy frame, the only hint of softness about her.

"My dad's talked to Reverend Nash, too. I mean, she just won't shut up about this . . . Just because she got vacuumed out once, or whatever, and never got over it, it's like no one else should."

"MOM, you want me to turn this off?"

Abby felt the steam from the pasta cool on her face, and she turned to the stove. The sauce had begun to spit out of the pot. "Yeah, please."

"I'll bring a book and sit in the hall or something while you talk to JoJo. Is it about that pregnant girl in eleventh grade? Kelly Price said she was in JoJo's Senior Fellowship youth group thing last year, and now some people in the church are blaming JoJo. Kelly's father's on some board there and . . . That couldn't happen. They couldn't really boot her because of something . . . because of someone else's bad move?"

"Why don't you call everyone to supper. Grab an apple or something because we need to leave now. Is that what you're going to wear?"

As they drove up to the church, Brendan talked at her, jumping from meaningless topic to meaningless topic. Guilt, she thought, at his ability to have gotten his own way. She didn't ask him any more about Tara or Kelly Price or the influential Mr. Price. She couldn't imagine what Jordanna would do if she were asked to leave this pulpit. Her job was all she had left. It was her entire identity. *Reverend Nash*. Jordanna had once told her that in the United Church of Christ you were only considered ordained while serving in a pulpit. *Reverend Nash* would just become another *Ms. Nash*. The thought of that seemingly brilliant ego disintegrating was unfathomable. No, Jordanna could rationalize or theologize her way back from almost any precipice. All would be subverted to maintain the theology. Life events would be reread, misread, reinterpreted, reinvented so as to make sense given the ideology. Abby wondered if there was anything, finally, that would force her sister to deal face-to-face with herself and her horrendous fortune, or if that wedge of denial and delusion was a permanent implant, a shunt for the steady delivery of the spurious. Abby wished she were a believer, then she could pray for Jordanna, and pray for herself to be forgiven her seeming hostility toward her sister. She didn't wish Jordanna ill, but she did, for once, want to see her prostrate in front of the truth, to see her felled by an honest thought or feeling. Some part of her was always hanging around waiting to witness that.

The beige program on the lectern in the narthex was titled "Service of the Bittersweet." Abby was relieved to see that there were no greeters here tonight. That was the part she disliked most about coming on a Sunday morning, the middle-aged men with their slicked-back hair and their oversize laminated name tags, the hearty handshake and all that eager fellowship so early in the morning. The lights were low in the sanctuary, and the altar was lit with white pillar candles. At the base of the altar were two large glass vases filled with orange and yellow bittersweet. Instead of the organ, someone was playing the piano. There were no more than twenty or thirty people scattered throughout the church.

Abby stopped at the third pew on the left, in front of the pulpit, and waited for Brendan to slide in. Instead, he genuflected, then crossed the aisle and sat down in his own pew. She hesitated for a second before taking her seat. Abby looked up at the one-story-high, walnut-colored cross behind the pulpit, so unlike the Unitarian Universalist church of their childhood. How had Jordanna gotten here from there? One minute she was working for AFS, arranging for American students to live abroad, occasionally traveling to the Mideast, and the next she was at Yale Divinity School. Abby didn't think she'd ever seen her sister pick up a Bible. Had she once mentioned that God even interested her half as much as Nostradamus? Had she talked about it with their parents? She remembered Jordanna explaining that the ministry was often a family business. A number of her classmates were the third or fourth generation to enter the ministry. More than a few had come to Divinity School as the thirteenth step of their twelve-step programs. The Peace Corps and Vietnam were the training grounds for most of the rest. Maybe that's what had made Abby wary of Jordanna's whole God thing in the first place. Where did it come from? Certainly not their upbringing. As Jim had told her once after attending a Christmas service with her parents at the Unitarian church in Whiting's Point, "you're all about as likely to worship a tree, or the sap running through it, as Jesus Christ, Our Lord and Savior. You're certainly not taking anything on faith here, not coming down on any one side. Unitarianism, the religion of 'whatever.'"

Their childhood had been infused with appreciation for the spirit, though. There was a rhythm to their lives as kids that Abby knew was deeply influenced by her parents' belief system. Sundays were sacred, because that was the day of the week reserved for exploring the natural world. When she was young, few stores were open on Sundays, and as that began to change, her father maneuvered their lives so that nothing commercial transpired on that day. They'd spend Sundays on the flats clamming, or berrying behind the old Cold Storage schoolhouse. Or they'd bike all the way to the Little Whiting River and back, even in the iciest wind. They'd hike over to the herring run in the spring, and in the summer they'd go to Payomet Beach. But unlike the tourists, they'd arrive late in the day, and stay until the moon came up, cooking their dinner over a fire made only from driftwood.

Jordanna emerged through the little door up on the altar and whispered something to the pianist, who kept on playing but nodded her head. Abby knew what would follow. Her sister would sit, eyes closed, for a few minutes, before bounding up and floating through the church in her vestments, the black robe accessorized with the woven "scarf," the deep colors of some more overtly sensual culture. She would stride down the aisle, raise her arms, tilt back her head and sing. She would breathe deeply, drawing those massive hands slowly up toward her face, as if everyone in the pews were just one more aroma for her to inhale. And again, Abby would be forced to consider if Jordanna had an inner life that differed from the outer. For all her seeming vulnerability, where was her fragility? It was as if she had both more and less feeling than your average woman. The day Abby found her in the kitchen with a martini, she'd almost seemed mortal for a while, and then, from nowhere, she was over-taken by the need to portray herself as invincible. Christ, what could be less genuine? Abby suspected that it was precisely this insistence on the public, clerical Jordanna standing in for the private, personal one that June had sniffed out. The ultimate lie—the minister was not really flesh and blood like the flock. What had Tara said about Rev-erend Nash, only this morning in her office? "It's like she's all the time about to say 'been there, done that' or something. Like she was there at the beginning of creation, and she's got the whole thing nailed. She thinks she's more like Jesus than one of his Disciples."

"This is a special service this evening. Mostly a service that will be conducted in silence." Jordanna's voice sounded hollow. She wasn't wearing that little microphone on her lapel, an accoutrement that always made Abby feel like she was in the audience of the Phil Don-ahue show.

"It is a service of remembrance. There will be a few readings, and then I will recite the names of all those in our church family who've passed away since last year." It was as if Jordanna were attempting to parse an ancient language, meant only to be read and no longer spo-ken. The syllables emerged oddly spaced and unstressed. Abby looked over at Brendan for confirmation. "After that, we will have a silent meditation, and then I will invite you to come up and write the names of those whose lives and spirits you are here to celebrate—on these slips of paper—and place them in this special Tibetan singing bowl."

Abby anxiously scanned the faces of the people who heard her sis-ter preach every week. She was working on the row behind her, searching for alarm or confusion, when she heard her name being called. Jordanna was standing at the edge of her pew, beckoning. The winglike sleeve of her robe obscured all the light behind her. "A reading from John 14:1–8," Jordanna said, in an attempt at her stagy minister voice.

"Gee, thanks," Abby whispered as she followed her sister up to the pulpit. Jordanna knew she hated any kind of public speaking.

When they reached the front of the church, Jordanna stopped and waited for Abby. She leaned in close as they took the steps together, and with her lips touching Abby's ear, she said, "I . . . can't."

Standing in the center of the altar was as close to being onstage as Abby ever got, and she was hot with the awareness of the audience behind her. Jordanna reached down and grabbed Abby's hand, her large workmanlike fingers oddly cold. Abby gripped back, firmly, kneading her fingers into the back of Jordanna's hand, palpating the raised veins, trying to make something circulate again. At first Abby thought she'd pressed too hard, because suddenly, before they had reached the pulpit, the opened Bible with the red satin strip like Christmas ribbon marking the reading, Jordanna let out a sob. The sound escaped from far back in her throat, as if it had been waiting for release for years. Jordanna stopped moving, except for the heaving of her shoulders, and Abby wondered if she were going to be sick, right there on the red carpet.

The pianist, a woman Abby recognized from the drive-up window at the bank, had taken a seat on the side of the altar. Abby nodded at her now, hoping that she possessed the power to signal to this woman to move toward the piano and start playing. Jordanna was sobbing softly, and through the rise and fall of her crying she looked up at the pianist and nodded once vigorously. The woman moved to the piano, her face flushed with the shock of being involved in an improvisation. Abby looked around the altar for that door, the door Jordanna always emerged from at the start of a service. Except for the twenty-foot, lighted wood cross on the back wall of the church, everything was white. She and Jordanna kept moving, slowly, toward the back, Abby's eyes alert for a seam, a knob, a hinge. From behind her she heard coughing and shuffling and then a pounding of feet, and for a moment she thought that Jordanna had fallen. But no, she was right there, hunched over, their hands still entwined, the sleeve of Jordanna's robe glancing the inside of Abby's wrist. Abby started when she heard a voice boom out, "Let not your hearts be troubled . . ." Someone was at the Bible, reading. They had moved now past the three armchairs along one side of the altar. And then she saw it, a small brass handle. Abby pulled open the door and guided her sister through.

"I need . . . to go . . . home," Jordanna said, as soon as they'd pulled the door closed behind them. They were in a cold dark hallway. The only light came from the exit sign above a header at the end of the hall. The tunnellike space confirmed Abby's suspicion that organized religion was riddled with secret passageways winding through the whole of it, chambers and catacombs the worshipers were never privy to, a secret society with a rigid hierarchy and a host of tricky handshakes and impenetrable codes.

"Abby," Jordanna said, her voice pleading, invoking her name as if it were synonymous with *help*.

"Where are the lights in here?"

Jordanna nodded in the direction of the exit sign, and the two began moving toward it. There was barely room for them to walk side by side, so Abby inched a bit ahead and, holding Jordanna's hand, began to lead her down the hall, the slippery sound of Jordanna's robe sliding along the painted cinderblock.

They exited through the undercroft, and when she opened the door to the parking lot, the wind gusted, blowing dead leaves into the vestibule. "Why don't you wait here while I get the car," she said to her sister.

"I need to go home. I just want to be home." Jordanna gripped the cuffs of Abby's sweater, and the two inched across the poorly lit parking lot to Abby's car.

"Brendan's still inside. I'm just going to unlock the—"

"Please. Take me home." Jordanna began to sob, and as Abby guided her into the passenger seat in the van, Jordanna pulled Abby to her. They stayed like that for a moment, Abby's face pressed to Jordanna's chest, the wind ripping through the open van door blowing Jordanna's hair across Abby's face.

"What's going on, Mom?" Brendan jogged toward them holding out Abby's coat to her.

Abby tucked Jordanna's clerical robe around her legs and shut the car door. "I don't know," she said as she and Brendan walked to the other side of the van.

The car radio, a murmuring backdrop when she and Brendan had driven up to the church, sounded distressingly loud in the silent van.

"Please," Jordanna moaned.

"Would you like to come stay at our house?"

"Abby." Jordanna's voice croaked and groaned under an enormous weight.

"Okay. It's okay," she said. A passing car honked as she turned up Hull Hill, and she realized she'd forgotten to put on her headlights.

Abby had barely pulled to a stop in front of the parsonage before Jordanna bolted up the brick walk, turned the handle of the front door and disappeared inside. Abby and Brendan sat in silence, waiting for lights to come on in the house.

"Mom, is JoJo okay?"

"Honestly, Bren, I don't know. I don't know what's going on. Why don't you stay here for a minute." Abby turned off the car and left the keys in the ignition.

When she stepped into the front hall, she saw a dark shape on the floor, and was forced to consider for at least a second or two that it was her sister. Kneeling down, she realized that it was just Jordanna's robe, spread out in the middle of the hall like a little black pond or an opened parachute. She gathered up the yards of material in her arms, then felt around on the front hall table for the lamp she thought was there. She moved up the stairs tracking the rest of Jordanna's clothes, clogs at the bottom, a lavender turtleneck farther up, purple silk trousers on the landing, bra and panties on the top two steps. She flicked on the light in the upstairs bathroom. The door to Jordanna's room was open, and she entered, the discarded clothing piled in her arms, as if she were doing what she did at home with her kids, picking up after them, folding, straightening, opening and closing bureau drawers, checking into those sometimes dark corners of their lives.

Jordanna was in bed under the covers, her bare freckled shoulders just visible above the quilt. Her eyes were open and she was staring, straight ahead, unblinking.

Abby stood over her for a moment and then sat on the edge of the bed. "What can I get you?"

Jordanna didn't respond. In fact, if Abby weren't studying the rise and fall of the covers, she wouldn't have been certain her sister was alive. She followed Jordanna's gaze. The shades were up on the windows, but it was impossible to see beyond their own reflections.

"Are you hungry? Thirsty? Aren't you cold? Would you like a nightgown?" She stood up and sighed. Catatonia . . . catatonia would be just cause to call 911.

"Don't go."

Abby shook her head. "I'm not going."

"Thank you."

"Is there anyone you want to talk to? Chip? He's home now, better. It's not that late." She sat down on the bed.

"It's not just me."

Abby turned so that she was facing Jordanna. She brought one leg up underneath the other and moved toward the middle of the bed.

"Did you notice?" Jordanna continued to stare at the opaque window.

"What?"

"Bev Congdon . . ."

Jordanna worked a fingernail into a loose thread on the quilt. "I thought that it was because of me." She shook her head slightly. "Everywhere. Inches from my mouth, my chest. Just right there. No room for anyone else." She spoke softly and without inflection, as if each word were equally meaningless. Her arms were tucked under the spread, and she reminded Abby of one of those stony-faced busts their old piano teacher used to give out as prizes at the end of the year.

"That mouse . . . never took up anyone's time or attention . . . she's monstrous, huge . . . a cloud that obscures everything good."

Abby reached for what she thought was Jordanna's knee under the spread and patted it. "Who, hon? Who are you talking about?" She tried to maintain an evenness in her own voice, the way she did when she was comforting one of the boys.

"She's louder dead. Very loud."

"I don't know who you're talking about," Abby said, resisting the urge to turn Jordanna's face toward her, to hold it and force some color and expression back into the cheeks, the eyes. "You're—"

"June," Jordanna said as if it should have been obvious. She turned her whole body in the bed, turned on her side to face Abby. "How did you feel in there, in the sanctuary? What sort of thoughts were you thinking?"

Abby pulled her hands back from massaging Jordanna's legs. What she was thinking now was that maybe she wouldn't have to call 911. Jordanna seemed to be coming back into focus. "You know me, I'm not a churchgoer. It's like classical music for me. My mind wanders."

"To good thoughts or bad?"

She'd been thinking about how her sister was too resilient, how she had a false bottom, like one of those trick Chinese boxes. How Tara Sears had said she had a Christ complex. Was thinking the truth the same as having negative thoughts? "I was just trying to figure things out. Isn't that mostly what we're always doing, following one train of thought, then another, trying on ideas, seeing which ones fit?"

"It was cold in there, wasn't it? It got so cold."

Abby remembered that her sister's hand had been unnaturally

cold. "Let me get you another blanket." She wanted to ask her sister why she was naked, but she wasn't sure she wanted to hear the answer. Abby got off the bed and walked into the hallway to the linen closet. She told herself that if Jordanna started talking about the devil and started sounding like something out of the Salem Witch Trials, she would call Scott Davis from the downstairs phone.

There were no extra blankets, only a few odd pillowcases, some hotel soaps and a very worn, down-filled sleeping bag. She pulled out the sleeping bag and a white log of a candle rolled toward her. It was the kind of candle they lit at christenings in Catholic churches. On one side there was a pale yellow lily and on the other a symbol she recognized from Jordanna's church letterhead. She ran her fingers over the raised red wax of the hieroglyph, another example of the fabricated mysteries of the faithful, like that cryptic rune that hung from Brendan's neck.

She spread the lumpy sleeping bag over Jordanna and placed the candle on the dresser next to the pictures of Alice and James. She lit the candle and breathed out the only kind of prayer she could muster: "Strengthen her."

"It's okay as long as it's not physical, isn't it?" Jordanna began loudly. "When it's just an idea, a feeling, a belief, a spirit . . ."

Abby sat down tentatively at the foot of the bed. She lifted the zipper end of the sleeping bag and tucked it under itself.

"But as soon as it crosses over into the material world, the body . . . so few can accept that. It's the whole problem. It's where I lose everybody."

Abby looked over at the clock radio on the nightstand. It was almost nine. "I'm not sure I really follow."

"If I pray, make a petition in my heart or my mind or even aloud, with words, that's acceptable. If I place my hands on someone, like a Tara Sears, place my hands on her head—"

"Did you do that? Did you pray over—"

"If the spiritual shifts over into the material, they think I've cheapened it. But the body—"

"Mom?"

Abby heard Brendan call from the stairs. She didn't want him in this room. Her sister seemed liable to do or say something disturbing. Abby got up from the bed and ducked her head into the upstairs hall.

"What's going on?" he said. "I was in the car for, like—"

Abby held up a finger to her lips.

"Is JoJo having a breakdown or something?" he said, his deep voice incapable of a whisper. "Maybe we should call Dad?"

Abby screwed up her face. "Why don't you go into the kitchen and make some tea for her, okay?"

"Tea? Right." He started back down the stairs and she could hear him mumble, "This is so far beyond tea."

Abby turned back toward Jordanna, who was staring at the candle. "My ordination candle," she said flatly.

"Oh, I'm sorry. We should blow it out."

Jordanna shook her head. "I've missed something."

Abby pulled the white rocking chair in the corner of the room to the side of Jordanna's bed.

"What lesson? What is it I'm being . . . You know I might lose my call? Did I tell you that?"

Abby shook her head. The candle on the dresser flared, then dwindled, and she resisted the impulse to get up and straighten the wick.

"Ben Hall and some others have called every member of the church, trying to get up some support. . . . They've formed a committee. When I got into my office today there was a sour cream coffee cake and a vase filled with flowers. Gael's typical bereavement package."

Abby stilled the rocker. "Are you certain you—"

"This spiraling down—June, Daniel, this pregnant girl in Senior P.F.—these things aren't accidents, you know?"

She was sounding like herself again, which wasn't as reassuring as Abby thought it would be. Pitying her sister, worrying about her, was so much more comfortable than having to register this itch of annoyance, which could so abruptly flare into a full-fledged irritation. "I'm not sure I know what you mean by *accident*."

"We're all connected." Jordanna sat up in bed now, excited. The spread fell from around her neck and slid to reveal the top of one breast. "It's all connected and intertwined. It's meant to be, and we are meant to understand that."

"Jordanna, those things happened to other people. I mean, apart from your marriage—you've just found yourself crossing paths with people in the midst of their own agonies. That's your job. That's what you do. But it's not about you, it's about them. You do see the difference, don't you?"

Abby thought back to what she knew about mania. Maybe the whole God trip was some kind of slow-growing, incipient mania. "You wouldn't want to dilute experience, the experience of the individual, by globalizing. Other people have different needs from yours, different perspectives. I mean, given that, how can things be so interdependent? It really doesn't make sense."

"There are things, Abby, that I'm . . . I see it all the time, the interconnectedness of events. I mean, this girl who's pregnant, what's come of that has been . . . there have been some truly amazing synchronicities there."

"That's such a sensitive area for you. Of course you're likely to view an unwanted pregnancy—"

"Oh, I don't think it's unwanted at all. That's just it. That pregnancy has released a truth into that family, a truth that really needed to be shared."

"It can't be easy for you to separate your longing . . ."

Jordanna looked down at her body under the spread and ran a thumb along the side of her underused breast. "My longing, my grief, is precisely why I'm good at my job."

Brendan appeared in the doorway holding a mug of tea at arm's length as if it were combustible. He rapped his knuckles on the doorframe of the bedroom.

Abby lunged toward her sister to pull the spread over her bare breast, nicking the soft white flesh under Jordanna's chin with her ring. "I'm sorry—"

"Oh," Jordanna gasped, "Bren, I forgot you were here."

"Where should I put this?"

Abby watched him stare at Jordanna's bare shoulders through the mist of steaming tea.

"Thank you, hon," Jordanna said. And for the first time tonight, Abby saw her sister smile.

"Right there, Brendan, on that little nightstand, on the books," Abby said.

"It's okay," Jordanna said, reaching her hand out to him. "I'm all right. I'm not going to—"

"It's chamomile," he said. You didn't have honey, so I just put some sugar in it. I know you like it sweet."

"Thank you," Jordanna said, squeezing his hand.

"Why don't you go down in the living room. You can read," Abby said, wondering if he had squeezed back.

The pillar candle on the dresser continued to flicker as if sending out some maddeningly long message to another boat at sea. Abby got up out of the rocking chair to blow it out. For a few moments the only light in the room was the indirect light from downstairs. "Sometimes I wonder if you realize how much power you have." She reached across the nightstand where the untouched tea rested and pulled the chain on the banker's lamp. "People make life decisions based—

"You're talking about June—"

"No. I'm talking about the girl in your church who's pregnant."

"Tara Sears?"

Abby nodded. "She's come to talk with me at school."

"You're her guidance counselor?"

Abby sighed and shook her head. "Not exactly."

"She's comfortable with you, then. That's good. I'm relieved. I was hoping she had some other adults in her life, apart from her parents, other people she could trust. That's good, Abby. Thank you."

Jesus, why did Jordanna do that, as if all of life were a party she was hosting, as if she were the guardian of the world. "No one could expect you to objectively counsel a kid about abortion. I mean, I understand that." Abby carried the rocking chair back to the corner of the bedroom where she'd first found it. "But part of counseling is zeroing yourself out, you know?"

"What are you saying?" Jordanna rubbed her great ringless fingers over the outlines of her thighs, as if she were both trainer and horse after a hard race.

"That girl is already sixteen weeks pregnant."

"You say it like it's my doing, Abby."

"Well, you've knocked her up pretty well with some of your ideas."

"What does that mean?"

"She came to my office this morning, Jordanna, and she told me that you told her that the greatest thing she could do now was to make some couple's dream come true."

"Why would I say that?"

"According to Tara, you made it sound like you wanted this baby yourself, which you really—"

"And you believed her?" Jordanna looked pale, propped up against the white pillows. "You really think I would wreck a kid's life, just because I couldn't distinguish between my loss and hers?"

"Not maliciously—"

"Are we even talking about the same girl, here? What makes you think that Tara Sears would listen to anything any adult told her? The girl's tough as nails—"

"I can only begin to imagine what it's like for you to listen to a kid who's pregnant, but why would you tell her that you know what she's . . . why would you twist your experience . . ." Abby expelled the air she'd been collecting by not breathing regularly. "That girl is under the impression that you had an abortion once and you don't want her to make the same regrettable choice. I mean, is that what you do in pastoral counseling?" Abby let herself go, and it was like being permitted to drop a heavy load. She'd spent so much time and energy worrying that it would slip from her, and there was an awesome power in willfully dumping it. "To drive home the empathy, the compassion, you just tell everyone you know how they feel—literally, because you've been there?"

Jordanna shook her head slowly back and forth against the pillow, and for a while it was the only sound in the house. "How's it possible that I respect you so much, and you respect me so little?" She rolled away from Abby and turned off the little lamp.

"I respect truth," Abby said from the doorway.

"Love, Abby. The ultimate truth is love."

Abby walked out of the bedroom and down the stairs so slowly that Brendan jumped when she appeared in the living room. When she thought about all this tomorrow, and the next day and the day after that, she would remember that she had exercised a great deal of control by not having said in that pitch-black bedroom what she now said aloud to herself: "You don't know what love is."

ഉ⊘ Chapter 20

I T was well after midnight when Jordanna unlocked the doors to the sanctuary. She slid an umbrella through the panic bar so that the door could not be opened from the outside. With the fluorescent light of the illuminated wooden cross as her guide, she walked through the darkened church, down the center aisle of the sanctuary, to the altar. The heat had been turned down and the cold pressed through the windows. The table full of white pillar candles had been left in the center of the altar. Hardened wax dotted the cloth from the Service of the Bittersweet earlier in the evening. She tripped on the middle step as she walked up to the altar to get the matches on the shelf beneath the lectern. She lit only a couple of the candles, just enough so that she could make out the singing bowl, still on the table cupping the names of the dead on folded slips of white paper. The upper reaches of the church, the choir loft and the forty feet of emptiness that roared above her were completely dark.

She had left the house sometime after Abby had because she needed cigarettes. That's what she told herself as she hopped on her bike dressed in nothing but a sweatshirt and sweatpants, no bra or underwear, no coat. But she hadn't bought the cigarettes. Instead, she'd pumped the old Raleigh out past the trailer park and the transfer station, across Osborne Bridge and down into Powell. The roads were empty and windless, and after a short while the rain felt neither cold nor wet. All she knew for sure was that she needed to be moving, closer to something. She biked and biked for hours without registering the darkened houses or stripped trees, the boarded-up farm stands or empty silos, the burbling streams or the late autumn lawns pooling with rainwater. It was only when she realized suddenly that she couldn't bike any farther that she looked for a landmark and found that she'd circled back onto the western edge of Bethel Road. She coasted down toward the church, her church, and used the key on her key ring to unlock the door.

She had already started to release her hold on this space. She was getting good at letting go of things and people. Standing in the cold dark of the sanctuary now, she remembered the lag time with James, the limbo between being told that the fully developed baby inside her was dead and actually delivering him. You weren't still pregnant once the baby was dead, you were just housing the fetal remains, the human equivalent of the mausoleums found in small-town cemeteries where the bodies of those who died in winter were stored until spring when proper graves could be dug. She was the dead thing now inside this space, this crypt. The church would go on, she would be expelled. If she'd made her way into any other church tonight, she might have been able to pray, but here the space had been permanently altered, just as her sense of her own body had changed forever in her failure to produce viable life. The whole room smelled to her now of failure and fear. The unlit corners of the sanctuary seemed infinite in their meanness.

She could let go of this place. She had relinquished much dearer things before. This was next to nothing. It was loosing yourself from people that was the problem, and she never did that until she was forced to. She never wrote people off, never gave up on anyone, not anyone. And to think that Abby had done that to her, who knows how long ago, was difficult to comprehend. Unrequited love was like howling into a void, giving it all up and over, this great gift of self, and waiting endlessly for the return flight. She couldn't remember a time when she hadn't adored her sister, when she hadn't wanted to be near her, to hear her voice, to touch her. How was it possible to respect someone so fully and have that person be so disdainful of you? How long had she not noticed that? Certainly that was one of the causes for her sister's repulsion. Since she wouldn't be able to stop loving Abby, this would be just one more unilateral relationship, ritualistic, cultic, theoretical.

She lowered herself into the first pew, exhausted but still too frightened to close her eyes, to sleep. From here she could barely make out the organ, and she wondered what she would do if a note sounded, if she started hearing music. What if the handbells up in the choir loft began to ring? Such things could happen in a world without end. She had tried to explain to Abby about June's presence, why she'd had to leave the service earlier tonight.

Evelyn Perry had been playing the piano softly as everyone came in. Jordanna had used that time to center in. She'd been seated on the altar, along the side, with her eyes closed, focusing on her breathing. The flow of the music into her feet and her ears was interspersed with the sound of zippers and snaps, coats and purses hitting the pews, the rustling of papers, the clasping of hands, some low talking, even some laughter. She thanked God for James and Alice, for the opportunity to be their mother for as long as she'd been allowed, and for their ongoing presence in her life now, however that might be manifested. She prayed for the soul of Mary Jane Krull, and then she tried to call June to mind and heart. She pictured her the last time she'd seen her, her lidded gaze, her unwashed hair, her unlovable self. She prayed that her body be found, that the family might have the comfort of a funeral. And then it was time to start, and she looked out at the thirty or forty people clustered throughout the candlelit church, and it was as if an errant wave, the kind that springs unsynchronized, unannounced, rushed toward her. An onslaught of grief sprang forth from the congregants, and she felt for a moment as if she were at some hideous man-made beach, a beach with walls. All the sorrow in that church raced at her headlong with no place to go. She was certain it would displace her, drown her. The grief was deafening as it roared toward her. And in the surging of that wave she could hear June's voice repeating Jordanna's own words to Daniel, "There's nothing for it." This was June's legacy. She felt it spread from her lower back down her legs and across her shoulders, despair, total, physical despair. And she was certain that June, in all her misunderstood pain, was present in the church. For the first time Jordanna knew what it meant to be haunted, to be forced to encounter that which you failed to fathom the first go-around.

In the moments before she hobbled out the side door of the sanctuary on her sister's arm, she had caught, for an instant, the specter of an inkling, the truth of which sent a pain shooting through her nose into her brain. That was it, a flash she'd barely been able to fathom, or had not wanted to.

She walked up to the pulpit now, rubbing her unadorned fingers together for warmth, and turned the opened Bible to Matthew 10:39. "He who loses his life for my sake will find it," she said aloud. It wasn't a ghost, but an idea, that had caused her to fold up, whimper, go silent. It was why she'd stripped off all her clothing, as if she could keep this realization from following her home, up the stairs, hosting on cotton and silk and wool, crawling from fiber to skin to soul.

She had let June die. June had died because of her sins. That tidal wave of nontranscendant grief she saw when she looked out over the congregation was the very perception that had made her as ill-prepared to deal with June as June was with herself. Spiritual life was dependent on conjuring. Belief was the active practice of a brand of alchemy that turned loss into insight, pain into compassion. She'd been able to fake it these past three years with just about everyone but June. The woman whose nerve endings seemed to have been cauterized was, in fact, the only one who'd sensed the lie. Jordanna was as stuck on her own loss as June was; she just hadn't killed herself over it, yet. Even with all the metaphysical stratagems at her disposal, Jordanna had not traveled beyond the stunning sensation that she'd lost two limbs and had the majority of her heart cut out. Personal loss was meaningless if it did not yield, finally, to true compassion, if its identity could not merge with the grief experienced by others. She had hoarded her loss, kept it close and warm, an incubus. Life was, in fact, cheap if the loss of it did not transport you, did not teach you to allow your heart to break, again and again, for a Tara Sears, or a June Nearing.

She blew out the candles on the altar, walked through the sanctuary and the narthex and unwedged the umbrella from the front doors. Nothing was random; she'd been right about that, after all. It was still raining, still dark, and she picked up her bike where she'd dropped it at the base of the front steps. There was a sense of relief in knowing so certainly what she needed to do now. She pedaled out of the church driveway onto Bethel Road, stuck out her tongue hoping for a few drops of cold rain and instinctively closed her eyes for the briefest of seconds so as to taste it better.

HER memory of the accident would never acquire a chronology. It would always remain a dreamy jumble of sensory images, none unpleasant. There was her body, all loose from wear, flying, not falling (she didn't remember that part). There was the luxuriant moisture of the air, on her face, her hair, the pavement. And mostly there was the ripe, stringy flesh of the misplaced jack-o'-lantern, the pungent smell of squash and all that pumpkins brought to mind.

THE light on the eastern side of the church filled the twenty-foot windows in grays and blues, setting off the white of the pew backs, the red of the cushions and the carpet. It was like coming to on the deck of a freshly painted boat, the steely Atlantic stretching out before her. Why had she never before noticed how like a ship the place was? A cubist *Mayflower*. So much unadorned white wood, the prowlike altar, the crucifix so like mast and boom.

"I think that was the end of your bike, JoJo."

She tried to lift her head.

"Better not."

It was Brendan. He was kneeling now, in front of where she lay in the last pew. She felt something damp and sticky at the edge of her hairline.

"You might need stitches," he said. "Maybe in a few places. I don't think anything is broken. Well, not your legs or anything. You might be dizzy. I mean, you threw up on my shirt, so you might have a concussion. So don't fall back asleep, okay?"

Jordanna braced an elbow beneath her and attempted to raise her shoulders. She let out a moan. She would make sure never to move her left arm again. A pile of scarves and coats slid off her chest onto the floor. Her nose was filled with the smell of rotting fruit. "What happened?" Her voice was scratchy, as if she'd been up smoking all night.

"You know, kids ride around town making pie out of people's jack-o'-lanterns. I guess you just skidded into some pumpkin pulp and . . ." Brendan replaced the jackets and sweaters back on her, as if she were a dresser top. "I called an ambulance from the phone downstairs."

"You should be in school."

"It's not even six A.M."

"Oh."

"I think you might have been out there awhile."

"Where?"

"I found you just around the corner, at the edge of the road. You're really cold. I just got all this stuff from the collection box in the front. I mean, JoJo, you weren't even wearing anything—"

"Why are you here?" This wasn't exactly what she wanted to say, but it was the best she could do.

"I was just out riding."

"So early."

"I had things on my mind, you know."

She did.

"Your mother will be worried," Jordanna said.

"She'll be worried about you. I know—"

"No," Jordanna said. She tried to clear her throat without jostling her arm. Anything not to feel that pain again. "No, Bren. No. This is . . . Please don't tell her. I'll be fine. I always am. Just tired."

"Don't close your eyes, JoJo. Keep talking to me."

She knew that her nephew was still there. She could hear his voice, but she couldn't make him out very well. He was reciting something, something familiar, the words of a song, or a poem, a nursery rhyme she'd taught him. No, that wasn't it. It had a lilt to it ". . . forgive us our debts as we forgive those who . . ." Yes, she knew that. She had taught that to all her children.

ᏣᎣ Chapter 21

A BBY saw Brendan slink down under the bare maple tree out-side her office window as she listened to the parents of a sopho-more accused of sending sexually explicit e-mails to a number of other males in his class. His sitting beneath that tree was the signal they'd agreed upon when he'd started high school back in Septem-ber. That way if he needed to talk with her during the day, he wouldn't be caught coming into her office, blurring the lines between home and school. She was to wave from her office window and then meet him by her car as soon as she could.

She'd been talking with these parents for almost twenty minutes. That was long enough. Aside from expressing shock and dismay, they hadn't proposed much in terms of monitoring their son's com-munications in the future. She explained the district's published rules about this kind of harassment, and waited for them, one more time, to pick up the PTA rhetoric, the idea of partnership between parents and teachers. No, it seemed that they wanted the public school sys-tem to do the parenting. She stood finally and extended her hand, and slowly they seemed to understand that this ineffectual meeting was over.

It was lunch period for most freshmen, and Abby grabbed her thermal sack from her briefcase and walked through the guidance office, down the corridor past the front office, out to the staff parking lot. When they'd left the parsonage last night, Brendan had demanded to know what was going on, what was wrong with Jordanna, what had been said to make them depart so abruptly, so coldly. All she had told him was that they were sisters and of course they fought sometimes, that was natural, wasn't it? They'd driven the rest of the way in silence. She was still expecting the guilt to kick in. Like knowing that everyone you'd shared a meal with had come down with food poisoning. She was waiting to feel sick. But she'd woken up this morning with a strange sense of freedom. She'd said what she'd wanted to her sister, and she'd been right. She'd been honest. She hadn't denied some part of herself in order to spare the whole of her sister. It was a relief, really.

She hadn't even felt guilty when Brendan had said, "You're all she's got, Mom, you know that." No, she hadn't felt guilty; instead she had acknowledged the genesis of the statement. It was something she had said to all the kids these past few years as a way of explaining the amount of time she spent with Jordanna, over the phone, over coffee, late at night over wine. How many times had she elbowed her children to make room for her sister? She had cleared whole mornings, hours and hours of attention and preoccupation. She had carved a space for this woman, while often putting her own young children on hold. She had sacrificed for Jordanna. Why? To what end? It had only served to make her angry. It was a sacrifice that would never be returned, never. She cosseted her sister so her sister could in turn, supposedly, go and cosset others. Where was the reciprocity in all this? Nowhere.

And what about her marriage? How often had she been forced to push Jim to the margins of her evenings or weekends to accommodate her sister? They included her now in all their family events. There was rarely a Saturday night when Abby didn't feel the need to extend an invitation to her sister, when she didn't think, as she and

Jim were setting off to the movies or dinner, whether her sister might want to join them. God, she'd been stupid. It had taken a surly, pregnant teenager for her to really see her sister's true nature, to understand the futility of making herself an instrument for changing and completing Jordanna. This older sister of hers, this beacon of sensuality and vitality, this Paul Bunyan of spirituality and optimism, the fucking heroine of their family, was damaged beyond repair. Nothing Abby did or said, no act or thought, word or deed, no intent or desire could make her whole. This was how it happened. This was how you liberated yourself from the bonds of repetitive injury. She was free of this sister.

Brendan was leaning against the side of the van, the tails of his flannel shirt dangling below the thrift store jacket, a surplus item once the property of some Scandinavian sailor. She indulged in the momentary deception of viewing him as merely just one more yawning, lanky freshman, rather than the shy boy she still so desperately wanted to hold close, keep safe and make happy.

She weaved her way through the tight row of cars and stopped herself from waving to him. "What's up?" she said, working at sounding casual.

"Have you called JoJo yet today?"

She squinted against the sunlight bouncing off the silver sedan parked beside them. She would handle this professionally. "No, I haven't."

He cupped one hand over his eyes. "Maybe you should."

"I know you think that, hon." She stared at the dark circles under his eyes. "I know you feel—"

"Don't do that, Mom."

"What?"

"That touchy-feely, psych-me-out crap." He shoved his hands into the sidecut pockets of his coat.

She placed her lunch on the hood of the van. There were times when she didn't notice that he was a head taller, and then times, like now, when everything about him, his intensity, his intelligence, his body, dwarfed her. "Why don't you tell me why you're so pissed off—how's that, is that better?"

"I'm worried about her, Mom. I—"

"Your aunt's pretty tough. I wouldn't spend too much time worrying about her."

"Did she do something to you? I mean, why are you so mad at her? 'Your aunt,' what's that all about?"

"I *am* mad at her, Bren. But it has nothing to do with you, quite frankly."

He turned slightly away from her and looked out toward a line of girls jogging from the gym up toward the soccer fields. "You're not going to like this, but if she loses her job . . . I think you should, like, offer for her to move in with us."

Abby exhaled loudly.

"Mom, I'm worried she—"

"What?"

Brendan looked down at the ragged hem of his cargo pants. "Do you think she might, I don't know, like, do something to herself?"

"Oh, Bren." She quickly recalled her fingers from the side of his face. "Is that what you've been thinking?"

"Mom, you have to help her." He took a small step back from Abby and leaned against the silver-colored car. "I think she's having a nervous breakdown. I mean, why did she just leave church last night right in the middle?"

"Brendan, Jordanna is human. She has her limitations." The sun was directly behind him now, and Abby closed her eyes against its brilliance. "She's under a great deal of stress right now. Getting divorced, some of the things that have happened in her congregation."

"Like Tara Sears?"

"Among others, yeah."

"Well, what are you going to do?"

"It's not my place to *do* anything." She opened her purse and began to feel around for her sunglasses.

"Jesus, you talk to loser kids all day, kids you're not even related to, and you, like, try to help them, supposedly. I mean, Jesus, JoJo."

"Stop saying 'Jesus.'"

He looked at her, teeming with something, she wasn't sure what, his face flushed and urgent. And without knowing why, she started to laugh. "I'm sorry," she said.

"I don't care."

"Look, Bren." She straightened out her mouth. "Jordanna and I need a little break from each other right now. I don't think I'm in a position to be helpful to her. But you're right, she does need . . . I'm sure your company would be . . . she'd be grateful for it."

"If I went over there, maybe even to stay for a few days . . . just to make sure . . . you wouldn't be mad?"

The bell rang to signal the next period. Out here it was muted, as if they were almost free, beyond the rules of the school. Of course, this was what he'd been after all along, her permission. Did her own son think she was so insecure as to be jealous of his attention to his aunt? "Don't worry, I can get over myself," she said, knowing she'd mangled a phrase beloved by his peer group.

SHE moved the grocery bags from Gabe's car seat to the floor of the van and reparked across the street from Miss Diane's. She hated getting caught in the day-care provider's driveway during the end-of-the-day evacuation. The goodbyes were never neat and clean, never efficient. There was always a message to relay, a game still to be won or, worse, a craft project to be bundled up and carried home. Abby waited for Sam's dad, who always smelled of the furnaces he repaired, to give up his spot on the threshold of the front door. Diane tapped her elbow and mouthed, *I have something to tell you.*

Abby looked through the slider to the fenced-in yard. Gabe and a little girl she didn't recognize were twisting the swings around and around and then letting them spin. Gabe was erupting in bursts of laughter, the fat pads of his cheeks all shiny red. It was cold outside, almost dark, and when he turned his back to the house, she could see crumbled brown leaves pressed into his hair and his bright blue fleece jacket. She prepared herself to hear him whine at being called away from his new friend, or moan that he was "starving to hunger." Or he might start in again about Cody, the boy who only came on Thursdays, and how he "was, too, going to Disney World, *again*." But she knew that he wouldn't question whether she was a good sister to her own sister. He wouldn't look at her with suspicion or doubt, hoping that she was in fact less than she purported herself to be.

"I was fixing a snack for the kids around four, and I just happened to pop on the TV in the kitchen." Diane squatted down in her lycra pants and reshelved *Richard Scarry's Busiest People Ever*. "Brad is supposed to be taking the scouts camping this weekend, and I wanted to see the weather. Anyway, there was something about your sister on the news, I think. I'm pretty sure they said Reverend Nash." She stood up and dusted some glitter off her turtleneck. "We all call her Reverend Jordanna at church. They definitely showed a picture of Hutchinson Congregational."

Abby realized she was clenching her teeth. She breathed out, lowered her shoulders, attempted to release her jaw. "I guess some people over there are less than happy with her in the pulpit and—"

Diane shook her head. She motioned Abby away from the slider and into the kitchen, just off the dining room. It always amazed Abby how clean the kitchen was. On any given day, Diane had up to seven kids in her home. A high chair and two boosters, all smelling of disinfectant, were grouped around the breakfast nook. "That's Carly Nearing out in the yard with Gabe. June Nearing's little girl. She just started here on Monday. The news on TV was about that."

"There's a little boy, too, a baby, right? Are you . . . does he come, too?"

Diane was confused by the non sequitur, but Abby was building in time, time that she needed to prepare herself for what she might hear next, what she was afraid to hear.

"No, I already have two under two, I couldn't take him. They think . . . the body might be up in Bethel Falls. You know part of it runs out behind the church. You ever see that little bridge back there?"

Abby shook her head. She could smell cornbread and oranges mixed in with the kitchen cleaner. The countertop beside the sink was lined with paper towels and upturned plastic cups and lids. "I better get him." Abby turned and slid open the door to the backyard.

She reached for the radio again and again on the way home, as if she had a tic. She knew that the local news would carry the local breaking story, but Gabe was humming in the backseat, and she couldn't bear that he might hear, too, not that he would have known Reverend Nash from Reverend Al. She entered the house cautiously, as if there were a trip wire across the door. Gabe pushed past her in the back hallway and ran to find his brothers. She hung up the jacket he'd thrown on the floor, and began to go through Michael's, and then Christopher's backpacks for any notes or rotting fruit. They weren't supposed to watch television in the afternoon. And they weren't allowed on the Internet unless a grown-up was around. But still, news filtered into their lives. There were radios and phones, and friends on the bus. There were a million pores.

"Brendan." She braced one foot against the bottom of the staircase and yelled up. "Bren? Christopher?"

A door opened somewhere up there. "Guess what, Mom?'

"Where's Brendan?"

"Out on his bike." Christopher slid across the upstairs hall and stopped at the top of the staircase.

"Where?"

He shrugged. "Mom, we're doing that President's Challenge thing in gym, and I did thirty-eight push-ups—the real kind."

Abby turned from the stairs and headed toward the kitchen. She stopped and walked back. "Wow," she said, trying to muster enthusiasm. "Anybody call, honey?"

He didn't answer. From where she was standing now, he was partially obscured by the spindles on the banister. He was lowering himself to the floor in the upstairs hallway. "See?" he yelled out, his breath constricted. "I get my chin—"

"Unbelievable," she said, walking away. "Maybe you could teach Gabe how to do that." She let her voice trail off as she went into the family room and turned on the television.

❧ Chapter 22

SHE had dreamt that they were out on the Widgeon, she and Abby, out beyond the breakwater, into the bay. It was a clear, bright day, but things were wrong with the boat. Oddly enough, the little Widgeon was gaff-rigged, with three sails, like a cutter. For some reason the centerboard kept popping back up into the hull, causing the boat to sail sideways. It was as if the wind were blowing them away. All that power, and yet they couldn't harness it to move forward. In the midst of this helplessness about sailing sideways was the nearly deafening slapping of the sails, which couldn't seem to hold the wind. The frenzied luffing sounded as if someone they couldn't quite see were getting a royal beating.

Jordanna woke to find herself kicking at the starched stiff hospital sheets. She reached up to her forhead, and recalled the rustling of the disposable razor being unwrapped, just this morning, as the nurse prepared to shave a half inch just at the hairline. Her heart raced now as if engaged in a dire struggle, seemingly unaware of her body's motionless circumstances. Everyone said she'd been fortunate. "Damn lucky he found you," the EMT had mumbled after wrapping her in a foil blanket and urging Brendan to go home rather than ride along with them to the hospital. The X-ray technician, even though she wasn't supposed to, told her that the fracture in her ulna was "unbelievably" clean. And after insisting that she be admitted overnight because of the trauma to her head, the ER physician capped off his sermon on bike helmets by pronouncing her relative well-being "a miracle."

"It really is your lucky day." Brendan wheeled his fancy bike into the hospital room. "Not only am *I* here, you're not going to believe what I found at this store down the street. Yoo-Hoo popsicles." He pulled a frost-covered bar from a white bag. "Did you even know they make these things?"

The slamming of her heart against her chest wall slowed as she stared over at her nephew and heard the urgency in his too-deep voice. "They let you bring that in?"

"You'll really need medical attention if I let you eat the crap they're dishing up in here."

She smiled. "No, I meant . . ." She nodded toward the bike, which he had just propped up against the far side of the empty bed.

"Leave this baby outside? No way."

"You rode here? You didn't need to. You could have called—"

He picked up the receiver from the phone by her bed and held it to her ear. "Not plugged in."

She'd told the nurse she didn't want any calls or visitors. It was an effort to talk. For some reason her voice was hoarse as if she'd spent all last night singing or shouting. She explained that people from her church might start trooping through or phoning. She didn't want the TV hooked up, either. She just wanted to rest. She wondered how Brendan had gotten in here. "What time is it?"

"Don't worry. I went to school. For the whole day. And if you go down past Snow's Lake, it's not even ten miles from the school lot to here."

"Let your dad pick you up. Okay?" His short blond hair was damp and his cheeks were flushed. As he moved closer, she could smell the mixture of sweat and wet wool from under his coat. "Promise me you won't ride back home."

"I just got here."

She smiled and patted the side of her bed with her good arm.

"You know, you're not really that bad off."

She lifted her eyebrows in response.

"I called the nurses' station before, during my lunch period, said I was your son and I needed to know when to pick you up, so they gave me the rundown. They're letting you stay as extra insurance or something. Treat the minister well, and then when we need her . . . You even got a double room, no roommate. You're getting special consideration."

She looked out the window into the attached parking garage. *Special consideration*. She had grown accustomed to that, in every small town where she'd had a pulpit. But if what had come to her last night (was it only last night?) were true, she would need to do without it now. Her title was getting in her way, a thick second skin, like the flesh-tone bandage on her forehead, protecting her from both love and pain.

"It's going to melt," Brendan said, pulling the other popsicle out of the silver-lined freezer bag and holding it out to her.

"I'm afraid I'm not very hungry." Jordanna stroked his hand, no longer pudgy like a boy's, but not yet topped with hair like a man's.

"Have you ever said those words before?" He laughed. "JoJo not hungry? Impossible. I had this baseball coach one year and whenever he would yell to me, 'Brendan, protect the plate, buddy, protect the plate,' I'd think of what it was like to eat a meal with you, hovering to snag our food."

She punched him weakly in the arm, and then picked up his hand again and brought it to her lips. "You didn't have to come. I'll be home tomorrow."

He placed one popsicle back in the bag and set it on the rolling tray table at the head of her bed. He unwrapped the other one, pulling at the paper in strips, as if he were peeling a banana. "I wanted to do it. I wanted to make sure. . . ."

"Don't feel you have to fill in for your mom, okay? I'm not your responsibility. I'm too . . . young to be the poor auntie you need to look after. You know what I'm saying, Bren?"

He stood up and tossed the wrapper in the plastic trash can on the far side of the empty bed. "You're going to be having canned corn for dinner. I can smell it. Four-thirty and they're starting to bring those trays around. Hospitals are so sad. Who wants canned corn when it's still light out?" He took a large bite from the curved top of the popsicle, and she watched as he negotiated the icy chunk between his tongue and the roof of his mouth. "I know you hate doctors and stuff, hospitals. And I know . . . well, my mother's told me . . . about Uncle Daniel. It sucks, JoJo. Everything that's happened to you sucks, and I think about it a lot."

"God works all things to good," she said quietly.

He sat down tentatively on the empty bed and, after looking around for a moment, lay back and put his feet up. "Do you really believe that?"

"*People* don't necessarily work all things to good, but yes, I believe God does, yes.

"When did you know?" Brendan asked.

She looked at him for a long time, wondering how he'd guessed. How had he figured out that she was going to leave her call?

He licked the underside of the popsicle just as it started to drip. "You know, that you wanted to . . . do something with God?"

Oh, she thought. She'd had no idea that this was what he was after. That this was what he might want from her. "Again and again," she said, taking her time to answer. "Some very rare people know it almost continually." She tried to clear her throat. "Once, long before I was old enough to understand the feeling, I remember being certain that I wasn't alone. I mean, I absolutely knew it, and I tried to tell my mother, and she thought I was talking about an imaginary friend, one that I'd invented for my own pleasure. And I remember being almost desperate with this need . . . to explain what I meant, to convince her of this *presence*. I was old, older, before I started listening to the voice that had been there all along—but that I'd been drowning out with other things, with other people." She wanted to tell him that that wasn't the end of it. It didn't stop there. It couldn't. If faith were really to guide your life, the awakening had to happen within you many, many times, just as it had for her last night.

Brendan had been watching her, staring at her as she spoke, but now that it was his turn he hopped up and threw out the bare popsicle stick. "It's getting dark."

She nodded. "Gets dark early.

He walked over to the window and flipped up the control panel on the vent. "I know that girl, the one who's . . . you know, got you in all that trouble at your church. She's in my school."

Jordanna's arm ached, down to her fingernails. She had refused the Percocet, when they'd offered it after setting the arm and stitching her forehead. No real sense in rubbing the cast. "What about her?"

"She's a junior, but I see her around. I mean, I just don't think it's fair that you're getting blamed for . . . her actions, you know?"

"It's complicated. I should probably have been more in tune with what was going on. Supposedly, the boy is in Senior P.F., as well. So, in that way—"

"He's not." Brendan flipped down the metal lid on the vent. "He's not in your youth group."

Jordanna stared at him, her firstborn nephew, her godson. "Tell me you're still a virgin?" It came out without thinking. "Oh . . . I'm sorry, hon." She laughed. "Really, I didn't—"

Brendan made a kind of squeaking noise and his face burned red out to his ears. "No. Jeez. He's in *my* youth group at Our Lady. Nick Montserrat. That's who it is. I'm not trying to gossip, really, JoJo. But if I don't speak out . . . I mean, if I know the truth, and you might lose your job . . ."

"Thank you, Brendan. Thank you. I appreciate that."

"I'm kind of telling you for a reason. I mean, telling you and not my mother. I mean, she'll want to know how I know, you know, and I . . . it's just weird."

"Thank you. I appreciate the information."

He hopped up on the windowsill and let his sneakers bang against the metal radiator cover. "A lot of people are really bad off in here, huh? The doors are open and . . . walking down the hall . . ." He stared up at a brightly colored woodcut entitled *Sur la Plage*. "Why were you riding around in the middle of the night like that?" he said, his voice sounding not quite so deep.

"Do you pray?" She tried to readjust herself in the bed. "I don't mean in church, when you're supposed to, when the priest says, 'Now, let us pray.' I mean spontaneously, on your own, as a way to figure things out?" She didn't wait for him to answer. "When I was your age, we didn't go to church much. It never happened for me there in the pews, ever. And no one told me it could happen other places. Sometimes, riding my bike brings me to that place where I can pray."

He walked over to the framed print to examine it more closely, nearly sticking his nose up to the glass. "Were you trying to kill yourself last night?"

"Is that what you think? Oh, Brendan."

"I had to ask you that." He still hadn't turned to face her.

"I'm sorry I—"

"No, you don't understand. I had to know because . . . you're the only person I know who really, really believes, and if you . . . I mean, I've been reading that guy you talk about all the time, that Nouwen guy, just on my own, and—"

"Reverend Nash?" The door creaked open, and a young nurse in a floral smock and mint slacks strode in. "The secretary from your church is incredibly insistent—" The young woman stopped and looked over at Brendan in the corner of the room.

"Oh, this is my nephew."

She gave a half smile. "Now that you're up, you might want to plug in the phone. Actually, the switchboard operator sent a message up here—saying that if anyone else calls for you . . . Something about some reporters wanting to talk to you, too. I guess the secretary from your church is making herself quite—"

"I'm sorry. We'll plug it in right now, okay?"

"Well, as long as I'm here I might as well check your vitals." She pulled the blood pressure cuff from its hook on the wall.

Jordanna placed her good hand on the nurse's arm. "My nephew is leaving in a minute. Would you mind if we just . . . He saved my life this morning and . . ." Jordanna started to cry.

"Oh, okay. Sure." She patted Jordanna on the back. "I'll be by in a few, then." She pulled the door closed behind her and Jordanna reached for a tissue.

Brendan knelt down by the bed and began to plug in the phone. "Reporters? The *Hutchinson Herald* must be having a slow news week. 'Minister Sideswipes Squash—' "

"Let's finish what we were talking about first. It seems . . ."

Brendan stood, the phone cord still in his hand.

"We were talking about belief, I think."

"Yeah." He let the cord drop on the linoleum floor and sat down on the other bed. "I don't really have anyone else to talk to about this. That Nouwen says everyone needs a spiritual guide. I mean, if I asked you to be my spiritual guide . . . I mean, is that something you could do?"

She reached across her body with her right arm for her Styrofoam cup of water. "I have a spiritual guide, Reverend Solloway. Maybe you've heard me talk about him. He's someone I can always talk to—about anything—not just about my faith journey. So many things in my personal life have not gone as I would have liked, and sometimes Reverend Solloway gives me practical advice on how to move forward, sometimes, spiritual advice. Sometimes he gives no advice, he just listens. And that may be the most powerful gift of all. That he would separate himself from all that he has to do, all that he might want to say, and just listen to me, be with me."

"I don't mean that counseling stuff my mother does." He looked down at his sneakers, the snaking phone cord, the salmon-colored floor. "I don't mean us just trying to talk when you come for dinner and Gabe is bouncing a ball off your head. I mean something regular, like where you give me books to read and I can talk to you about . . . what I think about . . . like, God and stuff."

She didn't want to cry now in front of him, though she couldn't help but acknowledge this moment of grace. Something precious, and so wholly unexpected, was occurring in this cold, cheerless room with the fading November light filtering through the metal blinds. She took another sip of water.

"Brendan, it's important that you understand something about this kind of relationship. I'm not the keeper of the answers, you know what I mean? It's not like I have something, and when you're ready I'll bequeath it to you. The 'truth' isn't some secret formula I guard until the right time and the right person comes along. . . . I am . . . flawed. Very flawed. Broken, even."

"Jordanna? Jordanna? Where exactly are you?" Gael's tinny voice was moving closer in the hallway outside. "Yell out, so I know which one you're in," she said, as if the third floor of Deerfield Hospital were a department store and Jordanna had vanished behind a dressing room door.

"Before you let her in, I need to tell you something," Jordanna whispered, and waved him closer.

He pushed himself up and off the hospital bed, as if dismounting from the parallel bars, landing awkwardly by her side.

"What I said to that nurse before is true. You saved my life today, maybe a couple of times over, just so you know. And also, I want to tell you . . . I need to tell you . . . how much I love you."

He leaned over her, his bony chin grazing her bruised face, and pressed his lips to her bandaged forehead.

❧ Chapter 23

"I N lieu of a sermon this morning, I feel called to be open with you about some things that have occurred in our church family this past week, and some decisions that I have come to." Jordanna stood at the bottom of the altar steps, looking out at the congregation. She had zipped up her robe with the sling inside, her broken arm in partial embrace, and now the left sleeve of her gown hung empty and limp.

"First, I wish to thank everyone who sent flowers, brought meals, said prayers following my accident on Wednesday night. As you can see, I'm fine. The doctors tell me I was very lucky. I should also mention that along with the wonderful home-cooked meals that arrived on my doorstep over the weekend, came four brand-new bike helmets. Yes, I have learned my lesson. Trust me, they will be put to good use." She paused for a moment and took a deep breath.

"For those of you who attended the Service of the Bittersweet on Wednesday, please, know that I feel . . . I know I let you down by leaving. It has gotten back to me that my abrupt departure during the service led to a lot of conjecture. Some people thought I was ill, having a nervous breakdown, or a fit of some kind. The truth was that I was overcome with a sudden and very profound realization.

What I experienced at the start of the Service of the Bittersweet, as I looked out on the mourners in our midst, was a powerful event in my faith life. It rendered me temporarily, very temporarily, speechless. Though, as you see, I'm making up for that today." She waited a moment, but no one laughed. The congregation seemed to have moved collectively to the edges of the pews. "What I received in terms of grace that night has all to do with understanding how to serve more fully." For the first time she allowed herself to lift her good arm and gesture. She paused again, reminding herself this needed to be done, these things needed to be said aloud.

"As most of you know by now, June Nearing's body was found on Thursday. The Nearings have been through an incredible trial these two months. I know that many of you here have helped to share that burden, truly shoulder it with them. While for some the finality of her death was an end to a hope you'd been tending day and night, for others the news was, perhaps, more of a beginning of a kind of peace.

"This is a small community, and concerns spread quickly, as they should. We *should* be connected enough to talk with passion about the things that matter. Some of you may have learned of certain disconcerting details surrounding the discovery of June's body. It was shocking for me to learn that when she was found she was wearing a jacket of mine. I had kept a wool shirt in the closet in my office, and I lent it to her one day, one cold spring day, when she needed it." Jordanna had planned to leave nothing unsaid to this congregation. All through the introit, the responsive reading and the unison prayer of invocation she remained convinced that she could deliver up the messy thing that was her still-developing heart. Standing here now before them, no ritual, no music, no form for passing along this particular truth, she was unsure.

The detective who had called the church office on Thursday had seemed to be doing so merely to break the news that June's body had been found. When he called back yesterday, it was to tell Jordanna that June hadn't died from drowning. There'd been narcotics in her system. The body had been found on the far side of Bethel Lake, shallow water. "The husband" was pretty sure that her outermost layer of clothing had belonged to Jordanna. There was a laundry mark up in the collar, *Greene*. "The husband says that's your maiden name or something."

Jordanna walked up to the lectern and bent down for her glass of water. The jacket she'd lent June one dreary day after Easter had been Daniel's. It must have been decades old when he'd bought it at a thrift shop in Middletown, back when they were both at Yale. It was cranberry-colored with flecks of tan and navy, and Jordanna had driven home with it draped around her shoulders last fall after she'd been to Maine to see him. It was the weekend they'd gone hiking, and Daniel had made fondue and they'd had sex on the floor of the living room, the little Sterno candle the only light in the room. She'd worn the jacket in her office all that week, she remembered, as if it were a letter sweater, a symbol of their intertwining. But by the afternoon six months later when she'd offered it to June, it had become more memento than talisman.

She had intended to tell her congregants the truth about that afternoon. The heat in her office had been insufficient. There had been a brittle freezing rain all day. The cold had settled on the floor and in the walls, and yet Jordanna had hesitated before slipping the jacket from its hanger to place it around June's shoulders. These congregants, some of whom still respected her, needed to know that for the rest of that counseling session Jordanna had been irked by June's indifference to the coat, the way those Christmas-colored sleeves hung inert from the ends of her motionless hands. How to publicly admonish herself for not having offered up the jacket sooner, or more heartily? After all, it was something concrete and effectual she was able to do for June, perhaps the only thing, make her just a little less cold. How to share with the people in the pews this morning that hearing about June dressed in her jacket was like God slapping her across the mouth? She was stung with the image of June's hair floating straight out from her head, the ruby wool arms of the coat draped across her open eyes.

Jordanna walked about a third of the way up the center aisle of the sanctuary. "This has been a deeply confusing time in our church community, and more than anything I do not wish to add to that confusion by what I am about to say."

Would it help them to know that she told Detective Wilroy she'd never given June pills of any kind? "I lent her a jacket," she'd said to him over the phone.

"People keep medicines in their purse, in desk drawers in their office."

"I rarely take—"

"Say you have a bad back, something like that, some pain pill for something like that."

"I do have a bad back. Mostly I just live with it. I don't believe in—"

"Ohh . . ." She'd heard him on the other end of the line fumbling to remember what he could about that religion with science in its title.

She needed this congregation to know that it didn't change her culpability one bit if someone had provided June with the pills she'd used to kill herself. Jordanna had been responsible for her soul, the navigational system of that broken self. Jordanna had failed to provide June with an adequate reason not to empty a bottle of pills into the vessel that was her body. She needed her church to know that she had failed by example.

No one coughed or moved. Perhaps it was too late; maybe they no longer cared what she said. At least three people on the Prudential Board were working furiously to terminate her position. On Friday afternoon Gael had told her that Ben Hall had been in touch with the Central Conference. And of all people, Seth Hardesty, the Divinity School intern, had stumbled upon a large group of church members in Phil Pangrossi's storefront accounting business in the IGA shopping center. Seth had called Jordanna last night to say he'd heard that a significant contingent of congregants had threatened to break away from Hutchinson Congregational if Jordanna wasn't removed as pastor. "Some people worry that you've opened the church up to a lawsuit, from the Nearings or even . . . well, if that girl did get pregnant during a church sponsored outing . . ." He was breathing noisily on the other end of the phone, as if he were holding the receiver too close to his mouth, something he tended to do with the mike during worship. Jordanna thanked him for extending himself to call her. Just before she hung up she said, "It's not always like this. Some ministers stay with a church their entire careers."

She was in the center aisle of the church, halfway down, which meant that her back was to some, but this seemed the right place to say what she had to say. "After deep, deep reflection, I have decided to leave this call." There was near-perfect stillness for a moment, then someone dropped a Bible, and almost in concert the congregation and the pastor took in a noisy deep breath. Jordanna looked up at the lit crucifix, the warm truth of it willing her to continue. "What came to me the other night, during the Service of the Bittersweet, what came through to me about the truth of grief—your grief"—she gestured to both sides of the church with her one arm—"and mine—has convinced me that I have not been hearing this call, in this church, in the way that I might, that I should, that I truly need to."

She had sat up last night at her kitchen table with a stack of index cards, attempting to get this just right. But as always happened with her, once she began speaking, the words themselves begot words. Precisely why she needed to step away from preaching for a time. Good works in the world, deeds not words, was her plan for her future. "We are all, each and every one of us, in pain, and we must acknowledge our covenant responsibility to tap into the Divine source of love within. To tend to one another's pain as if it were our own. And that, above all else, is who we are finally called to be and what we are ultimately called to do, pastors and lay people alike. We are called, called here into mortal, physical life so that our love can make a difference. I've been deaf to this call . . . though I suspect God is in the process of sharpening my hearing—"

"Excuse me . . ." A man cleared his throat. "Reverend Nash." She turned and looked behind her. It was Tara's father. Buck Sears. She couldn't even remember the last time she'd seen him at a worship service. He was wearing a summer shirt, short-sleeved, and a solid brown tie. He stood where he was, in the middle of the second-to-last pew. "Real brief. Two words. Just two words before you go. Thank you." He sat down, and people in the front turned to look at him. People along the sides rose up slightly from their sitting positions and craned their necks. There was much whispering and some blushing, as if what he had said somehow reflected on all who were present. Fred Rinehardt, who was up on the altar in a chair, stood now and called out, "Amen to that." Derek Taylor and Kim Brinckerhof and Amanda Wright, kids from Senior P.F., were together in the back, and they rose from their pew and began to clap. Corinne Jenkins stood in the third pew and waited for everyone's attention. She held up her hand to quiet the applause. Then, in her staccato old-lady voice, she said, "We have much to be thankful for in our minister, our loving and giving minister."

Jordanna was caught off guard by this display. She'd merely been trying to ensure that her departure from this church not be a foggy, embarrassing matter for the congregants, something that brought shame on her and them, something they never fully understood. She turned and nodded to the soloist.

"Just a minute, Reverend Nash." Ben Hall was climbing out of the fourth pew. "We need to hold on here a minute." He walked up to the lectern and switched on the mike. "I think that some of you may not understand—"

People began shouting, "We can't hear you." Ben looked over helplessly at Fred Rinehardt, who suggested he tap the mike. "Just so that another voice is heard—" The mike cut in and out, then squealed. A few people with hearing aids put their fingers in their ears. "Speaking on behalf of the Prudential Board, Reverend Nash might have come to us first, given us the common courtesy of informing us of this decision before making this kind of a general announcement. By now I assume all of you know the concerns we've had about Reverend Nash's service have been legitimate concerns. Concerns that she's carefully chosen not to mention this morning. Just in case anyone starts getting the idea we've somehow unfairly or unduly influenced this decision . . . well, while this may cause Reverend Nash some embarrassment, in the spirit of *openness*, which she seems to be so fond of, the Prudential Board would like the congregation to know that our minister, here, is getting divorced."

Jordanna pursed her lips and took a few steps backward, closer to the doors leading to the narthex and out to the lobby. Hundreds of little dialogues now erupted in the pews.

"I think it's important for the members of this church who have been through so much, and will be here long after this minister has gone, to know that the Prudential Board never intended to allow this congregation to be led by a divorced woman minister. A divorcee as a symbol of this church officiating at weddings, providing marriage counseling—"

"Ben." Grant Price stood up from his spot in the back of the choir. "This is so totally and thoroughly inappropriate—"

"She—" Ben began.

"Just a minute." Phil Pangrossi popped up on the left side of the church, a third of the way back. "Ben is only trying to bring up some important matters for this church. Matters that many of you, I know for a fact, are deeply upset about. I think we owe Ben—"

"I'm divorced." Dee Cimino stood up and tugged at her fuchsia blazer. "Does that make me spiritually unfit? Is that what you're saying?"

Jordanna didn't want to appear to be halting necessary open debate, but she couldn't imagine letting this go on. She walked up to the pulpit and breathed loudly into the mike. " 'Let us speak the truth in love,' Paul wrote in his letter to the Ephesians, 'so shall we fully grow up into Christ.' Perhaps we should still our hearts and continue this conversation downstairs, after our worship has concluded. Many of you remember Remi Stilltoe from grade school and high school. Well, we're really honored to have him back with us today as our soloist. Remi is studying at the Hart School of Music. He was planning to play one piece for us, but if I might . . ." Jordanna turned to Remi, who was coming up to the altar, his violin at his thigh. "I would like us to have a meditation today. I think we all need to ask for God's guidance. Remi, if you have some other music with you, something soothing, perhaps you could play for ten or twelve minutes." Jordanna strode the width of the altar and flicked off the lights. "I would like everyone to get into a comfortable position, as comfortable as you can be in a pew. Find a resting spot for your hands, your feet. Now close your eyes. . . ."

WHEN the postlude had ended, Jordanna walked down the aisle and pushed on the glass doors of the narthex. Just beyond, Fred Rinehardt swung open the two big double doors to the outside, and she saw that it was snowing. The air was crowded with fat white flakes, piling precariously on the hard tips of the November grass and the blank tree limbs. As the congregants began to file out of the sanctuary, the vestibule grew warm and moist. No one exited, not to the little storm outside nor down the stairs to the undercroft. It was as if they all wanted to get near her and stay there, an immense litter at feeding time.

"We won't let you go," Marge Price said, reaching over a throng and tapping her on the arm.

Larry Foley shook his head and ran his tongue over his teeth. "How do you get on the Prudential Board, anyway? Always been a mystery to me, like some secret society."

"They ought to be ashamed of themselves," Frank Leahy said.

"Ben Hall ever hear about casting the first stone?"

Jordanna nodded politely and shook hands. These were the ones who'd chosen to surround her. She knew there were others who were making their feelings known elsewhere right now. That was okay. She continued to greet people, clasping hands, offering hugs.

"I've never done that before," Nan Lowey said. "I'd say it was better than taking a nap, that meditation."

Jordanna nodded. She wondered if they knew, these men and women of her church, who fluttered around her now in that great give and take, that suckle and soothe, she wondered if they knew the blessings that they were. Did people really understand their own divinity? If she and her sister spoke to each other again, and she were to try to describe this moment, Abby would say that she was confusing spiritual communion with adulation. No, she'd tell her, it's so much greater than a one-way ego trip. It's proof. Proof of God's kingdom here on earth, a trailer for the feature yet to come.

ᘛᘚ Chapter 24

THE notice in the paper announcing a celebration of June Nearing's life at the Congdon family farm the day before Thanksgiving had not indicated that it was private, and Abby imagined that people would be piled up on the front porch, leaning in from the kitchen. It was conceivable that half the town might show up. She had come for Drew. They saw each other almost every day now at Miss Diane's. He'd become a friend.

She'd never been to a funeral in someone's living room before. The rented white folding chairs lined up in tapering rows through the downstairs made her think of the way hospital beds and commodes supplanted regular furniture when family members got sick. This was just the next practical step.

Abby stepped over three people as she slid into one of the last available seats. She looked around to see what everyone was doing with their coats. She hoped someone had remembered to unplug the phone. It seemed Drew's luck that a telemarketer would call in the middle of his wife's funeral. Abby placed her purse on the hardwood floor and began the slow process of inching her arm from her unforgiving dress coat. She craned her neck as she tried to slide out her elbow and caught a glimpse of her sister. They hadn't spoken since that hideous night after the Service of the Bittersweet three weeks ago. For a week or two, Abby had expected Jordanna to call or drop in at home or at school and apologize, or at least appease. Jordanna hated for Abby to be mad at her, or, as she called it, to "fall from favor." When it seemed that Jordanna wouldn't be coming by to smooth things over, even after Abby had sent over a lasagne with Brendan, who seemed to be practically living there ever since her "accident," Abby was sure it was only a matter of time before they ran into each other at the post office or the bank. But that hadn't happened, either.

Abby watched her sister now, moving through the crowded room, her arm still in a cast, her bulky shoulders tipping a small framed oil along the wall that separated the dining room from the kitchen. Abby had heard through Brendan that Jordanna was quitting as soon as a replacement could be found. The announcement was the cause for all kinds of turmoil among the faithful at Hutchinson Congregational. A few people on the Prudential Board had up and left the church altogether. The letters section of the *Hutchinson Herald,* which had hummed with church members' moral rectitude and righteous indignation for a few weeks, included a number of unabashed valentines to Jordanna in its most recent issue. Still, she thought, Jordanna had a lot of balls showing up here today. Jim had called Jordanna last week and invited her for Thanksgiving dinner tomorrow. Abby had been furious with him for doing so without telling her first, or asking her. And oddly, she hadn't been relieved when he relayed that Jordanna was going up to the Cape for Thanksgiving, even though their parents were coming to Hutchinson.

Abby looked down at the program. The photocopied picture of June on the front was the same one they'd used for those missing persons posters, a few of which could still be found clinging to phone poles around town. She scanned the program to see if her sister was supposed to speak, but it wasn't that kind of a program, instead it was like an adult's version of a high school yearbook page. There were quotes from famous people, lines of poetry, even some things June had written herself.

People were still talking when the first notes sounded. An oboe. Abby couldn't see all the way to the front of the room, but she heard the music, low and pleading. She closed her eyes and chided herself for having been afraid to come today. She'd never been to a funeral for someone who'd committed suicide, and she was worried that it would be disingenuous. The worst thing that could happen to you once you were already dead was to have an untrue funeral—one that was either inadequate to who you'd been in life, that didn't do that life justice, or one that glossed and fawned, as if currying favor with the dead were some kind of mandated sacrament.

The family filed down the narrow center aisle. The two brothers, one with a pregnant wife, then June's mother, gripping Lee's and Carly's hands, and finally Drew, carrying Ian. When they were seated, some other young men carried in the coffin. It was fashioned of rough planks, like the planks of the floor, but the wood was pale, almost white, unvarnished, unsanded. There was a wreath of bittersweet on the top, and as the pallbearers walked, the little orange berries rolled off the top of the casket onto the floor.

When the music stopped, June's mother smoothed her palms over the front of her navy dress and moved behind a little folding table, the kind people set their suppers on when they watch TV. "I would like to thank you all for coming today. It was important for us, for me and Drew and the children, Kent and Miles and Anna, to bring June back home one more time, and so we chose to do things this way this time. Reverend Nash assured me that any space could be made sacred enough to celebrate a life, to mark the close of a life."

Abby turned to look at Jordanna. Her head was bowed and her hair concealed her face. June's mother read some Bible passages, and then, as if on some invisible cue, one person after another stood and read—poems, psalms, the lyrics of a song. Abby waited for the eulogy, but this service lacked that kind of progression. It was just words, then more words, whatever anyone wanted to read, it seemed. The two girls stood in front of their mother's casket and sang a two-verse song about little boats on the ocean. And then Drew came forward. He took a handkerchief from his pocket and pushed at his eyes, then picked up a book from the little table and began to read slowly. His tongue, thick and dry, seemed to have trouble clearing some of the oddly clinical words.

Abby looked around her, gauging the responses. Drew was reading to them at his wife's funeral from a clinical essay on suicide prevention. Most people were studying their knees or the backs of the rented chairs with the Easy Rent-All sticker pasted off center on almost every one. Drew pushed his way over the mountainous sentences, occasionally his intonation alerting the audience that here, here was where they should attend to the words. People were extremely still for a long time while he read, but as it went on, Abby could hear Ian up front, sucking loudly on something. And then, as if his own oral gratification were a signal, the adults started moving, uncrossing their legs, blowing their noses, pulling on the elasticized straps of their watch bands. Abby looked over at Jordanna again, but her head was still down. When Drew finally concluded, he looked up at everyone, almost surprised to see they were still there in their seats in his mother-in-law's living room. "I really thought that you should all know," he said. "We didn't know what to look for, how to check. . . . If someone close to you, someone you love, someone you're responsible for . . . well, we're all responsible for each other . . . if someone is acting like some of the ways I just read—help them. Help them." He patted his handkerchief to his brow. "Bev is going to end this service with one more reading. It's a poem, a poem by Jane Kenyon that was meaningful to June. We printed it on the back of everyone's program because we thought these were words you should take home with you." Drew walked back to his seat, and June's mother came to the front of the room and looked out at everyone. She stood quietly for a moment, then closed her eyes and began to recite "Let Evening Come."

When she got to the last line, "God does not leave us / comfortless, so let evening come," June's mother opened her eyes, the tears streaming forth, and everyone fixed on her, as if to say, yes, this is what grief looks like. If loss were a presence, it would be this woman, in this moment. The oboe began, and June's mother stood there, until Lee walked up to her and pulled on her hand, calling, "Nana."

ABBY found Jordanna on the front porch, a mittened hand wrapped around a Styrofoam cup of hot cider. "A shot of bourbon and they might be able to call it a drink," Abby said, buttoning her coat and slinging her purse over her shoulder. Jordanna tucked her cup under her bad wing and reached the distance between them with her long right arm, touching Abby's coat sleeve, then quickly removing her hand, as if it had been a gesture that had gotten past her own defenses.

"You okay?" Abby said.

Jordanna nodded.

Abby sighed, and when she breathed in again deeply she smelled cider and cigarettes and something wafting toward them from the barn. She looked back at her sister, who smiled at her again.

"Nice service. Different," Abby said stupidly.

"June sent me that poem," Jordanna whispered, moving over to the railing at the front of the porch, away from the door leading into the house.

Abby followed, and tried not to pick at the peeling paint on the porch pillar. "What do you mean?"

"She left it to me . . . in her suicide note—as her suicide note to me."

"Jesus."

"What do you think of it?"

"As poetry?" Abby sank her teeth into the Styrofoam cup. "You have a cigarette?"

"What do you think it . . . conveys?" Jordanna unzipped a little black purse Abby didn't recognize and pulled out a pack of Marlboro Lights.

Abby looked around. "I'm not sure."

Jordanna cocked her head in the direction of the barn, and they walked together across the bristly pale grass and the already frozen ruts made by the fat tires of farm machinery. Jordanna stopped and cupped her mitten around Abby's cigarette as she lit it for her. "What do you think of . . ." She held her cigarette between her lips and pulled the funeral program from her pocket. "'God does not leave us comfortless'?"

"I don't know," Abby said. "You—" She stopped. She wanted to say, *You got left comfortless.* But she stopped.

Jordanna shook her head as if disagreeing with this unvoiced argument.

"What?"

"Do you think it's true?" Jordanna asked.

Abby turned and looked back at the white house with the delft blue shutters. The front porch looked as if it were sagging, badly. "If you believe in God, then it probably is true."

"What do you think she meant by sending it to me? If she really believed God doesn't leave us comfortless . . ."

"Then why did she kill herself?" Abby finished the thought.

"You'll get a charge out of the fact that until today, until I heard Bev recite the poem just now, I'd taken it, June's sending of it, as a hopeful sign, that somehow she'd found some real consolation in the end. But now, maybe, she was just getting me back, in a way. Maybe I missed the ironic intent in the words and the gesture. That would be like me, wouldn't it?"

Abby pulled hard on her cigarette. What was it about her sister that made it so tempting to hurt her and so utterly unfulfilling in the end? "Irony would lose its cachet if there weren't at least a few of your kind floating around."

"Hardly a resounding endorsement for faith."

"Maybe the poem was for you."

"What do you mean?" Jordanna rubbed out her cigarette with the sole of her black boot.

"Maybe she wasn't talking about herself. Maybe the poem was like a gift for you, telling you something she thought you needed to know. Maybe she really did believe that God would not leave *you* to struggle along in pain."

Jordanna slid her hand into her pocket and rubbed her thigh. "How are the girls doing? Bev told me they're in with Gabe in day care. How do you think they're faring?"

"Gabe likes that little Carly. Lee's in school most of the time. I don't know, really."

"And Drew?" Jordanna asked.

Abby shrugged. "Not too good, I don't think."

Jordanna blew her nose and then wiped her eyes.

"You driving up today? There'll be a lot of traffic, huh?" Abby said.

"How long are Mum and Dad staying? I should try to see them, at least for a while."

"Sunday. They'll be here until Sunday." Abby looked at her watch. "You got another one of these?" she said, taking the last drag and then stomping on the nub of the cigarette with her high heel. "Shit. Look. It'll suck without you tomorrow. Have dinner with us, okay?"

Abby felt her sister's mitten on her head. The soft patting was at once irritating and comforting, a gesture retrieved from a winter thirty years ago, a stake, a claim. And she wondered if Jordanna were channeling her to recall the words of that childhood hymn, "I Have Called You and You Are Mine."

"What do you need? I'd like to cook something," Jordanna said. "Just come."

Jordanna shook her head. "Tell me what the boys would like."

Abby watched the smoke from her cigarette disappear into the silver November afternoon. The sun was coming at them at a slant. The decks of the big houses to the east of the Congdons' farm were already in shadow. Abby and Jordanna had been moving slowly, unconsciously toward the barn, toward the lingering light. Abby slipped off her leather glove and reached up to her sister's forehead, just where the sun was touching it. "You think it'll leave a scar?" she said. Her fingertips warmed and she let them rest there longer than she should have.

⚘ Chapter 25

THE kids had asked her to sit up by the pulpit, but she insisted on being ministered to along with everyone else on this Youth Sunday. The Senior Pilgrim Fellowship had met at her house for pizza every Thursday night during January and February, and she had poured soda and picked up paper plates and listened as the preparation for this service evolved. They had chosen "Blessings" as their theme, and she had suggested that they divide the group into three smaller groups, one for the sermon, one for the liturgy and one for the music. She had let them decide for themselves, or in some cases for one another, about who should comprise each group. And week to week, as she stuffed oversize pizza boxes into her single-person trash can, she watched kids shuffling around, arguing that "consensus-building is just a PC form of bullying." She occasionally directed them to scripture, reminded them to stick to the theme and to mine it for all its multiple meanings, but mostly she had hoped that this would be an exercise in the responsibility of spiritual leadership.

Personal responsibility in spiritual leadership had been the emphasis of her interview with Karen Tiernan from the *Hartford*

Times. The reporter had spent the first week of Advent trailing Jordanna as she visited sick congregants, met with church staff, attended an interfaith council meeting. She knew that Tiernan had intended to write a follow-up piece about June's suicide and its rending effect on Hutchinson Congregational Church. When Tiernan arrived in Hutchinson for the Greening of the Church, Jordanna knew she wanted nothing more than to write a piece about how she was being ridden out on a rail. "Wear her down," Chip had advised over the phone. "Turn that considerable self of yours inside out and block her view of everything but your massively big heart and your abiding faith."

But Jordanna hadn't done that. Instead, she'd brought her to the Bible study at the prison, to the oncology floor at Deerfield Hospital and to a meeting with a young couple interested in joining the church. She gave her a tour of Hutchinson Cemetery and Bethel Lake, and she invited her to the parsonage for dinner. Jordanna explained to Karen that she felt it her responsibility to stay on until the congregation installed a new minister. She asked the reporter about her childhood faith, and about her life now, if she liked her job, what her deepest desire was and what she thought she was called to do in the world. Jordanna told her that she was following a lead on a job in New Haven working with trauma victims. Scott Davis had put her in touch with some colleagues at Yale. Jordanna didn't cook for Karen, but she ordered in pizza and opened a bottle of wine, and after dinner she brought down the photos of James and Alice. Jordanna waited through Christmas and New Year's and most of the winter for an article to appear, but it never did.

THERE was a little giggling now in the church as the musicians positioned themselves and their instruments up on the altar. Brendan, who'd begun spending most evenings at the parsonage, had written the anthem to fit the musical propensities of Kyle Martin, who played the violin, and Tina Brush, who played flute. Jordanna had told the kids again and again that she trusted them, that they did not need her to approve the music or the readings or the sermon. Something had happened to the group when she relinquished control. Her declaration of their independence had acted like a drug upon them. At first they were giddy, almost manic, then hyper-responsible, righteous and finally, when all that had worn off, they'd become rather solemn and, above all, unified.

Jordanna closed her eyes and felt the sun pour in through the eastern windows. It had snowed last night, and today was one of those high, clear winter days that sent piercing light in every direction, much of it collecting in the soaring white ceiling of this church. Jordanna had heard Brendan play the melody on his guitar one night when he was waiting for Jim to pick him up. She'd been wiping Dr Pepper off one of the hymnals the group had been using. She'd been thinking about Tara, about how she was glad she was back in Fellowship, even if her attitude was problematic. She was thinking about the workshop on Christian divorce she and Chip were going to lead in March in Atlanta, about whether there could be such a thing, though she knew there must be, about Daniel and his pregnant girlfriend, about how long it took to get divorced compared to how long it took to make a marriage. She was glad she had her back to Brendan, because she was crying, and it wasn't the cast of her thoughts, but the spell of his music that made her weep. There was an urgency to the tune. It rushed headlong from the strings, lifting the listener just beyond the edge of the conscious, the rational, to that other sphere, that was so often out of reach. "Make sure Mom and Dad come on the twenty-seventh," she'd said to him as he'd snapped the guitar into its case.

She hadn't yet caught sight of Abby or Jim this morning, but Gabe had run up to her before worship began, and Christopher and Michael had waved to her as they ran to bring him back. Kyle Martin snapped a string on his violin partway through the piece, but the congregation applauded, and then a few proud parents stood, and reluctantly, like a slow rip zigzagging through worn cloth, most of the rest of the congregation stood.

She had suggested to the kids that they offer an introduction to their scripture lesson, explain to the congregation that they would be acting it out. But Tara Sears, back when she'd been in the liturgy group, had convinced them all that doing so would drain it of its drama. Jordanna was pretty sure she'd overheard her say that the problem with organized religion was that it lacked the element of surprise. It seemed now that they'd all concurred. Jordanna was somewhat afraid that Derek Taylor's clown-size blue jeans would, in fact, be pulled down by Kelly Price as the unclean woman daring to touch his "hem."

The congregation shifted slightly toward the center aisle as everyone craned to see Kelly Price in a long brown dress reaching dramatically for the clueless Jesus. Matt List played the part of the ruler seeking Jesus' help in raising his daughter from the dead. Derek was forceful, if decidedly twentieth century, as he turned his gaze on the hemorrhaging Kelly and bellowed, "Take heart, daughter; your faith has made you well." Tina Brush played her flute and the rest of the class was the crowd attempting to make a "tumult." Sarah Hancock lay with her eyes closed on the second step leading up to the altar, the ruler's dead daughter. "Do you believe that I am able to do this?" Derek shouted at Kim Brinckerhof and Amanda Wright, taking the parts of the blind men. He reached out with his still-boyish fingers and placed them on their closed lids. "According to your faith, be it done to you." Kim rather dramatically flashed open her previously unseeing eyes and Amanda, who could barely tolerate having so many people focused on her, blinked a couple of times. Then Derek said, "See that no one knows it." Jordanna had heard them argue about this last line. Sarah had pointed out that Reverend Jordanna ended scripture readings wherever she wanted. You had to stop somewhere, and it did kind of change the emphasis of the whole thing in a way. Kelly had argued that Jesus' humility was, like, the whole thing.

After the offertory and a round of "When All Thy Mercies, O My God," Tara Sears remained alone on the altar. Jordanna had never seen her in a dress. And certainly no one in this church had ever seen someone so pregnant clothed in so little material. As she pounded across to the lectern, her black combat boots kicking at the carpet, Jordanna looked away. Nipples, belly button, everything was identifiable beneath that second skin of celadon spandex. Fred Rinehardt had left a little step at the lectern for her to stand on, but Jordanna saw that she kicked it to the side with the toe of her boot.

Initially, the kids had voted for Sarah Hancock to give the sermon. She was literary. Her poetry got published every year in the *Hutchinson High Folio*. But when Kim Brinckerhof and Kelly Price had come complaining to Jordanna about Tara Sears, Jordanna had enlisted them in figuring out where Tara's strengths might be best applied. Kelly had said, jail, and Kim had explained that when Tara's cells started multiplying to form that baby, her vicious attitude had multiplied right along with them. They refused to work with her. Jordanna offered to nudge Tara from the liturgy group to the sermon group. After one meeting, the sermon committee meted out the job of delivering the sermon to Tara, as if it were a fitting punishment. Jordanna advised her that a pulpit was an important public forum. "Let it rip. Get it all off your chest. Let us, finally, have it— but stick to the theme, *Blessings*, and remember, no profanity, no off-color stories."

When Jordanna stood in the pulpit at the start of a sermon and looked out at the crowd, she often detected a mass slackening, necks tilted back, barrettes loosened, a loafer or two slipped off. But this morning, even those who did not know Tara noticeably stiffened in their pews. The swollen belly, the military boots, the random streak of orange hair dye limning her side part, were sufficient to call the whole church to attention.

"In today's scripture lesson, Matthew 9:18–31, we get to see Jesus doing the things He will become famous for. It's the basic message of the Gospel, if you think about it. Jesus reaches out to everyone, the ruler and the unclean woman, the blind men. So that's the first part of the message. He's willing to reach out, not just in empty words, but really, physically, with His whole self. The touching is important. He puts his hands on them and they are healed. And in the case of the ruler's daughter, He brings the girl back to life."

Jordanna noticed that Tara had lost the little catch of terror in her voice and seemed to be easing into her role. She pulled the microphone a bit closer, stopped to take a sip of water, fixed her green-lidded eyes in a kind of frightening ownership on the whole of the church before her. *Reteaching Loveliness* was the decidedly un-Tara-like title of the sermon as printed in the bulletin. Kim and Amanda had designed the program, with a pointillist church on the front cover, a welcome departure from the line drawing of the old meeting house with a peace dove overhead that Jordanna and Gael relied on Sunday after Sunday. She'd counseled Tara that if she were foundering, to stick to scripture. Scripture was the map.

"But the thing I want you to notice this morning is what Jesus says. To the woman who's been bleeding for twelve years, He says 'Your faith has made you well.' You remember what she says right before that, right? She says, 'If only I touch his garment, I shall be made well.' He's telling her that the power is not His. He's telling her that she's got the ability to heal herself, that the blessing is a self-blessing.

"Blessings, that's the theme of our service today, and Reverend Nash kept on us about that, about sticking to the theme. The kids in charge of picking out the scripture reading picked out this one, which most people would say is about healing, about Jesus giving his blessing to all these people. But if you push at the thing a little harder, Matthew is really trying to tell us about faith. 'Your faith has made you well,' He says. And then, to the blind men, "Do you believe I am able to do this?' And when they say yes, He says, 'According to your faith be it done to you.' That's the blessing—or, as Reverend Nash would want me to say, *the gift*. Jesus' gift is to tell us that through our faith we are blessed, we can bless, we are healed, and we can heal, too.

"In trying to write this sermon, I was struggling and Reverend Nash, thinking she was helping me, said, 'Any good sermon reveals something about the minister. Tell a story or use your own life as an example.' Well . . ."

Jordanna watched now as Tara swung her arms and legs and took four huge strides to the center of the altar. She turned, in warped fashion-model style, to show off her astounding profile, then returned to the lectern.

"I'm not sure I would have understood this passage from Matthew a year ago. I wouldn't have identified much with the untouchables who Jesus touches, not back then. But in this town, being sixteen, in high school and expecting a baby—let's say the idea of a leper is a lot less foreign to me. But there were people around me who were not afraid to reach out and touch me. My parents. I think my parents have been just as radical as Jesus was. They've done something very hard. They've stuck by me, and more, much more. And there have been other people who have kept on reminding me that even though I made *this* mistake, and some others, I am loved. There have been people who have worked hard to show me their faith, to let me hitch a ride on their faith. And let me tell you, I wasn't always . . . I'm not always the most pleasant passenger. All the time, these people who helped me were telling me the same thing as Jesus. Even as they were reaching out to me, touching me, they were directing me toward myself, telling me that I would be able to rely on myself, that what was in me would heal me.

"I just want to end today with a poem Reverend Nash handed out to us last year in Senior P.F. It's by Galway Kinnell, and it's called "St. Francis and the Sow."

> The bud
> stands for all things,
> even for those things that don't flower,
> for everything flowers, from within, of self-blessing;
> though sometimes it is necessary
> to reteach a thing its loveliness,
> to put a hand on its brow

of the flower
and retell it in words and in touch
it is lovely
until it flowers again from within, of self-blessing;
as Saint Francis
put his hand on the creased forehead
of the sow, and told her in words and in touch
blessings of earth on the sow, and the sow
began remembering all down her thick length,
from the earthen snout all the way
through the fodder and slops to the spiritual curl of the tail,
from the hard spininess spiked out from the spine
down through the great broken heart
to the sheer blue milken dreaminess spurting and shuddering
from the fourteen teats into the fourteen mouths sucking and
blowing beneath them:
the long, perfect loveliness of sow.

It was probably only a few seconds, but when she finished speaking, no one moved, no one said anything. Tara left the lectern and sank into the armchair on the side of the pulpit. Slowly people began to stand, then some of the kids in the front, the kids from Senior P.F., whistled and hooted. Jordanna bounded up the altar steps, two at a time, and leaned down over Tara, whispering, "What a gift!"

⚫ The End

JORDANNA waited until the snow had all melted and Lent had come and almost gone before she pulled Mary Jane's two-seater bicycle out of the shed behind the house she was renting. The red and yellow tulips had sprung up sturdy and vibrant all around the circular drive at the front of Hutchinson Congregational. And even from there, she could hear Bethel Falls running under the little bridge in the back. As she bounced across the new grass leading from the church house down to the bridge, the front fender of Mary Jane's bike slapped against the box strapped to the handlebars.

Reverend Hough, the new minister, had called this morning to say that he'd found some of her things when he'd moved a file cabinet while settling into his office. If she came by after he was gone for the day, she would find everything in a box on his desk. She had cleaned out the parsonage a month ago so Mrs. Hough and the twin baby girls could move in. Jordanna had planned on moving to New Haven to be near her new job as a group facilitator in a counseling center for trauma victims. But Abby had said that the boys were increasingly upset at the thought of her being even forty minutes away, and that Brendan would miss her terribly. "He needs you, Jordanna, more than you know." Fred Rinehardt had invited her to come take a look at the converted barn on the edge of his farm. He'd intended it as a ceramics studio for his wife, and even though she died long before it was completed, he kept on with the construction. He had never been able to envision anyone else inhabiting it, not, of course, until he thought of Jordanna. The farm was eighteen acres, including a pond he stocked with trout. A perfect fit, he told her.

It was warm for the beginning of April, and the wood of the bridge had been steeping in the sun for the better part of the afternoon. She took off her helmet and placed it on top of the box. Judging from what was visible, she didn't think she'd left anything of value behind, just some books, mostly anthropology texts and a mouse pad that a congregant had brought back from Rome: Michelangelo's God and Adam reaching for one another across eight inches of thin foam. She lay down on her stomach, her chin on the backs of her folded hands, and inhaled the water, still scented with winter, snow and rock. The trees were bare, no leaves yet, no cherry or apple blossoms, just bark and bud, promise.

She'd preached her last sermon, at least for a while, two Sundays before. The title had been *Salvation*. "We move through our lives as if assigned a ladder on the day of our birth. We consider life an ascent, always climbing, moving from ignorance to wisdom, from earth, closer to God. And so here we are, each one of us, up on our individual ladders, a planet pocked with tilting fools . . . . But what if God predicates our personal salvation on the salvation of the group? What if personal salvation does not mean *individual* salvation? In Christ, we are all loved, together, at once. . . . And if we are to love one another as Jesus loves us, then we are to do so without comparison, without analogy, without the filter of self . . . Your joy must be my joy, too. . . . Could it be that we are, finally, so inextricably tied to one another, that all must be raised up before anyone can rise?"

The sun had just dipped behind the trees on the ridge above the falls. Jordanna sat up, rubbed her arms and pulled the carton toward her for inspection. She found her copy of Teilhard de Chardin's *The*

Divine Milieu, which she'd been looking for to give to Brendan. Wedged in a corner of the box and wrapped in copies of an old bulletin was the quahog shell she used to hold her hair clips. Her fingers grazed the bottom of the box and she slid some bobby pins into her palm. Reverend Hough was thorough. She pinched a stack of church letterhead with her name on it, of no use now, and began to replace the books in the box. Mixed in with the anthropology texts was a worn softcover poetry anthology. She set it aside on the bridge, as if she didn't have the right to open it. When the wind rifled its pages, she could see there were annotations, handwriting in blue and black ink. "Eve Congdon, English 412," it said in small block letters on the inside cover. She lifted the book and the volume flopped apart, the spine having been flattened there to the point of damage. The white space around "Let Evening Come" was filled with a large, though shaky, script, intermittently invisible, as if the ink were running dry: "This one, June. This is the one."

Jordanna buckled her helmet strap beneath her chin, tucked the box under one arm, and hopped onto the bicycle built for two.